PRAISE FOR
THE QUANTUM MAGICIAN

"A boldly ambitious debut."
SFX Magazine

"An audacious con job, scintillating future technology,
and meditations on the nature of fractured humanity."
Yoon Ha Lee

"Künsken has a wonderfully ingenious imagination."
Adam Roberts, *Locus*

"Technology changes us—even our bodies—in fundamental
ways, and Kunsken handles this wonderfully."
Cixin Liu

"I have no problems raving about this book. A truly wild
backdrop of space-opera with wormholes, big space-fleet
conflict and empires.... What could go wrong?"
Brad K. Horner

"This brainy sci-fi heist novel uses mathematics like magic to
pull you through a caper worthy of Jean-Pierre Melville."
The B&N SciFi and Fantasy Blog

"*The Quantum Magician* is the type of book
you go back to the beginning and read again once you
know how everything pans out and have those
'why didn't I see that the first time?' moments."
Strange Alliances

THE QUANTUM
GARDEN

DEREK KÜNSKEN

SOLARIS

First published 2019 by Solaris
an imprint of Rebellion Publishing Ltd,
Riverside House, Osney Mead,
Oxford, OX2 0ES, UK

www.solarisbooks.com

ISBN: 978 1 78108 571 4

10 9 8 7 6 5 4 3 2 1

A CIP catalogue record for this book is available
from the British Library.

Designed & typeset by Rebellion Publishing

Printed in Denmark

THE QUANTUM
GARDEN

To my parents,
who built me in many ways that I can see
and in many ways I cannot.

CHAPTER ONE

CAPITAINE ARSENAULT'S FACE was cool in the infrared, unperturbed. On the younger side of forty, with braided blond hair, she stood inscrutable on magnetic soles in the zero-g. She fingered the ridges of artfully symmetric acid scars on her cheeks as she considered the tactical display. As much as the Scarecrow could like anyone, he liked Arsenault. She had the controlled passions and equanimity to command a Congregate warship.

Les Rapides de Lachine was her command and the Scarecrow waited on her now. He'd given Arsenault the intelligence he was willing to share. While his recommendation was founded, it in no way obligated the naval arm of the Venusian Congregate.

Majeur Demers, *Les Rapides de Lachine*'s political officer, eschewed magnetic soles and floated with still grace in the middle of the bridge. The Scarecrow hated political officers, political commissars, envoys, advisers and ambassadors. Too slippery by half, they slithered among the factions of the Congregate Presidium, cluttering clean military and intelligence choices with spongy thinking.

"A clear signal must be sent," Demers said. A fashionable Venusian lilt colored the precision of her *français* 8.1. "The Congregate protested the Plutocracy's bioengineering of the

Homo eridanus. The Congregate *demarched* the Plutocracy when the *Homo pupa* were bioengineered. Now the Banks have engineered the *Homo quantus* and one of our own client nations is in rebellion, aided by the *Homo quantus,* probably aided by elements of the *Homo eridanus.*"

The Scarecrow's neck swiveled with the flexing of artificial, piezoelectric muscles and he creaked forward, imposing his weight on the conversation again. If he didn't, the political officer would drown them all in words.

"We hold prisoners and many records," the Scarecrow said, "but the intelligence teams need weeks, perhaps months to scour the *Homo quantus* nest deeply enough to be sure we leave nothing of value in the Garret."

Majeur Demers crossed her arms. "We can't leave warships over the Garret to protect you from Bank ships, Scarecrow. And waiting tells our rivals we thieve from a position of weakness rather than punish from a position of strength."

Capitaine Arsenault studiously ignored them, long enough that he and Demers quieted.

"I understand the political and intelligence concerns," Arsenault said, "but the Congregate does not stand or fall on politics and intelligence. Politically, a client nation is in open rebellion. Militarily, the dreadnought *Parizeau* was destroyed and we're certain the *Homo quantus* had a role. Military setbacks never go unavenged."

Demers smiled. Arsenault's choice was not timid. Although the situation had not swung his way, the Scarecrow sympathized with the capitaine's view. The Congregate thrived because its enemies feared its strength. The choice here today, Arsenault's choice, might precipitate a war with the Banks of the Plutocracy, and although they had not yet finished mopping up the rebellion of the Sub-Saharan Union, they acted from a position of strength.

"*Feu,*" Arsenault said to her bridge officers.

Les Rapides de Lachine was too massive for humans to feel the launch vibrations of even a missile as large as a *casse à face*, but not so the Scarecrow. The fibrous webs of variably conductive carbon making up the Scarecrow's muscles and nerves sensed the vibrations through tiny deviations in resistance and potential.

The holographic display showed the *casse à face* gaining speed, lancing at a massive asteroid looming on one side of the display. The image expanded quickly. The surface detail sharpened. Small features of the rock and ice regolith resolved, and then even patterns of decorative lights near a small port.

The explosion bleached the display. Chunks of asteroid hundreds of meters wide tumbled into space. Webs of fracture lines shot through the surface, erupting with super-heated plasma and dust. A fast-expanding cloud of debris bloomed into nothing, along with any chance of gathering more information from the *Homo quantus* habitat.

The home of the *Homo quantus* had been a spherical asteroid six hundred kilometers in diameter. Now a crater fifty kilometers deep was burned in its side, the center of the kilometer-deep fracture lines grasping all the way to the other face of the asteroid.

"*Bon,*" the Scarecrow said. "I will get my information through interrogation."

CHAPTER TWO

CHAPTER TWO

BELISARIUS AND CASSIE had finally decided to call the inflaton racer *The Calculated Risk*. They'd had a lot of choices, but felt this best described the last three months of their lives. The act of Saint Matthew's automata painting the name onto the bow gave them a tiny sense of belonging. The ship had been partial payment for moving a small fleet of Sub-Saharan Union warships across the Puppet wormhole, and the last three weeks hadn't been long enough to feel like it really belonged to them.

The Calculated Risk wasn't spacious. A hollow tube fifty-three meters long and three meters in diameter constituted the drive section. Other systems and spaces wrapped around the outside of the cylinder: the habitable areas, control and power networks, life support and information processing. The 'living' area shrank to a meter tall in many places, but expanded to as much as two in the cockpit and galley. A larger cargo area lay astern.

The inside of *The Calculated Risk* was not inviting, nor even comfortable, and he and Cassie had done nothing to make it any better. They had data and they wanted to begin modeling hypotheses. But the original mainframe of *The Calculated Risk* was entirely inadequate to the processing needs of a pair of *Homo quantus*. So they rebuilt it.

The new computer operated orders of magnitude faster than anything the Union had ever possessed, with multi-dimensional, geometry-heavy holographic interfaces suited to the way *Homo quantus* thought. Over the last two months, they'd both made an enormous amount of measurements and experiments on the Puppet Axis and the joined wormholes they'd stolen from the Union. The data they held now obliged them to reassess most of the known wormhole theories. Whole families of theories would have to be discarded or promoted, and vast series of mathematical symmetries needed new proofs. They couldn't wait.

They'd been jacked into their joint virtual workspace for a few hours through implants and wires. From within induced savant states that gave them prodigious mathematical abilities, they delighted in writing and rewriting the arrays of geometric structures containing each others' ideas. Their thoughts and ideas dove through the holographic space like dolphins leaping through waves. But a persistent voice interrupted their geometric thoughts.

"The telescopes are detecting a ship in high orbit of the Garret," Saint Matthew repeated.

The delusional artificial intelligence, stored in a service wristband, was plugged into the cockpit controls. A holographic head floated above the band, showing a stolid, white-bearded face patterned after the brush strokes of oil paints in Caravaggio's *Inspiration of Saint Matthew.* That the AI believed himself the literal reincarnation of the Apostle Saint Matthew didn't bother Belisarius much, although his religiosity did make it harder for him to get his help in confidence schemes. It didn't matter anymore. No more confidence schemes. He had wealth for a dozen lifetimes and a way to study the cosmos.

Belisarius reluctantly came out of savant, leaving behind the soaring geometries. He expanded the display to show the

Garret, as much as it could be expanded at a distance of three light minutes. Rendered in grainy detail, a ship hung over the place they'd been born. Cassie leaned on his shoulder.

"Does the Garret get visitors now?" he asked.

"No," she said.

"It's big," he said. His brain had already taken the reflectivity of the display, the strength of EM emissions, assumed its diameter at less than a hundred meters and corrected for a distance of three light minutes. "About eight hundred meters long."

"The right size for a Congregate warship," Saint Matthew said.

"Blockade?" Belisarius said.

No one dared guess. They stared at the display whose resolution inched better minute by minute. *The Calculated Risk's* drive emitted nothing in the electromagnetic, making the racer difficult to detect. They could get closer.

The Garret was Cassie's home. It had been Belisarius' home once. It was also home to four thousand *Homo quantus,* the sub-species of humanity genetically-engineered to possess quantum perceptions. The *Homo quantus* project had been launched with great fanfare by the Banks of the Anglo-Spanish Plutocracy, with investors and an Initial Coin Offering. Bank CEOs, market analysts, and Bank Generals had held high hopes for the invention of novel predictive powers within the planned new sub-species of humanity: military strategies, investment tactics, monetary policy calculations. Wealth and power.

But even eleven generations into the project, the *Homo quantus* were now a disappointing footnote in annual stock reports, one of the many blind alleys in corporate R&D. The *Homo quantus* couldn't predict the future any better than classical or quantum computers. Worse yet, their natures were contemplative and retiring, unsuitable for military and conflictive economic environments. They became a cautionary tale, the butt of R&D jokes. The Banks had not withdrawn their funding yet, but they'd let the *Homo quantus* retreat to a quiet asteroid far from the bustle of the Epsilon Indi system. Except for Belisarius and Cassie, none of the *Homo quantus* left the Garret. They shied away from loud interactions and reported their ongoing experiments to the Banks in writing.

"Maybe it's just passing by?" Cassie offered. Her voice had risen half an octave.

"It could even be a big freighter," Belisarius offered without conviction.

The ship orbited closer to the Garret than was efficient for off-loading supplies, well beneath the altitude suitable for low-energy transfer orbits. No one voiced the possibility that civilization had become interested in the *Homo quantus*.

"We need better telescopes," Belisarius said in frustration.

"Time will improve resolution," Saint Matthew said.

"We're forty hours away," Belisarius said. "We shouldn't accelerate until we know who that is."

"I might see it better from within the fugue," Cassie said. "Three light minutes isn't much."

It couldn't hurt, and she was good at the fugue. Better than him right now, and maybe forever; he didn't yet know how much his own experience of the fugue had changed.

An immense flash bloomed into a searing crescent around the Garret. Sensor graphs spiked in a range of wavelengths: visible light, hot infrared, gamma rays. Then small peaks of beta particles searing in at close to the speed of light collected as statistics on the readouts.

Someone had nuked the Garret three minutes ago.

Cassie's fingers tightened on his shoulder.

Their sub-surface home was radioactive ash. The green rolling hills. The quiet birds. The faint, colored lights. The still, shallow ponds. And the thousands of infuriating, impractical, naïve, obsessive scientists, doctors and genetic engineers. His throat tightened, and not just from loss.

He'd caused this. Guilt rotted in his stomach.

Weight pressed Belisarius harder into his seat. Cassie fell back in hers. Saint Matthew accelerated to two gravities. The painted holographic head of a saint dead twenty-four centuries leaned forward, like the figurehead on the prow of a ship.

"What are you doing?" Belisarius demanded.

His stomach still churned as his mind processed. Four thousand people. He'd grown up with them. His near perfect memory flashed hundreds of faces before his mind's eye. All of them gone.

"The warship is moving away," Saint Matthew said, his face spinning back. "We can cut our travel time to twelve hours, or many times less if you both get into the acceleration tanks. We can rescue as many of your people as we can."

The explosion bloomed multispectrally in the readouts, like news of a horrible event replaying over and over as particles of different speeds reached them: neutrons, alpha particles, plasma.

Belisarius' engineered brain was capable of imagining six- and seven-dimensional space—graphs, patterns, hyper-solid solutions to physics problems—but now that intellectual hardware unwillingly visualized the geometries of cindered bodies tumbling in precessing orbits around a shattered home. His brain identified vaporization rings beyond which diamond-bright water-ice chips would refract the bright shine of Epsilon Indi into rainbows coloring the charred, frozen dead.

Belisarius couldn't take thinking of them. He could count anything, quantify anything, except his own people. He sent a micro-current from electroplaques under his ribs, through conducting carbon nanotubes, to the left temporal area of his brain. The current impaired his social nuance and linguistic abilities. Savant didn't balm emotion, but smoothed the topography of some feelings, eroding their sharp peaks.

At the same time, the patterns of the world came into sharper relief: the acceleration curve of *The Calculated Risk*, the minuscule relativistic blue-shifting of the incoming particles, the shape and depth of the gamma-ray curve. And more sophisticated logical channels became available to him, ones better able to manipulate quantum possibilities.

"The radiation pattern matches the known patterns of a Congregate *casse à face* missile," Saint Matthew said.

The Congregate. They knew about Belisarius then. They knew his role in the Union break-out from the Puppet Axis. And they'd erased the footnote that was the *Homo quantus* project.

Cassie had no home because of him. The *Homo quantus* were ashes because of him. He and Cassie might be the last *Homo quantus*, heirs to the smoke and dust and blood of a stupid investment project. Might be.

The *Homo quantus* brain was necessarily multi-channeled, but sometimes pattern searches crossed the channels. While he absorbed the enormity of what he'd done, his brain was also graphing incoming data. In routine linkage analysis between the two, his brain showed him calculations of burn and asphyxiation rates, and of bone-breaking concussive force. Geometric conceptualizations and models overlapped in his thoughts, painful imagination and hard observation, real and unreal at once, evenly balanced. The imagined unreality was as terrible as what they'd already seen. Worse, but the imagined would move into reality as they neared, driving the aching spike of grief further into his heart.

Yet the quantum logic hard-wired into the *Homo quantus* tickled at his thoughts.

Imagining and observation.

The cat dead or alive.

"Cut acceleration!" Belisarius said. "Make a new course for our last hideout."

"There may be survivors!" Saint Matthew said.

"Set a new course," Belisarius said. "They'll all survive."

They would all survive the *casse à face* missile.

Maybe.

A quantum maybe.

"The deepest parts of the Garret might have a chance of survival," Saint Matthew said. "There may be hundreds of survivors if we hurry."

"We're saving all of them," Belisarius said emphatically.

Cassie pulled him towards her. He flinched from her glare, but only a bit. She was in savant as well. Cassie was probably running the same calculations. She shut off the sensors and the readouts around them.

No observer. No reality.

She was letting the unobserved overlapping probabilities grow, become more complex.

Saint Matthew's painted holographic face had an expression. Belisarius interpreted expressions poorly in savant, except for Saint Matthew's. A series of three hundred and fifteen brush strokes made up his face. The program the AI used to animate the face followed rules that were easy for a *Homo quantus* to deduce. Disappointment. Saint Matthew was disappointed, but he cut the acceleration and rotated the racer.

"We've observed the explosion," Belisarius said to him, "but that's all we observed. We're too far away to know its effects, including casualties or deaths. We have to get out of here now before we make an observation that narrows our options. We're going back in time to save them."

CHAPTER THREE

BELISARIUS FELT HE was suffocating. To human eyes, the stars lay frozen beyond the cockpit window, but as he struggled with his storm of thoughts, his engineered brain and eyes measured minutely changing angles as *The Calculated Risk* raced across the Epsilon Indi system. Panic dogged him as he traveled the length of the racer to the stern of the cramped living space, where an airlock led to the hold and the time travel device.

The galaxy was vast, so vast that some ancient forerunner species had constructed a series of stable wormholes to link the stars. Humanity had found some, but had yet to understand or even map them properly. Humanity called the network of wormholes the Axis Mundi, after the connection between heaven and earth found in so many human legends. Some Axis Mundi wormholes crossed a few light-years, but many bridged dozens or hundreds of light-years. They opened the stars to humanity.

Of the forty or fifty found by humanity, the large patron nations controlled all except for two.

The Puppets controlled one.

In the back of *The Calculated Risk,* Belisarius carried the other.

Forty years ago, an Expeditionary Force of Sub-Saharan Union warships had been sent by the Congregate, their patron nation, deep into Middle Kingdom space. They never returned. The Union Force had been assumed destroyed, but had in fact gone into hiding.

They'd discovered a pair of wormhole mouths that in the ancient past had collided with each other, disrupting their normal function and structure. One side of the conjoined wormholes led into the past, the other into the future. And rather than give this time travel device to their patrons, the Union Force had fled for deep space, to try to figure out how to send information into the past.

The Expeditionary Force did find a way, and spent forty years creating new propulsion systems and weapons, achieving ten times the progress by sending their research results back to themselves in the past. But after forty years, they found themselves at the opposite side of the only other wormhole not owned by a patron nation: the Puppet wormhole. And the problem was that the Puppets had wanted the Union fleet as much as the Sub-Saharan Union had wanted to get home.

Four months ago, with no military or political options, the Union hired Belisarius Arjona, a con man, to get the Expeditionary Force through the Puppet Axis by tricking the Puppets. Three weeks ago, Belisarius and Cassie, with the help of a half-dozen others, had gotten the Expeditionary Force through.

But three weeks ago Belisarius had also physically entered the Union's conjoined wormholes, traveling through the immensity of the interior to emerge about ten minutes before he'd entered, allowing him to steal the time gates from the Union.

The Union breakout from the Puppet Axis had handed the Congregate a major military setback and had torn apart the

Puppet Free City's port. Belisarius had expected to become a wanted man among the Puppets, and eventually to the Congregate.

He hadn't thought they'd fire a nuclear weapon on his home. His people were contemplatives, pacifists. They didn't have his skills. The explosion of ten minutes ago was his fault, something so enormous that it bordered on the unreal. And in fact, its reality was in question. Belisarius, as much as Cassie, was wired for quantum logic, and the quantum world interacted with the macroscopic world in many strange ways. If they could navigate that interaction, they might save the *Homo quantus*.

Belisarius and Cassie sealed their suits and cycled through the airlock into the hold. The time gates were hard to see from this angle. They were two ovals, fifteen meters on the long axis and ten on the short axis, with millimeters of apparent depth. At times they displayed the properties of solids, and at times, the properties of liquids, with tensions and elasticities that hinted at previously unknown quantum gravitational phenomena. The conjoined wormholes suffered themselves to be bent to fit inside the curved hold of *The Calculated Risk*.

Belisarius and Cassie had to edge along the curved floor of the racer's hold to get to the futureward face of the gates. Faint blue Cerenkov radiation hovered over the austere surface of the opening like a mist of light. Within the dark surface, streaks of purpled light snaked like shadows from some other present. The patches of dim colors flexed—hypnotic, elusive and inscrutable.

It was now him and Cassie against extinction. But he didn't know if his idea could even work. Extinctions happened all the time in the grand scheme of things, and if the *Homo quantus* really vanished, where did the blame stop? His mistakes were the immediate cause, but his mistakes were themselves engineered into his behavior by earlier generations in braided chains of cause and effect. Maybe, in all the genetic tinkering and false starts and frenetic striving to evolve the *Homo quantus,* the only meaningful emergent property to rise from that chaos was a species-level suicide switch, which he'd triggered. Maybe as a species, the *Homo quantus* would exist and vanish, like a virtual particle in the quantum foam of empty space-time. Unless he and Cassie could thread their way through the chaos to find the *Homo quantus* some other fate.

Cassie's helmet came close to his. Through two layers of glass, expressions were not so hard to endure. She was worried too.

"We have time," she said unironically, clasping his glove with hers.

"What am I supposed to do by myself?" Saint Matthew demanded.

"When Cassie and I enter the time gates, you go back to the hideout and wait for our signal. It might not be long."

The bottom corner of a monitor showed the date and time. March 13th, 2515, 11:12am, Indi Standard time. Belisarius' pulse throbbed faster, not with fear for his people, but with excitement. He hated his instincts.

Cassie slipped into the quantum fugue, the rational nirvana of the *Homo quantus,* where self, subjectivity and consciousness extinguished. The intellect occupying her body could perceive probability and quantum superposition without collapsing them. Cassie, the woman who had his heart, ceased to exist, and yet in a very strange sense she was more satisfied and fulfilled than when she'd been a person.

Yin and yang. Mutually exclusive. Subjective and objective. Person and object.

The quantum intellect in Cassie would need a few seconds to prepare for crossing the futureward mouth of the conjoined wormholes. In some ways, he envied the careless joy with which

Cassie threw herself into the quantum fugue. He had a complex relationship with the fugue. His instinct to learn had always outweighed his instinct for self-preservation, which would have eventually killed him.

He'd fled the Garret at sixteen in hopes of surviving. He'd become a con man, burying himself in the patternless economy of human greed to avoid his addiction to mathematical patterns. But his skill as a con man made the Sub-Saharan Union seek him out to move their warships across the Puppet Axis. And that put him near the time gates they secretly carried, a cosmological and mathematical temptation no *Homo quantus* could ever pass by. To steal the time gates Belisarius had needed to travel through them, backwards in time. That had done more than show him the naked hyperspace within.

The transit had precipitated a crisis that changed his nature. He was no longer like Cassie or any other *Homo quantus*, capable of being one of two mutually exclusive things: a conscious subjective being or an objective collection of interacting algorithms. The quantum fugue ran constantly in him now, in a partitioned part of his brain; the subjective Belisarius, the con man, coexisted simultaneously with the quantum objectivity. He hadn't figured out what that meant yet, how the objective and subjective would interact with the world. He didn't even know if this weird new coexistence was sustainable and survivable. In the past, to access his quantum perceptions, he would have simply extinguished his self like Cassandra had just done, replacing his intellect with another. But now, he negotiated with that other intellect inside him?

The Homo quantus and all they've learned are in danger, he said to the quantum intellect running in his brain. *We need to navigate the interior of the time gates again, to travel back in time two weeks. While you navigate, the Cassandra objectivity will record all it can of the hyper-spacial interior.*

The quantum intellect lacked consciousness, but like any computer program or set of algorithms, it possessed fundamental operating parameters and objectives. Through these, it could be manipulated, like all non-conscious things, and many conscious ones. The quantum intellect couldn't conceptualize team work or value the lives of the *Homo quantus*, but it valued the knowledge possessed by the *Homo quantus* in ways reminiscent of kin selection in evolution.

Acceptable, the intellect responded in Belisarius' thoughts.

Belisarius pushed them off the deck and they floated past the surface of the time gates, and for only the second time, he was a watching passenger, riding a life he had handed over to something alien.

CHAPTER FOUR

EVEN IN THE remoteness of prehistory, humanity had created temples by which to mediate brushes with the mysteries of the universe. From inaccessible cave paintings and megalithic observatories to widely-scattered pyramids to the great cathedrals and mosques, builders designed mirrors to reflect the infinities beyond human understanding. Those reflections inspired awe.

The time gates in the hold of *The Calculated Risk* were the cathedral to these first tentative generations of the *Homo quantus* and perhaps fittingly, they possessed the unplanned structure of the first caves. Two wormhole mouths had collided in the ancient past and stuck together. The interference of their throats had uncurled the seven dimensions of space that were curled into undetectability in normal space-time. Physics worked differently in eleven dimensions.

Belisarius had been protected from the alien strangeness on his first passage through by the fact that he hadn't been a conscious being at all. For most of his trip, he'd been a piece of flesh driven by his own quantum intellect. For the last portions, once he and the objectivity had figured out how to coexist simultaneously, most of his senses had been routed through the quantum intellect. He'd experienced only what he could see with his eyes.

Now, his eyes struggled to focus on eerie purples and faint blues, shining light coming from dimensions his brain could not quickly model. Perspective bloated, as if lenses migrated between him and a misty scape of gray leavened with kaleidoscopic glints of orphaned colors. Weird sounds echoed faintly outside his helmet, phantom sensations. Electromagnetic fields pattered over the magnetosomes embedded in the muscle cells of his arms and legs, hinting at the higher-dimensional enormity of space-time within the gates that eyes could not perceive. Insignificance skewered him, causing even his guilt over his people to diminish and recede. Worldly concerns and even self-preservation withered in this cosmological temple.

His most precise sense, the magnetic one, was faint. The partitioned region of his brain where the thinking objectivity expanded its quantum perceptions hoarded the magnetic sensory input. He only glimpsed the vast world, but even this limited sharing of two intellects was something his genetic engineers had never intended.

The quantum intellect fed him navigational instructions which he followed as if he were nothing more than the drive program on a shopping drone. Six hundred meters forward. Full stop. Rotate forty-five degree through the x-axis. Two hundred meters. Full stop. Rotate ninety degrees through p- and m-axes.

The misalignment of the wormhole interiors sent some directions to spatial or temporal dead ends, minor singularities that even his quantum intellect could not yet model mathematically. The complex space-time topography generated strange forces, currents of gravitation and electromagnetism that required avoidance or circumnavigation. While inconvenient for travel, those imperfections would be the lenses through which the *Homo quantus* would decipher the fabric of the cosmos.

Belisarius risked a brief glance at his helmet dashboard. They'd slaved Cassie's suit to his, and her cold jets pushed her in his wake. Her temperature had risen to forty-one degrees. His own fugue fever had gone past forty. Since his change three weeks ago in the time gates, his body now ran a low-level fever of thirty-eight and a half degrees all the time, but the quantum intellect in him was running hard, processing enormous amounts of information and generating heat. He could last for a while longer, long enough to lead them out of the time gates, but Cassie's fever was becoming dangerous.

He triggered an injection of neural inhibitors in her brain, a packet of molecular agonists to force a hard exit from the fugue. She could have survived a higher, longer fever, but they didn't know what they'd need of each other in the past and a fever could slow them down.

Cassie gasped and resumed a panting human rhythm of breathing, instead of the slow, shallow breaths of the quantum intellect. She groaned.

"You okay?" he asked.

"It's so beautiful," she said wonderingly, "and there's so much."

"I know."

"There's more." She sounded breathy, struggling with the nauseous come-down from fugue fever. But like him, she might also be working despite the vastness of the awe. "I have to verify the math."

"We're almost through," Belisarius said.

"I don't want it to be a false positive, Bel," she said with a longing, plaintive note.

The genetic engineers who had built the *Homo quantus* for generations had dialed up mathematical and geometric ability and pattern recognition. Capable of tremendous theoretical discoveries, false positives and heart-breaking chimeras nonetheless haunted the *Homo quantus*.

What had she seen that had pulled that plaintive note from her?

He stopped on cold jets again, in a region of the hyperspace where streaks of iridescent green shot through the darkness like veins beneath skin. Belisarius and Cassie rotated ninety degrees across a final axis, bringing into sight a line before them. As they rotated, the line fattened, assuming texture and misty detail, growing into the oval they recognized as one of the mouths of the time gates, hovering dark against a gray, formless background.

"This should open onto three hundred and forty-eight hours ago," Belisarius said. "Ready?"

"I haven't felt ready for anything," she said distantly, her fevered breathing becoming more shallow in his earpiece, "but that hasn't stopped me yet."

They drifted through the pastward mouth of the gates. Belisarius' perceptions narrowed. From eleven dimensions of hyperspace, his world shrank to three dimensions of space and one of time. Despite his *Homo quantus* nature, palpable relief washed through him. Every *Homo quantus* would ache to worship at the hyperspacial cathedral, but it was an experience to withstand, not delight in.

Their helmet lamps lit the hold of *The Calculated Risk*, as if they'd never left, except now they faced the external bay doors instead of the floor. And they had weight, the third of a gravity he was used to. Belisarius wrapped his glove around a handhold. Three hundred and forty-eight hours in the past, *The Calculated Risk* sat in the hold of a large Puppet freighter Belisarius had rented at Port Blackmore.

The Belisarius and Cassie of this time would be asleep, zipped into sleep sacs near the cockpit as they waited for clearance to leave the port. The Saint Matthew of this time would be in the cockpit. Belisarius hooked into the ship's systems, which would immediately suggest to Saint Matthew that he had a security breach.

"Saint Matthew, this is Belisarius," he said. "Don't set off any alarms, or wake me or Cassie, because you'll produce a causality violation."

"What?" Saint Matthew replied, at the same time that the lights clicked on in the hold. Cameras focused on Cassie and him. Saint Matthew's automata woke and skittered along the walls, towards the door, then away, then towards the door again. Belisarius waved. Multispectrum cameras swiveled their way.

"One way to confirm what I'm saying is to check the suit IDs," Belisarius said. "These identical suits should be in the locker."

Long moments of silence dragged out. Then a long-suffering sigh sounded in their ear pieces.

"Good morning, Mister Arjona," Saint Matthew grumbled.

"You aren't asking me for more proof of who I am?" Belisarius asked.

"No one else would do this to me," the AI said.

"It's a mark of our friendship," Belisarius said.

"I won't be party to a causality violation," Saint Matthew said tersely.

"After all this is done, you could become the patron saint of time travelers, not just the patron saint of banks."

"That's not funny!" Saint Matthew said. "What are you doing? Are you from the past or future? Wait! I take that back. Don't tell me. Don't tell me anything!"

"We won't. Cassie and I just need to get out of here and into the Free City. Can you help?"

"We're still on the wreckage of the Free City port," Saint Matthew said.

"Great. You can open a hatch for us, somewhere, right?" Belisarius asked.

"If it gets you farther away, I can get one of my automata to open something for you."

"We'll get out of your hair."

"Very funny," the AI replied. The bald head of Caravaggio's Saint Matthew shone as a hatch opened at the stern of the hold.

"Thank you, Saint Matthew," Cassie said.

"Good luck," the AI said with the tone of someone looking to close the door quickly.

Belisarius and Cassie stepped to the hatch and peeked into the big hold. *The Calculated Risk* was just a small part of the cargo in the big cylindrical freighter. Iron beams, finished steel plates, aluminum plating, cabling, and satellite struts filled the hold, as well as two small tugboats. Belisarius and Cassie climbed out and closed the hatch behind them.

A hundred and eighty meters away, on the far side of the hold beside an emergency outer hatch, one of Saint Matthew's spidery automata signaled them with a flashing red light. The disapproving face of Caravaggio's Saint Matthew bloomed in miniature over the automaton. Belisarius and Cassie moved along the webbing that held *The Calculated Risk* in place, past stacks of beams. By the time they reached the automaton, the hatch was open and Saint Matthew's glower had deepened.

"We get it, Saint Matthew," Belisarius said.

The view beyond was ugly. The normal chaos of the port had been blown to pieces. Above them, where once the mouth of the Puppet Axis had opened into a cavernous space of cleanly-chopped ice bristling with gantries, bays, doorways and cannons, all under the umbrella of immense armored doors, the points of stars now shone in a black sky. Lines of scorched black or shining pink-white criss-crossed the walls of the port from the Axis all the way to the surface. Layers of weapons were melted or buried in sudden flows of ice, or simply incinerated. The observation and passenger waiting areas of the port gaped like empty egg shells.

It was humbling.

This was war. Belisarius hadn't caused it, but he'd opened the door to let through the people who had. It was like living with the fugue; things happened out of his control, but he was necessary, a midwife for events too immense to take in. The Puppets had wanted to extort the Union. The Congregate had wanted to keep the Union as a client nation. The Union had wanted to be free. And Belisarius had given them terrain on which to meet.

How many Puppets and humans had died as the Union force had blasted its way out of the Axis? The Congregate had paid too. One of their giant warships, the dreadnought *Parizeau*, had been destroyed with all hands. Belisarius had ceased to be a bystander belonging to no side. He'd become the enemy of all parties.

Puppets worked in crews, operating big construction machinery with dangerous and inefficient abandon, and in big-wheeled vacuum trucks. Puppets in battle armor also patrolled, watching the skies, but also unloading cargo.

Belisarius and Cassie hopped from the hatch. They shouldered twisted pieces of metal and began walking towards what looked like airlocks. A couple of full-sized humans working in the port might be uncommon, but in this chaos, probably large sections of the human population of the Puppet Free City were doing uncommon things.

In a large crater of shiny new ice, they reached an airlock that looked like it had barely survived a strike on what might have once been an artillery emplacement. White clouds blew out of the sides of the chamber beyond the airlock. Over the leaks, Puppet workers in space suits sprayed water that froze into new ice to hold the breathable air in the city.

A Puppet stepped towards him, trying different frequencies to speak to Belisarius. Belisarius mimed that he wasn't receiving and dropped his piece of metal. The other Puppets, who in Puppet fashion, stopped working as soon as anything happened around them, watched his fiction. Belisarius continued towards the airlock, but the Puppet grabbed his arm.

Belisarius eyed him for three point one seconds before pressing a money card into the Puppet's gloved hand. The Puppet regarded it suspiciously and pocketed it with a conspiratorial look at his companions. Belisarius cycled the airlock. The Puppet with the new money card watched them indecisively and then turned back to the work crew.

Inside, Belisarius and Cassie found a corridor that ought to have been lit. Their helmet lamps revealed exposed wires in the ceiling that they could feel with their magnetosomes. Lots of live wires, just centimeters from shorting. The wiring looked like it had been cannibalized to skip the nearby junction box, but not in a safe way. A couple of empty old tool boxes lay dusty in the corner. He handed one to Cassie and took the other. They moved deeper into the Free City.

They made their way into better lit and ventilated parts of the Puppet Free City. A café without coffee or tea or food, but with network access, seemed as good a place as any to stop. They removed their helmets at the table, but not their insulated cowls.

The pressure had definitely dropped below one atmosphere,

and the smell of burnt plastic laced odd air currents. Cassie's fugue fever glowed hot from her cheeks in the infrared. She popped two anti-pyretics. Belisarius did the same.

He accessed the public network. The display greened as he made contact with one of his sub-AIs. He instructed it to find three big freighters capable of inducing their own temporary wormholes. The Puppet Theocracy had an anemic economy, partly because of the embargo they lived under. Usually, freighters idled and were cheap, but most of them would now be leased for years as the Free City rebuilt. He authorized the sub-AI to outbid other potential customers, or even buy the freighters outright, and then left it to work.

"Are you okay?" he asked. She was sweating even in the cold, and she shivered slightly.

She nodded with fever-laced enthusiasm. "The interior was..." her voice trailed off.

He nodded, but he envied her and maybe she saw that. There weren't many things he could hide from her. She put a hand on his, clammy hot flesh on clammy hot flesh.

"What was it for you?" she said. "How did you interact with your quantum intellect?"

"I don't know. I don't understand it. It feels really partitioned, but it meant I couldn't see anything, not the real quantum world. I may not be your next step in *Homo quantus* evolution."

"You didn't get any sensory input?"

She was referring to his magnetic sense. To the *Homo quantus* the other senses were mostly irrelevant. He shook his head.

"You and the intellect set up the partition. There must be a way to partition it differently."

The touch of her hand on his irritated in the body ache of the fever. He pulled his hand away from beneath hers.

"When we have time, we can explore the partition together.

Find out what it means," he said. "Now, I'm getting some ships."

"Can you be traced?" Cassie asked.

"The Free City is nothing but clandestine channels," he said. "The three hundred Puppet micro-states don't trust each other. They don't police their networks. They just live out the normal kind of Puppet chaos. Over the years, I've hidden anonymous pockets of money and dormant sub-AIs throughout the city."

The display began running long lists of information.

"We have three big ships," Belisarius said, as the money for several years of leases transferred out of his accounts.

"How much money do you have?" Cassie said.

"This is most of it," he admitted. "But in a week we'll have plenty."

"A week in our past," she said, "and a week in the future. We need new grammar."

An incoming message from another of his sub-AIs winked on in his helmet. A hologram displayed his face and Cassie's, as well as those of Marie Phocas and the *Homo eridanus* Vincent Stills. Arrest warrants accompanied the holograms. Nothing on William Gander or Antonio Del Casal. William was dead, and Del Casal was missing.

"The Congregate has warrants and rewards for our arrest," he said. "Let's not spend a lot of time here."

THE FREIGHTERS BELISARIUS had leased were neither habitable nor in good repair. He and Cassie lost a day slaving the navigational controls of all three together before setting out. They set robotic systems to refitting the cargo holds, sealing leaks in the hulls, and building cubicle-sized rooms in the huge space; rows stacked upon rows—uncomfortable, poorly-lit, and indifferently ventilated. It was exhausting work, and sometimes intellectually tasking, even for *Homo quantus*.

Partway through that first day, in an exhausted moment, Belisarius drifted to the cockpit and floated before the tiny window, staring at stars that didn't move, letting his frenetic brain cool. The starscape was quiet. His brain matched patterns and constructed orbital curves of the stars, the satellites and ship traffic.

He couldn't see it, but he looked toward the exact location of their secret hideout. Their present selves, with Saint Matthew, were making their way to the hideout. From here though, their present selves were invisible, and to one accustomed to quantum logic, perhaps not entirely real.

The ships of the Sub-Saharan Union and of the Congregate were also too invisibly distant to feel real, even if he stepped up his vision. Those two mismatched fleets were finishing their battle over the Freyja Axis Mundi right now. Theoretical, academic, probable, like the destruction of the Garret, and unlike the certainty of the debris field of the *Parizeau* shining above Oler.

Dirty ice regolith and churned surface roads gave way to great blast craters of shining white. New flash-frozen ice melt lay like silvery-pink rivers of molten rock, forming sudden five meter high obstacles to the surviving surface cars hauling steel and finished parts from the gaping hollow of the port just at the edge of Belisarius' view. He didn't step up his vision to get a better view.

How many Puppets had died? How many humans? Belisarius hadn't wanted this. He'd known what would play out; he wasn't naïve. But prior to seeing the destruction, he'd justified, putting the moral responsibility on others.

The Puppets were responsible for extorting the Union. The

Congregate was responsible for refusing to surrender political hegemony. The Union was responsible for their willingness to kill for independence. All of them owned their sins. What did he own?

Nothing?

The Union chose to rebel. And he wasn't the Congregate; Belisarius didn't rule over other nations. And most importantly, Belisarius couldn't find any guilt for stealing the time gates, no matter how he tried. The engineers who'd made the *Homo quantus* hadn't added a moral element into the engineered instincts. They simply made a species of people whose curiosity and pattern-seeking instincts were unnaturally strong, disproportionate to evolutionary advantage. Competing perspectives withered around the pattern-seeking instincts. Belisarius was a monster engineered to not regret having stolen the time gates, even if it resulted in the Garret being blasted to atoms.

A faint magnetism pressed against the muscles in his arms and legs. Cassie floated in behind him. She drifted to the port hole and regarded the stars. Their brains liked the star patterns. She put her smudged hands onto the grips and followed his eyes down to the broken surface of Oler.

"What are you doing?" Cassie asked.

"Thinking about what we are," he said.

"And?"

"The *Homo quantus* need to understand the universe."

"That's pretty innocuous," she said.

"On our own, in the Garret, under controlled circumstances, we're innocuous, but when our instincts are set free in the universe, we enable monstrous things. The Numenarchy thought they were making something innocuous when they made the Puppets. The *Homo quantus* and the Puppets are invasive species that escaped the lab."

Derek Künsken

Cassie made a face. She despised any comparison that put the *Homo quantus* and the Puppets in the same breath.

"Do you think we're dangerous, Bel?"

"I got the Garret blown up," he said.

She touched his cheek. "We did that together, Bel. We need the time gates. Nobody else needs them like we do. And we'll save everyone in the Garret."

Her insistence didn't make it better. She wasn't giving him a line, but neither was she convincing. His throat tightened. His eyes became hot and wet. He tried to stop it, and wiped at his eyes with his own smudged hands. It didn't help. Cassie moved to float against him, holding them together with her legs and a hand on his shoulder. She thumbed at his tears with her other hand.

"We should have been stronger," he said. "We're not just our instincts. We should have said no."

"Any of the *Homo quantus* in our place would have made the same choice, and would have died trying. No *Homo quantus* could have pulled the con you did, Bel."

"If they'd died trying to do what I did, the rest of the *Homo quantus* would still be alive."

"They still are in this past, Bel."

The hollow in his stomach, the tight knot in his throat belied her faith, and his. The *Homo quantus* no longer played with physics problems. He was no con man playing a mark. Even if they got to the Garret in time and managed to evacuate them all, they would be leaving all the things the *Homo quantus* were good at. How would they survive as refugees in the wide world? After what he and Cassie had done, every nation in civilization would be after them.

Cassie put her smudged hands on his cheeks. Her eyes teared.

"In an hour, we'll be underway to the Garret," she said.

"There's nothing to do until the coils get up to strength. Let's not tie ourselves in knots. All we can do is be ourselves."

He kissed her. Her arms slipped around his back and neck. She responded, then pulled back, smiling.

"What?" he asked.

"In the time gates, I made some weird observations," she said. "While we reprogrammed the navigational systems, I finished triple-checking my calculations."

If it had taken her this long to mentally check her calculations, the analysis must be complex. Against his will, the ugliness in his chest receded, displaced by the promise of discovery. And she became momentarily shy. She worshiped at the ornately bent space-time topology of the time gates as much as he. She navigated a religious awe with memories that, in her perspective, simply appeared while she vanished from consciousness.

"I found signs of strange quantum entanglements," she said.

"Interior entanglement structure?"

"No," she said. "When I looked at the time gates as a single quantum object, I found paths of quantum entanglement leading away from the time gates out into space. Lots of them."

"How far?"

"I probed at one of the paths," she said, "and I measured how it resonated. I took those measurements and calculated what would be entangled with it to explain the resonances. I think the time gates are entangled to another wormhole of the Axis Mundi network."

A cautious elation crept into his chest, engineered endorphins released in response to the mental state associated with discovery.

"There's more. I think I have a rough sense of where that other wormhole is," she said.

Belisarius realized he was gaping and that time had passed. He'd been processing the astonishing thing she'd said.

"I couldn't have done that analysis if I hadn't guided the induced wormhole into the Puppet Axis three weeks ago," she said. "Quantum entanglement between wormholes was very different than entanglement between particles."

"You can find another wormhole of the Axis Mundi?" he said in astonishment.

"I'm wondering if I can find more than one."

She grinned. Her eyes were bright. He grinned too.

CHAPTER FIVE

BELISARIUS AND CASSIE stepped into the smell of moist grass and trees in the Garret. Long hours of working the freighters, reprogramming their systems and robots, had left them dirty and sweaty, incongruous with the Garret. Gentle landscaped hills rolled from their feet all the way to where the winking blue, green, yellow and red lights on the roof of the icy cavern met the north wall of the Garret. Quiet birds flew shyly from tree to tree. For all that Belisarius disagreed with the *Homo quantus* who lived as isolated contemplatives, the Garret was a work of art and felt like home. Except that he was the corruption come to paradise.

No one came to meet them; that wasn't the way of the *Homo quantus*. They were all researching, or planning the directed evolution of the next generations, in savant or even the quantum fugue, solitary activities at their core.

One paved footpath led to a round administrative building tucked close to the western wall of the colony. Lightly-colored glass in aluminum frames gave a soothingly simple geometry to the walls, while the roof overflowed with bright, faintly-scented flowers. The glass doors slid open, revealing maintenance and engineering offices.

The *Homo quantus*, while highly creative in their scientific pursuits, preferred a pedestrian touch to their architecture and decorations. They named the rooms of the municipal building after the colors of the windows: the yellow board room, the violet, blue, and orange offices. And, at the end of the small building, the mayor's office was the green room, after its green windows. Belisarius and Cassie walked to the green room.

Mayor Lina Arjona smiled and bowed slightly to Cassie. Lina led the *Homo quantus* project. Like Belisarius, Afro-Colombian and mestizo blood from Earth mixed in the mayor. Despite being born into the ninth generation, with the same organs and modifications Cassie and Belisarius carried, Lina was one of the many who couldn't enter the quantum fugue.

"Welcome home, Cassandra. We missed you." Lina looked at him. "And you came back again, Belisarius. I hope it's for good?"

Belisarius glanced to Cassie for help. She looked uncomfortable. Some people collected behind them.

"Let's sit and catch up," the mayor said.

Lina's office had a table with six chairs. A few people brought extra chairs from other offices. He met colony Councilors Agustín Uribe, Beatríz Pachón, Nícola Samper, and assistants Tatiana Melendez and Marcelo Arciniegas. Brief bows accompanied each introduction. Many *Homo quantus* reacted poorly to physical contact, partly from their introverted natures, partly because not everyone could control their electroplaques as well as he did. Contact discharges could be painful.

They spoke. Some of it was small talk. At one level, his brain absorbed the information, made the appropriate gestures and responses, but on another, his brain panicked, trying to find a way to tell this, to make it better. All his con man skills seemed to fail him; nothing came to him.

He cared about the *Homo quantus*. He and Cassie had agreed that she should try to explain the danger to them. He'd left the Garret at sixteen, a decision many in the project took as a betrayal, while Cassie was one of their darlings. And yet, in the moment, she seemed not only out of place covered in dirt and smudges, but as nervous as he. And yet he couldn't speak. They wouldn't believe him.

"Where have you been, Cassandra?" the mayor asked. "What's the wide world like?"

Cassie smiled awkwardly.

"Three months ago, Bel offered me data if I helped him on a job."

The mayor leaned forward when Cassie said 'data'. Belisarius did too.

"Bel showed me evidence that his employers, the Union, had found a time travel device," Cassie said.

Eyebrows rose. The mayor lost her *Homo quantus* expression of double-processing. Someone said "What?"

"I didn't believe him right away," she said. "I went with him because of our previous collaborations, and because of the data he brought."

The mayor and her councilors eyed Belisarius uncertainly.

"A time travel device?" Arciniegas said.

"The Sub-Saharan Union had a small fleet on the other side of the Puppet Axis," Cassie said. "The Puppets wouldn't let the Union through unless they turned over half the fleet in payment. So using the theories Bel and I had developed a decade ago, and data from the Union fleet, we connected an induced wormhole to the mid-throat of the Puppet Axis."

The mayor's mouth gaped open. Some councilors made sounds that weren't words. Most remained silent, mentally digging up their knowledge of space-time geometries. They were all brilliant mathematicians and capable astrophysicists, but none were wormhole experts. Wormhole physics was too applied a discipline for most *Homo quantus*.

"I directed the induced wormhole from within the fugue," Cassie said, "guiding my perceptions, following lines of entanglement as navigational guides through hyperspace. While I did this, Bel stole the time travel device from the Union."

Eyes turned on him, at once horrified and approving.

A time travel device.

Every one of them hungered for knowledge the way he did.

"That can't be possible," the mayor said. "Nothing can travel back in time."

"I transited the... device myself," Belisarius said, feeling guilty at referring to something so spiritually sublime with the banal word device. "I went back fifteen minutes."

They looked at him like he'd grown another head.

"I navigated through it from within the fugue," he said. "The interior is naked hyperspace, two eleven-dimensional regions of space-time that together make a twisted mess of twenty-two dimensions."

"Bel and his quantum intellect changed inside the time gates," Cassie said. "He and the intellect coexist in his brain all the time by some kind of partitioning. He may be the next step in the evolution of the *Homo quantus*."

The mayor rose slightly in her chair. "You haven't been hooking him up to monitoring equipment to study this? We've been wasting time talking? What if this effect is temporary?"

Cassie looked stricken. A tear traced a curve down one cheek.

"There's been no time, Lina," she said. "Yes, we took the time travel device... the time gates. Yes, Bel has some strange partitioning in his brain hinting at the future of the *Homo quantus*. But this pulled Bel and I into the conflict between the

Congregate, the Union and the Puppet Theocracies. The Union wants their wormholes back."

"You led them here?" Uribe said with an expression of dawning understanding.

Cassie shook her head.

"Everyone knew where the Garret was."

Cassie waited. She'd changed in the last three months. She'd become harder. More confident. Like him. He didn't really want that anymore. He'd rather become more like her; in control of his instincts, just a researcher, not a con man.

"The Union will come here?" the mayor asked. "They'll use us as bargaining chips to get the time gates back?"

"It's worse than that," Cassie said. "Congregate spies know that two *Homo quantus*, Bel and I, helped the Union."

"The Congregate is looking for you?" the mayor asked quietly.

"Everyone who has business to know these things has realized that the *Homo quantus* have become a military asset," Cassie said. "All the *Homo quantus*."

Lina's expression melted.

"The Congregate..." the mayor said finally. "You've destroyed us."

Cassie nodded. "We really have. In twelve days, the Congregate will arrive at the Garret. They'll destroy it."

The mayor deflated.

"You know this because you somehow broke into their plans?" she asked guardedly.

Cassie said nothing. The mayor looked at Belisarius. He shook his head. Lina looked away with a dreamy, stunned expression.

"You've both come from the future," the mayor concluded.

"Yes," Belisarius said.

"Why?" the mayor asked in a low voice. Her face and hands

had cooled. She wilted as he watched. They'd brought her the best and worst news of her life. New evolution. New knowledge. And extinction. "We can't change anything."

"We observed the destruction of the Garret," Belisarius said. "We were too far away to see any *Homo quantus* die. We can run away with all of you before that happens, and still be consistent with the observations in the future."

"Paradoxes," Samper said. She looked queasy at the word.

"This is *mierda!*" Uribe said, rising and flinging his chair away. He stomped out of the office. His footsteps faltered four meters down the hall, but he didn't come back. He just couldn't be in the same room as them with this news.

Cassie touched Lina's arm. "We haven't given you any information that will change the observations we made twelve days in the future. If we move quickly, we can save the *Homo quantus* without violating causality."

"Where would we go?" Samper asked angrily. "The Banks will protect us. They'll keep funding the *Homo quantus* project."

The whole room existed within a held breath.

"If we run to the Banks, the *Homo quantus* will become a military project," Belisarius said. "The *Homo quantus* have become militarily relevant. No one will ever believe otherwise again."

The mayor put her forehead in her hands.

"This is the end of us," she whispered.

She was right. No more quietly retiring to contemplate and engineer themselves. Events were thrusting the *Homo quantus* onto the stage. No, not events—*his* actions. He'd gone into the wide world with the gifts and curses of the *Homo quantus* and shown civilization that they were not children anymore.

But neither had the *Homo quantus* grown into adulthood. They were fragile, in-between, lacking most of the abilities needed to truly protect themselves. He and Cassie were their only guides in this terrifying new world.

"We brought three freighters," Belisarius said. "They won't be comfortable, but there's just about room for us all. We can jump away by induced wormhole, far enough that the Congregate won't find us."

"Freighters?" the mayor asked.

"Like refugees," Arciniegas said.

"Where will we go?" the mayor asked. "How will we live?"

"We don't have all the answers," Belisarius said, "but we can make sure no *Homo quantus* are here in twelve days."

"You left the Garret!" the mayor said. "You rejected us! And now you've come back, dragging this... destruction to our door!"

Lina's words resonated with his imaginings of the dead Puppets in the Free City, with the silence of the crew on the *Parizeau* and all the others who would have been alive but for his actions.

"You asked me to convince Bel to come home, Lina," Cassie said. "I went with him for the data, and the chance at more. We brought back much, much more, but Bel didn't know this would happen."

The mayor was crying, shaking her head. Thin tears met under Cassie's chin. Belisarius found his cheeks wet too.

"Lina," Cassie said, "this is awful news, but right now we need to keep people alive. We need to evacuate now."

"Where could we possibly go where the Congregate wouldn't find us?" the mayor said in a daze.

CHAPTER SIX

THE WORST WERE not the crying children. It made sense that children, frightened and disoriented at the idea of leaving their homes, would be reduced to tears. The tears of the adults bit Belisarius more deeply. The Garret had always been a dangerous place for Belisarius' engineered instincts. His nature had forced him away, and he'd had years in the Puppet Free City to grieve his leaving. Nothing in the Garret could have prepared any of the *Homo quantus* for this. And so everyone mourned the Garret right now.

Belisarius might have dealt better with them yelling at him, throwing things, but they'd gone numb, overwhelmed and disbelieving the message Belisarius and Cassandra brought from the future. Between fits of grieving for the home they would be leaving, the *Homo quantus* became automata, unable to process the world beyond their fingertips, free of self-consciousness for moments, as if they'd hidden in a fugue of fear. A people designed to one day see the future suddenly couldn't see an hour ahead.

He and Cassie shared the small bed in her suite, huddling each night like two little animals frightened of the world outside their nest. Their moods swung wildly. At times, they could take the despondency no more and they fled into savant and mathematics.

Within that numbing state, they had a rich theoretical world to model. They still didn't understand all of what Cassie had seen in the interior of the time gates. Instead of sleeping, she sometimes went into savant, raking through the memories left by her quantum intellect, turning the puzzle pieces over and over. Belisarius couldn't help, even though he wanted more than anything to stop thinking about the evacuation.

"I need to be able to enter the quantum fugue in some way," he said, "otherwise I'm no more useful to us than any of the bioengineers and geneticists. We need to understand what you observed more quickly than we are."

Cassandra had been laying back, complex holographic geometries above her constructed from datasets in her brain that he couldn't access. His own quantum intellect had taken different measurements, had navigated. His data was valuable, but she was looking at things he didn't understand, true basic exploratory science, and he was jealous, left out. Cassandra's holograms stilled and she slowly rolled to face him. The distant expression in her eyes cleared as she emerged from savant.

"Let go of all your resentment, Bel. The *Homo quantus* project isn't your enemy. We were built for a reason, with a purpose, and you might be the next evolutionary step, but none of our steps come easy. You have to explore what you are now, to yourself and to the quantum intellect. There's a whole village of scientists here who will want to help you, once we're out of here."

He nodded.

"Do you have any hope for the *Homo quantus* project?" she asked.

"Before the time gates, before someone tried to kill them all, I would have said no. Blood runs deeper than I thought."

Cassandra smiled and lay back on the narrow bed, and

resumed the manipulation of models he didn't understand. And their rhythm of evacuation work during the day and theorizing at night continued, although he turned more and more to the question of what he was and what it meant for he and the quantum intellect to coexist.

After three days, Cassie had scraped enough data from her memories to make a model. He felt anxious to see what she'd made. They sat in their old shared office in the Museum. Holographic projectors represented eleven dimensional space-time using angles, color gradients, holographic perspective and electromagnetic fields to depict them all. Visualizing six or seven dimensions was routine for *Homo quantus,* but eleven was challenging.

Cassandra had modeled the time gates as a single quantum object, a lumpy, uneven central blob of probability, with hundreds of thousands of lines of quantum entanglement streaming outwards, some bright and clear, others faint and blurry. Other lines of entanglement looped from one face of the time gates and back into the other, quantum events stitching and restitching themselves through time. The mathematical beauty and ambition of Cassie's thinking was awe-inspiring and humbling. She'd grown past him many times over in the years he'd been a con man, and he regretted part of his flight from the Garret.

"I think the lines of entanglement lead to other wormhole mouths of the Axis Mundi," Cassie said. "In healthy wormholes, we might never notice because the entanglement is so smooth. But the time gates are damaged, so the entanglement structure is easier to detect for our quantum intellects."

Belisarius' heart expanded with a kind of elation. Her theory was so vast, maybe the first thinking in all of humanity to understand the Axis Mundi network left by the forerunners. And flashes of possible patterns winked from the geometric tangle of dimensions in the hologram.

"There," she said at the same time as he traced a finger along one of the bright lines of entangled probability in their model. Another node, its own lines of entanglement radiating outward like the invisible solar wind from a star. "I think that's another wormhole of the Axis Mundi network."

He could guess at others, in the far distance of her projection. The model was limited by the data, and the data was just what Cassandra had grabbed on her first experience through the time gates. Quantum entanglement illuminated the architecture of the Axis Mundi network. She rotated the projection and three other bright nodes became clear in the cloudy image. Something looked strange.

"Do you recognize anything?" she asked.

Fevered excitement had crept into her voice. His brain tested model after model of the nodes. No correlation. No correlation. No correlation. Then something greened in his mind. He gasped.

"See?" she said.

Five bright nodes. Out of all that entanglement noise, he could match the geometric relationship of four nodes with the locations of the four mouths of the Axis Mundi in the Epsilon Indi system. The Puppet Axis. The Freyja Axis. The Delta Pavonis Axis. And the Congregate's Axis to Polaris.

And one bright node hovered in her model, unassigned. They neared the projection, tracing the filmy details with their eyes. A gentle magnetic pressure touched his arms and hands; Cassandra examining the last node in the electromagnetic. He hardened the magnetic field projected by his magnetosomes, and felt at the brightness, the spongy hardness, and Cassandra's magnetic field.

"The fifth Axis," she said, smiling.

The mouths of the Axis Mundi seemed to almost always come in sets of five. That wasn't to say that orbital dynamics over astronomical time hadn't ejected some Axes forever into interplanetary space, or into their sun, or that some still hadn't yet been found. The patron nations expected Epsilon Indi to have five Axes, but no one had ever found the fifth. But Cassandra may have. And if no one else knew of it, they may be able to flee through it with the *Homo quantus*.

Hope.

"It's beautiful," he said, "but one passage, through a single wormhole, is only a temporary solution. Sooner or later, someone will find this Axis. We need to go farther."

They looked for a long time at the projection, seeking, searching for more information, but like equations with too many unknowns, they'd reached the limit of what this data set could tell them. They needed more data, and not just because they were *Homo quantus*. This could save their people. And so those bright moments in the Museum stifled them under the full weight of their predicament as time wore down. Eight days to flee, and ten days until the Congregate arrived, and the *Homo quantus* were not mobilizing quickly.

Cassie cried in the mornings before going out to shepherd their people. She occupied a weird interstitial space of being the only one who could really get through to their people and being the only one truly capable of being angry with him. She'd seen the wide world, and that gave her the strength to be sullen and lash out.

What had he been thinking in getting involved with the Union? Only an idiot wouldn't have seen the dangers in helping the Union rebel. What gave him the right? It didn't matter that she'd played a part. He agreed with her. He'd come to this because he'd wanted to live. And then he'd become greedy for the time gates.

But part of Cassie's anger turned selfward. He'd been a con man long enough to know that her instincts were at war. She loved her people. This was her home. And unlike the rest of the

Homo quantus, she hadn't the luxury of denial. The destruction of the Garret had burned itself into her perfect memory. But she was *Homo quantus*, with all the engineered instinct for pattern-recognition and curiosity. She couldn't set aside the value of the time gates, or the things she'd seen and discovered within the fugue, even for a moment, something that would have let her regret the exchange. That told her something of the kind of person she was, and her instincts trapped her in an ambivalence surely as bitter as his.

Cassie was washing her face on the fourth morning, and tying her hair back.

"Lina can't do it," Cassie said abruptly, like she'd been puzzling over something for a long time. "She's coming apart."

Belisarius sat in a chair, feeling like he was filled with heavy, viscous tar. Of course Lina was coming apart. The mayor had been elected to administer a stable research outpost, not oversee its destruction.

"The *Homo quantus* need to hear that if we move quickly, they'll be safe, that we'll find them a home," she said.

He said nothing.

"They listen to me," she said, "but they won't believe me on this."

"You're one of them," he said.

"I don't know the world. They need to hear it from you, Bel."

"I don't know how to find them a home," he said. "I couldn't find myself a home."

"You've survived the wide world."

"I had Saint Matthew."

"William said that when he found you, you didn't know anything, that everything scared you," Cassie said. Her banked anger was dry for now, like her tears. "Every *Homo quantus* is there right now, Bel. Even me."

"I'm not responsible enough for this, Cassie. I never was."

"You took responsibility for everyone in the Expeditionary Force when you moved them across the Puppet Axis," she said.

He shook his head. Picked at his fingernails. He felt like he was curdling. He couldn't look at Cassie anymore.

"Everyone who worked the con accepted the dangers," he said. "You did. Even Will. General Rudo was responsible for the Expeditionary Force. She brought them home. I was just the ferryman."

"Like it or not Bel, whether the *Homo quantus* hate you or not for what's happened, you have to be the one to tell them it'll be okay. You have to tell them you'll lead them somewhere safe."

"It's not true," he said. He met her eyes. She'd not given up, but she was handing this to him.

"You're a con man," she said, without irony or judgment. "Your profession is lying. Exercise your profession now, or the *Homo quantus* will never leave the Garret. Pretend to be a leader."

He stood, and moved to take her hands. She didn't let him.

"Cassie, precisely because I'm a liar, they can never believe me," he said. "People think there's something magical about a lie, like it's about the lie itself, as if you make up a good enough lie, it will work. For a lie to work, the liar needs to be trusted. And no one trusts me."

"I do," she said.

He didn't want anyone's faith.

"I don't want to lie to anyone. They trust you, Cassie. They'll believe you because they want to. And they have to be angry at someone. Let them stay mad at me."

After a time, they walked from her small room to the cafeteria, ate briefly in a cubicle, surrounded by other hushed cubicle eaters. Then they made their way to the low office buildings, heavy under a funereal mood. Lina Arjona received them numbly. Councilors Uribe and Samper were morosely slumped in her office too. The five of them sat in silence for a time. This was supposed to be the morning meeting to deal with the problems of the fourth day of the preparations for the exodus.

"Lina," Belisarius said finally, "have you thought of asking Cassie to lead the evacuation for you?"

The mayor's dark eyes regarded Cassie dully, then drifted to Belisarius without expression.

"Can I appoint you mayor?" Lina asked quietly.

"Me?" Cassie asked incredulously.

Lina's limp stare leaned on her. Uribe and Samper, councilors who ought to have had some claim to the mayoralty, seemed relieved at the direction of the conversation.

"For the evacuation, and until we find a new home, it should be Bel?" Cassie said.

She'd chickened out.

"No one trusts me, Cassie," Belisarius said.

The mayor and the two councilors regarded him. Their expressions did not disagree with him, but neither did they look like they had alternatives. He saw what they wanted. They feared the unknown beyond the Garret. They couldn't imagine getting food and shelter that wasn't grown here or provided by the Banks, much less founding a new home. They thought he could. They wanted him to tell them what to do.

"I'll help you, Cassie," he said. "I'll be your advisor on the outside world."

"Legally, it isn't difficult," Uribe said. "The mayor appoints Cassandra deputy mayor, and then resigns."

"Cassie would make a great mayor," Belisarius said.

Cassie squeezed his hand. His heartbeat and breathing fell into resonance with hers, as if she were spotting him in the fugue.

CHAPTER SEVEN

ONE THOUSAND, THREE hundred and twelve *Homo quantus* assembled around the municipal building, looking up to the garden roof to watch Cassie's swearing in ceremony. Belisarius had never been watched by so many people at once. His hands and knees trembled. He wanted to hide, in savant, or even in the fugue. But their predicament was his fault and they all knew it by now, so he had to be here.

He was something of a prop too, now. They did trust Cassie, moreso because she'd been into the wide world. But they were angry and resentful, and he was the lightning rod. They could direct all that resentment towards him, leaving Cassie to be the one they would look up to and listen to. It was a bit of an emotional con, playing specifically on the highly developed *Homo quantus* ability to think in multiple channels. They could feel in multiple channels too.

And in a sense, they wanted to be conned. Desperate marks stood out there, as desperate as people greedy for money or recognition or power. The more desperate the mark, the easier they were to con. Cassie just had to find what was important to them, and con them with the truth. Cassandra Mejía took the oath of office, becoming the sixth mayor of the Garret, and the last.

She began her speech, haltingly. They'd written it together, using her knowledge of their people and Belisarius' knowledge of the con. She didn't have notes; her memory meant she didn't need them. Her hesitation was her reaction to all the people looking at her.

"We've been quiet and safe here, even ignored," Cassie said, "but the universe has noticed us. We made ourselves the gifts that enable us to study the cosmos. There are those who would use our gifts for war. We have to run, find some place to hide, forever."

The crowd hung on her words. Their faces were often guilelessly expressive and with his augmented eyes and overactive brain, Belisarius could analyze dozens of reactions at once, graphing them in his mind.

"I'm not a good pick for mayor," Cassie admitted, "but I can lead you in exile. I can find us a new home. Finding and building a new home will be hard, but when our grandparents first came to the Garret, it was just ice. We'll start with more. We're tenth and eleventh and twelfth generation *Homo quantus*. We've navigated the quantum fugue. And we're taking all our data and learning with us. None of it will be lost. We're leaving the Garret with the most important things: ourselves and all our learning. We'll never stop pushing at the cosmos until it gives us all it knows."

They were listening, really listening. Cassie was appealing to their artificially-strengthened curiosity and pattern-recognition. She went off-script, feeling their desperation, reacting to it, reassuring them, as good as any con man would have. Belisarius was lost in sweep of her words. When Cassie reached the end, no one clapped. The *Homo quantus* disliked noise, but he could tell she'd moved them. The *Homo quantus* drifted away, mildly uplifted, warily open to hoping, if only for a few hours.

After a time, Belisarius and Cassie went down to the mayor's office, Cassie's office, until the Congregate blew it up. They sat in the chairs in front of the desk, instead of either one taking the mayor's place. He kissed her.

"You did better than I could have, Cass."

"I can pretend to fix what you've done."

He sat back in surprise. "You're good at placing all the blame on me," he said with a touch of heat, "but didn't you see this coming? What did you think the *Homo quantus* project was about? Eventually this would have happened."

She shook her head, standing and moving away from him. Something was bothering her. Or catching up with her.

"The *Homo quantus* project is about understanding the universe, Bel," she said. "We provide knowledge and understanding to humanity."

Belisarius knew denial when he heard it. It was mana to a con man. She'd swept up the people of the Garret with her words, but in the best multi-channel *Homo quantus* thinking, she was second-guessing herself, picking apart arguments, attacking her own confidence; turning that to anger. But the same was happening to him. They were a day later, and now this all really was on them. She was the mayor, and he her advisor.

"The project is nothing of the sort, Cassie. The Plutocracy's Banks invested millions of pesos over eight decades to create people with quantum perceptions. They hoped their investments would buy them economic and military maps for the future. We're economic and military technology. Our day had to come. The world has noticed the weapons the Banks have created."

"We aren't dangerous."

"You moved a squadron of warships past militarized borders, Cass! What do you think we mean to the generals of the patron nations?"

"It didn't have to be now," she said. "We could have waited. We could have not taken the job."

He envied the quiet life she'd led, one that hadn't required her to build skills to push through difficult social situations, moral dilemmas and angry people. A cosseted life. A good life where the biggest arguments could be settled with data or statistical modeling. The wide world was chaotic and scary. He came close, but didn't touch her. He lowered his voice.

"That might not have changed much, Cass. At least now, the *Homo quantus* have you and me. We've been in the world. We're the dangerous ones. If the *Homo quantus* have a chance at surviving, it's us."

CHAPTER EIGHT

CASSANDRA WATCHED THE embarkation of the *Homo quantus* onto the three freighters, one day ahead of schedule and with a sinking heart. The robots from the freighters and the Garret were still working around the clock and although they hadn't finished remodeling the insides of the freighters, they were at least habitable. Water storage on the inside of the hull would shield them from radiation, but no ecosystem had been built, so for now, they chemically recycled the air and installed the colony's bioreactors. The larger problem was that with all the stowed scientific and industrial factories there was a lot less space for the people.

The *Homo quantus* boarded with haunted expressions—dejected, stunned, angry. Cassandra didn't like feeling the dread in her stomach and wanted to be away from here. Away from the people, lost in mathematics and discovery.

Nearly thirty-seven hundred people were boarded and unhappy, but a few hundred *Homo quantus* flatly refused to leave. They gathered at the port, trying to convince the others not to go. They'd changed the minds of a dozen. But finally, the last of the *Homo quantus* in exile were aboard.

Bel faced the hundreds refusing to come with them with

Cassie at his side. He argued with them. He pleaded with them. He reminded them of all the data they would lose access to if they stayed. He described the fireball that would devastate the Garret. But they wouldn't budge. What could anyone do?

They were rational, but they'd taken the information and come to different conclusions.

Based on those conclusions, Cassandra and these few hundred would live two very different, mutually exclusive lives. One path taken. One path not. It was the closest she would ever come to a true multiworlds cosmos, where a single choice dictated so much. But their choices were made, and each side would now live out the implications.

Belisarius was still trying to convince them. Cassie pulled on his arm and shook her head.

"Go into savant," she said.

"I can't convince anyone in savant."

"It's not for convincing, Bel," she said, wiping her eyes. "It's to get the work done. Let the emotions go."

He frowned. Uncomfortable. The resisters around them sensed something happening.

"My feelings won't go away in savant, Cassie."

But she had already entered savant. The arguments and grief and loss washed over her, prickling, but not really getting to the core. The mathematics became clearer. Time ticked. The freighters had to be away.

Belisarius turned from the doomed few who had chosen to stay and walked towards the boarding ramps.

"That's it?" Constanza yelled after him. Not at Cassandra, but at him. Constanza had helped run the telescopes for years, someone with whom Cassandra and Bel had crossed paths many times.

Belisarius kept walking.

"That's it," Cassandra said, following him.

Terrifying feelings of separation, abandonment and betrayal washed distantly over her, refusing to define themselves. She should have been screaming, dragging these people with her, but they could not come. They were real and would soon be dead, and she was walking away.

Once they had boarded, the umbilicals detached behind them. They were already likely under observation right now by the Congregate, and maybe even the Banks, but no one would be suspecting that the three freighters were anything but what they appeared. The patron nations were only now piecing together the *Homo quantus* involvement in the breakout of the Union from the Puppet Axis.

The freighter Belisarius and Cassie had boarded, *Blue,* rocked as they lifted off from the Garret's small port. They'd named the freighters *Red, Blue* and *Green* after quantum chromodynamics; the colors that bound quarks together in protons. The *Homo quantus* children had come up with the naming system as a kind of totem to make sure no one was lost.

They stood on the bridge of the *Blue* with a few of the councillors and engineers. From behind them, deeper in the freighter, cries emerged from children and adults who'd never left home, never felt any acceleration other than the gravity of the Garret.

When Cassandra had left the Garret, she'd been afraid, but she'd left with Bel, the boy she'd loved as a girl, and whom she might love again as a woman. She'd left the Garret with the confidence that she could always come home. Now, they were all refugees.

Cassie's pad buzzed. Pads buzzed all around her. Personal computers. Comms. Service bands. A message from Bel rung on every device in the fleet. The message contained data they had gathered about the wormholes; mathematical problems about the modeling of eleven-dimensional space. A sudden elation filled her, and she smiled. The *Homo quantus* might be terrified, homesick and mourning, but they were still *Homo quantus*, easily drawn into geometric problems. They didn't particularly like applied questions, but that might not matter now. More problems and deeper questions appeared on their devices— the stability of induced wormholes; the six-dimension hyper-structure of wormhole throats, and stress problems; spaceship blackbody radiation interference questions. She even saw some of the basic entanglement models they'd started building for the Axis Mundi. Cassie smiled.

Most *Homo quantus* would never have worked on anything like this, but Bel had included enough references that they could go back, learn the math and assumptions, imagine the geometries, and begin making progress. Probably in a few hours. Other messages appeared on her screen. Working groups started establishing themselves. Problems and assumption testing elements were divided up. It was hope, a sign that they might survive.

"That's very thoughtful of you, Bel," she whispered.

He smiled wanly. The acceleration cut and they floated free in their seats. More grunts and exclamations came from the stacks of cubicles sternward. The freighters were far enough from the Garret's weak gravity and blackbody radiation to induce the wormhole they'd preprogrammed. Cassie rubbed Belisarius' arm encouragingly, trying to banish the image of those they'd left behind. She couldn't of course, and neither could he.

"We're escaping, Bel," she whispered.

He pursed his lips and pulled her closer, touching his hot forehead to hers.

"This is just hiding," he said. "We have to find them something better."

CHAPTER NINE

CONGREGATE MARINES IN powered armor bearing shoulder-mounted particle cannons emerged from the airlocks into the eerie stillness of the Garret. The Epsilon Indi Scarecrow followed them into the cavern. Its piezoelectric musculature whirred beneath carbon steel cloth. Zooming cameras in its face rotated, spotting the same thing as the marines: infrared signatures. Warm, breathing bodies. Radar frequencies penetrated the plastic and sintered regolith of the houses and apartment complexes on the rolling green hills.

Two hundred and seventy people.

Intelligence sources had estimated four thousand. There were dwellings for that many.

The marines fanned out, securing common buildings and installations, those most likely to contain electronic records. Second and third waves followed, moving from house to house, breaking in and pulling the crying families into custody. Ultrasounds of the captives' torsos revealed the presence of electroplaques beneath their ribs, confirming their *Homo quantus* natures. Most captives were anesthetized, fitted with helmets to interrupt electrical or magnetic signals and then carted back to the airlocks and onto the Congregate dropship.

Some, however, were brought to the Scarecrow.

"Where are the rest of the *Homo quantus*?" the Scarecrow asked in last century's *français*.

"They left," one woman stammered.

"Why?" the Scarecrow demanded.

"Belisarius Arjona came back," the woman said. "He warned us that we had to leave, that he'd seen that the Congregate was going to blow up the Garret."

"How did he know that?"

"He said he traveled back in time."

"Did you believe that he did?"

"I don't know. I don't think so. Time travel is impossible. I should have listened."

"Because it is possible?"

"Because you came."

"Where is Arjona? Where are the other *Homo quantus*?"

She shook her head. "I don't know. They left in ships."

"How long ago?"

"Two days ago."

The woman sobbed, hugging her child. The Scarecrow relayed the information he'd been given to Capitaine Arsenault on *Les Rapides de Lachine*.

"You'll all be coming with us," the Scarecrow said, turning back to the *Homo quantus*, "for more extensive interviews about these incredible stories about Arjona, and about your quantum abilities."

"I don't have any quantum abilities," she said, eyes widening. "Most of us don't. Every generation has a few more functional *Homo quantus*, but I'm only generation ten."

The woman was anesthetized and loaded with the others. Intelligence officers and political officers descended from *Les Rapides de Lachine*, systematically dismantling the Garret. The

Homo quantus had left a great deal of information, mostly useless reformulations of physical theories and genetic records, but they'd also left in such a hurry that they hadn't grabbed all the backups of how they'd inched forward in developing this new and dangerous sub-species of humanity.

"This will anger the Banks," Majeur Demers said.

"Let it," the Scarecrow said. "The Banks should have kept a tighter leash on their pet projects. We've no doubt already pre-empted their anger with a million-franc bounty on any *Homo quantus* brought to us alive. Politically, we can accuse the Banks of engineering terrorists."

"What do you make of the story, that Arjona had come from the future?" Demers asked.

The Scarecrow had been turning this over too.

"No technology we know of would enable time travel," the Scarecrow said. "But if the *Homo quantus* have figured out some way to do it, that might start to explain the Union break-out of the Puppet Axis. Our spies saw no Union ships entering the Axis at Port Stubbs. Somehow the *Homo quantus* engineered this. And if we have four thousand genetically-modified Anglo-Spanish weapons capable of seeing the future, then the capture of Arjona and the remaining *Homo quantus* has to be one of the highest priorities of the Presidium."

CHAPTER TEN

BELISARIUS FELT AN unreasoning relief four days later when they rendezvoused with Saint Matthew in the empty fastness of space almost a light-hour above the ecliptic. This oughtn't have been in doubt, but the reality of leaving the Garret and the misery of the *Homo quantus* had amplified risks in his mind. The Garret was gone. They'd pointed passive telescopes towards solar south and watched their home vanish in a slow-motion replay of their original observations. Hundreds of *Homo quantus* were now dead.

Belisarius and Cassie transferred to *The Calculated Risk*. Cassie's models would only prove their worth once they'd collected more data. They had to know if the time gates were really maps to other mouths of the Axis Mundi.

"You did it," Saint Matthew said in wonder.

"Barely," Cassie said.

"This might be the closest thing I've seen to a miracle."

"We've performed nothing but since Bel convinced me to leave the Garret."

Belisarius didn't feel that they'd done anything miraculous. He couldn't even fit the word into his thinking now that he'd really been inside the hyperspacial interior of the time gates.

Every moment since Major Iekanjika walked into his life felt like frantic improvising. And the Garret had paid for his risks. He didn't know how to get things to safe and right.

As he and Cassie entered the cramped hold, Saint Matthew's automata skittered on the walls, lighting the way. Soft brackets held the time gates in a gentle curve, and they drifted towards them, feeling the awe of being before the gates of their temple again. They ached to enter.

Cassie slaved her suit's thrusters to his, and took his hand. He loved the pressure, even through their layered gloves. But as quickly as the squeeze came, it went. Cassie had already ceased to be a person. She'd leapt into the quantum fugue and once again he was alone. Of course she'd be rushed to begin. The quantum world flooded into the *Homo quantus* through their magnetosomes. In the first moments of the fugue, the quantum intellect would begin to receive overlapping inputs, waves and particles, whole spreads of probability. At first, these were just from nearby sources. But because the *Homo quantus* felt electromagnetic fields, the scale of Cassie's perceptions would expand one light-second per second, and the scale of her senses would enlarge through entanglement much faster than that. Reluctantly, Belisarius released her hand.

He activated the suit jets, nudging them past the horizon and into the space-time hyper-volume of the time gates. Sight expanded in strange directions. Sounds and ghostly touches from nowhere pattered on his perceptions. Magnetism and electrical charge felt mushy and distant; his quantum intellect was hoarding most of the measurements it was making. It reported some observations to him, although not many. If it shared more, Belisarius would collapse many of the overlapping probabilities he saw. But the two quantum intellects, Belisarius' and Cassie's, could share indeterminate quantum data with each other without collapsing the overlapping probabilities.

"What do you see?" Belisarius asked the two quantum intellects.

The intellects were probably speaking to each other via electromagnetic signals, in a language of equations, partial observations, mathematics and new hypotheses. His own quantum intellect began feeding him minor data points, not direct observations. Belisarius couldn't have access to those without collapsing the probabilities. He felt left out, moreso because despite everything, he still lived to discover and understand.

The data points appeared; hundreds of stars, bereft of hints of spectroscopy or luminosity. Belisarius tried to match the pattern to the geometries of star fields. None of this data mapped to any of the star maps he knew. He was seeing only a fraction of what the quantum intellects were perceiving, but it was enough. As the pattern thickened, his brain toggled through possibilities of orientation, geometric system and scale. Abruptly, his brain started matching these to the structures of large quasar groups, those collections of galaxies named for the super-massive black holes that held them together.

He didn't reach any conclusions. Genetic engineers had dialed pattern-recognition in the *Homo quantus* so high that they suffered many false positives, finding things that, heart-breakingly, weren't there. But if these initial patterns held, what did it mean? Why would quantum entanglement at the time gates lead to the centers of distant galaxies?

The intellect gave him more data, even as he ached to actually see it unfiltered. The new data points increased the resolution of his modeling. Each individual point soon resolved into a haze of fine points, and the new data allowed a kind of magnification into that haze. There was a lot of data now, but if he was receiving a thousandth of what the quantum intellects perceived, what were they seeing? Each point in those vast mists possessed the kinds of quantum features they'd seen in the Puppet Axis.

Every point seemed to be another mouth of the Axis Mundi network.

And there were so many points that they formed a hazy cloud that, from a distance looked like a single pinprick of lights, and of those, there were millions, across great chains of galaxies. The scale beggared his *Homo quantus* sanguine calm. Theoretical modeling took on the weight of a near-religious experience. What he was glimpsing might mean that millions of wormholes were knit together by quantum entanglement into the super-galactic structure of the large quasar groups.

Civilization knew of fifty or sixty wormholes. Here were millions, only visible through the lens of quantum entanglement, something he and Cassie had practiced to pull a confidence scheme.

More data rolled in.

The large quasar groups themselves, despite containing quadrillions of stars, were only the building blocks of the walls, filaments and sheets of galaxies in the observable universe. The pattern of accumulating points began assuming a shape Belisarius recognized: the Hercules-Corona Borealis Great Wall. This vast collection of galaxies strung across twenty billion light years of sky was the largest known structure in the universe. Lines of entanglement seemed to lead to billions of points all across this vast structure.

But if every line of entanglement they were seeing led to a mouth of the forerunners' Axis Mundi wormhole network, then that network was immensely more vast than anyone had ever imagined. The forerunners might have colonized a sizable fraction of the known universe. They might not even be extinct.

There might be so many mouths to the Axis Mundi that the forerunners might simply have lost track of the few dozen that humanity had found.

Belisarius' brain raced, thinking about how the expansion of the universe might affect time and simultaneity around the wormholes. They couldn't all be synchronized. Simple drift during the expansion of the universe would put some wormholes in the relative pasts and relative futures of the other wormholes. How might the forerunners live around this immense network? What might their society be like, at that size, encompassing a sizable portion of the entire universe?

"Quantum intellects," Belisarius said to the two objectivities, "we don't know if these are mouths of the Axis Mundi or something else. We need to examine the nearer ones in more resolution, in the Epsilon Indi system, or Bachwezi or Earth, or nearby systems we already know."

The quantum intellects were not dumb. They would eventually have come to the same conclusion, but the pattern-recognition instincts they took from the *Homo quantus* made them just as likely as Belisarius to drift off into idle observation of the mathematical and physical beauty of the cosmos.

The quantum intellect in his brain began feeding him different information. Instead of the immensity of the Hercules-Corona Borealis Great Wall, something much smaller formed: five points, without reference to anything else, without scale, with no real sense that they mapped in any linear way to the real world.

"What is this?" Belisarius asked.

Bachwezi, came his own voice, devoid of expression or feeling.

Bachwezi: the system where only one Axis Mundi mouth had ever been found, a kind of dead end. The Congregate had given the system to the Sub-Saharan Union. In the seventy years they'd been there, despite a great deal of searching, no one had ever found another Axis Mundi. The quantum intellects were following the trail of five lines of quantum entanglement, but without reference to anything physically observable.

The information was scale-free. The five points of entanglement in Bachwezi might be an uneven ring a single astronomical unit in diameter, or a light-year across. They might not even be simultaneous with Belisarius' now. Quantum entanglement didn't treat time the same way that matter, and people, did. The image of Bachwezi contained no information they could use.

"Can you show Epsilon Indi?" Belisarius said.

The data distribution changed after a few seconds, showing five different points of light. Only four Axes had ever been found in Epsilon Indi. The Anglo-Spanish Plutocracy had one, the Congregate had one, the Sub-Saharan Union had recently taken one from the Congregate, and the Puppets had a subsurface one. The fifth Axis was the Holy Grail or the sucker's bet of Epsilon Indi, depending on one's point of view. Whichever nation found the undiscovered Axis mouth would be politically, economically, and militarily strengthened.

The quantum intellects showed five points, but there was no reason to think that entanglement might map real-world order and orientation. They needed to find the equations to transform entanglement information into astronomical positions in space-time.

A series of equations and data points and logical statements appeared in Belisarius' helmet display. Cassie's quantum intellect transmitted readings on the Puppet Axis, something it had studied closely. The characteristics of the Puppet Axis matched the quantum properties of one of the five points. Her quantum intellect was suggesting that was the Puppet Axis.

Belisarius' brain played with the geometry, experimenting with orientations and scales. After long seconds of mentally flipping and transforming the geometry, he came up with a hypothesis that might account for the positions of the Congregate Axis, the Anglo-Spanish Axis, and the Freyja Axis. The last point, unattached to anything, lay far out in empty space, beyond the orbit of Epsilon Indi's two stellar companions. He had a theorized location relative to the other wormholes in Epsilon Indi.

An alarm had been sounding in Belisarius' helmet for long seconds. Cassie's temperature was forty degrees. He swore. He'd ignored it, and so had her own quantum intellect. The anti-pyretics had done almost no good. As much as he didn't want to return to the real world, given the value of the data here, Cassie's quantum intellect might not let go before her fever got dangerous.

"Record," Belisarius told the two quantum intellects. "We're exiting the time gates."

The pace of Cassie's breathing shifted, shallowed, as if she were waking. Belisarius activated the cold jets on their suits and they retreated. They crossed the gray, insubstantial disk of the horizon and emerged into the hold of *The Calculated Risk*.

Her uneven breathing sounded labored in his earpiece and he took her hand. She gripped it and held tight. He pulled her back to the airlock. In the crew area, he cracked the seals on his suit and took hers off, before removing his. Then they lay still, strapped lightly to the two pilot chairs. Saint Matthew had learned not to make chit chat with the pair of *Homo quantus* after they'd been in the fugue, or even when they were in savant. Their deep obsessions responded poorly to distractions.

Belisarius' brain was stuffed with new data he wasn't sure how to begin processing, all that he'd missed during the fugue. He turned on the holographic displays in their common work area, where they could draw their geometric ideas, translate equations, run iterative and chaotic processes in front of each other, with all the graphical short-hand the *Homo quantus* used to visualize up to seven or eight dimensions of space-time. He jacked himself in and began dumping data sets. Groaning, Cassie jacked herself in by wire and began creating images as she flooded their workspace with data points. The jack could only transfer so much per second, so some minutes passed before the image made by the points looked even closer to the structure of the Hercules-Corona Borealis Great Wall than he'd seen. Billions of data points.

"Could this really be a map of all the mouths of the Axis Mundi?" he asked.

Cassie's lips parted in gentle, unselfconscious breathing, her eyes hypnotized by the image she was making. She was in savant, socially prickly, but mathematically prodigious. She frowned, processing his question.

"It's a map of quantum entanglement," she said, "to the points we could perceive from the time gates. If that isn't a proxy to all the other permanent wormholes made by the forerunners, what would the time gates be entangled with?"

Belisarius absorbed the patterns and summoned a three-dimensional map of the universe blending infrared, radio, luminous, ultraviolet, and x-ray and gamma-ray sources. For a few minutes, neither spoke.

"At the largest scales, the lines of entanglement lead mostly to quasars, neutron stars and pulsars," Cassie finally said, "and with some transformations, the mapping seems almost linear. With errors of a few AU to a few light-years, the pattern matches the map of the universe."

She adjusted the view, zooming dizzyingly down from the entire visible universe to the local group of galaxies, to just the Milky Way, down to just the Orion Arm, and then to the apparently minuscule web of human civilization, and finally down to the Bachwezi system. Five luminous points shone in the hologram, and one shone in the actual map of the system.

Both saw the problem. Although the map of entangled bodies they'd found by looking through the time gates was mostly linear on the large scale, at the scale of a single solar system, the errors involved meant they could make almost no predictions of the locations of individual wormholes. In Epsilon Indi, they'd already known of four and used elimination. In Bachwezi, where they knew only of one, that wouldn't work. The five points they saw might be rotated through any of the four axes of space-time, and the scale might be anything at all, from light-seconds to light-minutes to light-hours.

"So many Axes Mundi," Cassie said. "Enough for the *Homo quantus* to study for dozens of lifetimes."

"Or to escape through," Belisarius said. "The patron nations could maybe follow us through one Axis. But the chances of them finding two or three Axes only we knew about is tiny, centuries or millennia away. We need some way to calibrate."

They modeled different equations and graphical displays and even chaotic space-time expansion drift scenarios, looking for something that might show them how to map from quantum entanglement to physical coordinates. After an hour, they'd come up with classes of candidate relations, but nothing concrete.

Cassie changed the view, from the Bachwezi system to Epsilon Indi, where they could compare the locations of four known mouths to the Axis Mundi to the map of entanglement. Here, they could test their models, eliminating one class of relations after another until only one remained. They stared at it for long seconds, a remarkable pattern that no one but the two of them in all of humanity knew about. The awe of discovery washed through their fevered minds.

Their new relation depended on one important parameter. If they knew that parameter to extreme detail, they could consistently translate Cassie's quantum entanglement map into real world coordinates in space-time. And what they needed to measure was the time difference across the two mouths of the time gates, the time difference across the futureward and pastward mouths.

But they had no way to measure that time difference without keeping the gates relatively unmoving for several decades. The shorter the period of measurement, the larger the error, and even small errors translated into light-minutes or light-hours of differences in the prediction. And the *Homo quantus* didn't have that much time to wait to get away from the Congregate and the Banks.

To very accurately measure the natural time difference across the two mouths of the time gates, they needed to measure it across thousands of years. Only one place and time had the information they needed, and Belisarius didn't want to mention it to Cassie yet. It was too much to even consider. Instead, he gave Saint Matthew the predicted coordinates of the fifth Axis Mundi of the Epsilon Indi system and asked him to fly there without being observed.

CHAPTER ELEVEN

By SPY CAMERA, in a ready room, Colonel Ayen Iekanjika watched the government officials enter the *Mutapa*'s stateroom to meet with Lieutenant-General Rudo, recently promoted to Commander of the Navy. The first was Charles Nanyonga, the Minister of Defense. Daudi Echweru, the Minister of the Interior, accompanied him. Nanyonga wore a business suit cut in the latest Venusian fashion: dark pin-stripes with ruffles at the cuffs and neck. Echweru wore a long, flowing kandu robe, tied at the ankles against the lack of gravity. They strapped themselves into chairs around the meeting table.

Lieutenant-General Rudo did not often leave the *Mutapa*. She considered the risk of assassination too high. With all the Congregate spies and agents riddling the government of Bachwezi, that was certainly justified. And it was just as well. For Cabinet ministers coming to the *Mutapa* it was like walking into history. They posted pictures of themselves posing against the forty-year-old flags in the meeting rooms. They gave speeches to their constituents about having spoken to the Lieutenant-General, peppering their public comments with things like "much like I saw on the *Mutapa*." No doubt it played well. The crews of the Sixth Expeditionary Force were heroes.

Low-level heroes were fine. But highly-visible heroes were a double-edged weapon to the Cabinet: the politicians gained popularity by association, but could just as easily be eclipsed. The Lieutenant-General had been offered several political positions, as had Iekanjika, but they'd both opted to stay in the navy. Far more factions moved behind the scenes than she could have imagined.

The Lieutenant-General greeted the ministers formally, and briefed them on the latest intelligence and military information. The ministers asked questions. The Lieutenant-General answered factually and completely.

The questions the Lieutenant-General posed were, in Iekanjika's view, far more pertinent to the war effort. Supply lines. Positions. Defensive range and offensive projection capabilities. True targets and valueless targets. After a time, the Minister of the Defense put his pad back into his vest pocket, and folded his hands before him. The Lieutenant-General put away hers too.

"I'd like to come back to the theft of the time gates," Minister Nanyonga said.

"I'd be pleased to amplify my report in any way you desire, Minister," Rudo said.

"The Cabinet is having a bit of trouble coming to grips with the loss, General," he said. "We are wondering what might have been done differently."

"Arjona fooled us all," Rudo said. "I can offer no other explanation. He was the right man to get the Sixth Expeditionary Force to Epsilon Indi, but he robbed us."

"We can't find him and get them back?" Minister Echweru asked.

"Arjona has disappeared," Rudo said. "He is a magician. There's no longer even a record of his art gallery in the Puppet Free City."

"This is a serious failure, General," Nanyonga said.

Iekanjika's hands turned into fists, impotently, in front of the display in the ready room. Could she have hidden this reaction in person? Rudo didn't flinch.

"I brought the Sixth Expeditionary Force home with new weaponry and propulsions systems, destroyed the Congregate Dreadnought *Parizeau*, captured the Freyja Axis, and destroyed all Congregate fortifications in the Bachwezi system," Rudo said. "Perhaps you could contextualize the failure for me?"

"This seems to be more the failure of judgment of Colonel Iekanjika," Echweru said placatingly. "She was your effective commander left behind in the Stubbs system. She was responsible for Arjona and the time gates. A failure of the magnitude of the loss of the time gates cannot stand unaddressed."

"I was the Commanding Officer of the Expeditionary Force. I have conducted my own investigation and pressed no charges nor issued reprimands. If the Cabinet wishes to judge *my* failure in this, they are free to do so."

"You mistake our words, General Rudo," Nanyonga said. "Of course this matter, when balanced with all others, is manageable."

"My apologies," Rudo said. "I heard you incorrectly."

The two Cabinet Ministers exchanged more pleasantries and planned a speech for the Prime Minister for the following day, then unstrapped themselves and departed. After a delay, Iekanjika shut off the spy camera and entered the board room.

"Thank you for defending me, ma'am," Iekanjika said.

"No need for thanking," Rudo said. "I was only twenty-two when I left Bachwezi with the Sixth Expeditionary Force, but even then, the Union government had its corruptions and politics. It hasn't changed. It could yet kill us all."

"I doubt it will have the time, ma'am," Iekanjika said.

"Let's hope your new pilots can slow down the Congregate," Rudo said.

CHAPTER TWELVE

STILLS PULLED FIFTY-eight sphincter-clenching gees in the brand new Union fighter. Twenty-nine other mongrel pilots flew tight on his ass like they wanted to hide something in there. Even though his body was adapted to live at benthic ocean depths and was sealed in a hyper-pressurized tank of water, the gees gnawed at the limits of what even he could stand. His electroplaques sputtered a war howl in the electrical language of the Tribe of the Mongrel. His squadron echoed back twenty-nine chaotic *fucks yous*. Two of his pilots were sucking wind, falling behind, accelerating at just fifty-five gees.

"Come on, dog-fuckers!" he yelled. "Last one to the party sucks my cock!"

"If anybody can find it!" some twat said, chasing that with hooting noises.

The entire squadron started hooting and accelerating at fifty-nine gees, crowding him so dangerously that he had to itch his drive to sixty gees. Something hurt in his gut. The fighter creaked around him.

Ahead, two Congregate destroyers and their fighter squadrons had gotten close enough to the mouth of the Freyja Axis to lob heavy artillery, but not close enough for the smaller Union guns to drive them away without moving into withering fire.

"Union fuckers don't think we can do this," Stills said. "Fuck them!"

The tribe's roaring drowned out everything else on the channel. Didn't matter. They mostly used the common channel to throw insults. Mongrels weren't strong on formation fighting anyway. The major jerk-off who'd accepted the job of being the commanding officer of the mongrel squadron was probably giving orders. He'd been pretty insistent on formations and tactics.

Fuck him.

Mongrel employment with the Union was so new that the Union had installed scuttle switches on all the fighters. If any mongrel tried to make a run for it with the new Union fighters, major cock-munch could turn the craft to ashes. The Union didn't trust so much, but neither had Stills' last employers, the Congregate. And if a mongrel wanted to fly the absolute best fucking fighters in civilization, this was where they had to fly: at the pointy end of a David and Goliath war. That was how Stills had convinced the other twenty-nine pilots to come with him and offer their services to the Union. *Tabernak* but they leapt at the chance to piss in the Congregate's mouth! The Congregate hadn't mistreated them or anything. The Way of the Mongrel was The Way of the Mongrel: *Piss on every leg. Bite every hand.*

Congregate particle beams reached to stroke the mongrel squadron, but missed. The firing systems weren't fast enough to accurately lead their fire on fighters that could accelerate at sixty gees. And even when the Congregate gunners and their programs got close, Stills' pilots would spin, and accelerate as hard laterally. Growing up in the oceans, three-dimensional thinking was the default mental map. It made the mongrels dangerous at fighting in the vacuum of space.

Major deep swallow was still yammering like he didn't need to breathe. He was giving orders, most of them directed at Stills. He was on the *Nhialic*, too far away and too slow to make a difference.

If Stills followed the major's orders, they would lose the advantage the mongrels brought: they were faster than anyone else and as predictable as rabid dogs. Stills was gonna have to ask for a more hands-off commanding officer, maybe somebody on the edge of retirement, or maybe an uncertain second lieutenant who could be pushed around.

Stills surveyed the electrical signals in his cockpit: the positions of the two Congregate destroyers, the arcs of the particle beams, the lasers, and the clouds of fighters, crewed on the Congregate side by other mongrels. Stills had flown picket with those mongrel fighter pilots on the destroyers. He knew most of their capabilities. But they and their employers had no fucking clue what was coming for them.

"Balls flight," Stills said, "strafe the *Sainte-Foy* at point blank. Climb into their ass and shoot something while you're there. Put those engines out of commission. Cock flight, fuck up the *Portneuf*. Ass flight, break into syndicates. We're greasing some of their officers."

Electrical howls of approval filled the channel. Their major was probably protesting, but Stills'd be fucked if he could even hear any of it. He tight-waved a quick "yes, sir" to the major to shut his cake hole. Then he dove into his run.

The next ten minutes were some of the hottest of Stills' life. Nobody had a faster fighter than the Union and nobody was tougher than the Congregate. The Congregate had brought its best kit, including its experimental and advanced shit. They even shot anti-matter. Usually they only uncased AM when the Congregate really wanted to fuck up something bad. Stills had only worked peacetime fighter pilot contracts for the Congregate with the occasional asymmetric fuck-somebody-up skirmishes. He'd never seen them live-fire AM before today. This was wall-to-wall bullets to the head.

The mongrels pilots flying for the Congregate were superb. Great shit-eating clouds of them, flying *tonnère* fighters, easily pulling twenty-five to thirty gees. They fought intuitively, better than the Congregate gunners. They were probably paying as much attention to their orders as Stills. They adapted as they could to Stills' capabilities, which saved them from a rout. Stills' squadron broke formation, weaving through the web of particle fire and laser tracking, following no plan and probably givin' major ass-wipe a coronary.

That was the major's problem. Mongrel pilots didn't need to be told how to get somewhere. Tell them where and when the fuck you wanted them and what you wanted blown to bits and then sashay the fuck out of the way. When left to their own devices, the mongrels fought a modern berserker strategy, pressing forward an uncoordinated cloud of violence, half my-prick-is-bigger, half suicidal, and half crazy-train, never letting the enemy know what the fuck any mongrel pilot might do at any time.

As a case in point, the mongrels liked knowing where shit was on Congregate destroyers, not just munitions and fuel, but where they kept the officers and the bridge. It wasn't fair to say that nobody else knew, but Stills bet no one else could get so close as to make a difference. Ripping past the *Portneuf* at a hundred kilometers per second, Stills unloaded one of the pissy low-yield Union missiles, right over the Congregate bridge. There was too much armor for him to break through, but the second pilot behind him, an arrogant little twat called Vincent Fletcher, landed a second missile in the same spot.

Fuckin' felcher. Stills'd never hear the end of it. Merced Hillman and Vincent Tork shot their loads, but Stills was already too gone to see. He was cranking his acceleration in a new direction, swinging wide and fast around the *Portneuf's* chaff arc, to make a run straight for the *Sainte-Foy*.

Laser comms started crackling on his display.

What the fuck? The Union didn't have tech to keep a secure laser on a ship moving this fast, so he wasn't equipped. But it felt like there were words in it. Was his ship mistaking Congregate laser targeting for comms? Where the fuck were they sighting from?

He spun, changed vector, and found no attack. But the comms laser kept on him. For this much crackling, it must be far. How the fuck was a laser tracking him from that far? He was moving too fast. His ship wasn't reading it as comms. The defensive system was registering it as a targeting laser. And there were words in it. Modulations in the laser. And then it hit him. It was mongrel speech, the electrical patterns they used to speak to each other in the crushing depths through their electroplaques. Who the hell?

"Stills," the message crackled, "this is Belisarius."

Stills raced towards the *Sainte-Foy*, unloading two missiles straight at the plating over the captain and bridge. Antimatter beams sizzled across his hull, shuddering the ship and launching it into a spin. He recovered.

Felt like a few hundred nanograms might have hit him. Anything bigger and he would have been a big shit stain all over the *Sainte-Foy's* shiny hull. *Malparidos*! He hated antimatter. Felcher, Hillman, Tork and Fuckhead followed fast, their targeting brag-worthy.

"Felcher, you lead! Rinse and repeat, you fuckers!" Stills said, pulling his ship out of the informal volume of the battle.

The Congregate destroyers were big, but Stills' dogs were fast, dropping their ordnance near the officers and the engines. If he could psyche out the officers or bust the engines, the Congregate would either fuck off or get taken apart by conventional Union missiles. Cock and Balls flights still worked over the engines. The battle buzzed like a wasp nest ass-fucking a hornet nest.

Stills targeted his laser comms back at the signal he'd received. "Arjona, where the fuck are you? I'm kinda busy licking my knob here. Is this important?"

Unlike the pure electrical signals he used to speak with other mongrels, his voice was being translated into Anglo-Spanish. He could have given his voice more depth and tonal expression with a simple program, but he liked messing with people and set the translator to inflect only the swearing.

"I need to talk with Iekanjika," the *Homo quantus* said. "I have a business deal to offer her. You too."

"I'm not a messenger, *malparido*. What the fuck do I want with a message?"

"You will when you hear what I'm offering."

"I got what I want, *patron*."

Stills turned his fighter wide and yelled at his pilots on the other channel. Fuckin' Cock flight wasn't makin' much headway. Withering Congregate fire was slowing them. "Dive in, you fuckers!" He lanced towards them, firing his particle weapons, blowing two Congregate fighters to shit, and zeroing in for a run on the engines.

"Have I ever over-promised you yet?" Arjona interrupted.

"Shit, no, *patron,* that you haven't, but I still ain't no messenger."

"Tell Iekanjika I want to talk to her."

"Based on how much shit I had to eat when tryin' to volunteer for their cocked-up war, I got the impression she hates your guts."

Stills swooped hard, accelerating at sixty gees as he circled the stern of the *Portneuf*, unloading a shit sandwich of missiles at the big nuclear engines. He even squirted off a shot from his little particle cannon. It blistered the cowling of the engine just before his missiles tried to ass-fuck the destroyer. He didn't get to see the results, but it would take a few more direct hits before they started bustin' the plating.

He'd have to tell Iekanjika he wanted bigger missiles and a new CO. This reminded him to transmit a quick "yes, sir" to his major. He did that.

"Your impression is right," Belisarius said, "but I'm offering her something bigger. An Axis. I'm transmitting the coordinates."

Arjona said more, but the nugget of the message was pretty goddamn show-stopping. At first, Stills thought he heard wrong, or that the flack and static of battle was fuckin' with him. Or that Arjona was fucking with him. But Arjona wouldn't know a joke if it slapped him.

"No shit," was all Stills could think to answer.

A new Axis? Arjona had found an Axis and was giving it to Iekanjika? What the fuck did he want? The bill wouldn't be light. "You're rich now, prancy-pants. Go frolic on your mountain top."

"I need this," Arjona said. "And I need your help again. I have a bigger con."

Don't ask.

Don't ask.

Don't. Fucking. Ask.

"What's the con?" Stills asked.

Fuck me.

"I'm going to hide the *Homo quantus*."

"All of them?" Stills said sarcastically.

"Yup. And I need a pilot."

"Good. I thought this was gonna be tempting or something. I'm already altruisted out, saving the Union. They got the best flying. Sorry."

"I need a pilot to fly me through time," Arjona said.

Malparido hijoeputa. "Are you shitting me?"

"I never have," Arjona said.

"For the love of.... Goddamn! Can't you ever just rob a bank or something?"

CHAPTER THIRTEEN

THE *SAINTE-FOY* and the *Portneuf* withdrew after a harried hour. They were scratched and bruised and even damaged deeply in spots and hadn't gotten anywhere near the Freyja Axis or the Union cruisers. Stills' squadron lost eight pilots. The twenty-two surviving ships looked like they'd been chewed on by a big cat, swallowed and squeezed out the other side. But they'd proven themselves. The Union could take them on long term contracts. Or eat shit.

Stills had ideas about new tactics. They'd pissed away some tactical opportunities because the Union didn't trust the mongrels enough to risk their big kit. That was fine. Mongrels got the ass end of most deals. But with a bit better stuff, he could win something rather than stalemate.

His squadron landed on the *Nhialic* and the *Batembuzi*. As soon as the bay doors started closing, his CO was on his ass. Stills hadn't followed any of his approved plans. Stills hadn't answered any questions during the battle. Stills hadn't followed any new orders nor had he withdrawn his pilots when ordered. Stills had played far too risky. The major was receiving serious flack from his superiors.

"I got a message for Colonel Iekanjika," Stills said flatly.

"I'm your commanding officer. I deal with you."

"I didn't say I want to talk with Iekanjika. I said I got a message for her. Someone contacted me during the battle by laser."

"You contacted the enemy while in combat?"

"No, *comemierda*," Stills said slowly, "I got a message. I'm just passing it the fuck on 'cause I don't like playing messenger."

"Give me the message," major ass-for-brains said.

"I know when a message is ears only, fuckhead. I worked with her before. She's gonna want to hear this one personally, so get me a meeting or give me your fucking name and serial number so when I do meet her, I can tell her which scrotum-faced moron wasted her chance."

"I won't tolerate insubordination, Stills."

"Can you fucking tolerate success?" Stills asked. "My mongrels pushed back two fully-kitted Congregate destroyers."

"You have to work within our rules."

"I'm working with you. Read my contract. And remember I'm a contractor. If you want to go flagellate somebody, go punish one of your own. I did good today. And if you don't get me a meeting with Iekanjika pronto, your CO'll hear about it. If you want to make the meeting happen faster, give her the name Arjona."

CHAPTER FOURTEEN

To: Detachment Commander,
           Congregate Counter-Insurgency Operations
           51st Intelligence Division
           Epsilon Indi

13 March, 2515

Subject: Report X156JWR78 – Interrogation of Captured
           Homo quantus

1. Detained Intelligence Targets: On 12 March 2515, one hundred and fifty-five Anglo-Spanish Plutocracy shareholders were taken into custody under article 76(3)(c) of The Official Secrets Act. These detainees are members of the human sub-species known as the *Homo quantus*. All 155 were interrogated for (a) general intelligence on the *Homo quantus* project, and (b) the Union emergence, and (c) specific intelligence regarding the *Homo quantus* Belisarius Arjona. All *Homo quantus* survived and are available for further mechanical and surgical interrogation.

They are being shipped directly to the Ministry of Intelligence, 1st Division at Venus. Heavy naval escort was requisitioned as per the emergency subsections of article 40 of the OSA, in case Anglo-Spanish assets seek to recover the detainees.

2. Outstanding Intelligence Targets: Approximately three thousand, eight hundred and thirty *Homo quantus* are unaccounted for. An all-points alert has been issued to naval and intelligence assets in Epsilon Indi and Axis-adjacent systems. Elements of the 12th Fleet have been deployed on fast reconnaissance missions in multiple directions within two light years of Epsilon Indi. This effort is wholly inadequate, but most 12th Fleet assets are occupied with rebel activity around the Freyja Axis. Additional naval assets are urgently required to track down the remaining *Homo quantus* before they rendezvous with Anglo-Spanish forces.

3. Preliminary findings:

    a) Many of the *Homo quantus* were resistant to probes and torture. Extensive physiological, neurological and genetic changes are evident in all detainees.

    b) No evidence of weapons development was found at the *Homo quantus* base, called the Garret. The entirety of the Anglo-Spanish *Homo quantus* project seems to be devoted to developing mental capacities and perceptions in the *Homo quantus* that would have predictive military and economic value.

    c) None of the detainees appeared to be capable of entering the predictive state they call the "quantum fugue." They claim it is a rare state, a bioengineering success in approximately 19% of all *Homo quantus*. The names of all *Homo quantus* capable of achieving this predictive state are appended (Appendix A).

4. Belisarius Arjona:

a) Detainees consistently claim that Belisarius Arjona is capable of achieving that predictive state, and that he was absent from the Garret for twelve years. This is consistent with other intelligence reports that have placed Arjona in the Puppet Free City and at times in Epsilon Indi Congregate territories. Arjona was suspected of involvement in a prison break that freed a former Congregate Special Forces Sergeant Marie Phocas from the Epsilon Indi *Maison d'éducation correctionnelle*. DNA records at the Garret confirm Arjona's presence at the *Maison*.

b) Previous reports co-locate Arjona with Sub-Saharan Union Major Iekanjika (see report X156JWP47 for details on this major for whom no records exist at the Union Academy at Harare) at the Puppet Free City and Blackmore Station. The interrogations also identified a *Homo quantus* accomplice: Cassandra Mejía. Mejía is regarded by detainees as highly competent in the *Homo quantus* predictive state, at the level of Arjona or higher. Investigations at both the Puppet Free City and Blackmore Station are ongoing.

c) On March 3rd, Arjona and Mejía returned to the Garret after a three month absence. They claimed to have *traveled back in time two weeks* after having seen the Garret destroyed by a Congregate nuclear device, thought to have been a *casse à face* missile. The date and time given by all detainees correspond exactly to when Capitaine Arsenault actually fired on the Garret. The detainees were sedated while these actions were being taken and they would have had no way to have known Arsenault's decision or timing ahead of time as Arsenault made the decision just before firing. It is unknown if this knowledge is some kind of trick, whether this was a genuine military prediction from within the *Homo quantus* fugue state, or if this is evidence of the claim of time travel.

d) This impossibility of time travel was acknowledged by all detainees, and apparently by the missing 3,830 other *Homo quantus*. However, only the 155 *Homo quantus* taken into custody elected to disbelieve this story enough stay behind after the warning. The remainder are reported to have fled in old cargo freighters.

5. The warrant for Arjona's capture has been elevated to first priority and a reward of five million francs attached. A warrant for Mejía's capture has been issued at the first priority and a reward of five million francs attached. The warrant for Phocas' arrest has been amended, elevated to first priority and a reward of one million francs attached. The potential political complications of the Phocas warrant should be examined by 1st Division and measures taken.

6. Analysis: The *Homo quantus* as bioweapons: if the *Homo quantus* possess true predictive powers, they are possibly the most dangerous weapons in civilization

and under no circumstances can the Banks be allowed any access to them. Far more unlikely, but far more dangerous, if the *Homo quantus* really have discovered some way to travel through time, no military or economic assumptions can survive. The capture of all *Homo quantus* should be a military and intelligence priority, above even the recapture of the Axis.

7. Analysis: The Congregate has historically eschewed human bioengineering, but now we cannot afford to sit out this new arms race. At the very least, we must understand the full capabilities of the *Homo quantus*. But the Congregate cannot afford to have a bioweapons gap. The Congregate must reverse engineer the *Homo quantus* and then develop a better, stronger *Homo quantus*.

8. Analysis: We do not yet know how the Union's Sixth Expeditionary Force managed to exit the Puppet Axis at the Free City without having entered at Port Blackmore. No matter how it was done, the security of all Congregate Axes can no longer be assumed. The only way to properly estimate our tactical and strategic exposure is to capture and interrogate Arjona and Mejía.

Scarecrow
Mobile Counter-Insurgency Operations
Epsilon Indi

CHAPTER FIFTEEN

STILLS GOT HIS meeting with Iekanjika the next day. He didn't expect it to go well. When he'd come to the Freyja Axis two weeks ago with thirty-nine other mongrel pilots, offering their services, he'd leaned on his knowing Iekanjika. Without her, there had been a good chance that all the mongrels with him woulda been blown into fish chow.

Iekanjika had been angry. Something about Arjona had her majorly pissed, even though as far as he could see, it had been an unqualified fucking success for the Union side. They'd not only gotten through to Epsilon Indi but they'd face-fucked the Congregate and taken the Freyja Axis.

But Iekanjika had been pissed about something and wanted to track down Arjona. She'd even offered Stills a giant reward for Arjona's capture. Not that Stills wouldn't throw Arjona under the bus, but you can't draw blood from stone. Damned if he knew where Arjona had hidden himself away and it wasn't any of his business anyway.

Stills was in a smaller tank, just himself, the kind they used to transport mongrels or isolate them if they got sick. The rest of the mongrels were in a much bigger pressurized water tank that had been built into the *Nhialic*.

Iekanjika came to the bay by herself. She was different from a lot of other officers. Lots of officers were professionals whose field happened to be soldiering. Iekanjika radiated warriorness first; she just happened to also be a professional.

She might have made a good mongrel. Fearless. Smart. Dangerous. Didn't care what people thought.

"Good fight," she said. The systems translated her voice into the electrical signals mongrels could hear in their magnetosomes.

"Good start," Stills said.

"You have a message for me."

"Arjona lasered me during the battle."

"He's a wanted man," she said. "You want a reward?"

"I'm no bounty hunter. And I'm no messenger either. Out of affection I'm makin' nice and not pissin' on the rug."

Iekanjika barked a laugh.

"He told me to tell you he's got a business offer for you."

"Are you really working for the Union now, Stills?"

"Have I given you a reason to fuckin' doubt me? I dodged a shit-load of bullets and Congregate missiles yesterday and scared off two destroyers. Does her august Majesty desire me to fucking bleed to prove myself?"

"If you're completely loyal, I can tell you that I want Arjona's head. Badly. I want it attached to his body until I get back what he took from me, but after that, I'll take it off his neck."

"Look, you want me to seek and destroy Arjona? Order it. He's a sneaky bastard, so I don't know if I can get him, but if you want me to try, I will. But before you make up your mind, you want to hear his message? Nothing pisses me off more than a commander who changes her fucking mind when I'm midway through shooting someone's ass off."

"What's the message?"

"He told me to give you these coordinates," Stills said,

transmitting them to Iekanjika's personal system. "He says it's the location of the fifth Axis in Epsilon Indi, a fucking goodwill gift to you. He said he might be able to give you the locations of ten other mouths of the Axis Mundi in Bachwezi and in a neighboring node."

"Did you check this?" she demanded.

"I'm the hired muscle, sweet-cheeks. I just wait for orders."

"Does anyone else know about this?"

"Why? You gonna kill the messenger?"

"These coordinates aren't near anything in Epsilon Indi," she said. "How fast a recce could you fly without drawing any attention?"

"Solo, I can do close to sixty gees the whole way. I can take a circuitous route to obscure my trail for anyone trying to track me."

"I want you take a member of my staff," Iekanjika said.

"I appreciate the *cojones* of the Union and all, but that ups the fucking risk, don't it? If you want me flyin' a fighter with a military observer, even in an acceleration couch, you gotta know that you guys start to smear at thirty gees. If I have to pull more than that to escape detection or escape an ambush, I'm bringin' you home a staff officer slurry."

"Thirty gees is faster than Congregate missiles."

"Not all of them."

"Can you get my observer there and back without alerting the Congregate or the Banks?"

"Just don't get used to me playing taxi or carryin' around fucking messages. I'm a fighter pilot."

CHAPTER SIXTEEN

AN HOUR LATER, Stills' closed pressure tank was transferred into the cargo area of a command fighter and networked into the control systems. A Union major called Kuur was jacked into the ship's systems from within a gel-filled acceleration chamber. Kuur was one of Iekanjika's people, although that didn't say much. That other major, the ass-licker, was also Iekanjika's.

Command fighters outweighed the faster fighters, and didn't play to mongrel strengths, but from the bigger craft a pilot could carry a group commander to direct a fighter squadron. Its inflaton tube was slightly larger, and the superstructure and weapons more numerous, but not enough for Stills to want to show his balls if he ran into a Congregate force by himself. Stills didn't like sneaking missions, but this one ran straight through a war zone, so he couldn't complain. He launched.

"So *mamacita* sent a major," Stills said conversationally in his electrical speech. The computer translated. "I asked her to send someone who'd shut up like a lieutenant, or someone useful like a sergeant."

"The Chief of Staff is named Colonel Iekanjika," Kuur said.

"Sorry," Stills said, not sorry at all. "I knew her when she was just a measly major. You puke much?"

"Of course not."

"You might be in for a surprise."

Stills rammed the acceleration to twenty-two gees, something he could just feel, stored as he was in the pressure tank, and reinforced in every part of his mongrel physiology.

"Your bones all still good?" Stills asked. "If you want to say uncle or call me papa bear, we can fly slower."

Major Kuur responded slowly, as if having trouble forming words with his brain. "You... have a problem with officers?"

Stills ramped the acceleration up to twenty-six gees.

"No," Stills said, "I love you guys. It's great having the smartest people around all the time."

"In the Union, pilots are officers," Kuur said slowly. "I heard the mongrels turned down commissions and insisted on designing their own ranks."

"Ain't a mongrel alive who could live down wearing an officer's bar or taking a fuckin' salute," Stills said. "God fuck, but I'd love some dog to do it though. I'd make sure he never lived down the embarrassment. Fuck, his kids' kids would still be gettin' razzed about it a hundred years later."

"Flight-sergeant suits you?" Kuur asked.

Stills accelerated.

"You ain't called me papa bear yet, so I edged up to twenty-eight gees. You still okay?"

"Officers take responsibility, Flight-Sergeant. You're smart. You ready to take responsibility?"

"Thirty gees and you're still conscious," Stills said. "Good for you! And don't ever think I don't take responsibility. When Iekanjika asks me why four of your ribs snapped and gang-banged your lungs, I'll tell her it was me."

"Enough," Major Kuur said finally.

"My mongrel rank isn't really Flight-Sergeant," Stills said.

"That's your translation. My rank is Papa Bear. You gotta say Papa Bear."

After a long delay, Major Kuur responded. "Please slow down, Papa Bear."

Stills laughed electrically and eased down to twenty-two gees. The major said nothing, but his heart rate, blood pressure and stress hormones dropped. From then on, when Stills had to course change to throw off any possible surveillance by Congregate telescopes or radar, he warned the major and made the changes below thirty gravities of acceleration.

Probably for the best. Stills didn't know how many ass-hats Iekanjika had laying around who could be quickly turned into major ass-hats.

Six hours of evasive stealthy flight got them to Arjona's coordinates. Stills brought the command fighter down to orbiting speed for this distance from Epsilon Indi's sun and shut down the inflaton drive. Stills wasn't sure what he'd expected. Every other Axis Mundi wormhole he'd seen had been heavily fortified. What would a naked wormhole look like in space? More fuckin' space?

"It's really there," Major Kuur said. "An Axis. Thirty kilometers away."

Stills focused his sensors, finding the same faint thermal source Kuur did, only a few degrees above the background radiation of the universe. The sensors also picked up a faint, changing light source. Cherenkov radiation, just a bit, something that would be drowned out by the wash of starlight from only a few thousand kilometers away. This was it, the fifth Axis of the Epsilon Indi system. People had been looking for it for centuries.

"Fucked if I know how that prancy contemplative little shit does it," Stills said in wonder.

CHAPTER SEVENTEEN

STILLS WASN'T SURE how to read Iekanjika. Most baseline humans were spineless and chicken-shit, and he could only hear them in translation anyway. Iekanjika wasn't soft and had never been talky. She seemed to have no interest in being the center of attention, and he suspected she held civilians in contempt. He guessed, if he thought about it at all, that she held the same finger up to the world that he did. When Major Kuur reported back to her, she asked Stills what he thought. Fucked if he had an opinion on strategic politics, but he didn't think she was asking to blow sunshine up his ass. He didn't think that anyone should fortify it yet. No one knew it was there and it was undetectable except up-close. And the Union didn't have the firepower to protect another Axis.

"And what if I want to talk to Arjona?" she asked next.

"I suppose the little pecker'll be in touch," Stills said. "He wants a deal. He wouldn'a left off if he didn't have a way to get an answer."

"Presumably you," she said.

"Maybe."

"So we set up a meeting with him. He wants to talk to me, probably alone. Say he's setting a trap for me. How would you do it if you were Arjona?"

"If I wanted to trap you? Fuck. We got superior speed and firepower if it's just the two ships. There are two ways to shit on our chances. Either cut our firepower advantage or cut our speed advantage. He could do both with backup, but I don't see it. You think he's workin' for someone else?"

"He stole from me and he's now one of the most hunted people in civilization. Maybe he cut a deal with whoever caught him. To get to me or the Lieutenant-General."

Fuckin' shit on a stick, he hated the way the Union talked about their CO. *The Lieutenant-General* or *The Old Lady*, like they were honored to be allowed to refer to her. Well *zarba!* Her Highness crapped in a tube like everybody else in space. Wasn't his business though. Fucking cultists.

"Say you fly me close enough to talk to Arjona," Iekanjika said. "After we're done talking, can you catch him?"

"In a big command fighter?" Stills asked. "I could catch anything except a real inflaton fighter, but he ain't got one of those. Shit, even if he did, I'd lay money on me catchin' one of them. Wouldn't be pretty for you. You'd be a colonel soup when I was done."

"I can take any acceleration Arjona can take," she said.

She probably could at that. He had no idea what kind of military augments she was carrying. Hardened bone. Reinforced organs. Probably pressure-activated interstitial shock proteins.

"Do you have any split loyalties about this?" she asked.

"I got no loyalties to start with. Arjona hired me for a job. Now you did. I just want something to fly and something to fight."

"I'll make sure you don't run out of either any time soon," she said.

Iekanjika got pensive. She was a big shit now. Not the highest-ranking officer in the navy, but when she talked everyone knew to jump.

"Go back out with your squadron," Iekanjika said. "Set me up a meeting with Arjona."

CHAPTER EIGHTEEN

THE SCARECROW PORED over the database backups from the Garret. There was more here than, and more to the *Homo quantus* than first glance might suggest. The intellectual capacities and memories of the *Homo quantus*, even from a young age, were considerable. Their memories in fact were reportedly as perfectly crystalline at a Scarecrow's, no small feat.

Many people remember back to the age of four and sometimes three, but not all memories survive the processes of petrification and vitrification involved in making the Scarecrow brains. The furthest the Scarecrow could remember was of being a twelve-year old on Sillery, one of the big floating towns of Venus.

Sillery was, still is, a globe of carbon, glass and diamond suspended in perfect buoyancy forty-two kilometers above the surface of Venus, below the lowest cloud deck, but still within the haze. As a factory town, automated engines of manufacturing provided ballast, extracting carbon from the atmosphere to produce building materials as varied as multi-fullerene fibers and acid-resistant diamond. Robots ran the industries and farmed the crops, leaving the four thousand inhabitants free to think and create. Sillery, like many Congregate towns, was not only a hotbed of political discourse and analysis of foreign threats, but a major seat of artistic expression.

But that wasn't what the Scarecrow remembered. That was just tone and background to the twelve-year old. The boys and girls were neither political analysts nor foreign policy afficionados. Instead, they wore survival suits and leapt into the acid clouds, the engines on their stubby wings shrieking as they played tag at a hundred kilometers per hour, darting through patches of mist, looping, spiralling, climbing, stalling, diving, laughing.

Since becoming a Scarecrow, he remembered nearly every moment, like the *Homo quantus*. But most of what lay earlier was gone; except for a brother, the Scarecrow couldn't remember the names of the friends. Petrification preserved attitudes more than events, feelings more than people. But he remembered the laughing shrieking of his brother Adéodat, the thrilling joy of winging through the hot clouds, the simple happiness of childhood. His petrified brain of silicate semi-conductors and atomic-scale metal threading preserved the feeling. Few of the blows and slings of the world could matter to the Scarecrow as long as Venus lay protected and safe from her enemies and that feeling existed somewhere, redeemable in her encircling clouds.

CHAPTER NINETEEN

IEKANJIKA SLIPPED INTO the oxygel acceleration tank and plugged the neural feed into the jack behind her ear. The gel pressed against her ears and eyes, slithered into her throat and lungs. Long practice could only do so much against the instinctual fear of drowning, but she forced her body to breathe and go limp.

Inhale gel, exhale air. Inhale gel, exhale air.

Stills flew them out of the *Nhialic*.

The Lieutenant-General had been hard to read. Iekanjika was more than her Chief-of-Staff; she was Lieutenant-General Rudo's junior spouse. Iekanjika carried political and social importance far beyond her rank and position. The Lieutenant-General didn't have many people she could trust completely. That was why Iekanjika had been sent out to find Arjona in the first place, to hire him to get the lost Sixth Expeditionary Force across the Puppet Axis. Their middle spouse, Major-General Wakikonda effectively commanded all the defenses of the Bachwezi system and had no time to spare for anything else. Iekanjika had been the Lieutenant-General's eyes and ears before. Now the Lieutenant-General was sending out her eyes and ears and voice to speak with Arjona again, after he'd betrayed them.

Stills had set up the rendezvous. Iekanjika and Stills had wanted something relatively close to the Freyja Axis, somewhere they could pull in reinforcements and catch him. She'd expected Stills to have to negotiate for this, something she wasn't sure he knew how to do. But Arjona had accepted Stills' first proposal.

They reached the rendezvous point forty minutes of hard acceleration later. The Congregate didn't have enough ships yet to set up a tight picket, nor were their ships fast enough to catch a fighter. The Union had a few weeks before overwhelming Congregate firepower would neutralize the Union's technological advantage. That fact loomed over all her thinking.

"He's a tricky little fuck," Stills said, "with dog-sized *cojones*."

"You can't pull too many tricks in open space," Iekanjika said. "The laws of physics are the laws of physics."

"Yeah," Stills said with a robotic tone of dubiousness. "I ain't got a signal though. I'm pinging directional radar, but fuck all is comin' back."

Stills brought them to a stop relative to the distant Freyja Axis and the Union fortifications. Space was naked around them. "No Arjona," Stills said. "Maybe he smells a trap."

Maybe. The neural jack fed her customized scans of the fighter's systems and sensor data. Nothing anywhere responded to their pings. Arjona wasn't within a light second of them.

"Arjona to Iekanjika," came through the comms system.

Clearly.

"Where is he?" she asked Stills.

"Radar's givin' me nothin'," he said. "Comms thinks it's comin' from dead ahead."

"Find him," she said, before transmitting. "Arjona, this is Iekanjika. Where are you?"

There was a delay. Seven seconds.

"I get that you're angry, Colonel," Arjona said. "I stole something from you. Trust me when I say that I can do things with it that can only be done by the *Homo quantus*."

"I want it back," she said.

Stills drifted the fighter forward on cold jets and Arjona's signal started fading. It should have gotten stronger, not weaker. Stills drifted back to the exact position Arjona had given them.

"Let me put it this way," Arjona said after a delay. "Would you rather have the small gates I took from you that you can barely send signals through, or do you want the locations of ten mouths of the Axis Mundi?"

Stills drifted the command fighter solar southward, and the signal weakened again. When he gently reversed course on cold jets, the same happened. No matter which direction they went, the signal strength dropped. Still nothing on radar. No nearby transmitter. He couldn't understand it.

"That isn't my decision to make," she said, "nor do I see it as an either-or proposition."

"Is this Rudo's decision?" Arjona said after a slight delay.

"Lieutenant-General Rudo. Yes." She switched to Stills' channel. "Where the hell is he?"

"Then perhaps I should speak with her again," Arjona said.

"Cunning little fucker," Stills said appreciatively.

"What?" Iekanjika demanded of the mongrel.

"Cunning little cock-sucker!" Stills said in tonally-flat wonder. "We ain't gonna catch him. He's light-seconds from here."

"How?"

"I'm no big head, but prancy-pants is a *Homo quantus*. He probably pisses quantum interference patterns."

"I don't follow," Iekanjika said.

"There's only one way our signal strength could drop off in every direction. The signal we're getting is a standing wave, localized right fucking here. The only way you get a standing wave is by mixing together a bunch of other waves. Arjona's split up his signal wherever the hell he is, and he's beaming it by different paths, probably reflecting it off of micro-satellites, and it gets recreated right here, right where we are, by constructive interference."

"Who has that technology?" Iekanjika said.

"Fucked if I know. Maybe he's doin' it with his own head. Fuck, he's tricky!"

"How did you guess that?" she demanded.

"Most people know wave theory," Stills said, "but when you grow up in an ocean, you don't call it wave theory. You call it hearing."

She'd underestimated Arjona before. And now she'd underestimated Stills. She had dangerous blind spots.

She switched on the transmitter. "We'd be delighted to host," she said.

"I'll be alone. The time gates will remain hidden and I won't know where they are," Arjona said. "And I'm aware of the political history of the Union. Torture won't work on the *Homo quantus*. If need be, I can mentally activate a suicide switch and then you'll have neither the gates nor the Axes I'm offering."

CHAPTER TWENTY

Level III Top Secret – Navy Commander's Eyes Only
Log, Commander Sixth Expeditionary Force, 17 August 2475

FOR MY FINAL log entry, I wish to comment upon my actions, which must be reviewed posthumously by the general staff. This may not occur for three or four years while the Force hides, puzzling out our prize and weaponizing it, but every officer has an opportunity to make a statement during a review and time won't change mine.

I take personal responsibility for violating the Congregate-Union Patron Accord. Many other officers were involved in executing my orders, but the decision was mine. As soon as we found the conjoined wormholes, I chose not to request new orders from the Senior Congregate Political Commissar as required by article 41(1) of the Patron Accord. I was the one who ordered the arrest of all Political Commissars, as well as the detention of engineering crews. I authorized summary trials of the commissars and sympathizers, including sentences of long-term confinement and death.

Hundreds have died and many thousands may die, but I do not regret my choices. The key to Union independence fell into my hands and I am a patriot. I only regret that I am not strong enough to finish what I began. My cancer has advanced quickly. At headquarters it might have been treatable. The Force medical officers can only slow it, so I've refused treatment. It's better to have a new Commander installed quickly than to suffer the instability of an acting commander. I will be promoting Brigadier Takatafare to Major-General at midnight and transferring command to her. This is not an ideal choice, but there is nothing for it.

Brigadier Takatafare and Brigadier Iekanjika are both flawed officers, lacking the seasoning for a long term command of this size, and so much moreso for leading a rebellion. The political tensions between these two officers and others have also been apparent from the beginning.

Takatafare's alliances and marriage connections make her popular among Rozvi Party sympathizers, and even among my own Korekore adherents. She is pitiless to her political enemies, making it difficult for some cruiser commanders to trust her. I've done what I can to limit her power, but I expect her to begin positioning her own people into positions of greater power and to reduce the influence of anyone outside of the Rozvi alliance. Brigadier Iekanjika is talented, skilled at manipulation, and a forceful organizer. Although the Makoni Party is smaller, Iekanjika is more highly placed as the junior wife of the Justice Minister. Several cruisers carry her rabid supporters and I do not see her taking well the elevation of Rozvi sympathizers around her.

I had hoped that my Korekore Party members might have continued to act as a buffer, but the stupidity of Colonel Bantya has discredited us, and my own death will leave Korekore with no senior leadership. Soon, in days or weeks, Rozvi and Makoni party activists will be grinding against each other. Iekanjika remains powerful enough to challenge Takatafare, regardless of my wishes. And Takatafare may yet drive her to it.

While this was just a ten-month mission, these tensions were under control. But we are far from home and the political stakes are high. Whoever brings back the conjoined wormholes to the Union will be in a position to dictate terms and probably choose the party that holds the prime ministership. And yet whoever brings them back will also precipitate a war with our Congregate patrons.

We don't have the Congregate's numbers, nor their industrial strength, so we will have to take our independence on some other field. We will have to remain hidden from civilization until we can pry from our discovery that key to victory.

The victors will scrutinize each of us, judging what we did for our independence.

I set us on this road.

Major-General Kutenda Nandoro

CHAPTER TWENTY-ONE

BELISARIUS EMERGED FROM the airlock of the inflaton racer into open space. The weightlessness was vast. The sound of his slow breathing and the crinkle of his suit sounded hollow in his helmet. *The Calculated Risk,* holding Saint Matthew, Cassie and the time gates sped away. In moments it was gone.

Blackness all around. Nothing above him. Nothing beneath. Emptiness, with only Epsilon Indi's faint magnetosphere pressing lightly against every muscle cell. His heart slowed. Guilt receded. He existed alone in the void, without obligations or moral concerns, referent-free.

Except that wasn't entirely true. His capacity for denial was pulling a con on his guilt, playing on his own desperation. People fell for cons because they wanted a quick fix, a magic bullet, something to shortcut slow suffering. He wanted to be conned, but he knew he couldn't. He had to take responsibility for all that he'd done, intentional or not. He didn't know if he could. He felt like he might crumble when he thought too much about what he'd done and what he had to do.

A big Union fighter appeared in the darkness. He felt it magnetically before he saw it, but barely. The inflaton drives emitted no EM and the running lights were extinguished. It pulled alongside him and neutralized their relative movement. The near side of the hull had an airlock. Belisarius approached on cold jets and cycled through. The interior was dark, but the EM from the inner wiring and control systems pressed on his magnetosomes faintly.

"Stills?" he said into his helmet microphone.

"Take the pilot seat, Arjona," Stills' false voice said in his ear. "I ain't gonna go fast unless the Congregate decides to keep us company."

Belisarius went to the front and strapped himself in. "Thanks for working this out," he said.

"No sweat on me. You got your own problems with Iekanjika and her people."

"Yeah." Two gravities of acceleration pressed Belisarius against the pilot seat. He groaned.

"You swiped something pretty important?" Stills asked.

"Yeah."

"I don't care either way, but shouldn't part of your plan have been to never again see the people you stole from, or am I missing something?"

"That was the plan."

"You fucked the dog on that one," Stills said.

"The Congregate blew up the Garret."

"Shitty. How many survived? None?"

"All of them."

"How the fuck do you do this? You really are a fucking magician."

"They're not safe. I might find them a safe place to stay if I can make a deal with Rudo."

Talking about it congealed the worry in his stomach. Think of other things. Think of other things. But he couldn't. His brain stuttered in the face of so much terror, so much guilt, pushing his thoughts off their path every few seconds. He stopped fighting it. Taking responsibility meant feeling the paralyzing enormity of the stakes. Taking responsibility meant just suffering and wishing for it to end.

Stills rotated the fighter and began decelerating twenty minutes later. The countdown to arrival finally gave Belisarius something emotions couldn't derail. Time. Metronomic and precise and mildly numbing.

Stills flew through the Freyja Axis. They emerged seventy-five light years away in the Bachwezi system. A series of half-constructed fortifications surrounded the Axis mouth, spotted with the mid-sized Union battle cruisers and the small battleship *Mutapa*. He couldn't tell more than that because the controls in front of him were all off.

The *Mutapa* sharpened in detail as Stills edged them towards the flagship. Laser scars striped its hull like talon marks dragged hundreds of meters over the plating. New shielding made a patchwork of color tones across the hull, from blasted black to shiny unblemished steel. Sentry craft accompanied them and turret cannons turned slowly, so that Belisarius could stare down their dark lengths the whole approach. Stills nuzzled the big fighter into a cradle under the flagship. They weren't even letting them enter a bay. How dangerous did they think Belisarius was?

A pair of military police met him at the top of the umbilical. In the zero-g they removed his survival suit right there, down to naked skin, and sealed his equipment in a locker. They deep and shallow scanned him before giving him a pair of loose pants and a plain sweater. Finally they brought him through discolored plastic corridors to a state room where, four months and about four hundred light years away, he'd first met Kudzanai Rudo.

Rudo still appeared remarkably short, surrounded by the

towering men and women of her crews, but she had hard, cunning eyes, and her officers floated in obvious awe of her. She'd seen battle. New scars had overwritten older ones on her face and neck and fingers. A wicked burn scar still ran from the front to the back of her scalp, even though plastic surgery could have fixed it relatively easily.

Scars were better than medals to soldiers, but in her case, it might not matter. In capturing the Freyja Axis, she'd made military history. She sat stone-faced across the table from him, strapped to her chair. Iekanjika sat near her. Two military police in body armor and magnetized boots stood with pistols drawn on either side of the two officers.

Warm welcome.

He strapped himself into one of the seats.

"You found the new Axis?" Belisarius asked.

"We don't consider that payment for what you stole," Rudo said.

"As long as you don't think you're getting back what I took, this conversation can go on," he said. Rudo stared back at him.

"What do you think this conversation is, Mister Arjona?" she asked finally.

"My employment with the Union has been costly," he said. "The Congregate and the Banks are after the *Homo quantus*. The Congregate blew up the Garret. I barely had time to get my people out. Now they're in hiding. I need to find a place to hide them permanently, otherwise they're all dead."

"We can offer your people asylum here," Rudo said. "It's possible we have things to offer each other. Your feats of..." she waved her hand lazily, "magic were impressive. If your people can do this too..."

"I don't think you or I consider Bachwezi safe," Belisarius said. "And I'm thinking further afield than a quick alliance. I've found a way to locate the mouths of the Axis Mundi through the time gates."

"That makes the *Homo quantus* incredibly valuable and incredibly dangerous," Rudo said, "and your theft that much more bitter."

"It's not anything that your people could do. Nor most of mine. My people are introspective, reclusive, mostly inept, in need of protection," Belisarius said.

"You're not like that," Iekanjika said.

"Cassandra and I are outliers, and the two of us can't protect the *Homo quantus*. I intend to hide my people three or four nodes out in the Axis Mundi network where no one will threaten them."

"So do it," Rudo said.

"I can't yet. The time gates can show me other Axes, but there's no scale. My view isn't calibrated. We found the fifth Axis in Epsilon Indi because we oriented our measurements to the four known wormholes. But we can't do that elsewhere. I can tell that the Bachwezi system contains five mouths of the Axis Mundi, but without calibrating, I can't tell you where they are."

"What do you need?" Rudo asked.

"You found the time gates on a planetoid," Belisarius said. "You took core drillings. What data do you have on those?"

"What do you know about those?" Iekanjika said heatedly.

"We don't have the cores or the data anymore, Mister Arjona," Rudo said.

"So there's no deal then?" Iekanjika said.

Rudo smiled coldly. "Mister Arjona didn't come here expecting us to carry core samples across forty years in the wilderness. He has another plan. Don't you?"

"You already know what it is?" Belisarius asked, as a tickle of unease snuck up his spine.

Rudo nodded slowly.

"And I think you know why," Rudo said.

The unease became gooseflesh up his neck and down his arms.

Iekanjika looked from Rudo to Belisarius, trying to understand what they meant. She couldn't possibly guess. Rudo signaled the MPs to leave. They frowned, holstered their sidearms. They looked pointedly at Iekanjika for some signal to stay or for acknowledgment that she was assuming the protection of Rudo. The hatch closed behind them. He, Iekanjika and Rudo were alone. Fear slithered in his stomach.

"We're going to make a deal with Mister Arjona," Rudo said to Iekanjika. The colonel schooled her expressions inexpertly.

"He robbed us once, ma'am," Iekanjika said, tamping her anger as much as she could.

"Mister Arjona can do more than find wormholes with the time gates," Rudo said. "He can go back in time with them."

"Eleven years?" Iekanjika said.

"Thirty-nine years," Rudo said.

Hackles rose on Belisarius' neck.

"Do you have me at a disadvantage, General?" he asked.

"I'm sure I do," Rudo said. "We didn't meet four months ago, Mister Arjona. You and I met thirty-nine years ago, on Nyanga, the planetoid where we found the time gates."

"What?" Iekanjika blurted.

"Where did the idea to use Mister Arjona come from?" Rudo asked the colonel slowly.

"Babedi," Iekanjika said, from behind a guarded expression.

"I had instructed Brigadier Wakikonda to discreetly suggest Mister Arjona's name to Mister Babedi," Rudo said.

"You knew him," Iekanjika said.

"The fact that I met him and you thirty-nine years ago meant that I knew he would get us across the Puppet Axis."

Belisarius felt played, on a scale he found hard to swallow. He'd played everyone in the room to get the Sixth Expeditionary Force to Epsilon Indi. He'd been smarter than everyone else. But now he didn't feel that smart.

"Me?" Iekanjika asked. Her anger seemed to have faded. Her voice had the same tone of creeping fear as his.

"We know enough about avoiding paradoxes to know that Mister Arjona has to go back," Rudo said, "and so do you."

"We came to you for help?" Belisarius said.

"Yes," the lieutenant-general said.

"Something must have kept you from shooting us when we spoke to you," Belisarius said.

A flicker of pain crossed Rudo's face.

"Yes," she said, "something convinced me you came with the blessing of my future self."

"What?" Iekanjika asked.

Rudo stared at her fingers for long seconds. The air vents hummed.

"My name isn't really Kudzanai Rudo."

"What?" Iekanjika said in astonishment.

"I was born with the name Vimbiso Tangwerai in Murombedzi," Rudo said quietly, "one of the teeming millions looking to get out of the political chaos of the Sub-Saharan Union. I knew Kudzanai Rudo, and that she'd been selected to go to the Union Academy at Harare. Forty-five years ago, I killed her. I falsified her genetic records. I took her identity. I became Officer Cadet Kudzanai Rudo."

Iekanjika gaped.

"No one has ever known this," Rudo said. "Now only the two of you know. If you're smart, you'll take this secret to your graves."

"You're not Rudo," Iekanjika said in a daze, looking like a tent pole had been removed from her life.

"I am Lieutenant-General Rudo," the older woman said. "I lived every part of this military career, from the first day at the academy, through the forty years of the Sixth Expeditionary Force, through the break-out, until now. The late Miss Rudo's only contributions to this career were her political connections to get into the academy. The rest is just a label. I have been Kudzanai Rudo longer than either of you have been alive, and longer than the original."

"Why did we go to you in the past?" Belisarius asked. "Because we could tell you the truth or because you could get us where we needed to be?"

"You wouldn't have lasted a day on Nyanga without inside help," Rudo said. "It was a dark time for the Sixth Expeditionary Force. We'd captured or killed all of the political officers, and most of the Congregate sleeper agents infiltrating the Expeditionary Force, but we could never be sure. We were paranoid, but not just against the Congregate. Political factions in the Expeditionary Force moved against each other for control of the Force and the time gates."

"You know when we arrive in the past," Belisarius said.

"Your window isn't large," Rudo said. "We found the surface of Nyanga pristine, so you couldn't go back before the arrival of the Expeditionary Force to take a sample. And then we left with the time gates just ahead of stellar flares from the brown dwarf primary. The only time you and the colonel could get onto the surface for a sample was while the Force was there, with all the players watching all the other players for signs of betrayal. To get onto the surface, you need identities and covers. I was a young captain back then, but in internal affairs we had disproportionately high security clearances."

Iekanjika breathed, looking straight ahead, still deflating. "We're not going back in time because Arjona wants to, or even because we want to," she said numbly. "We're going back because we have to."

"To avoid a grandfather paradox," Belisarius said.

CHAPTER TWENTY-TWO

STILLS FLEW BELISARIUS back to the rendezvous point and left him floating in space. Fifteen minutes later, Saint Matthew arrived with *The Calculated Risk*. As expected, Belisarius found three transmitters in his vacuum suit. This slowed them down as he removed the bugs and left them drifting off on misleading paths. He didn't begrudge the time though. He didn't really want to face any of the *Homo quantus*.

Belisarius hadn't seen a lot of suffering in his life, not real suffering. The orbital pathway of his existence had been designed to avoid emotional content. Love. Hate. Passion. He already had too much passion in his engineered addiction to curiosity. He'd only succeeded in fighting that instinct by living a quiet life deprived of mathematical and scientific stimulation. The other *Homo quantus* didn't need to hide from their curiosity. Theirs were not as strong as his. They could indulge their other emotions too, as he did not. Anguish. Loss. Depression.

Saint Matthew flew him to the fifth Axis and through it. Then, it was a short voyage at high acceleration across the system to the orbit where they'd set the freighters: ugly boxes of abraded metal with lumpy engines and small cockpits. They were not made for long-term life support. They'd improvised radiation shielding, but at some point atmospheric integrity would go. The four thousand *Homo quantus* had two thousand emergency vacuum suits and only a few hundred standard ones. Perhaps worst of all, the inelegant lines of the ships resisted modeling in any deterministic or non-determination geometric system.

They were cobbled together as a poor optimization of cost and functionality, distracting patches of color, without even rudimentary colored lights inside or out. They'd gone from living in a bright green garden full of quiet life to a series of creaking steel and aluminum boxes.

Belisarius was both the cause of this suffering and the only one they could turn to with their anger and need for reassurance. His people were dead-eyed, haunted, and turned away as he passed the stacks and stacks of cubicles.

Belisarius averted his eyes, not looking at the people watching him. At the bridge of *Red,* he met with Cassie and told her of his conversation with Rudo. Then, they messaged Nicola Samper.

Samper was one of the more pragmatic councilors, aged twenty-nine years, eleventh generation of the *Homo quantus* like Belisarius and Cassandra, although she wasn't capable of entering the fugue. She'd taken a number of roles in managing the Garret and one day might have naturally expected to reach the unwanted pinnacle of administrative responsibility: the mayoralty. She arrived six point four minutes later and strapped warily into a chair. The stars beyond the scratched cockpit window moved with lazy, linear precision.

"I need you to be deputy mayor," Cassie said.

Samper eyed her with growing suspicion. "I thought Belisarius was deputy mayor."

"He has to go with me," Cassie said.

"You're leaving us?"

"I need to find a safe place for the *Homo quantus*. I need Bel's help. It may be just for a week."

"You're abandoning us!"

Belisarius leaned in, conspiratorially, trusting, using body language the way he'd learned in confidence schemes. "I've got a line on a place, where no one will find the *Homo quantus*. We'll be able to live in peace and quiet for centuries."

"If you know the place, why not just take us there?" Samper asked, puzzled.

"I don't have the information, but I know where to get it."

Samper frowned. "Is this another trick? You shoot off with your fast ship and your time travel wormholes and leave us stranded here?"

"No trick!" Belisarius said. "We have to work out the way to get where we're going, but I don't have all the information."

"This doesn't sound very good for us."

"We'll be gone three, four days," Cassie said. "But if we're not back after that time, you have some choices to make."

"If you're not back?" Samper asked. "You are leaving us!"

"Getting the information might be dangerous," Belisarius said. "If we're not back in four days, we're probably dead. In that case, everyone in civilization will still be after the *Homo quantus*. Your safest bet is probably coming back to Epsilon Indi and inducing wormholes all the way to Alhambra. There, turn yourselves over to the Banks. I'm not sure how free you'll be, but they'll protect you."

Samper swallowed. "This is rotten. I knew we couldn't trust you."

A sadness seeped through Belisarius, swallowing him piece by piece.

"I'm not running," he said. "I'm getting what we need to ensure our future. This will make us safe."

Samper unstrapped herself and maneuvered to the door.

"I wish I believed you," she said.

She spun the door latch, heaved it open on squeaking hinges, and left Belisarius and Cassie in the ugly cockpit.

CHAPTER TWENTY-THREE

BELISARIUS, CASSIE AND Saint Matthew rendezvoused with Iekanjika and Stills' cargo much the same way Belisarius had been picked up last time: floating in space. It took Iekanjika and Belisarius twenty minutes to transfer Stills in his unwieldy tank into the lower hold of *The Calculated Risk* and hook him into the racer's systems. They'd added a third acceleration chamber to the cockpit for Iekanjika, making it even more cramped than before. Iekanjika handed Belisarius a data wafer.

"These are all the security codes and procedures we still had on record," she said. "These are not the kinds of things we keep for forty years, but they were backed up in auditing records. They won't cover the entire base, nor even all paths completely through the base, but they'll get us started."

"You guys are fuckin' insane," Stills offered through the comms system.

"This is the only way," Belisarius said.

"Walking into a Union base in disguise, in the past, seems beyond the risks even I'd take," Stills said. "I don't know shit about time travel, but it seems to me that if some cocksucker sneezes wrong, history puts our *huevos* in the cutter."

Out of the corner of his eye, Belisarius observed Cassie. She was tense, anxious. She agreed with Stills. For that matter, *he* agreed with Stills. But there wasn't another way, or even a better way to measure the time difference across the gates and how that difference had changed over geological time. She smiled at him encouragingly despite her reservations.

"Many theories say the past we know is established and robust," Cassie said to Stills. "The past happened and the Union came back to civilization. That shouldn't change."

She didn't add *what happens to Bel, Iekanjika and Saint Matthew in the past is another question,* but the thought sort of hung between them.

"We'll be careful," Belisarius said. "Interact as little as possible. But you'll both have to be as careful."

Cassie shrugged.

"Fuck that," Stills said. "We're just the getaway car."

"Waiting in twenty-two dimensional space-time," Belisarius said.

"Number of dimensions don't matter shit if we're just parking."

"Once we're inside," Belisarius said to Iekanjika, "you'll see why no one but the *Homo quantus* could navigate the interior."

"I'm more concerned with you successfully passing as a member of the Expeditionary Force," Iekanjika said.

She unpacked two uniforms and two standard-issue vac suits from four decades ago. He started putting his on. His skin had already darkened significantly. He'd been taking cosmetic supplements to stimulate his skin into producing more melanin, darkening it from the Afro-Colombian brown he'd been born with to something closer to the typical skin color of the citizens of the Sub-Saharan Union. He'd also learned the accent and idiosyncrasies of the Union French of forty years ago and the entirety of the Shona language.

"Antiques?" Belisarius asked.

"Refurbished," she said. "They'll look good enough for us to move around."

Belisarius thumbed the raised ridge of the rank insignia on the uniform she'd gotten him. "Private. I'm honored."

"The people you meet won't expect much from a private."

"What rank did you give yourself?" Stills asked.

"Corporal," she said.

"A workin' man," Stills growled in electrical approval. "It'll show you how the better half lives. Don't say anything fancy in the enlisted mess. We fuckin' hate that and you'll be marked as somebody needin' to be taken down a peg. Especially you, quantum boy."

"I'll keep him quiet," Iekanjika said with no irony Belisarius could detect.

"Approaching target," Saint Matthew said.

The AI had already turned the racer stern-first to decelerate at one gravity. The holographic display showed a bi-lobed asteroid. Each lobe was about two kilometers in diameter, joined at the waist by a deep pile of rubble. Although the asteroid seemed to be a gently-formed contact binary, one lobe had ancient fracture lines which ran dozens of meters deep. Saint Matthew stopped the racer, and then matched the asteroid's ponderous rotation.

"Nice pad," Stills said. "Fix it up yourself?"

"While we go into the past, we need to leave the time gates somewhere safe," Belisarius said. "No one would ever accuse Epsilon Indi of being asteroid-poor, so hiding the time gates in a crevasse for a while is a safe bet."

"You keep them here?" Stills said.

The racer vibrated as the doors of the hold opened into space. Belisarius switched on the bay view in the cabin.

"He carried them around with him," Iekanjika said with a touch of bitterness.

"That's it?" Stills said. "I thought you said they were wormholes. Those are tiny."

"Fifteen meters wide, ten meters high," Belisarius said. "Small enough to fit in the hold with a bit of bending."

Stills might have had a quip or something insulting to say, maybe along the lines of *'You fucking bent a wormhole?'* but maybe a sliver of awe could wiggle its way even through his layers of blubber and muscle.

Saint Matthew's robotic spidery automata unloaded the time gates and propelled them into a deep crevasse twenty meters wide and blanketed in shadow. A holographic schematic appeared, showing the walls of the crevasse, the entire contact asteroid structure and the time gates.

"Can you compensate for the lumpy gravitational field, Mister Stills?" Saint Matthew asked.

"Fuck off, wrist-sweat," Stills said.

"Transferring control to you then," Saint Matthew said.

"What do you want, prancy-pants?"

"As soon as you enter the wormhole, your instruments won't make any sense," Belisarius said. "Use dead reckoning to come to a full stop a hundred meters after you clear the mouth. Cassie will navigate from then on."

For no reason other than apparently to bother them, Stills twitched the controls to get the feel of the cold jets. They all had to grab something. Then, Stills drifted them towards the flat face of the time gates, compensating for the uneven gravity with deft touches to the jets.

"I guess you don't want me scuffing the paint of your pretty ship on the sides of the wormhole?" Stills said.

Belisarius didn't answer. The mongrel was fishing for compliments or just challenging him. Stills had thirty to fifty centimeters clearance even at the widest section of *The Calculated*

Risk. He would never have made a piloting error any more than he would have lost a race. Too much pride. Stills piloted them through and space changed. The dead visual stillness of the shadowed asteroid gave way to an eerie subconscious throbbing that made Iekanjika wince.

"*Puta!*" Stills said over the comms.

Human nerves had evolved to respond to a very narrow set of visual, auditory, chemical and pressure cues. Setting out to colonize other worlds had sometimes left some senses unfulfilled as people lived in tiny, artificial habitats. Here, the opposite was true. In this eleven-dimensional cathedral, every kind of nerve was triggered from within by phenomena that had nothing to do with human senses. Blotches of purple spattered sight like interference on a transmitted visual, while an unwholesome stew of phantom tastes hit them all. *Homo quantus* brains could create algorithms to subtract false signals, and even retreat into savant if they had to. Iekanjika, Stills and even Saint Matthew were exposed though.

Iekanjika was tight-lipped and wide-eyed. But she mastered her reactions quickly, walking her expression back until even Belisarius couldn't tell she was disturbed. Beside him, Cassie, in savant, began calling out navigational instructions.

Full stop. Forty-five degree rotation around the q-axis. Full stop. Ninety degree rotation across the r-axis. Two hundred meters per second for twenty-eight seconds, spin the racer one hundred and eighty degrees for braking, then full stop and the next rotations...

Belisarius watched Iekanjika. He couldn't afford to have her harmed by exposure to being in here. Beyond the cockpit window was a weird, alien space, mostly impenetrable to baseline human eyes, and even most kinds of sensors. Shifting curtains of light crept through the dark interior of the time gates. And while it was as cold as a shadowed asteroidal crater, stray gamma rays and the occasional anti-particle zipped past. Stranger than the view were the eerie sensations of additional dimensions opening around them. Iekanjika probably felt the small twists in her stomach, in her balance and in her vision without knowing what they were.

And it would be a lie to say that he and Cassie were immune to exposure to hyperspace. They were equipped to rationalize and compartmentalize the sensations, but their novel senses made new vulnerabilities too. Gravity and electromagnetism traveled differently in eleven dimensions, and even moreso depending on which axes of the interior they followed. Portions of their trajectory briefly gave them two temporal dimensions instead of one, which Belisarius felt through his magnetosomes and disliked.

He wondered what Iekanjika thought of all this. Did she still resent that all this hostile space and time could have been hers? Or was she not even thinking about where they were and instead busying her mind with what they'd find thirty-nine years ago? Only her fingers, tight on the arm rests of her seat, betrayed her tension.

"Mister Arjona," Saint Matthew said into Belisarius' ear implant. "The colonel's data wafer contains a sleeper virus that is programmed to infect the racer. At some point, it is supposed to start sending homing signals to the Union."

You've neutralized it? Belisarius typed into his data pad.

"Of course," the AI responded. "But if we can't trust her..."

We never expected to, and she doesn't trust me.

"What a fucked up place," Stills said.

"Are you alright?" Belisarius asked.

"I'm always fuckin' A-okay, but I got weird sensor shadows. Have you pulled a physics theory out of your ass to explain why the place reflects back images of ourselves?"

"I don't see anything."

"It's faint and inconsistent, sometimes bigger, sometimes smaller," Stills said, changing the view in the projection to a fuzzy, tube shape kilometers behind them that grew and shrank. It was almost identical in size to the *The Calculated Risk,* but additional dimensions did strange things to perspective and relativity.

"I got a good sense for echoes and that ain't an echo."

Whatever it was vanished and didn't return.

"We haven't figured out all the kinds of visual and electrical echoes inside the time gates when we move across time axes," Cassie said with the distant enthusiasm of a *homo quantus* in savant. "We're staying away from those to avoid paradoxes. What if what you just saw was us, on the way back?"

Belisarius watched the empty image, checked it in other spectra and watched contaminated data roll in from sensors not made to work in this environment. Nothing.

"Fuuuuuuck," Stills said. "Don't pull that shit with me, princess. I ain't lookin' to meet another me."

Cassandra continued issuing navigational instructions. The stops and starts, the rotations around strange dimensions made even Belisarius a little queasy. But at last the projection changed, and a flattened oval appeared about two hundred meters before them. As *The Calculated Risk* rotated around its final axis, the disk expanded into the familiar shape of the time gates.

"The pastward mouth?" Saint Matthew asked quietly.

"Opening thirty-nine years in the past, on the planet where the Union found the time gates," Belisarius said.

No one spoke. A directionless sense of dread crept over him.

"Well, shit!" Stills said loudly. "No one'll ever believe this."

Belisarius briefly took Cassie's hand, and despite being in savant, she squeezed it back.

"Are you ready, colonel?" Belisarius asked.

Iekanjika squinted, peering into the gloomy weirdness beyond the cockpit. She nodded curtly.

Belisarius and Iekanjika sealed the chests, hoses and gloves of their vacuum suits. Belisarius became Private Wedu Abugalo and Iekanjika became Corporal Upenyu Manyika. Iekanjika's hands shook slightly; not so much that anyone else would notice, even Cassie in savant. Cassie hadn't trained herself to read meaning in people's behavior. Will Gander had trained Belisarius to interpret all the cues and tells his marks showed, so he picked up on Iekanjika's nerves.

Belisarius took Saint Matthew from the cockpit console and put him around his wrist as a service band. They'd modified the band to match the style that the Union wore forty years ago. Cassie exhaled a long breath, the kind she made when emerging from savant. She unstrapped and came close, putting her hand on the neck ring of his suit. Her eyes were worried.

"We'll wait here for the next hour," she said. "Then we'll move onto an axis where we can see the wormhole mouth across a broad stretch of time, so whether you're back in two hours or two weeks or two months, we'll see you and move to pick you up."

"If you can figure out any of that, prancy-pants," Stills said, "power to you."

"Come back," Cassie whispered to Belisarius.

"I will," Belisarius said.

She pressed her lips to his until his heart started beating more quickly. Hers did too, in the resonance that *Homo quantus* learned as children to help with fugue spotting.

"I will," he said.

CHAPTER TWENTY-FOUR

IF TIME INSERTED intervening distances between moments, separating events from one another, then the vitrification and petrification processes collapsed time. Events separated by fifty years, or a hundred, maintained an unnatural clarity, as if seen through a telescope. In a petrified brain, life and memory were connected by lenses rather than time.

Many of the lenses in Scarecrow memory revealed informants, those bricks and mortar of espionage work. As a young intelligence officer posted off Venus, he'd cultivated his own informants, inherited others from his superiors. He'd plied them, bribed them, threatened them for information. Their likenesses were sharp-lined in memory, as if under glassy water, but they had no names. They all had code-names, or names he could no longer remember.

His own name was gone too, as if he were just someone's informant too, some part in the great chain of intelligence and espionage. His name wasn't important though. The Congregate was greater than the sum of the Houses and families floating in the clouds of Venus and knowing what Venusian House he came from might dilute the Scarecrow's loyalty to the Congregate.

Bribing informants in the Congregate was increasingly

difficult. The Congregate was born of scarcity, but for decades had been moving into a new post-scarcity world. The people of Venus were born of generations of separatists, who themselves were born of other separatists, and forced to move out to one of the most inhospitable places in the solar system under the thumbs of the Banks. No one who lived through that period of want and poverty could forget it, but a society could forget it, trading memories away as the price of raising children in the light of wealth.

The Scarecrow had lived on both sides of the divide. Haunted-eyed parents and all the old *ma tantes* and *mon oncles* obliged him to remember their sacrifices, all that came before his games of tag in the clouds, back when the Banks had tried to own and invade them. It was old history to him, but he learned.

The bright side of the scarcity divide was a strange world. He didn't need to work. He didn't need to do anything. But where was meaning in such a world? He found it in service to the Congregate, in the espionage forces, but that cut him off, first from all those who did no service, like his brother Adéodat, and parents he could no longer remember, and second from all those who harbored discontent with the Congregate in their hearts.

Bribing informants in this new world was hard. Loyalty became a new currency, coming with social status and its own set of dividends. And among his peers, the other new currency was immortality, as a Scarecrow. His fellow intelligence officers strove to prove their loyalty, for advancement, better postings, and maybe for one day being born in a second petrified, vitrified life. He hadn't. He'd never believed he had what it took, nor believed he was any better than his fellow intelligence officers.

He was good with informants, a talent that hadn't faded with age or petrification. And one of his informants had spotted the *Homo quantus* Arjona on the Union flagship with one of the high-level rebels, Colonel Ayen Iekanjika. The substance of their conversation was unknown. Arjona later left the *Mutapa*, and a day later Colonel Iekanjika did so as well.

The Scarecrow had followed the colonel's command fighter, running in stealth mode, nearly invisible against the stars. He rode in the casing of a *casse à face* missile fitted with an experimental reactionless drive. The Scarecrow needed no air, no life support, or even space beyond its robotic body. The drive burned no fuel, so only active radar pings would reveal it, but the colonel moved too stealthily for that.

The command fighter made for one of the deep-system relays, an artificial satellite of Epsilon Indi that boosted communication signals on their way across the solar system. The fighter came to a stop, and for long minutes, waited at the satellite before it darted back the way it had come. The Scarecrow would have followed it, but it detected new emissions from the satellite. Thermal. Something human-sized emitted infrared near body temperature, alongside a large, cooler object. The command fighter had disembarked someone with equipment.

The Scarecrow weighed its options. The weaponized AI was capable of complex espionage and counter-intelligence functions, but its primary role was counter-insurgency. The command fighter was far enough from its forward base that it might be captured for intelligence analysis. But intelligence was not the same as rooting out the rebellion. The Scarecrow transmitted a progress report to its team on the cruiser *Port-Cartier*, twenty light-minutes away, and waited.

Fifteen minutes later, a larger craft approached, decelerating at five gravities. It had low reflectivity and IR emission and no running lights of EM emissions from its drive. It was a very quiet inflaton ship, trying to be even more quiet. It stopped at the satellite and loaded the secretive passenger and the cargo. Then, it accelerated away at four gravities. The Scarecrow followed at a distance, and transmitted another tight-beam report to the *Port-Cartier.*

The inflaton ship made a number of course changes, some drastic, and the Scarecrow had to run on silent and make corresponding maneuvers long after the inflaton ship had pulled far ahead. After three hours of this, the inflaton ship decelerated near C99312, a chondritic, bi-lobed asteroid. The Scarecrow did the same, maintaining telescopic distance.

The small bay doors on the inflaton craft opened, removing something from its hold. The EM emissions were strangely inconclusive, colder than the rest of the inflation ship. The object's luminosity was faint and variable, with a spattering of x-rays. Through their faint infrared emissions, the Scarecrow watched robotic automata move this cargo into a shadowed ravine. Shortly, the inflaton ship closed its bay doors, turned and entered the ravine.

Then the Scarecrow could not detect it.

The Scarecrow scrutinized its telescopic observations, but only the slow cooling of the robotic automata was visible. No ship. Had it entered the asteroid? Not likely. The asteroid would have been hotter in the infrared if it had housed even a lookout station. The Scarecrow reviewed its telescopic observations again. The thing they'd taken out of the hold was far colder than the ship. And it emitted faint radiation and scattered x-rays of a very peculiar kind.

Strange.

Delicately, on cold jets, the Scarecrow approached C99312. From fifty kilometers, the Scarecrow lasered the little robots in the ravine, enough to burn them out, but not enough to melt them and destroy the possibility of conducting a forensic examination on their inner workings. A faint magnetic field centered on the asteroid, so faint that at fifty kilometers, Epsilon Indi's own field almost swamped it.

The Scarecrow reached the ravine, ready to respond to any attack, but nothing moved or signaled. A few meters away from the nose of the *casse à face* missile, the inscrutable Cherenkov radiation and trace x-rays shimmered.

No observers had ever recorded any wormhole so small, so small that only a narrow shuttle or missile could fit through, and the inflaton ship had vanished. The Scarecrow shot a tight-beam report to the *Port-Cartier,* with instructions to secure C99312 immediately. The message would reach the destroyer in twenty minutes, and it might need another ten minutes to induce a temporary wormhole and arrive on full alert. But by then, the trail of the Union colonel might be cold on the other side. And the colonel was either with Arjona or could lead him to the *Homo quantus.* The Scarecrows were not grown to feel trepidation or fear, only unwavering loyalty to the Congregate and deep affront when faced with threats. Although the far side of the Axis might be defended, high-value intelligence was on the other side.

The Scarecrow crossed the insubstantial surface of the wormhole mouth.

Everything became immediately incomprehensible, with nonsensical visual, gravimetric and electrical signals. Automated system diagnostics activated, showing weird time discrepancies, energy readings and impossible internal pingback delays. The Scarecrow came to a stop. This was no normal wormhole. It lacked a throat structure. Instead, a vast, trackless space opened, and readings made no sense.

The inflaton ship floated, barely visible, a kilometer ahead. It had also stopped and was rotating on cold jets. But as the Scarecrow watched, the inflaton ship shrank and vanished. It didn't recede. It didn't pass through the horizon of a wormhole mouth. It shrank along an axis, squashing and vanishing.

The Scarecrow moved precisely on cold jets to the last position of the inflaton ship with readied weapons. The region, although writhing with weird, sourceless energies, was empty, bereft of obstacles or any cover where the ship might have hidden. There was no such thing as a cloaking effect, unless the *Homo quantus* had invented one.

Where had they gone?

The Scarecrow rotated exactly as it had seen the inflaton ship do. The view of the interior of the weird space changed. Some colors shrank and disappeared. Others kaleidescoped through frequency and apparent direction. Despite being an AI with powerful processing capacities, the Scarecrow hadn't been so disoriented since its construction decades ago.

The kaleidescoping effect pulled an image of the inflaton ship into visibility, six hundred meters ahead; at first minuscule, then small, then growing to full size as the Scarecrow completed its rotation. The stern of the inflaton ship was visible, moving off.

The Scarecrow couldn't understand the shrinking and growing ship. No element of perspective or movement could explain it. Nor could anything explain the strange time discrepancies with the speed of internal diagnostic pingbacks within the missile system. Something very, very strange was at play.

The Scarecrow didn't understand this space and what it saw, nor the speed of its internal pingbacks. And it also realized, with unfamiliar dread, that it couldn't see the wormhole mouth anymore. It had only advanced a couple of kilometers into the Axis, yet the Scarecrow hadn't controlled its drift precisely in its urgency, so even reversing its course exactly would not necessarily bring it back to the wormhole mouth, if it could ever even find it again.

The inflaton ship was rotating again. Its pilot knew how to navigate this space. How long had the Union and the *Homo quantus* been working on this treason?

It didn't matter. The *Port-Cartier* would secure one side of these bizarre wormholes. Then the Congregate would have decades and centuries to peel the layers away from their secrets, perhaps with the help of the *Homo quantus* the Scarecrow had captured. And perhaps with the help of the Union colonel. The Scarecrow couldn't navigate the interior of this place, but it could repeat all the rotations and accelerations it saw in the inflaton ship. Once it found the other side of the wormhole, it could get a star fix and signal the Congregate.

CHAPTER TWENTY-FIVE

IEKANJIKA SNAPPED CLOSED the seals on her helmet, ignoring the puppy love between the two *Homo quantus*. She'd never experienced that kind of innocent affection. She'd had lovers from time to time, trysts, but nothing like the needy insecurity Arjona and Mejía displayed. When she was relatively young she had been joined into a powerful triple marriage to Lieutenant-General Rudo and Brigadier Wakikonda, both significantly older. She'd always respected Wakikonda, and she revered Lieutenant-General Rudo's military cunning, her commanding leadership, and her unflagging belief that they would return home. Despite Iekanjika's own failure in losing the time gates, she'd been so proud when Rudo had been promoted and given command of the Navy.

Iekanjika's loyalty had been unshakable since childhood, but the last three days had dislocated her life, tilting everything askew. Lieutenant-General Rudo wasn't Rudo, not really, but a name didn't matter. The woman they'd called Rudo all these years was the same person, and had been since before Iekanjika had been born.

Yet names did matter, as much as actions.

The Union named its warships after places and people that

meant something to them: *Mutapa, Limpopo, Kampala, Gbudue, Batembuzi*; names bound to their history and identity. The Venusian Congregate did the same, honoring names from a colonial Québec inflated by time and steeped in legend. Zimbabwe, the central power of the Union, had itself taken its name from an Iron Age kingdom precisely because names had power.

So the young woman, Vimbiso Tangwerai, had taken the name Kudzanai Rudo, a name with the totemic power to enter the academy. And she'd transformed that name into a charm spoken with reverence by her fleet, with respect by Union politicians, and with frustration by the Congregate.

So maybe the Lieutenant-General had been right to take Rudo's place in history. What were the chances that the original Rudo would have accomplished as much as the woman who had stolen her life? If the murdered Rudo was anything like the Union's social elite Iekanjika had met since their return to Bachwezi, those chances were tiny.

Iekanjika moved to the airlock. The dislocation of her life had not run its course; it was worsening. She was dislocated in history now too, stepping into a legendary time, when her slightest error could abort their rebellion four decades in the past.

Arjona joined her in the cramped airlock; Iekanjika cycled it and the door swung into the surreal space outside the racer: a slate-gray shot through with elusive, oily moments of sourceless color; flashes of sweet tastes and painfully loud bursts of white noise. All points around them touched her eyes as if they were at three different distances at once.

The racer, while solid enough, shifted in this eerie space, moving in and out of focus, with sourceless green and blue glints shooting under its opaque surface. Her own gloved hands

Derek Künsken

shimmered and when she moved them to dispel the effect, they seemed to foreshorten. Arjona seemed not to have the same trouble and focusing on him seemed to reduce the field of strangeness. His darkened face looked at her from within the halo of his faceplate.

"Ready, colonel?" he asked.

She could deal with this if he could. She wasn't *Homo quantus,* but she was proud of her officer status; that didn't change in a strange hyperspace, nor in the past.

Arjona activated the cold jets on his suit and moved without trouble, like he'd been born here. That was a dangerous notion. For months she'd considered him a brilliant, underhanded criminal. That assessment, perhaps wrong, might have come by measuring him outside of his proper setting. Aboard the *Mutapa* and the *Jonglei,* and in the Puppet Free City, Arjona never seemed quite to belong. But he and Mejía possessed the ease of the children born to this chaos.

She followed hesitantly, slowing as he stopped just above the red-shot surface of the wormhole mouth. Disconcertingly, he pressed his face through that horizon, as if pushing his faceplate into a liquid. He pulled back and looked at her.

"The coast is as clear as I think it's going to get," he said. "I lasered the nearest watchtower with our identification."

He took her upper arm and she matched his trajectory with her cold jets, bracing herself for the transition, but she felt nothing as they crossed the horizon. Hard spotlights cast harsh shadows. Gravity pulled her onto concrete-hard water ice overrun with drifts of melt-welded pollen, powdered with carbon dioxide snow and wreathed in faint mists of methane and nitrogen.

She'd never walked this ice, but a strange sense of ownership shivered in her. Somewhere among the Union forces were the

155

mother and father she'd never met. Overhead loomed the fat brown dwarf she'd been born under, squatting across fifteen degrees of the sky like a great glowing ember. Once, stars determined lives and fates. Dusty threads of metallic oxides—of vanadium, iron and aluminum—striated her star's windy upper atmosphere, while deeper clouds of titanium oxide were slow-moving bruises over the inflamed red beneath.

Behind her, the lower edge of the wormhole was frozen into the surface of the ice. In a wide circle centered on the portal stood rudely-built pillars of ice, topped with bright spotlights. They shone on an oily black scum covering much of the ground, a vacuum-living slick that photosynthesized the infrared from the young brown dwarf. Farther from the time gates, other photosynthesizers sprouted from the ground, assuming fractal shapes reminiscent of trees and bushes, oily black films webbing the branches to one another. But strangest of all was the herd of motile creatures, the ones called the vegetable intelligences in all the reports.

At first glance, they appeared utterly still, but after only a few moments her combat-trained senses noticed slow, inching shifts of weight. They were four-legged, with barrel-like body structures. Icy black fronds splayed above them, catching the dim infrared of the brown dwarf and the fine pollen that emerged from the time gates; except that no pollen emerged from the time gates anymore.

"You named the planet Nyanga," Belisarius said.

The Lieutenant-General had only said the name twice, but Arjona never forgot anything. The name was sacred, and neither she nor anyone in the rest of the Expeditionary Force ever spoke it lightly. It sounded strange coming from his lips, like an intrusive familiarity.

"The name is a dark joke," she said. "Nyanga is a national

park in Zimbabwe. Does this look like a national park to you?"

Arjona looked around with the same awe as she did.

"It does feel like a garden," he said slowly, "a garden grown under the ember of a failed star."

She didn't know how to take the tone of reverence in his voice. She didn't know the *Homo quantus* and what they might honor. And until he'd said it that way, it had never occurred to her that she'd been born under a failed star.

"About one minute until the cameras wake up from the override Rudo gave us," the AI said.

They walked from the time gates briskly, skirting the individual vegetable intelligences; if any had noticed their passage, they made no sign. In the distance, the outlines of crude buildings masked the stars and spilled their own illumination onto the ice. There some fifty people were widely scattered on the surface of the ice, bustling with activity.

Iekanjika's and Belisarius' helmets picked up radio traffic— uncoded orders, security detail check-ins, assignment changes. She listened to each message, feeling the press of history. If the Union survived breaking away from the Congregate, this would be their founding myth and she was standing at its inception, listening to its pedestrian humanity.

They passed the occasional worker. Most paid them no attention, or eyed them sidewise with masked suspicion. This was the Force's first of forty years on the run, using the time gates to accelerate the design of new propulsion and weapons technologies. But it was also the end of an ugly period of rooting out spies, sleeper agents, and traitors with loyalties to the Congregate. It had taken five years to outgrow that distrust, five years in which Rudo grew into prominence in the Expeditionary Force, helping forge a single, loyal unit focused on freeing the Sub-Saharan Union from the hegemony of the

Congregate. Iekanjika had been raised in that unified fleet and knew nothing of crossed loyalties, until they had come home and seen the politics of the Union, the squabbles in the Cabinet, the jockeying for position and blame. Did she even have the skills to navigate this time?

Perhaps not, but Captain Rudo did.

Sets of orders from security volleyed back and forth. She absorbed as much as she could, but lacked many of the referents. Then she heard, "Iekanjika said to clear them out. Kill them."

She froze, her heart beating hard. Arjona hurried her along.

"Keep moving! They're not talking about you."

She shook off his arm.

"I know that," she said through gritted teeth. "Who did my mother just order killed?"

"There's a lot of chatter," Arjona said, "but I'm pretty sure they're talking about the vegetable intelligences."

Relief washed through her. "Plants."

"Maybe."

Dirty gray ice peeked from beneath the oily black skin of the ground as they drew close to the buildings of ice and plastic. They walked past the MP tower, around the research coordinating center, behind the big supply hut, and came to the ground HQ. Everything seemed smaller and meaner than in the maps she'd studied. The buildings were built of warped and patched plastic and sprayed with ice to seal in the atmosphere. They'd been slapped together without an eye for efficiency, just a need to make-do. Iekanjika was used to living with deprivation. In the Force, they'd had very little. But even during the times of eating unflavored bioreactor produce for months on end, even after years of no chance to mine and build new parts, the crews of the Sixth Expeditionary Force had taken pride in their work. She saw no pride in any work here.

Iekanjika showed her service band to one of door scanners, punched in a code and the airlock opened for them. Nothing had so far impeded their progress; their temporary codes were working like a dream. She hung her helmet in an open locker and then started stripping off her vacuum suit down to her inner work clothes. Arjona disrobed too. He would pass well enough for a member of the Expeditionary Force, perhaps even in conversation. He was a cunning liar.

She adjusted her webbing and holster and began down the hall. Arjona followed, matching her attitude and pace. They passed soldiers, NCOs and officers, and saluted or nodded as appropriate, pressing deeper into the complex. The icy walls and floors chilled the air, lending everyone's movements a cold briskness. Off an underused side corridor in the second basement, they found a cluster of cubicles carved into the ice, housing two or three crew at a time, working on 2D screens or pads. Near the end of the hallway, thin light spilled from beneath a door.

Anxiety crept into Iekanjika, in a way she hadn't experienced even before combat. Hesitation in soldiers and commanders could be fatal. She'd been trained from a young age to overcome hesitation with brisk, reasoned movement. But no one had ever trained her for infiltrating the past. Habit dragged her hesitant hand to knock anyway.

A young voice bade them enter. Against a sudden nervousness that came close to nausea, Iekanjika opened the door.

The room was tiny, a couple of meters square, roughly ground from the ice so that there wasn't a neat corner or straight edge in sight. Behind a small table covered with data-pads and a scratched surface screen, looking up at her from an impossibly young face, was a diminutive captain.

This woman would be her wife in the future, but thirty-nine

years earlier, *now*, she was a marvelous stranger. Iekanjika had prepared herself for this, had studied old photos, but even so, she had to will her hand not to shake as she saluted. Arjona repeated the gesture behind her.

"Yes, corporal?" Rudo said.

Iekanjika hesitated so long that the young Rudo began to look suspicious. The precocious captain's face was smooth, her short tight curls night black. The scars were gone too; the one that looked like a river delta on the side of her neck and face, and the long wrinkled burn crease on the left side of her scalp where a sleeper agent had tried to assassinate her were yet to come. Thirty-nine years in the future, Lieutenant-General Rudo wouldn't leave the flagship for fear of assassination. Iekanjika now stood in a time before Rudo was worth killing.

"Ma'am," Iekanjika said softly, "I've been sent by a friend to ask for a favor."

Iekanjika stepped forward and Arjona crowded awkwardly behind her and closed the door. Rudo had to crane her neck to look Iekanjika in the eye, but she did this commandingly, leaning back in her plastic seat with a certain amount of cockiness.

"We're all comrades here," Rudo said.

Captain Rudo has yet to develop the polish of the executive and commander. Iekanjika recognized the new officer's swaggering assumption that respect was hers by right.

"May I sit?" Iekanjika asked.

"Ma'am?" Rudo asked archly.

"Ma'am," Iekanjika said.

"Speak your peace and go, corporal. I'm busy."

She sat anyway. She exhaled deeply and the words that she'd rehearsed before now seemed wooden in her mind.

"My name is Iekanjika. Ayen Iekanjika."

Rudo regarded her dubiously. "We both know there's no such

person on the Force's manifest."

Iekanjika balked at the insanity of what she had to say, then pressed on. "I'm from the future," she said. "I'm the daughter of Brigadier Iekanjika."

Listening to herself, she could tell it sounded like a bad joke. Yet everyone in the Expeditionary Force, whether they knew it or not, had worked around the time travel device they'd found on Nyanga. Everyone who knew of its presence had carefully thought through the possibilities and perils of time travel. They'd designed an entire administrative structure to hermetically separate knowledge, so that causality would never be violated, accidentally or on purpose.

Rudo slowly drew her sidearm and rested her hand on the table.

"You first," Rudo said, lifting the barrel to point directly at Iekanjika's chest, "then him, carefully."

Iekanjika removed her sidearm with two fingers and laid it on the table. Arjona did the same. Without taking her eyes from them, Rudo pressed a button on the desk. One of the lights above them reddened. She'd secured the room. She regarded them, as if steeling herself.

"You look to be in your thirties, Corporal Iekanjika," Rudo said finally. "Given that the Brigadier is pregnant right now, you're asking me to believe that you've come from more than thirty years in the future. That's not how the gates work. They send things back eleven years."

"In the decades the Expeditionary Force has had them, we've learned to control them a bit better," Iekanjika said. "I'm thirty-nine years old."

"Convenient. You didn't come without proof, did you?"

"You could run my DNA against my mother's," Iekanjika said, "but that might draw attention. You sent me from the future with something simpler."

"I did?" Rudo asked, eyebrow arching. "Thirty-nine years from now, I'm giving you orders?"

Iekanjika stared back at her young wife to be, trying to see the same person in the breezy tone of the twenty-two year old compared to the stately dignity she knew from the *de facto* leader of the Union's armed forces.

"Go on," Rudo said finally, waving her hand casually, as if she were doing Iekanjika a favor.

"I've known Kudzanai Rudo my entire life. She even took me as her junior wife, a deeply moving and humbling moment for me," Iekanjika said. "Then, a few days ago, for this mission, she told me her name isn't really Rudo."

Captain Rudo's expression crumbled and the pistol rose until Iekanjika stared down the barrel.

"I suppose she remembered that this had convinced her that I really came from the future," Iekanjika said. Rudo looked increasingly horrified. A weird feeling of protectiveness for this young incarnation of her wife stole into Iekanjika's heart.

Rudo swallowed, loud in the silence.

"If you're not lying," Captain Rudo croaked, "my future self must have given you a name?"

"Vimbiso Tangwerai."

Rudo grimaced, but the sidearm didn't waver.

"I thought I'd covered my tracks," Rudo said, "but obviously someone found out and has been holding this in reserve. That sounds like something a Congregate sleeper agent might do."

The barrel of Rudo's pistol trembled and her finger tightened on the trigger.

"This is what you told me to say!" Iekanjika said, angry panic welling up.

"You have nothing else?"

"I can tell you all about your future, but that won't convince you of anything," Iekanjika said. "You didn't give me any more secrets."

"Then you'll both tell me where you really got this information, and who else knows."

"Twelve years ago, you took me as your youngest wife," Iekanjika said in Shona. "All marriages are political alliances, but you've been kind to me, mentored me. One of the things you like about me is my affinity with the Shona language. You've asked me to help you practice your own, to rid you of your accent. You've told me that when I speak it, it reminds you of the last bits of the language you heard growing up." Iekanjika halted. "You have a favorite song from when you were a girl, *Dai ndiri shiri*."

Rudo grimaced. The pistol continued to tremble. If she fired now, she was as likely to blow off Iekanjika's shoulder as her head. Iekanjika didn't blame her; she barely believed what was going on herself.

"That's everyone's favorite," Rudo answered finally in Shona, and a note of doubt had entered her voice. Rudo's lips twisted as if fighting for the courage to say something to master the situation.

"Who's he?" she asked with a quick wave of the muzzle towards Belisarius.

"Someone with whom you enter into a business partnership in my time."

"You trust him?"

"No. He's too slippery."

"Funny that you'd take him into the past."

"Your choice, not mine," Iekanjika said flatly.

"Do you have a ma'am to finish that, corporal?"

Iekanjika stared at the young captain until Rudo's glare softened.

"I'm a full colonel in my time," Iekanjika said, "so I'm not sure how to address you. This isn't exactly in the manual."

Rudo regarded her uncertainly, before turning her gaze on the *Homo quantus*.

"What's your name, stranger?"

"Belisarius Arjona."

"Anglo-Spanish."

"Yes."

"So we at least make contact with the Banks in the future," Rudo said.

"You believe me?" Iekanjika said.

"Because of the name? Or the song?" Rudo said. "No, neither of those things."

"What tipped it?" Iekanjika asked.

"Your Shona. It's too good, better than the Shona of anyone in the Force, probably better than anyone in the whole Sub-Saharan Union. You sound like you've been speaking it for years. And your French is strangely accented, like you learned it as an afterthought."

"You didn't warn me to watch my French when you sent me back in time."

"That might have been on purpose," Rudo said.

The hackles rose on Iekanjika's neck as lines of logic, deception and causality fell into place. Lieutenant-General Rudo had omitted this detail on purpose.

"What happened to my marriage to Okonkwo and Zivai?" Rudo asked.

"You expect me to answer that?" Iekanjika said.

Rudo lowered her pistol and laid it carefully on the table, but still within easy reach. She exhaled noisily.

"So we figure out how to travel through time," Rudo said, "while I'm still alive."

Iekanjika kept her face studiously neutral. It would be too much to let the bitterness out, to tell young Rudo that there was no 'we' in this, that Arjona had stolen the time gates and he'd figured out how to use them, and that perhaps he and Mejía were the only people who ever could. Rudo frowned.

"You came *through* the time gates, didn't you?" she asked. "Did you just emerge onto the ice in the middle of our security perimeter, or have you been here since before we set it up?"

"An hour ago," Iekanjika said. "You kept some passwords and security channel frequencies all these years, no doubt for this reason. We used them to mask our arrival."

Rudo stared for a long time, considering perhaps how she would do such a thing, how this might or might not be a grandfather paradox.

"Why are you here? This is dangerous," Rudo asked finally in French.

Although neither of them enjoyed using the French of the hegemonic patron nation, its complex verb tenses and modes made speaking about time easier, in a way that, even forty years later, Shona had not matched.

This era was not just the military and scientific birth of the Sub-Saharan Union. The forty years in the wilderness had also midwived a linguistic renaissance and the Union's national creation story. That in Iekanjika's time Shona had not completed its growth any more than the Union had achieved its military independence meant only that the creation story had not yet run its course.

Iekanjika now straddled both beginning and middle. She couldn't escape the feeling that her mission here would decide whether the story became a true national myth told by her descendants or a cautionary tale told by others over Union corpses.

"We need core samples of the crustal ice," Iekanjika said, "going back as far as we can."

"Just like that?" Rudo said, her French sarcastic. *Juste de même?* "Carting tons of ice samples back through the security perimeter?"

Iekanjika wasn't used to a Rudo this... expressive. Anger flowed just beneath the surface of Captain Rudo's facade, over a palpable need to prove herself. But mixed into Rudo's manner was also a trembling confidence—uncertain and chrysalis-wet. This was dangerous, not just for the Union, but for Rudo. The Rudo of this era possessed a fragility Iekanjika hadn't known. This visit from her poised and commanding future wife could cement Rudo's confidence and faith in herself and the future, or weaken it.

No. Iekanjika knew Lieutenant-General Rudo. Whatever doubts she'd had about herself and her place in the world were long conquered and buried. Or were, until she'd had to tell Iekanjika her secret. Iekanjika leaned forward.

"Kudzanai," she said softly, "in the future you need this. I can't tell you why, but in the future, it could cement Union independence. We decided to gamble me on this. That's all I can tell you."

"Are you gambling him too?" Rudo asked. "What Anglo-Spanish Bank have we gotten into bed with?"

"Arjona is a scientific consultant, a kind of expert on wormholes."

Rudo's eyes bored into her. "He's more than that. What are you holding back?"

"Everything!" Iekanjika said, throwing her hands up in exasperation. "This is no controlled message being sent to the past, vetted by a dozen logicians! I'm trying not to burst causality with a misspoken word."

Rudo flinched from the outburst, and Iekanjika was ashamed.

This was her future wife's first impression of her and she was losing control of herself. The captain was quiet for a time, eyes on the scatter of data-pads.

"I can't get you to the core samples we've already taken," Rudo said. "They're with the research teams."

"Can we steal them?" Iekanjika said. "They're not a state secret under guard."

Rudo stared at her as if puzzling at a child. "How naive are you? How did you get picked as my wife?"

"I don't know anymore why you wanted me as a wife," Iekanjika said, frustration pulling the words out of her before she could stop them.

After a slow, awkward start to her career as an officer, Iekanjika had been promoted quickly to captain and then to major. Then had come the offer of a position on Rudo's staff and the baffling invitation to join the most powerful political marriage in the Expeditionary Force. She'd been a new major at the time, and there was no shortage of choice among the young colonels commanding warships who might have expected to be invited into Rudo's marriage. Iekanjika had been forced to interpret Rudo's marriage proposal as a sign of an excellence she didn't see in herself. Over the years, she proved to herself that she deserved what she'd been given, even if she didn't believe it.

But the last few days had undermined all the proving she'd done over the years, congealing new suspicions of why Rudo had taken her as a spouse. None of them knew what would really happen if they precipitated a time travel paradox. No one wanted to risk it. And now Iekanjika knew that from the time she was a captain, Rudo had carried memories of a young colonel visiting her in the past, telling her that she was to be one of her spouses. Regardless of Iekanjika's competence or other qualities, this information alone would force any careful commander to take Iekanjika as a wife, even if it created one of those odd bits of cyclic causality, where cause triggered effect and effect triggered cause.

As difficult as it might be for Captain Rudo to accept, the information about her future came from nowhere. And as painful as it might be for Iekanjika, her marriage and career similarly came from nowhere. Maybe Iekanjika was married to Rudo because she was married to Rudo. Maybe Iekanjika was a colonel in her present because she'd been a colonel in her past. Who she was, what she offered as a spouse or as an officer, might be irrelevant. Captain Rudo's caustic words breathed life into all those maybes.

"I'm trying to find a solution, Kudzanai," Iekanjika said with a touch of heat. "That's what colonels do."

Rudo's eyes narrowed at the rebuke.

"I don't know what things are like when you come from, colonel, but here," she said, tapping the table, "everything is secure. We arrested all the Political Commissars the Congregate assigned to the Force. We think we've caught all the sleeper agents the Congregate hid in our crews, but now political factions in the Fleet are positioning for control. Everyone is watching everyone else."

"I thought Takatafare had taken command of the Force after Nandoro died," Iekanjika said.

"She did, but many officers remain loyal to Brigadier Iekanjika. Takatafare doesn't know if she can trust them. You don't know all this?"

"I know dates. I know promotions and assignments, matters of record."

"Odd that my future self didn't give you a fuller briefing," Rudo said.

That stung. She'd been given maps, codes, layouts, schedules, personnel records and shift rotations. She and Lieutenant-General Rudo had been focusing on moving through the past without being noticed, as if making contact with young Rudo was all she needed to do. Why hadn't she gotten a better briefing? Knowledge of the past didn't create paradoxes. Did Lieutenant-General Rudo really not trust her?

"We need core samples," Iekanjika said. "What do you think we should do?"

Rudo examined her for a long time, as if trying to establish dominance. If Iekanjika had been facing Lieutenant-General Rudo with this tension, this might have been an uncomfortable few moments. But she found nothing intimidating in this captain promoted before her time, despite the shadow of the general who waited for the both of them. Rudo was unproven, to herself and to everyone else; a young officer, like Iekanjika, pulled into a political marriage early. Rudo looked away.

"This will take a lot of preparation," the captain said. "Days. Hopefully not weeks. Do either of you have identification or any place to stay or belong?"

"We came to you for that," Iekanjika said.

"Space on the surface is tight. A lot of crews have come down on different projects," Rudo said, "and I have no way to issue security IDs. That's done through Takatafare's MPs."

"That's where I think your future self can help," Iekanjika said. She slid a silicate data wafer across the table. "As an auditor, you had access to records of expired security codes. This wafer contains the codes for the main security network for this week. You kept them all these years."

Rudo's eyes widened slightly, but she didn't take the wafer.

"Breaking into a network is a capital offense," she said.

"I know."

"It's a good sting. You say the wafer contains the passcodes so when I try them, I'm detected, arrested and executed."

"No sting," Iekanjika said. "If some other faction wanted to remove you, couldn't they already have done that with your real name?"

"Let Iekanjika do it," Arjona said in perfectly-accented African French. "If it doesn't work, you arrest both of us and you become the hero who caught two spies trying to break into the network. If it does work, we get temporary identities attached to your unit."

Captain Rudo considered Arjona. "Cunning," she said.

"Is he right?" Iekanjika asked.

"If you are really from the future, and I give you identities for a few days, then that gives me two operatives I can use to solve a problem."

"What?" Iekanjika said.

"I'll give you the identities," Rudo said. "For twenty-four hours."

Arjona's suit crinkled as he stiffened.

"I'll give you another twenty-four hours when I hear that a particular man is dead."

"Are you insane?" Arjona said. "We have to avoid modifying the past at all costs. Any changes here could affect your future, not just ours."

"Do you know a Lieutenant Zesiro Nabwire in the future?" Rudo asked her.

The captain's hands had steadied. Her face showed a new sense of shaky determination.

"I guess not," Rudo said, looking then to Arjona. "I suppose he's not that important to history then, or that he really did die here, at your hand."

"You can't take that ris—" Arjona began.

"I'm not an assassin," Iekanjika said, cutting him off.

"You're a soldier, colonel," Rudo said. "We do our duty."

"This is an extrajudicial killing. If Nabwire deserves justice, give him to Command or MilSec."

"You know how intelligence and counter-intelligence work, don't you?" Rudo said. "The proof will be circumstantial, deniable enough to survive a court martial and do political damage to everyone."

"Hit him yourself," Iekanjika said.

Captain Rudo's expression wavered. Then she leaned forward.

"I have you for twenty-four hours. He'll be on the north comms trunk later today with his crew. Kill him and you get another twenty-four hours."

"Do you not realize how important it is to get those samples?" Iekanjika said, rising from her hard seat. "This is the Union's freedom."

"So is this," Rudo hissed, glaring up at Iekanjika. Steely resolve showed beneath Rudo's doubts. "Your mother, if that's true, is bed-ridden right now. It's been a bad pregnancy from the rumors I hear. She's gracefully accepted Takatafare's command of the Force, but her followers haven't. Nabwire is organizing false charges that will fall on people who, among others, happen to be my wife and my husband."

"Why aren't your wife and husband handling this?" Iekanjika said. "They're both senior to you. Prove that the charges are false."

"This isn't their forte. And it will take months to sort out the truth and clear ourselves. The charges are about trust. If Takatafare can't trust us, even for a while, the damage is done."

"There has to be another way," Iekanjika said.

"There isn't a more effective way," Rudo said, "and this is the way I'm telling you to do it."

Arjona put his hand on Iekanjika's shoulder.

"You aren't seriously considering this, are you?" he asked.

"Is my mother involved?" Iekanjika asked.

"Does it matter?" Rudo asked with an edge of contempt.

"Yes."

"For what it's worth," Rudo said, "I don't think so. But her followers aren't happy Takatafare got command of the Force."

"You're not an assassin, colonel," Arjona said.

"Do you see another way?" Iekanjika asked.

Arjona turned her to face him. He stared straight back at her.

"We do this our way," he said, "with our resources. We're not killers."

Iekanjika shook off his arm and faced Rudo.

"Twenty-four hours," Iekanjika said, "and Nabwire."

Rudo holstered her sidearm and moved to a shelf overflowing with old data-pads. She handed one to Iekanjika. Arjona turned his back on the both of them.

"Enter your code, colonel," Rudo said to her.

Iekanjika grabbed the pad. It was old, to her. She'd been tutored on some old holographic interface pads as a very young child, but even then, Force engineers had needed all obsolete equipment for parts or recycling, so very few old things survived the decades. She connected the pad to the main base network and logged in with an administrative passcode. She navigated to personnel systems, causing holographic orange authentication challenges to blink. The display greened when she entered the pass-code Lieutenant-General Rudo had given her.

"I really didn't believe it," Rudo said, her eyes wide.

Iekanjika turned the pad back to the captain.

"Get us a couple of serviceable identities," Iekanjika said tersely.

Rudo remained frozen, eyes on the data-pad. This break-in, more than anything else, seemed to have convinced her. She was in deep now, with no way out, whether she was facing time travelers or a sting. She sat, but didn't touch the pad.

Iekanjika sat and crossed her arms, matching Rudo's stare until the captain looked away. Little of the great military commander showed in the twenty-two year old, try as she might to see the substance beneath skin become unfamiliar in its smoothness. A fire smoldered beneath Rudo's doubts and secrets, but the burning faith with which she would carry the Expeditionary Force all the way through the Puppet Axis was absent. Iekanjika had come back in time, trusting that she'd be led by Rudo, and instead she got this. And Nabwire.

She ought to have prepared herself better. Lieutenant-General Rudo must have known that her past self was too fragile a fulcrum upon which to lay the hopes of their war effort. But what if the Lieutenant-General was less concerned with the war than avoiding paradoxes? The Rudo of the future knew she had to send Iekanjika back. It was possible that Rudo remembered Iekanjika failing and perhaps dying in the past and was just making sure that past observations were preserved. Maybe Iekanjika and Nabwire shared sacrificial roles.

She leaned forward, until Rudo met her eyes over the table.

"Kudzanai, get started before we get arrested for spending too much time in your office," she said finally. "Get us bunks and places to be. Then, start to get us the authorizations for surface work to get new samples."

Rudo inhaled deeply, and set to work. It took her ten minutes to create personnel files and the associated records for two enlisted crew—a corporal and a private, transferred to the surface base from the *Juba,* one of the cruisers on distant sentry duty. She got them bunks in Barracks D, which had no crew from the *Juba,* and assigned them to external labor duties with the auditing team. The familiar administrative work seemed to fortify the captain.

"Stay out of everyone's way," Rudo said, and handed

Iekanjika a data wafer. "Get out of the barracks during the day. I'll keep my eye on MilSec notices for Nabwire. When I see that, I'll extend your passes. It will take a couple of days for me to frame the right kind of audit to requisition the drilling equipment you'll need."

"What if we need to contact you?" Iekanjika said.

"Make sure you don't need to."

She heard something of her wife in Rudo's tone. Iekanjika picked up the two sidearms on the table and pushed one into Arjona's hand. A glance at Rudo didn't encourage her to make their goodbye elaborate, so she opened the door and shouldered past the con man. He followed in silence. At the airlock, they suited up. Only outside, twenty meters from the building did he speak by laser.

"We're not assassins!" he said.

She didn't disagree. But discussing it wouldn't make it easier. Ice fragments crunched under her boots.

"She has us over a barrel," Iekanjika said.

"Trick her!" Arjona said. "Make her think we did it. We've got the tech to pull that off."

Fury rose in her. She wanted to hit something. Or someone. She stopped.

"A con man," she said in disgust. "That's all you are! A small thieving man with small grasping goals. This is war. Not a swindle."

"This isn't war, colonel! Your Lieutenant-General sent us back to this and didn't tell us everything. She didn't forget the details! This has to be a test for you. Young Rudo can order all she wants, but we don't have to do any of it. You're older, more experienced. General Rudo isn't the same person we just saw in there. Maybe you've been sent to save her from herself."

Iekanjika grabbed the front of his suit.

"Get your head out of your ass, Arjona! We aren't betting over cards and interesting thought experiments. My people will die if I fail here. And unless you've forgotten, so will yours! This isn't the time for fancy; it's the time for expediency. The exchange of one man for two nations is a good trade."

"This isn't your call, colonel. We each get a vote here, including Saint Matthew."

"Your mad AI?"

"I'm not anyone's AI, and I'm no more mad than anyone else," Saint Matthew said.

"You have nothing to say on this, AI," Iekanjika said. "I read up on Saint Matthew when we first met. The Patron of banks. The turncoat tax collector. A man who collaborated with his conquerors. The Expeditionary Force shoots people like that."

Iekanjika released Arjona. She continued in the direction they'd been moving and he followed.

An uncomfortable silence fell.

"That isn't what your marriage is like, is it?" Arjona said.

They crunched another dozen steps. Her hatred of Arjona was becoming uncomfortably complex. He'd tricked the Puppets and gotten them across the Puppet Axis. And he'd stolen the most precious of their nation's treasures from them. But she'd seen the insides of the time gates now, the tremendously alien and terrifying space that the human mind could not comprehend, or even properly perceive. Arjona and Mejía could withstand and navigate that world outside of time. And, still shaken by her journey through that strange realm, she'd brought him home, so to speak, to the most intimate of conversations she might ever have. Her connection to Arjona didn't orbit about an axis; it precessed chaotically. And he was the only one here to help her in the past.

"I'm not married to that woman back there," she said slowly.

Saying it aloud crystallized a disappointment that had been silently uncertain in her. Family mattered. Rudo and Wakikonda were the only family she'd ever known. In normal families, pasts could be buried by consent. Staring too hard into the past did not build trust, and didn't feel exactly fair. Rudo hadn't asked for a woman to come from the future and judge her on standards she had no way of meeting for another thirty years. Captain Rudo was a product of her times, as was Lieutenant-General Rudo in the future.

"I'm close to the Lieutenant-General Rudo and our husband. Our marriage is a political one fenced by contracts and trust built over time. But none of that relationship infrastructure exists here. We'll be strangers for another twenty-five years."

"Is that why you didn't tell her about Saint Matthew?" Arjona asked.

Iekanjika stopped. Arjona peered at her, his expression revealing none of the cunning in his question.

"You know what he can do," Arjona said. "Saint Matthew could probably have gotten the mining equipment tonight."

The young brown dwarf glared a directionless orange glow onto the oily black surface around them.

"Theft of one kind or another is all the same to you, I'm sure," she said, "but one will draw attention to us, and one won't. You come from a clean world with rules. Theft and sneaking is a matter of technology to you. Here, in this period of the Expeditionary Force, eyes, snitches and informants are everywhere. I'm not equipped to navigate this world. Rudo is."

"What I saw in your fleet in the future is what you call trust?" he asked incredulously.

"In the future, we don't trust outsiders," she said. "Here we don't trust each other."

CHAPTER TWENTY-SIX

BELISARIUS DIDN'T LIKE Barracks D. The air was below freezing, colder than the Puppet Free City. He felt like he would never be warm again. Yet despite this, the barracks stank of sweat, fear, resignation, and the simple will to endure. He knew a lot about fear and desperation. They were strings he'd plucked to fleece marks. So he understood what he was seeing in Iekanjika. She didn't see another way out. Wasn't even looking for another way. Simple fear was driving her to murder.

He saw the same thing in Rudo too—a sense of being in over her head—but she and Iekanjika weren't the same. The wave of pressure on the colonel broke against an unwavering sense of mission, and a loyalty to her superiors that had never been divided. Rudo had none of that. She was a captain, trying to play at a table where she didn't understand the stakes. Rudo might break.

And could he handle it? When would he break?

He might freeze first.

The Union crews had built not only the commissary out of ice, but also the tables and benches. Pots of soup, mushy stews and bioreactor paste steamed flavorlessly over electric stoves along one wall. Iekanjika slopped generous helpings into a bowl she scraped clean with a half-frozen piece of flat bread.

Belisarius disconsolately spooned a single portion of rubbery stew into the bowl he'd surreptitiously wiped with his sleeve. Even though the stew smelled faintly of bleach, his brain unhelpfully calculated bacterial growth curves, microbial adaptation to non-neutral pH, the potential selection coefficients for psychrophilic characteristics. That didn't take more than a few seconds and then he couldn't get the likely bacterial count out of his head.

Iekanjika wolfed down the contents of her bowl before she'd finished walking out of the serving area, dropping her bowl and spoon back into scummy disinfectant. Belisarius forced himself to chew the squishy chunks while standing, and to swallow a few yeasty mouthfuls. The flat bread was hard, tasting of cardboard and chlorine.

He followed Iekanjika to the dispensary for sheets, and then to the two bunks they'd been assigned. The sleepers in the last shift were just getting up and leaving with their sheets. Belisarius laid out his sheets and resisted the urge to sniff suspiciously at the cooling blankets.

Belisarius lay straight and stiff and cold, acutely aware of Iekanjika, looking for some cue on how to handle this. But it was like she didn't notice so many sleeping, shifting, smelling bodies around them.

He couldn't stop being aware of them all. He couldn't sleep like this. But this was how his people were sleeping, thirty-nine years from now and about five hundred light-years away, in cramped freighters that weren't meant to house people. His stomach tightened.

He backed away from that feeling by imagining the kind of block-time geometry of space that could hold all the time and space that separated him from his people. Although he was *Homo quantus,* his head spun at the immensity of where and when he was. Nothing had prepared him for walking in the past, for traveling the wrong way through time. Iekanjika had to be feeling the same, but shortly after suffering an arguably life-changing experience, she put her head on her rolled towel and snored softly.

How could she do that?

"Saint Matthew," he sub-vocalized.

"Are you alright, Mister Arjona?" the AI answered in Belisarius' subdermal auditory implant.

"Maybe not," he said silently to the AI. "Murder shouldn't be a part of the price of saving the *Homo quantus*."

"You don't need to help her."

"The *Homo quantus* need a home. Can I go back and tell them I couldn't get them one because I stopped one stranger from killing another stranger?"

"No one is a stranger, Mister Arjona," Saint Matthew said. "That's why you're doing this for your people."

"I don't know that I could stop Iekanjika if I tried. And without her we can't get the samples."

Belisarius hid his face under the blanket that smelled of many other people. The geometry of space time was still in his mind's eye, and a much larger image—the hyperspace in the interior of the time gates—came to join it, although he couldn't picture its entirety.

Moral problems. Logical problems. Geometric problems.

"I can't put anything in perspective," Belisarius said. "We're talking murder versus extinction, but we're in the past where the murder already happened. We've left everything we were evolved for, or even designed for. We traveled through naked hyperspace. Things don't fit, yet there's so much awe too. How do you fit it all in your mind?"

"I don't," Saint Matthew said.

"I feel like I'm holding onto reason by fingertips. I feel I might fall."

"I did."

"Said the AI who believes that he's the reincarnation of an Apostle."

"Irrationality is a state of mind."

"Nonsense."

"Mister Arjona, at some point you'll make observations that not only can't be incorporated into any theory, but that contradict proven facts. That's not irrationality. That's a consequence of the way we're built. That's the way awe enters our lives."

"You embraced an irrational religion."

"I embraced the things I could prove and explain, as well as the things I could not."

"You can't do that!"

"The world has different ways of showing itself."

Belisarius took a deep breath, chilling his lungs.

"Are you suggesting I accept irrationality and rationality?"

"Those labels aren't helpful where we are now, *when* we are now."

"I can't live like that," Belisarius said.

"We live with lots of things we can't live with."

BELISARIUS SAT UP an hour before he had to get out of the bunk. By then, many men and women moved into cold, short showers that Belisarius didn't want to touch. He followed them uncertainly, trying not to think about all the bacteria and viruses he might exposing his feet to. Shivering people stood near the walls, frothing themselves with harsh ammoniac soap under limp drizzles of cold water; so finally he did too. The low fever he'd borne for weeks made the icy air and water that much more painful. He shivered back to his bunk, dressed and got back under the covers, trying to warm up.

Iekanjika rolled straight out of sleep, apparently fully rested. She stripped down unhesitatingly in the chill air, walked to the showers and washed quickly with the rest of the bathers. She toweled off and hung sheet and towel on the end of the bunk. She didn't shiver as she dressed.

They didn't speak through breakfast or wait around in the barracks; the next shift of sleepers was already shuffling in, grabbing food and beds. In vacuum suits, Belisarius and Iekanjika cycled out of one of the big airlocks with twenty other crew who dispersed to their duties on the surface. He and Iekanjika walked out onto the ice. The dim, spongy light of the brown dwarf hadn't changed. Nyanga was tidally locked, so the failed star would never move, like time stood still here. It gave a soothing, dreamy feel to Nyanga.

After two hundred and sixty-six steps, Belisarius stopped and poked at the oily black ground. The flat patches reflected like oil, as hard as frozen taffy. Stems festooned other areas where no one had walked. The darkness cloaked them here; the spotlights focused at the perimeter, or at the time gates.

"Have you thought of what we talked about?" he asked her.

"My mind is clear."

"You're going to kill him."

"Sometimes to win a battle, a commander sacrifices individual units," she said.

"Saint Mathew can get us the supplies to do the drilling."

"Will he also orally brief the watch officers?" she demanded. "Will he write it in pencil on today's authorized work details? Will our drilling, our very obvious and very loud drilling, mysteriously pass the morning order verifications, when the section heads are asked to verify the orders they gave? Rudo wasn't lying. Everyone watches everyone else out here. You're too dependent on computer tricks."

"So this poor lieutenant dies."

"I've never heard of him, so he obviously didn't survive to my time," Iekanjika said. "It might be that I really did kill him in my history, and I'm only finding out about my role in it now."

"That's a lot to take on faith in a captain you don't know."

"Faith is for you and your AI."

"I hope you're not expecting me to help you."

"Your lack of military training makes you a danger to a real op, Arjona. You need to stay out of the way. I have sixteen hours to save your people and mine."

"You can choose not to do it and let Rudo figure out if she still wants to deal with this lieutenant," he said, a little nervously. "You don't have to make it easy for her. And if you still want to help her... I'll stop you."

Iekanjika laughed so loudly that he had to dial down the volume in his earpieces. But he stood his ground. He had his sidearm and his electroplaques. She had decades of training. He had intellect. She adjusted her stance, still grinning in her helmet. One of her hands neared her pistol grip. The other arm hung loose, and no doubt the real, deadly threat.

"You're going to get hurt, Arjona."

"Mister Arjona," Saint Matthew said in his ear implant, "this isn't the best way to reach her."

"Are you going to do something, Arjona?" Iekanjika asked.

He darted in, reaching to touch her hand. Instead of avoiding him, her hand snaked out, cobra-fast, grabbing his. He released a ninety milliamp current, enough to knock out even an augmented human. The current sizzled through the fingers of his vacuum suit, crisping it and burning his fingertips.

Arcs of electricity shone briefly on fine wires leading down her suit.

Her suit was grounded.

And he was burning. He wanted to shake the heat away, but she held his hand tightly. Then she punched him in the stomach and he doubled over, emptied of air. He saw spots for long seconds as panic set in, before he was finally able to take a breath.

"Get yourself a new glove before your air leaks out and you do yourself a serious injury," she said, letting him collapse onto the ice. "Then stay outside, out of everyone's way. Go look at the flowers or something. I'll come back for you later."

Iekanjika stalked off silently across the ice. Belisarius tucked his now cold hands under his armpits. Air hissed from the burnt tips of his gloves.

CHAPTER TWENTY-SEVEN

IEKANJIKA TREMBLED AFTER leaving Arjona on the ice. She'd hurt him. She'd wanted to hurt him for some time; to take him down a peg, to make him pay for what he'd stolen. But beating him had been effortless. She didn't feel like he'd gotten what was coming to him.

She'd been a bully, letting a fight happen with someone who could never win. She'd been measured and fair her whole life, with all her subordinates. And now she'd pushed a contemplative into a corner until he hurt himself. The fault wasn't his. In all that mattered, he was an idiot, and she was commanding this mission. He was her responsibility.

But that wasn't the worst of it. What stung was that she wasn't in even the right. Soldiers killed. Soldiers followed orders from duly commissioned officers, who themselves derived their authority from the government. The Sixth Expeditionary Force had gone rogue for forty years, with no oversight, but never with self-interest in its heart. Each commanding officer, from Nandoro to Takatafare to Rudo, had been working for the Union, and behaved as if they could be called to account at any time.

Captain Rudo ordering an extra-judicial execution was alien

to her. Iekanjika didn't know Lieutenant Nabwire or what he'd done to cross Rudo or her allies. And unlike a soldier on the ground or crew on a ship, she had no license to just follow orders on faith in her superiors. She had a professional duty as an officer to understand her orders, or trust that her commander did. She had no commander and she'd agreed to assassinate a man.

The Sub-Saharan Union was poor, and its navy moreso. The Sixth Expeditionary Force had learned to eat of duty and drink of honor. They had nothing else with which to face the very real possibility of total destruction in the coming months. The officers and crew of the Sixth Expeditionary Force did their duty in the future, with honor.

And she was here. It had been easy for her to quantify this and throw it in Arjona's face. One man. One man didn't outweigh the lives and freedoms of two nations. She'd sent people to their deaths on purpose for tactical gain. This was the same—trading death for strategic gain. But that comfort was hollow.

Lieutenant Nabwire was Rudo's price, not the price of the advantage itself. And the cost in quantity was not the whole cost. Committing a murder would make Iekanjika a criminal. An extra-judicial killing was a dishonor that could be neither erased nor redeemed. And more deeply, to know that Captain Rudo's ordering of the killing was the suitable response for this time, that this was the way things were done at the birth of Union nationhood, only further tilted the ground beneath her feet. What did she stand on when her new nation was born of this swamp, bereft of honor and duty?

Victory? Freedom? For whom? For the politicians posturing on Bachwezi? Or for the people positioning here for control of the Expeditionary Force? Did they deserve the victory Iekanjika might deliver if she could not stand on honor or duty?

But maybe she held her honor too highly. She could sacrifice herself for her people, so why price her honor above that?

Iekanjika came to the air-fill station beside the general HQ. MilSec secured many parts of the surface base, but the air-fill station wasn't one of them. A simple key-card swipe and tanks could be refilled without going inside. The system cross-referenced to the supply system and the personnel system, so air use could be accounted for and audited. They'd set it up this way in the hopes that accounting would net them a few unwary Congregate sleeper agents. She connected a hose to one of her tanks, pulled out a pad and began reading the files behind the refill accounting system.

Lieutenant-General Rudo had given her many small passwords and administrator codes in addition to the big one she'd used yesterday. She logged onto the system with a low-level auditor code, crossed virtually to the personnel system, and queried for Lieutenant Nabwire.

Information appeared. Lieutenant Zesiro Nabwire. Male. Aged 26 years. Engineering specialist. Posted to the *Ngundeng* at the launch of the Sixth Expeditionary Force as a junior security officer. Attached to MilSec on Nyanga.

None of the unimportant information was there. The record didn't list his favorite color or why he'd joined the navy, or whether a spouse and children waited for him. He wasn't a person, and she didn't need him to be to kill him. If he had a family, they would wait in vain, like all the families of the Sixth Expeditionary Force, until, in about fifteen years, the loss of the Force was declassified and a mass *in absentia* funeral was held. On behalf of the Sixth Expeditionary Force, she'd visited the graveyard on Bachwezi. It had been an eerie, hollow experience, being fêted like a returning hero in a place she'd never been, near the empty grave of her mother. The Lieutenant Nabwire living now certainly had an empty grave there too.

And the Nabwire living now had an unsurprising schedule. A lot of power, comms and network systems had to run along the ice from building to building and to the transmitters and antennae. He lead a crew to maintain the hardware and inspect it for security breaches.

He and a team of MilSec technicians were due outside this evening. It didn't say what they'd be doing, but parts of their work schedule lay outside camera range. She studied the map of the terrain. Tactical possibilities bloomed in her thoughts. Angles of fire and vision, separation of lights and people. She could make this work.

CHAPTER TWENTY-EIGHT

BELISARIUS TRUDGED BACK to Barracks D. His fingers hurt, but the pain wasn't overwhelming. He could route sensation to different parts of his brain and create filters, as much as he could in the interior of the time gates. He'd failed to save a man's life. It wasn't about that man though. He'd seen humans and Puppets die before. He was perhaps a terrible person because death hadn't mattered so much to him then. Now it did because it was chasing down his own people, like a lion stalking a herd of gazelle. Every death seemed enormous.

"That didn't go well," Saint Matthew said.

"No."

"I'm sorry, Mister Arjona."

He cycled through the airlock into the kit area. Some air had escaped his suit, but he'd cranked his tank feed up to maintain internal pressure. He cracked the seal on his neck and took off his helmet.

Beyond the kit area, quiet snores and slow breathing filled the barracks. Among the hanging vacuum suits and tools and small equipment, a few insomniacs huddled around a card game played on an ice block. One of them, a private, saw Belisarius' fingers sheltered under his arm and turned suspiciously. They might think he had a weapon. Belisarius exposed his glove with the blackened fingertips and the man put down his cards.

"Whoa, you need help?" the private said in accented Shona.

"Looks worse than it is," Belisarius answered in similarly halting Shona. Finding the right level of linguistic inexpertise was more challenging than just learning a language properly, but he'd built an algorithm to introduce common mistakes and mispronunciations, and that helped. "The electrical cable shouldn't have been live."

Indignation flared across the private's face. "You want to report this?" he said, switching to French in his anger. "Whoever cocked this up should be pulling some serious shit jobs."

Belisarius shook his head, following the private into the African-accented French of four decades past. "It was my mistake."

Belisarius snapped open the seals on the glove and took it off. Angry red blisters covered his fingertips.

"Doesn't look too bad," Belisarius ventured in French.

"Hmm," the private said. "No need for your sergeant to hear about this, I guess?"

"I learned my lesson."

"I think Jumisse keeps a box of mismatched suit parts. Hey, Jumisse!" the private hissed at the players.

In short order, they brought him to the first aid station and found him a second glove for his vacuum suit. While he bandaged his fingers, his brain analyzed their card game. He didn't recognize it, but Jumisse was deftly bottom-dealing and a woman called Pojok was trying to count the cards. The others weren't bad. He very quickly inferred the rules with ninety-five percent confidence. He could have easily won. He longed to sink himself into probability and statistics for a time. But that wasn't why he was here, and it would also have blown his flimsy cover.

He resealed his suit, thanked the private and was soon resolutely out on the ice.

The *Homo quantus* as a species suffered from intellectual impatience, but Will Gander had taught him to fight it. Confidence schemes demanded patience. The mark had to come to think the con was their idea. Greed had to simmer before boiling. And while the marks simmered, the con man had to feign indifference. Belisarius wasn't conning anyone right now, but he knew he had to be patient.

Luckily, an alien garden blossomed all around him in the weird, faint magnetic interference from the time gates. The only sensing device in civilization with the resolution to feel the interference waves was the set of billions of magnetosomes in the billions of *Homo quantus* muscle cells. The tactile press hinted at a world built of the things humanity couldn't see.

Belisarius stopped about three hundred meters from the time gates, at the limit of most cameras and sensors. The faint light from the brown dwarf offered little illumination, especially with the surface covered with dark plants. He knelt. Thin, fragile stems and tiny fanning canopies of pitch-colored leaves covered the ground. Boots had recently crushed nearby plants and torn the surface film, revealing a mix of crushed ice and oily black tar. The geometries of the image fascinated his eye. His brain rotated and flipped the images a dozen different ways as if trying to see how the puzzle fit together. But this became too limiting and his brain represented the pieces as smaller shapes and ran arrayed linkage analyses.

Anatomical and biochemical hypotheses formed in his mind, that the oily black plastic was the plant itself. Like the vines, it had no structure capable of holding itself above the ground. It had to climb onto something to get to the weak dwarf light before competing plants did. The Nyanga version of weight-bearing plant stems were rods of branching water ice. The plants were hollow, living on the outside, but the ice structures themselves were not naturally occurring. They had plant shapes, a sign of convergent evolution. Any time iteration, selection and competition played with each other, certain branching shapes became predictable.

His brain ran a series of parallel models, weighing and discarding, mixing and matching possible growth algorithms and energy budgets until he found something that might explain the shapes of the ice. The black, tarry plants could absorb infrared from the brown dwarf, using the energy to melt minute quantities of water. In the moments before the water refroze, the plants moved the liquid upward, shaping the stem-like substrate upon which they could grow.

The possibility that the plants of Nyanga could use dwarf heat to sculpt the surface of their world was beautiful. They rode their own ice sculptures to compete for light. The idea was hopeful, haunting and quiet.

Farther from the well-trodden paths, the plants grew into larger bushes and even low, fragile trees. In the anemic gravity and the thin atmosphere, the trees and bushes needed only the finest of stems and branches to reach out to catch the red and infrared light of the brown dwarf. Belisarius walked between the taller plants. He tried not to touch them, but in places they were so closely-spaced that the breaking branches sounded faint and blurry on an atmosphere too thin to carry the sharp snapping of ice.

He neared the spotlighted security perimeter around the time gates and stopped. Any closer and he would trigger alarms, but he was still close enough to see the high-standing fronds of hundreds and hundreds of vegetable intelligences. After a few moments, their glacial movements became apparent.

On the nearest, a stumpy leg swung forward in achingly slow motion, the whole body leaning. After thirty-eight seconds, the foot touched the ground, slowly rocked the body, lifting the trailing foot. The joint of that trailing leg took another five hundred and twelve seconds to melt enough so that gravity could help lower the foot.

Those that moved lumbered around the time gates, fanning large fronds above themselves. Belisarius zoomed in with his ocular implants, stepping up the gain in the infrared and ultraviolet. The gasping wind moving towards the time gates pulled light pollen from the fronds, carrying it into the past. Nyanga's faint atmosphere was denser in the future, which drove a slow wind backwards across time.

On minimum energy paths through the interior of the time gates, the pollen would emerge eleven years in the past, about a decade before the Sixth Expeditionary Force would discover Nyanga. Yet no pollen emerged on the wind arriving from eleven years in the future anymore. The Union would shortly steal the time gates and would hold them for thirty-nine years. Eleven years in the future, there were no vegetable intelligences to send their pollen back. And in about twelve years, the scientists of the Expeditionary Force would begin sending scientific results into the past, encoded in synthetic pollen. Belisarius was a participant in all this, because in thirty-nine years, he would acquire the time gates in another act of theft.

Something tickled at the back of his thoughts, something that didn't add up. His brain was running other calculations, modelling ecological energy budgets. The plant life received so many watts per hour of insolation from the brown dwarf, but they needed more calories than that to melt and shape minute quantities of ice for the movement he was seeing, to say nothing of running intelligence. He had no precise figures for the energy budgets, because he didn't know what chemical systems they were using, but they would have to be remarkably efficient to do all those things under a brown dwarf.

The cosmos was a great heat engine, distributing and mixing energy. Life eddied in those flows, briefly diverting energy for their own purposes. Most of the time they did this remarkably inefficiently. Any signs of highly efficient energy use hinted at the involvement of the quantum world. Photosynthesis in Earth plants was far more efficient than it ought to have been; its electron transfer processes incorporated the equivalent of quantum tunneling. Nyanga's anemic ecosystem probably couldn't power movement and intelligence without the involvement of quantum processes. And the nature of the intelligence here would affect his estimates.

He strengthened the microcurrent from his electroplaques to the millions of magnetosomes in his body, increasing his sensitivity to the ambient magnetic field. The brown dwarf's tense field lines were stable and distant, but the textured magnetic field of the time gates pressed at him slightly differently than he'd felt around the time gates in the future. The field was more richly timbred, but so subtle that he hadn't noticed until now.

Was the nature of the quantum interference around the time gates different in the past?

The thought teased. He watched the field of vegetable intelligences, wondering how their quantum processes might work. Their glacial movements hinted at some other time scale they might inhabit, like slow-growing trees and still lichens. All the human bustle around them might be flashes of quick light, and the coming flare that would melt this face of the planet in months might feel like tomorrow to them.

If he'd had better access to the quantum fugue and all of its parallel processing power and sensory insight, he might have been able to puzzle it out, but he wasn't even sure how to interact with those senses anymore. The Union records he'd broken into on the *Mutapa* had mentioned that the Union had found a mechanical way to speak to them, but at the time, he hadn't followed that thread.

He wanted to speak to the vegetable intelligences.

"Mister Arjona," Saint Matthew said, "someone is approaching. It's not Colonel Iekanjika."

Belisarius' brain clung to the strange interference patterns, using up most of his processing power, but he looked back in irritation. A private strode through the low thicket of bushes, stomping straight over them, shattering everything in his path under thick soles. The man was thickly built and stood at almost a hundred and ninety centimeters. He stopped in front of Belisarius and pointed a sidearm at him.

Belisarius had no cover story. He'd been trusting Iekanjika for that. Rudo had told them to stay outside and be inconspicuous. The only work he had to look inconspicuous with was trying to come up with a cover story.

"Stay on a low local channel," the man said in choppy Shona. "Someone wants to talk to you, but if you make any fuss, I can blow a hole in your chest."

Belisarius lifted his hands warily. The big man took his sidearm and discreetly led him across the ice. The private kept his sidearm holstered, but his hand stayed close to it. They crunched along the plain, along a track of broken frozen bushes and plant tar that had been trampled by countless sets of boots. The other surface workers and security cameras in the distance wouldn't notice anything wrong. Belisarius could try to shock the man with his unburnt fingers, but the private was just a symptom. Who wanted to see him?

"Got any ideas?" Belisarius subvocalized to Saint Matthew.

"I can only think that if you hadn't taken the original job," Saint Matthew said, "we wouldn't be in this mess."

"You'd be sitting in an empty chapel in *Saguenay Station*, and I'd be sitting by myself in the Puppet Free City."

"This is better? I haven't spread the faith to a single person. The *Homo quantus* are homeless. And this goon is bringing you to a shallow grave!"

"They can't kill us."

"Sure they can!"

"Yes, they can," Belisarius admitted.

They neared a small hut in the dark. It was only a few meters on each side. He made out an airlock in grainy low-light magnification.

"Cycle it, soldier," the private said in his helmet.

Belisarius opened the outer airlock door and they squeezed in together. The man had his sidearm out again, and Belisarius could feel steely muscles pressing the muzzle against him, a lot more muscles than was needed to keep the gun on him even if Belisarius struggled. An electrical discharge could probably take the man out, but the resulting seizure might also cause the trigger finger to convulse.

Belisarius spun the second door and stumbled into a small lit space. The private followed him and shut the airlock behind them. Then he holstered his sidearm. A short figure in a vacuum suit stood in the corner of the hut.

"Take off your helmet," Captain Rudo transmitted.

His suit measured point seven atmospheres of air at minus forty Celsius. That was probably the warmest the hut could do against the hundred below outside. Belisarius cracked his helmet seal, took it off. The icy air touched him. Rudo did the same. The brute beside him didn't.

"He won't hear us," Rudo said.

Of course. White noise was probably playing in the man's ear pieces.

Rudo gave a signal and a heavy fist rammed into Belisarius' side. Air whooshed out of him and he crumpled. He didn't drop far. The private held Belisarius up with one hand and drove his first into Belisarius' stomach, so hard that he would have vomited if he'd actually eaten anything.

"Mister Arjona!" Saint Matthew said in his ear. "Do something!"

The private looked back at Rudo, as if doubtful about whether he should go on. Belisarius had wilted. Rudo nodded and the private punched him so hard that he fell to his knees, clutching his stomach as he tried to breathe. Belisarius' helmet rolled on the icy floor. The man's boots stepped back two paces.

"You're no soldier," Captain Rudo said.

"I... get that a lot," Belisarius gasped.

"What kind of consultant are you? Who hired you?"

Belisarius rolled back to a sitting position, wincing. He leaned against the wall and groaned. He snapped the seals on his gloves, dropping them both onto the ice and probed at his ribs.

"Answer or he uses boots," Captain Rudo said.

"I'm a science consultant," he said slowly. "You don't want to know much else about the future, do you?"

"I want to know everything about the future."

"Are you some kind of idiot?"

He didn't see the signal, but the big man's boot, heavy and fast, hit him. Belisarius blocked with his arm. It numbed with pain. He didn't hear a snap, but that wasn't a convincing diagnosis.

"Talk fast," Rudo said.

"Mister Arjona!" Saint Matthew said. "Say something! Even if it's a lie. We can't kill her, but she can kill us all she wants without creating a grandfather paradox!"

"Whether I tell you lies or truth," Belisarius said, "it could change your future, and mine."

"You think I can't avoid a causal paradox?" Rudo demanded. "We found a fucking time machine! Every order, every op, every bit of research is scrutinized to make sure we don't mess up."

"I don't see a time ethics committee around here. Unless he's it," Belisarius said, gesturing to the private, "but he doesn't look that smart."

This time he saw the signal, but his numb arm couldn't do much. The private's boot snapped something. Belisarius vomited. It froze into a concrete-hard greenish pancake on the floor. Belisarius struggled to his feet, leaning against the wall.

He gave the private the finger.

"Mister Arjona!" Saint Matthew said in his ear.

The man's fist slammed into his cheek. His head rebounded from the wall. Pain exploded behind his eyes, amid a fireworks of false images that his brain graphed and subjected to regression analysis in the time it took to taste the blood in his mouth. The private smiled in his helmet, but this wasn't over.

Belisarius was *Homo quantus*. His brain had been engineered to run on multiple channels at once, any of which could be isolated at need. His mind was already split multiple ways, with a whole intellect running in one partition. He rerouted the pain signals to the objectivity running in his brain. The objectivity wasn't conscious. Belisarius' pain wasn't pain to the objectivity, just data, and uninteresting data at that, quickly erased.

"You don't even believe we're from the future, do you?" Belisarius said in perfect Shona, like he'd been speaking it all his life, a quality of Shona that wouldn't exist for another decade or more in the Sixth Expeditionary Force. "That's half of what this is about, isn't it?"

Rudo's assured expression wavered in the face of a foreigner speaking with perfect authenticity the old language the Expeditionary Force nursed in intensive care. She was surely aching to be sure about something and here he stood before her, an impossible data point.

She signaled the private again. The fist darted forward like a striking snake. Belisarius' brain had already calculated weight, acceleration, and corrected for the weak gravity. His own hand was in motion; to them, Belisarius' reflexes might look supernatural.

His fingertips described a trajectory arching under the man's arm, brushing gently as one hundred milliamps of current at three hundred volts burned from fingertip to suit. The ice under the man's feet was only weakly conductive, but the full current arced from him to the airlock. The private's momentum carried him, convulsing, past Belisarius and to the floor, hard enough to crack his faceplate. The back of his suit was scorched.

Rudo stared wide-eyed at Belisarius for a split second before acting. He'd been counting on more than a split-second, but her physical and psychological reflexes were fast. And he was slower than he wanted. He'd probably broken a rib. His organs throbbed. He watched her draw her pistol. The muzzle cleared the holster as he touched the metal seal between her sleeve and glove.

She'd been stepping back, right against the wall. The current shot up her arm, cooking through the internal wiring used to heat the suit, and then into the grounded metal frame of the hut. She cried out and fell, holding her arm. Belisarius stepped on her pistol.

He took the charred and flaming bandages off his fingers with the slightly burnt fingertips of his other hand. Surging current through his fingertips usually just made shallow burns, but anytime they were covered, the current charred the material, which did far more harm.

"I thought you cared about the Expeditionary Force," he said to her in perfect Shona.

"I do," she said, body still trembling, though her voice remained stridently forceful.

"Could have fooled me," he said. "Somebody smarter than you came from the future with a mission that will make or break everything, and you're messing it up instead of helping."

"If you're from the future, you could be on my side or you could be an enemy faction."

"There are no factions in the future."

Belisarius kicked her sidearm away and then started slipping his gloves on gingerly.

"Are you getting us the equipment and permits, or are you just using Iekanjika to settle some scores here?" he asked.

"I want information."

"You either believe us or you don't. If you do, you're helping yourself in the future."

"And consultants too?"

He winced, snapping one wrist seal tight.

"My interests are broadly aligned with yours," he said. "It's not a perfect fit. Iekanjika would admit that. But for now, we live or die together."

"You sound like an enemy."

He snapped the second wrist seal tight.

"Why are you here?" she demanded. "Who brought you?"

He maneuvered the helmet over his head and sealed the neck.

"Who brought you?" she said.

"You did."

She rose shakily.

"I did? I hired you? I sent you both back? Who am I in the future?"

"You're more of a team player, that's for sure," he said, picking up his own pistol and sliding it into his holster. He spun the airlock handle. "A lot of lives are riding on how fast you become that person. Hurry up."

He cycled out into the dark. By partitioning some of the pain, he could limp away from the hut well enough. He couldn't go back to his bunk for another couple of hours. He needed to find something to do to look inconspicuous, somewhere he could lay low.

He hobbled to a tool shed four hundred meters away. No one was in it. Among many other things, he found metal detectors, seismic sensing equipment, and heavy picks for breaking ice possessing the hardness of concrete. He took the lightest metal detector, strapped it on, and wandered along the edges of the higher plant growth, slowly swinging the detector back and forth without even turning it on. Instead, he studied the magnetic interference patterns in the faint field from the time gates and kept the pain routed to the intellect that couldn't feel pain.

CHAPTER TWENTY-NINE

(Translated from *français* 7.1)

To: Chairman
          Congregate Presidium
          Security Committee
          Venus

10 May, 2499

Subject: Recruitment Report R312HBR21

1.   Pursuant to article 106, clauses (a) and (d) of the Official Secrets Act, the Ministry of Intelligence reports on the recruitment of the thirty-first Scarecrow. Petrification subject is intelligence operative 1D446 (personnel files, medical and psychological tests, and field assessments annexed).

2.   1D446 has led an exemplary career as an operative, and was instrumental in operations O417TCH34 and O414TCL98. His loyalty was tested using standard (see psychological reports R616BGV13

and R616BGV66) and uncommon (see psychological report R616BGV79) methods, yielding the combination of results considered highly attractive for potential recruitment to the Scarecrow corps.

3. 1D446 was gravely injured in an operation (eyes-only classified in report R419JJY01), which even with prosthetics, would render him unserviceable for any other intelligence service objectives.

4. Exercising authority under clause 106, C-I Ops Commanding Officer initiated the petrification and vitrification procedures to begin the Scarecrow process. The process is expected to take 10 months. 1D446 will be kept under sedation for the entirety of the process, and then woken to see if consciousness has survived and is suitable for arming and training.

5. 1D446's new status will trigger an upgrade in reporting procedures and oversight by this office to the Security Committee and ought to be added as a standing agenda item to briefings and testimony by the Commanding Officer and senior C-I staff to fulfill the requirements of article 106.

General Pierre Audet
Commanding Officer
Counter-Insurgency Operations, 1st Division
Ministry of Intelligence
Venus

CHAPTER THIRTY

IEKANJIKA LAY ON the ice on the north arc of the surface base. A major trunk of comms wiring ran to a series of communication dishes. The radio and microwaves could be intense, so a full two kilometers separated them from the base. The cabling laying on the ice at a hundred below zero superconducted without any special effort on their part, other than keeping it buried.

Even at that, the tiny heat it gave off mimicked what the local plants could absorb from the brown dwarf. Plants constantly tried to grow over the cable. Normal maintenance procedures included clearing the icy growths. Normal maintenance did not include whatever devices Nabwire and one of his techs were clipping to the trunk.

Iekanjika had covered herself in old plant fragments in a shadowed area between lights to mask her temperature. The distance was at the effective range of her pistol, and she had no worries of missing; she was a good shot.

She recognized the unauthorized devices they were installing. Nabwire and one of his crew were bugging the comms trunk. Whatever Captain Rudo had thought Nabwire was up to, he'd started. That didn't make her feel better. Whatever he was doing offended her as a colonel. She was required and empowered as an officer to arrest anyone involved in a crime. She'd been trained for it. She'd done it.

But she wasn't empowered here in the past.

She had only her ethics and honor.

And a pistol.

It would be simple. One shot. The rest of Nabwire's crew would scatter, and in the confusion she would make her way back through a series of sensor blind spots Lieutenant-General Rudo had given her. Nabwire would be at extreme range for another thirty or forty seconds.

Simple, but not right.

But did right have a place in these stakes? Or was it all just mechanical? However uncomfortable she might be playing a part in that mechanical process, she had no real choice. Lieutenant Nabwire, whoever he was, whatever his loyalties, was dead in her time. She'd never met him, never heard of him. All the struggles of whether he would live or die had ended long ago.

In the past she was now inhabiting.

Lieutenant-General Rudo never would have ordered her to kill another officer. The Expeditionary Force had lived under the rule of law for as long as Iekanjika could remember. And yet the Lieutenant-General knew the past, knew that Captain Rudo would give this order to her, make the murder of Lieutenant Nabwire a condition of help. And the Lieutenant-General had said nothing about it. Why?

Was the lieutenant-general proud of the captain she'd been?

Maybe Rudo had been preparing Iekanjika for this mission all her life, not going into the past to recover a core sample, but to save Rudo from herself. Iekanjika had been considering Captain Rudo's reactions to a visitor from the future in terms of the overwhelming intellectual blow of the travel itself, not as a moral shock.

Iekanjika had trouble sometimes thinking about herself in terms of being important to Lieutenant-General Rudo, of trying to put her staff officer position and political marriage into context. Iekanjika never considered herself worthy of those things. And the knowledge that Captain Rudo had known her in the past had deepened her doubts. But what if she was more important to Lieutenant-General Rudo than she let herself believe? What if meeting Colonel Iekanjika had changed not just events, but Captain Rudo the person? It was hard to swallow, and perhaps wishful thinking. Wishful thinking was dangerous to any op.

But if Rudo the person had changed, was it a vision or faith in the future, or was it just foreknowledge? Iekanjika had always tried to emulate Rudo's unflinching resolve, the commander's conviction that they would get home. Rudo's faith had given Iekanjika faith, had given unbreakable faith to the entire Sixth Expeditionary Force: faith they'd needed four hundred light years from home. But maybe Rudo had no faith. Rudo had met the people from the future, had known that she had a hand in the Expeditionary Force's success.

Lieutenant Nabwire rose, having finished whatever illicit things he'd been doing to the comms trunk. His heart beat in the sights of a single trigger finger. He was leaving. Now was the time to clear up this one problem of the past. This was Iekanjika's own proof of faith. Nabwire stood there for a few seconds, talking to the crewman.

Iekanjika laid her pistol back onto the ice.

Nabwire would pay for his crimes through a court martial convened under the authority of the Code of Service Discipline, not through the skill of an assassin. She waited until Nabwire and the crewman had moved far enough out of sight and then rose from the tinkling pile of fine ice fragments.

Her feet dragged her towards ground HQ. It didn't feel like history anymore. The awe of walking at the true birth of the Sub-Saharan Union, what they sometimes called the seed born in the garden, was gone. Nyanga was no garden. It was just dark and cold and mean.

At ground HQ, she presented her service band at the airlock and cycled in. She hung up her helmet in the cold air, but didn't take off her suit. She wouldn't be here long. She retraced her steps deeper into the icy warren of offices and work spaces. She had to knock twice before the door opened. Captain Rudo looked around Iekanjika into the hallway and then ushered her in with a jerk of her head.

"What are you doing here?" Captain Rudo demanded after she'd locked the door. "People will see you! There's no reason your cover identity would see or know me!"

"I need to talk to you," Iekanjika said.

Iekanjika's voice was level. She needed to accept that she was older and more experienced. She was talking to a captain, not a general.

"You don't talk to me!" Rudo said, leveling a finger at her. "Meetings create questions."

"As many as having a man killed?"

Rudo's eyes narrowed. "Are you blackmailing me?"

"I didn't kill him."

"Then why are you here?"

"I'm not an assassin, and you shouldn't be either. This is no example you're setting. There's no honor in any of this, nothing that will make people follow you."

"I don't need people to follow me," Rudo said.

"The Rudo I know wouldn't dishonor herself like that."

Rudo looked honestly baffled, like she couldn't grasp the argument Iekanjika was trying to make.

"And what are you?" Rudo said. "And that Arjona? I've never seen augments like that before."

"What augments?"

"The hand-mounted shockers. Whatever you're carrying."

"What did Arjona do?"

"Get out!" Rudo said. "I never want to see you again! I think they're monitoring my channels now."

"Get us the equipment and the permits, or I'll be in here a whole lot. Everything you want in life is waiting for you in the future," Iekanjika said, "except one missing piece. I can't get it without your help. If you're going to shoot yourself in the foot, do me a favor and do it now. Maybe the timeline will rewrite itself with someone else stepping up to do their job."

CHAPTER THIRTY-ONE

BELISARIUS FORCED DOWN the bland food and collapsed on his recently-liberated bunk in Barracks D. He didn't wash and instead lay shivering under his covers. A few minutes before the lights were to go out for his sleep shift, Iekanjika appeared and knelt beside him.

"Oh, hi," he said in a low, conversational voice. "Did you finish your chore?"

"What did you do?" she asked in a light tone, keeping her eyes on the other bunks.

Belisarius shifted and winced. "Before or after her goon jumped me?"

Her face was impassive, but Belisarius had mixed the art of the confidence scheme with *Homo quantus* observational powers. The degree of tension in the forty-three facial muscles and some of the larger neck muscles revealed the simmering frustration beneath the surface, even though her body language didn't shift.

"I didn't do it," she said.

A wave of relief washed through him, out of proportion to how little they trusted one another. He could overlook his differences with a soldier, but he really hadn't wanted Iekanjika to be a murderer. In hushed tones, he told Iekanjika everything that had happened, and after a pause, she told him of her weird meeting with Captain Rudo. They both quieted, digesting. Unlike the colonel, Belisarius could think many thoughts at once, but it didn't help him. His brain could see no pattern in any of this.

"Is she authorizing the work?" he asked.

"I don't know."

The lights went out. Quiet conversations around them faltered.

Belisarius held his breath.

"Do you have a Plan B?" he asked.

"I have several, but there are reasons they aren't Plan A."

"She's not the same person," he said.

"No."

Belisarius would have liked to have comforted her, and by extension himself. He would have liked to have said that some of this had to work itself out, that the future waited for them, but that reasoning didn't hold. Lieutenant-General Rudo remembered meeting Iekanjika and him in the past. If they hadn't come back in time, they would have triggered a grandfather paradox. But that was the only causally necessary part of all these events. Iekanjika and Belisarius could both die or fail in the past without affecting the timeline.

"When do we go to plan B?" he asked.

"When plan A fails," she said. After a moment, she added, "Even if she started today, it will take several days for authorizations to collect the right signatures."

Irrational as it was considering time travel, delays still felt urgent, perilous. He couldn't just sit around, like all the *Homo quantus* sitting in the *Red, Blue,* and *Green.* They needed him to hurry.

"Tomorrow I'm talking to the vegetable intelligences," he said.

"Why?" She frowned.

"We have to do something on the surface. The Expeditionary Force might have been the first to discover real intelligent aliens anywhere."

"I've read the reports. Despite the poetic musings of a few officers, the vegetable intelligences are underwhelming. Vegetable is the key word."

"Then there's no harm in me talking to them."

She pursed her lips as if looking for a reason to object, but apparently found none. She went to her bunk, rolled herself into the blanket and shortly began snoring. Belisarius' mind quietly calculated soothing nonsense patterns from the colors in the icy ceiling.

CHAPTER THIRTY-TWO

BELISARIUS STEPPED DOWN his vision and turned his face up at the glowering brown dwarf. Dwarfs were dim, steady objects, stellar embers mostly cooling in stately quiescence in the visible spectrum. But even from more than half a million kilometers away, the knotting of its magnetic field lines faintly tilted the angles of billions of magnetosomes in his body. Brown dwarfs didn't flare often, and even when they did, they often flared weakly. But from time to time, these failed stars could blast out enough energy to melt vast parts of Nyanga. All that destruction was going to visit the vegetable intelligences, forever silencing them.

During the night, Saint Matthew had discreetly queried the quartermaster systems and found the devices used to translate vegetable intelligence speech. The translator had been designed, built and then left aside when the Expeditionary Force found out the vegetable intelligences had nothing useful to tell them. The vegetable intelligences were actually of such low priority that the lockers storing the translators were in one of the minimum-security tool sheds.

A half dozen other crew starting their shifts were already in the shed kitting up. Belisarius waited his turn. Iekanjika shouldered past him and pushed past another crewman. She dragged

Belisarius in her wake, pulling past cursing soldiers and to the locker. Saint Matthew opened the lock, falsifying credentials and the associated work order. They pulled out two big translator packs and then pushed their way out of the shed again.

The vegetable intelligences formed a large circular herd of perhaps three thousand beings centered on the time gates. Under less light than a full moon, and from a distance, glacial movements rocked their pitch-colored fronds, fooling the human brain into seeing the nighttime waving of grass-tops.

The Expeditionary Force let the vegetable intelligences walk around the time gates, because they posed no threat. Slow-moving and incredibly fragile, a single crewman with a metal bar could have demolished the entire herd. But MilSec was nervous enough that they didn't allow unauthorized people around the gates. Belisarius and Iekanjika stopped beyond the illumination of the spotlights, fifty meters from a lightly populated area.

The vegetable intelligences had a strange speech. They had photoreceptors, but signaling to each other with light or even infrared took more energy than they could spare. Nyanga's thin atmosphere attenuated sound, making speech impossible. And they produced no electrical signals, so they communicated by smell.

In the vanishing atmosphere of Nyanga, smells at least traveled in straight lines. Months ago, the Union deciphered about a thousand individual odors of the vegetable intelligence language. The translating devices organized these logograms, these picture scents, into a lexicon. The Expeditionary Force synthesized the smells, loaded them into a thousand tiny sprayers, and built a receptor plate to receive the 'words' sent by the vegetable intelligences. While crude, their translators had served at least to tell the Expeditionary Force that these creatures were too alien and primitive to be militarily or scientifically useful.

"The flaring Rudo mentioned," Belisarius said, looking at the clouds of iron skating through the upper atmosphere of the brown dwarf, "it's going to be bad isn't it?"

"The records of our core samples show periods of melting dozens to hundreds of meters of depth," she said, "including periods overlapping with the vegetable intelligences. They've had their entire species completely melted many times in their evolutionary history."

"But this time you took the time gates," he said. "Aren't they using them?"

"They didn't get violent, if that's what you're asking."

"That's not what I'm asking. You're bitter at me for taking the time gates to research the universe, but you stole them from a garden to make weapons."

She didn't answer, but he doubted he'd made a point. He crunched slowly across the ice again, into the vegetable intelligence herd. Iekanjika followed. They emerged from the waist-high black alien plants onto a broad plain where all the ground cover had been trampled. Here, the tirelessly lumbering feet moved the vegetable intelligences around from the faint wind that dragged their pollen into the past to the gasping, empty wind from the future. Many more vegetable intelligences stood on the margins of the slow procession, absorbing the shine of the spotlights. Belisarius moved towards a few big, weathered vegetable intelligences basking under a spotlight tower.

"Where do they come from?" Belisarius asked Iekanjika. "The dwarf is too young for them to have evolved here."

As soon as he said it, he realized that all assumptions of astronomical or evolutionary time had to be thrown out when the system included a time travel device. The Expeditionary Force had made impossible leaps in weapons and propulsion technology in just forty years. For all he knew, the vegetable intelligences had evolved from nothing to mobility and language in a few thousand years around the time gates, perhaps several times over due to the instability of the brown dwarf.

"Genetically-related, sessile, unthinking forms infest the comets of this system," she said, "but that's it."

The intelligences reacted to his presence, with fronds slowly tilting towards him. Despite the insulation of the vacuum suit, he was probably leaking enough heat to appear bright in the infrared. What did the vegetable intelligences think of humans? Was he one of many hot, fast-moving angelic beings? If irony was especially cruel to the vegetable intelligences, perhaps. Iekanjika and he were the next two owners of their time gates.

The vegetable intelligences possessed an eerie beauty. Their legs had two joints, like ankle and knee, but no real foot, just a hard black pad. Their four radially symmetric legs splayed at ninety degrees to each other. That radial symmetry carried upward into a big vase-shaped torso that was just a barrel of icy ribs with black skin pulled drum-tight across them. In places, damaged skin revealed bright ice beneath. Flowering crowns of fronds stood high above the chests, taller than Belisarius. It was from these that pollen launched itself onto the ghostly wind. No face was apparent to hint at which side Belisarius should speak to. Yet that facelessness comforted, rather than bothered him.

Their glacial movements suggested pensive deliberateness, contemplation, like the *Homo quantus*. They might have other similarities to the *Homo quantus* too. Union records showed that the environment under the brown dwarf varied so much that the vegetable intelligences experimented with the number of chromosomes they carried, like flowers. Union biologists commonly observed pollen with four or even eight sets of chromosomes, meaning that some vegetable intelligences carried eight to sixteen copies of their genetic information. So genetically, they were like a superposition of states, a mix of possibilities, trying all genetic combinations at once. The image appealed to the quantum logic hardwired into Belisarius' brain.

Belisarius brought up the translation software onto his helmet projector. An empty display area floated in front of his sight, and the possible words he could use were in a column along on side. The chest plate carried only nine hundred and seventy-eight olfactory logograms, a small vocabulary for a conversation. He triggered emission of the smell for *communicate*. The chest plate hissed momentarily. On his display, the word appeared in the middle of the blank workspace.

One of the vegetable intelligences moved, turning slightly to Belisarius. Fragments of ice clung to dangling bits of inky skin. The slight movement made them knock together silently. He imagined the sound of chandelier crystal tinkling.

The word *communicate* hadn't faded. Union researchers had tested the chemistry and neurology of discarded skins. Unlike human neurons, the nervous cells of the vegetable intelligences did not relax quickly after firing; they felt stimuli for longer. A flash of light to Belisarius might be a sober still life lasting minutes to the vegetable intelligences, overlapping with other sensations that might come many seconds before or after, making a fiction of simultaneity and blurring causality. The very concept of the present probably meant something different to them.

Words appeared on his display, near his own word *communicate*.
Elder.
Gene/word.
Right parentage/truth.

He wasn't sure what to make of the second or third word unit. The Union had attached to a single smell two meanings: gene and word. And the display was counter-intuitive. He'd expected the Cartesian thinking of the Expeditionary Force to have laid out the words in vertical or horizontal lines. However, the words clustered radially, gently drifting, *elder* and *gene/word* slowly gravitating towards his word, which was fading imperceptibly.

Why had the Union organized the display like this? He'd seen their other display styles. All Cartesian. So it had to be something relevant to communicating with the vegetable intelligences. His engineered brain snuffled for patterns and hypotheses.

He'd offered to communicate. They had responded with *elder,* either referring to themselves, or asking about him. They didn't have a word for name, but maybe they were asking what he was. What was he? *Homo quantus* was meaningless to them, and he didn't have the logograms to explain it anyway. Human wasn't any simpler to communicate. And as much as he didn't like it, he was now one of the leaders of an offshoot of humanity.

Elder, he sent, causing his chest plate to briefly hiss. *Variant parentage,* he added.

He was different from the vegetable intelligences and from Iekanjika. His first word *communicate* was still fading, but his *variant parentage* overwrote the words *right parentage/truth* as if the question had never been asked. He hadn't expected that.

He had erased some of their words. He and the vegetable intelligences were writing a conversation only loosely associated with causality. The history of the conversation was not fixed. It was a very quantum way of thinking.

He rethought his assumptions. The long relaxation time of the vegetable intelligence neural cells wasn't the only thing expanding their present. What must perception and time be like for intelligences who routinely received reproductive material from the future, and sent it to the past? They lived under a cooling brown dwarf that, no matter how stable, would eventually flare, radically rewriting their environment.

The pollen the vegetable intelligences sent back in time contained genetic information about what had survived the unpredictable future. This genetic feedback loop would accelerate adaptation. And it would tend to create a conceptual space where the future not only affected the past, but changed what language and information could mean.

Billions and trillions of pollen grains traveling to the past were statistical information. The vegetable intelligences didn't send hard facts back in time, but probabilities, a language the *Homo quantus* spoke very well. If the information from eleven years in the future and past were considered sensory input, then the present perceived by the vegetable intelligences might be immense. The real-time exchange of information might make their concept of the present twenty-two years wide, a great rolling cylinder of *now*.

From the leading edge/future, the vegetable intelligences said in their scent-based language. These words appeared over *variant parentage* but did not overwrite it. Both phrases occupied the same space, making them hard to read. Their phrase clarified his, but didn't erase it; they interfered like quantum probabilities. Was this their way of posing questions? Both states existed until a choice was made, like Schrödinger's Cat.

Leading edge, Belisarius said, which translated into smells that hissed out of the tiny stomata covering his chest plate. His answer made the overlapping phrases vanish. And their conversation, the consensus reality they built became *elder, leading edge, communicate.* The rest vanished, as if it had never been under consideration, or as if the final conversation emerged from a pool of possibilities after an observer collapsed the superposition of states.

The word *people* appeared on his screen, to the right of the cluster they'd made, semi-faded.

A question?

Distant, he replied.

He tried to write *in danger* but the lexicon of logograms had no match. The closest was *shadowed/absence of pollen*, and he used it. The two words appeared on his helmet display, above and below *people*. His people were distant and shadowed. And he was the *leading edge elder*, seeking to *communicate*.

The fronds of one of the elder vegetable intelligences tipped towards the time gates, where pollen streamed from now into the past, and yet nothing emerged from the future.

Wait and *pollen/wisdom* appeared on his display, between the two clusters of words.

Was that advice, or a statement of what they were doing? Were they waiting for their present to reach the future so that they would know why their future had stopped sending pollen back in time? They associated *pollen* and *wisdom*. Did that mean they understood that their wisdom was statistical in nature, buried in gene frequencies contained in the pollen? The vegetable intelligences might be more similar to him than the humans with whom he traveled, creatures of questions and probabilistic knowledge.

Unfortunately, his knowledge wasn't probabilistic in this case. He knew with near-certainty why their pollen had stopped. Either the impending flare or the theft of the time gates would end the pollen because there would be no more vegetable intelligences in the future to send pollen back in time. Some spores and pollen might survive in the ice, but these elders and their wisdom would be sanded away by the flare, restarting their culture from zero. He tried keeping in mind that this had all happened thirty-nine years ago, that he moved among events frozen in the amber of the past, but it wasn't easy.

Wait, Belisarius added, reinforcing their *wait*, in agreement.

That was what he was doing. That was what his people were doing.

"Patrol," Iekanjika said. "Let's get back to the shed and get less conspicuous tools."

There was no logogram for goodbye, nor any similar concept, so he backed away, wondering what the vegetable intelligences saw or thought as Iekanjika led him away. Did they see retreating angels, minor astronomical phenomena, or monsters?

"That was a waste," Iekanjika said. "We should get started on thinking about where to drill."

At a smaller tool camp between some crude buildings, they set down their chest-packs. The rush of shift change was behind them, and they picked up surveying equipment and a pair of picks for quick and dirty sample collection. When Rudo could get them the heavy drilling equipment, they would want to start right away.

If she got them the equipment.

They walked back out onto the ice. Belisarius had read the equivalent of a master's degree in ice planetology sublimation and sedimentation before they'd left the future, and here, his restless brain had already played with calculations of brown dwarf luminosity, planetary albedo, interaction with surface plants and average flare activity. It was barely interesting enough to keep his attention as they walked.

The time gates were located in a wide valley a hundred kilometers in diameter whose edges sliced the starview at the horizon. Nyanga was tidally locked, always presenting one face, so that the ice under high noon sublimated constantly, layer by molecular layer. Some of this thin new atmosphere traveled into the past through the gates, but most expanded outward, cooled, and snowed onto the edges of the valley. The pollen measurements in the Expeditionary Force's crude ice cores suggested that the time gates and the vegetable intelligences had been here for more than a hundred thousand years. Several sites in the valley would give him the data he needed to calibrate the time distance across the gates. It depended now on where would give them the most cover and draw the least amount of attention.

As they surveyed across the dark, plant-encrusted surface, part of his brain kept pondering the vegetable intelligences. The more he measured the faint light from the brown dwarf, the more certain he became that quantum effects were at the core of the metabolic pathways keeping the vegetation on this world alive.

He modeled different molecular pathways of photosynthesis for Nyanga, from possible receptors to electron carrier mechanisms. None of them were efficient enough to turn the weak infrared into enough energy for movement and intelligence. The only way the energy budgets for life could work is if their metabolic efficiency was above ninety-nine percent. Terrestrial photosynthesis achieved this through a kind of quantum coherence, and it wasn't that surprising that the evolution of a photosynthetic lifeform would converge on the same solution as those on Earth.

But that was still nowhere near enough energy for intelligence too.

"Your people studied vegetable intelligence anatomy?" Belisarius said. "Did they have any chemical energy sources or energy storage organs?"

"You're still thinking of them?" she said.

He didn't answer, but examined the terrain from a crouched position.

"Researchers dissected a number of corpses," Iekanjika said. "I never read anything that they were other than photosynthesizers. That's why they move slowly."

Maybe he was coming at this the wrong way. Mammalian brains at thirty-seven degrees needed a lot of energy. His brain was so active now that he had a low fever all the time. But the vegetable intelligences weren't mammalian brains; they ran at a hundred degrees below zero. The metabolic math would be very different.

"What did you find in their brains?" he asked, marking the location in their pads as a possible drill site.

"Neurons?" she said.

"Go on," he said, facing her.

"This is a *Homo quantus* behavior, colonel," Saint Matthew said to both of them. "They have great difficulty in letting go of puzzles."

"I'm asking because I think it's important," Belisarius said with a bit of heat. "How many neurons?"

"Colonel..." Saint Matthew said.

"Don't patronize me, Saint Matthew!"

"A few hundred million," she said, waving her hand dismissively. "A billion in some."

Iekanjika led them to the next possible site with their rudimentary equipment, and Belisarius mentally fretted at his models. The vegetable intelligences had one percent of the neurons he had, although that wasn't a strong measure of intellect. But it focused his mathematical modeling. Brains a hundred times smaller than his running at the temperature of dry ice certainly needed less energy, but still wouldn't have enough processing power for abstraction and speech.

In classical computation.

Quantum computation was a kind of quantum coherence that used less energy and processed its operations in parallel, meaning it could need fewer components.

Iekanjika stopped them in a small depression somewhat

sheltered by the high-growing plants from the view of cameras and other crews. They drew at the nutrient tubes in their helmets.

"The Union never named them?" Belisarius said.

"Why would we?"

"I'm going to call them the *Hortus quantus*," he said.

"Why?"

"You're *Homo sapiens*. I'm *Homo quantus*. We should call them something."

"Does it mean anything?"

"It translates into *français* 8.1 as *le jardin quantique,* or into Anglo-Spanish as the quantum garden," he said.

They ate in silence. She was patronizing him. So was Saint Matthew.

"It's been thirty-six hours," he ventured.

"Yes."

"Do you think Rudo has had a change of heart?"

"If Captain Rudo wasn't going to help us, Lieutenant-General Rudo wouldn't have sent us."

"That doesn't follow," Belisarius said. "Captain Rudo has been obstructive and even dangerous. I don't know if she'll play ball. It might be that we have to figure out everything on our own. That wouldn't be something that General Rudo would need to tell us about. In fact, the less we know about our personal futures, the more General Rudo is shielded from paradoxes."

"We can make ourselves dizzy with second-guessing, Arjona," she said.

"We can also discreetly check if we should take over."

"What are you proposing?"

"You have powerful pass-codes," he said. "Saint Matthew is faster than any processor this era is carrying. He could look into

Derek Künsken

Rudo's communications, see if she's ratting us out, or if she's working on getting authorization for us to drill."

The rhythm of her breathing didn't tell him much of her thinking. Nor did the long pause.

"This is a suspicious time, Arjona," she said finally. "The Expeditionary Force had factions. One proposed taking the time gates and going home. Another said we should study them here and make weapons. A very small faction said we should run away with the gates and make our own nation, never to meet up with civilization again. The general officers and even some warship captains were vying for power. Political tension almost broke the fleet apart after the death of its first commander. Some factions watched every query and keystroke. Any queries we make could draw attention."

"What if Saint Matthew could move behind all those precautions?"

She didn't answer for a long time. The bruised eye of the brown dwarf glowered at them. Belisarius' engineered brain and ocular implants puzzled out spectra and temperatures. High clouds of chromium and vanadium oxide streamed over hazy molten iron mist that traced the lines of deep magnetic storms. Beautiful, but pregnant with destruction.

"It must be hard not to trust Rudo," he said.

"I don't trust you."

She picked at a latch on the surveyor laser mounting.

"I trust the woman she becomes," Iekanjika said.

Her dark skin in the shadow of the helmet made her expression hard to read. He dialed up the gain on his ocular implants, giving false illumination with patches of gray pixilation. But he saw.

"No, you don't," he said.

"I beg your pardon?"

227

"People get over some lies," he said, "but not others. Rudo lied to everyone for decades. I don't think you've decided if you can accept that."

"You know all about trust, I suppose?"

"Trust is at the heart of all confidence schemes."

"Yes, you pulled one on me," she said bitterly.

"You never trusted me. You obeyed orders."

"Maybe Rudo didn't trust you either," Iekanjika said, rising. The threat of physical violence was barely contained in her tense stance. "She hired you in the future because I came to the past with you. Our presence in the past forces her hand in the future. Maybe no one in the Union ever wanted you or trusted you, and we're only working with you to avoid a grandfather paradox. Maybe this is one of those cyclic causal structures. And maybe this trip to the past isn't even about the core sample and you're still playing us. If that's the case, maybe that's something I can fix."

"I thought you and Rudo were suicidal patriots!" he said. "I didn't know you were going to win! Can you blame me for thinking the Congregate would make short work of you? If you had failed, I was ready to try to hide for a while, while everyone's questions led to dead ends. But because you succeeded, I'm now the most hunted fugitive in civilization and the *Homo quantus* have been sucked into that with me. I'm trying to save my people, and you need those other Axis Mundi."

"I don't know where your people are," Iekanjika said. "I don't know that they really got away from the Congregate. I don't know that you care about them or anyone else. All I have is your word, and I know that isn't worth the air you're breathing."

"We need each other. I don't trust you not to shoot me, but I trust you to act in the interests of the Union. And if Saint

Matthew can look into Rudo's work during sleep shift changes, we reduce the risk of being noticed."

"Give her more time," Iekanjika said finally. "If we haven't heard from her by the morning shift change, I'll green-light a quick, low-risk reconnaissance."

CHAPTER THIRTY-THREE

IEKANJIKA ROSE TO the sound of the early showers, twenty minutes before lights on. She always rolled out of her sleep sack completely awake, a useful quality for a soldier. Nothing was overtly different in what she saw or heard, just soldiers rubbing scratchy eyes and taking their morning pisses, but the air whispered tension. The crews said nothing overt and she wasn't plugged into the confidences. If she'd belonged to this era, she could have asked another corporal or her sergeant. Hell, in a lot of squads, the privates got the best gossip. But she didn't belong to this world.

She checked her service band. No message from Captain Rudo. She'd hoped. She'd hoped by now to have come back to a place of trust in herself at least. But she wasn't there and she was the one who had to make this mission work. Instructing the AI to look in on Captain Rudo's work would crystallize her doubts.

She didn't normally vacillate over tactical decisions. She had a lot of practice pushing aside fear, anxiety, pride and elation; those got in the way. But wondering if her commander was committed to the mission was new. The emotional muscles required to push those anxieties aside felt soft.

And reason was hard to apply. Everything told her that Rudo wanted the same thing: the independence of the Union. Rudo had lied to her, to everyone, for a long time. Iekanjika responded to lies reflexively and she didn't know how to turn that response off. She didn't doubt her mission. She never doubted her mission.

Push feelings aside.

Focus on reason.

Assess risk.

Her mission here might tip the success or failure of the entire rebellion. How would she be behaving if her contact wasn't her wife? Wasn't her hero? How would she deal with a flawed officer, a tool of unknown reliability?

She had three choices: use the officer, replace the officer, go around the officer.

Focus on reason.

Assess risk.

Push feelings aside. Deal with this like a mission commander.

Arjona looked groggy and unrested again. That didn't matter. She kicked him lightly and he groaned. "Get up," she said in a low voice. "Even the saints have to work today."

Arjona shivered and sat up. The AI had surely heard her and was even now breaking into whatever systems he needed to access.

She and Arjona dressed warmly, grabbed food packs for now and for insertion into the food slots in their suits. Shortly afterwards, they were on the surface of Nyanga, heading to the tool tables and sheds under the inflamed stare of the motionless brown dwarf. She connected their suits by private laser communication.

"You didn't get anything from Rudo?" Arjona asked.

"What did your AI find out?"

"I'm not anyone's AI," Saint Matthew said indignantly.

"What did you find out?" she said. Carrying picks and sonar equipment, they'd reached the uneven tailings of one of the sites where cores had been drilled out of the ice. Compared to the smooth waves of the slowly sublimating plain, the sharp fragments of bright ice stood out like a wound.

"I couldn't break into Rudo's comms records with the pass-codes you gave me," the AI said.

"Didn't the Lieutenant-General give you an all-access pass-code?" Arjona asked.

"She did," Iekanjika said.

"Captain Rudo had additional layers of encryption around her comms, something I've seen in other parts of the larger network."

"Everyone has veto over access to their accounts?" Arjona asked.

"It was a suspicious time, Arjona," Iekanjika said. She crouched, looking down the narrow channel in the ice with its perfectly-cored walls. The shine of her wrist lamp disappeared into that claustrophobic gloom.

"A time of fortified camps might be a more accurate description of the architecture," the AI said. "There must be a lot of non-networked systems. The network I can see doesn't account for all the computer functions for a base this size."

"So you didn't get in," Arjona said.

"Of course I got in," the AI said, "just not with the codes you gave me. Even the quantum encryption technology of this era is crackable with the tools from forty years in the future."

Iekanjika's anger briefly flared with the realization that their systems would be so easily passed by this AI. Maybe Arjona had outmaneuvered her and stolen their time gates, her birthright, but maybe she ought to take his mad AI. But she couldn't pay back all the debts owed. Not yet. Patience.

"Is she getting us the drilling equipment?" Iekanjika asked.

"She's in the process of setting up the order structure," the AI said. "She looks to be almost done. She's creating layers of signatures to authorize it, but from what I can tell, she's not letting her superiors know. Which is good, correct?"

"How long?" Iekanjika asked.

"It looks like it should be today."

"You weren't noticed?" Iekanjika asked.

"Not by these systems," the AI said with a hint of pique.

A tiny glow of relief began to bloom in her chest; for the mission, for her wife.

"There are two other problems," the AI said.

"What?" Iekanjika demanded.

"Last night, MilSec found an illicit transmitter on the northern comms trunk," the AI said, producing an electric anxiety in her stomach. "It's MilSec equipment and it's set to intercept signals from Bioweapons to the fleet."

"Major-General Takatafare is spying on Brigadier Iekanjika's communications," she said. She could have stopped this. "This will raise tensions."

"It's worse," the AI said. "The tech crews have been arrested, among them Lieutenant Nabwire."

"Takatafare is trying to cover it up, trying to look like she's not involved," Iekanjika said.

"No," the AI said. "The codes and equipment used don't match the ones used by MilSec, Major-General Takatafare's units. Someone tried to frame Takatafare and they got caught."

"Is there anyone other than your mother who would stand to gain by Takatafare being caught spying?" Arjona asked.

Iekanjika pursed her lips. She'd had a chance to kill Lieutenant Nabwire last night. The assassination of a junior officer would have been less disruptive than this. Under interrogation, Nabwire would admit to have been working for months in MilSec, but on behalf of Brigadier Iekanjika's faction. All fingers would point to her mother.

"Rudo wanted me to kill Nabwire after his shift," she mused, "possibly to draw attention to what he'd planted on the comms trunk. MilSec was better than she thought. They found the transmitter anyway."

"It's a double-cross," Arjona said. "Takatafare engineered this, or someone did on her behalf."

"Why?" the AI said.

Iekanjika recognized in that moment that, despite how gruff and occasionally tedious Saint Matthew was, he possessed a remarkable naïveté. Arjona had understood her right away. Iekanjika had understood as soon as she'd thought like the politicians on Bachwezi.

"To destabilize the Expeditionary Force," Iekanjika said, "to force even loyal, uninvolved crews and officers into camps, especially if it looks like Brigadier Iekanjika was trying to frame Takatafare."

Neither Arjona nor the AI commented on that grim note.

"What's the second problem?" she asked.

"I found things in Captain Rudo's virtual work area that shouldn't have been there," the AI said.

"What do you mean?" Iekanjika demanded.

"Hidden beneath Captain Rudo's personal encryption was a secret shared work area. It looks like a space where she and at least three other people have been discussing illicit things, in code."

"It looks like?" Iekanjika said. "I suppose you broke this code too?"

"Yes."

"Well?"

"She and three others have a plot to kill Brigadier Iekanjika."

The wind left her. In her past, her mother had died. She'd set aside that historical fact for the duration of this mission. She hadn't nourished the thought that her mother was alive right now, less than a kilometer away. Breathing. Thinking. That too was a fact, possessing the same kind of eerie reality that history did, but seemingly at odds with the first fact. That her mother was alive now and would be dead soon didn't fit comfortably in her head. Now that Rudo might have somehow been involved tipped her world on its side.

"How sure are you?"

"It wasn't faked in her account," the AI said. "It's her."

"I'm so sorry," Arjona said, reaching a hand out in the cold. She smacked it aside, hurting him. She looked away and exhaled long and slow.

"Treason," Iekanjika said. Her voice sounded unexpectedly calm in her helmet.

"Can we finish the job today?" the AI said. "Chaos will make our work harder. We have to get out quickly."

Far above them, tiny lights moved across the starry sky, parts of the Sixth Expeditionary Force. She knew the ships inside and out in her time, but four decades earlier, they were just second-hand kit given to the Union by the Congregate in exchange for service; vessels that wouldn't have lasted fifteen minutes against even mid-sized Congregate ships.

"How well did you know your mother, colonel?" Arjona asked softly.

The Expeditionary Force hadn't yet discovered the inflaton drive and the inflaton cannon in this time. They were nothing special, just a lost fleet with unreasonable ambitions. None of these people had yet passed through their chrysalis. Most alive today never would.

"Congregate sleeper agents reached my mother not long after I was born."

"I'm sorry," Arjona said.

Iekanjika tried to shrug in her vacuum suit. "I never knew her. A lot of children grew up in the Expeditionary Force missing parents. I knew I was coming back to these events."

"Did Rudo know you would find out she is involved?" Arjona pressed. "She's deep in another faction."

"Or she's being framed too."

Arjona looked at her askance through his faceplate.

"Even as a junior officer Rudo was the target of assassination attempts by sleeper agents," Iekanjika said. "She was promoted to captain and brought into an influential triptych marriage in large part for her role in uncovering a highly-placed agent who had managed to signal the Congregate."

"Rudo aside, we may have a bigger problem," the AI said. "When were you born, colonel?"

"February 34th, 2476."

"Everything I see in Rudo's hidden work space points to the assassination of Brigadier Iekanjika on February 28th."

Two days from now.

"Was your mother killed in a way that might have allowed her to survive that long on life support?" Arjona asked.

"Execution. Head and chest," she said briskly.

"We have a causality problem," Arjona said.

"Or there's more going on than I know," Iekanjika said.

"Why didn't Rudo tell you about this?" Arjona said with frustration.

"I'm her youngest spouse," Iekanjika said with contained heat. She might have dark doubts about her commanding officer, but she'd be damned if anyone criticized Rudo without proof. "I'm her chief of staff, her strategist. I know she cares about me. Before we traveled back in time, she alluded to the sins and errors of this era. Maybe she hoped I wouldn't find out. Maybe she never knew that I found out."

"I'm so sorry, Ayen."

"I'm not interested in your sympathy, Arjona. I never knew my mother. My father was some sort of convicted criminal. I might have spent my life toiling as a deckhand with no security clearance. The Lieutenant-General selected me for officer training. The Lieutenant-General is the unifying spirit of the Expeditionary Force. She freed our people. I owe her everything. I don't know my mother any more than these vegetable beings who are the product of pollen from fathers they'll never know."

"You're a human being, Ayen," Arjona said. "All of this would be hard for anyone to face."

"Don't lecture me about humanity, *Homo quantus*," she said. "Never doubt that I can do my job. Let's get the locations of the other Axes Mundi."

"This causal problem is serious, colonel," he said. "If Rudo or her confederates kill your mother before you're born, the results will be catastrophic."

"It didn't happen, Arjona," she said. "I'm here."

"But we don't know how much we ourselves directly contributed to you having survived," Arjona said.

Iekanjika walked off a few paces. Too much. Too fast. From doubting her commanding officer and senior wife for lying, she was now faced with the thought of her wife being her mother's assassin. She didn't know where to start to hold this. Where did reason start and emotion end? What was the tactical and strategic terrain? Arjona left her to walk alone.

CHAPTER THIRTY-FOUR

BELISARIUS WATCHED IEKANJIKA for a time before turning his face once again up to the cool brown dwarf, feeling the slow, distant movements of its magnetic field washing over all the magnetism of the base. But his thinking was far afield. He was starting to turn his observations of the *Hortus quantus* into models and theories. He was almost convinced that not only did the *Hortus quantus* incorporate some quantum phenomena into their life cycle, but that this was mediated through the time gates. He didn't understand the mechanisms, but his models couldn't work unless this was the case. Something very special and unique lived here under a kind of death sentence and he didn't know what to do about it.

"You can't just stand here, Mister Arjona," Saint Matthew interrupted. "It looks suspicious."

"This is all a disaster. Maybe you were right. Maybe I shouldn't have taken the job."

"Well, you did. And so did I. We can't change the past. We can only come to terms with it."

Belisarius walked towards Iekanjika, but she was already turning towards them. "We have the drilling equipment," she said with a trace of exhaustion in her tone. "Let's get the core sample."

She led them across the black skin of plant growth covering the frozen valley, to the quartermaster's building. It stood eight meters tall, made of thick blocks of ice. Outside the building, she showed her service band to a scanner and the door slid open. Maps appeared on their service bands, leading them to one of several automated compounds half a kilometer away in a field of industrial equipment and chips to run them.

The Sixth Expeditionary Force had certainly not traveled with the tractors and bulldozers and drills in this lot; they'd been a squadron doing fast armed reconnaissance. They must have built all the equipment beneath this failed star with asteroid-mined metals. They'd done so much in such a short time. They were impressive.

Iekanjika inserted the control chips into a metal-wheeled truck with a large flat bed and a front loading arm. She drove it slowly to an area where drilling attachments, extra batteries and metal core tubes were stacked with other kinds of construction equipment, and programmed the arm to load the truck. It would take a while.

Belisarius neared the colonel as she surveyed the job. He wanted to press her further about her mother and Rudo. She might act on whatever conflicting emotions tangled in her and he could help. And selfishly, part of reaching out, making contact, might calm the roiling of his own worries. But they didn't have that kind of relationship. Reaching out would be worse than leaving her alone.

"What happens to the *Hortus quantus* after you leave?" he finally asked.

"I don't know," she said. "We took specimens of a few with us, to keep the pollen flowing into the past for another ten years, to make sure that we didn't disturb what we observed when we first arrived on the planet. I suppose that those that stayed behind did whatever they always do after their dwarf flares. They must get back on their feet after being knocked down."

"Yes," he said uncertainly, "but in the other cases, the *Hortus quantus* had the time gates around to resume their reproductive cycles. What happened to them when you took it away?"

"They can reproduce with or without the time gates."

"But not the way they do now. And I'm starting to think that their intelligence may be an evolutionary response to having a time travel device in their life cycle. And their life cycle is wrapped around it. We just don't know how. The solar flare is a habitat stress, but losing the time gates is habitat destruction."

"I've only so much pity to go around, Arjona," she said. "A moment's distraction on my part could mean the death of a Union soldier, the loss of a ship, or the loss of the single Axis we hold. The strong survive and the weak die out. That's always been true and maybe this is the end for the vegetable intelligences. It's a pity, but I have no tears to shed for them. Their end by the flare would have come whether we'd found them or not."

"But that's the thing. An active brown dwarf can flare every few thousand years. The *Hortus quantus* haven't been wiped out, and they can't have evolved intelligence in the few thousand years since the last big flare. Somehow, with the time gates, the *Hortus quantus* can survive on both sides of the disaster."

"That doesn't make sense, Arjona. If they're wiped out in the present, they're wiped out in the future."

Belisarius struggled with the concepts mixing quantum logic and causality, things that didn't usually go together. At the edges of what even his engineered brain could hold together, his thoughts leapt between extrapolations, balancing on theories and hypotheses extended past what could be proven.

"There's more to the *Hortus quantus* than just their bodies,"

Belisarius said. "The bodies that will be melted in the flare might be the least important part of them. The interaction of genetic information across time may be like quantum interference patterns. A single environmental event can influence that, but not destroy it."

"I don't understand the point of this conversation, Arjona," she said. "It's all academic."

"Information can't interact and interfere across time without the time gates."

"You have the time gates now, Arjona! Give them back if you feel that strongly. But the Expeditionary Force needs them right now, so we're going to take them," Iekanjika said. "That's history. Observed history. After the flare, who knows where the time gates would have been. Frozen under ten meters of ice? Blasted off into space? The gates won't be a tunnel for a gentle wind."

"Your people found that the gates have been here, and that pollen has been blowing through them, for a hundred thousand years, through flares and calm periods," he said, finding something to hold onto in her words. "What kept the time gates oriented during all that time? Maybe the fact that information is flowing across twenty-two years of time stabilizes the position and orientation of the gates, like a kind of angular momentum."

"I'm not interested in your maybes and mights and could bes, Arjona! I have a practical objective to achieve. Are you proposing we leave the gates here and change the timeline? Fine, let's do that! Then you don't get to steal them and we don't get to come back here. I find it ironic that I have to explain causal paradoxes to the great quantum con man."

Belisarius stood uncertainly as she kept moving. All he had was intuition and feeling. This kind of mental space, where he had to create patterns without data, was unfamiliar. He hurried after her, catching up. He had to lay out facts and principles for both of them.

"The events of history are set," he said, listing them on puffy gloved fingers in front of her. "The Union took the time gates. We came back here. You were born. Your mother was assassinated. But parts of history are unwritten. We can touch those. Maybe we can preserve something of the *Hortus quantus*."

"There's nothing we can do right now except endanger the future of my people and yours with distractions, Arjona."

Belisarius grasped for something else to say, something to make her feel the same unease, the same tickling sense of unresolved mystery, but a gulf of biology yawned between them. They were no longer the same species. He had thousands of additional genes and hundreds of anatomical differences. She could lean on instinct and reason that had been tested by *Homo sapiens* over two hundred thousand years of human existence. The *Homo quantus* could easily tilt at windmills with false positives in their hunt for patterns and relationships. He couldn't even be sure of the patterns he found.

CHAPTER THIRTY-FIVE

THE INTELLIGENCE OPERATIVE, shorn of name, came to a kind of consciousness cold and grating. Painful sounds crackled, limbs creaked, and raw light punched helplessly unclosing eyes. The world was not spongy from half-sleep but possessed of a marrow brittle and hard.

A face came into sharp focus behind the spidery limbs of auto-surgeons. The woman's face hung over his, rendered in gritty, pixilated detail, washing false colors of ultraviolet and infrared over pale features. Virtual reality?

"1D446," she said. Her voice broke into digital information, divided by sampling into approximated amplitudes, tones and frequencies, and rendered into graphics annotated with physiological responses testing for falsehoods. "*Réponds*, 1D446."

"1..." he began, but the electronic voice he heard stopped him. The sound of it was graphed beside hers, narrow bars, monotonal distributions, digital to digital. "1..." he tried again. It was his voice. He was speaking through a prosthesis. Where was his mouth? His face?

"*Réponds,* 1D446," she repeated. She sounded slow. He felt instants between the syllables, but the pacing of her speech

245

hadn't changed. He was thinking faster, in a digitally surreal awareness.

"1D446," he finally said and the alien voice filled his ears. More graphs crowded his thoughts.

After long long moments, her face withdrew, saying only "*Bon.*"

He was alone with graphs and the hard light and the harsh tread of thought. An internal chronometer counting microseconds spun relentlessly in the deep internal displays in his thoughts. Long seconds ticked past.

Then another face filled his vision, a Scarecrow, an early model. The metal and carbon mesh cloth over its head was lumpy under its painted mouth and nose. One camera eye bulged, as if ready to burst open as it considered him. And in that lens, he saw only mats of wires and lenses and electrical busses in the reflection. Where was he?

"1D446," the Scarecrow said.

"*Oui.*"

"Are you prepared to serve?" the Scarecrow said.

"*Oui,*" he said desperately.

"In all ways," the Scarecrow said, the motto of the Intelligence Service.

"*Oui.*"

"What do you remember?" the Scarecrow said.

"I..." There was no way to complete the sentence. The crackle of his own electronic voice, analyzed through machines, was graphed and plugged into his inflexible brain... this wasn't *I*. He remembered being an intelligence operative. He remembered the enemies of the Venusian state. He remembered flying through the clouds. "1D446 is prepared to serve in all ways."

"1D446 is gone," the Scarecrow said. "The Scarecrow Corps needs new operatives, loyal operatives."

Scarecrow Corps.

They wanted him to be a Scarecrow? Why him? He didn't deserve it and he didn't want it. Was there any 'he' left? Scarecrows were all machine, AIs grown on biological templates. For a new Scarecrow to exist, 1D446 must be gone, destroyed in the building process.

Destroyed. He was gone. What he'd been, a man, was gone. And no one mourned intelligence operatives. They just vanished. Their numbers were retired. 1D446 was gone, man, name, body and legacy consumed like anything that fell into the acid clouds of home.

"Prepare for testing," the other Scarecrow said.

Testing. Hard, sharp thoughts circled the word, transformed it, looked for synonyms and definitions. He couldn't possibly pass the testing of the Scarecrow Corps. He'd never wanted this. He wasn't made of the stuff needed for Scarecrows. He didn't want immortality.

New images were forcefully presented to his brain. New sounds began to fall upon him, a torrent of sound and feeling and information, faces, names, intercepted messages, movements of people and money, associations and grouping of spies, traitors and insurgents, all falling over his brain in an unending cataract.

"Begin testing," the other Scarecrow said.

CHAPTER THIRTY-SIX

CASSANDRA'S STOMACH FLUTTERED a bit. The pilot's chair and its straps felt confining. The recycled air smelled of charcoal, humidity and sweat. The fans, while quiet, had discordances and chaotic rhythms that only the brains of the *Homo quantus* would ever notice. She wasn't used to this. To any of this. Roughing it, like a soldier or... she didn't know what. She'd been raised in an environment where comfort was the base condition so that thinking would be undistracted. Not even the birds made noise in the Garret. The economical construction, hard seats and expedient angles of *The Calculated Risk* were off-putting and distracting.

This very minor bit of self-pity immediately stung. At least she was out getting new data. How many *Homo quantus* were in comfort now? The Garret was gone. They were all running for their lives, perhaps even Bel. And she, the mayor, was sitting here, safe in the most vast cosmological experimental chamber in all the universe. The surreal flashes of light, dopplering to the blue or red even as she watched, hinted at gravitational features that had no analogues in four-dimensional space. It was fascinating and compelling, and more than enough to push aside discomforts, even as her gorge kept rising due to the lack of gravity.

Stills didn't complain. Maybe he was used to roughing it. She was somewhat glad that he was locked in a pressurized chamber at eight hundred atmospheres. She wouldn't have known what to talk to him about, or better yet, how to politely ask him to be quiet while she thought.

But he'd followed her navigational instructions with taciturn precision, settling them within sight of the pastward mouth of the time gates. Instead of watching it in three spacial dimensions, she'd had him rotate *The Calculated Risk* forty-five degrees across a temporal axis, so that the wormhole mouth was revealed in two and a half dimensions of space, and one and a half dimensions of time. Visually, the pastward mouth was partly smeared like a finger-painting, but ghostly secondary images stacked before and behind it, like the image was reflected in layers of glass. The precise combination of partial dimensionalities determined the number and spacing of the images, something she and Bel had worked out on the way, but Stills hadn't seemed that interested in the mathematical explanations. So she'd dropped the topic and told him to monitor a set of sensors.

The geometry she'd chosen made time pass differently in *The Calculated Risk*. No matter when Belisarius, Iekanjika and Saint Matthew entered the mouth of the time gate over their next subjective two months, Cassandra and Stills would see them, while only a fraction of that time would pass in *The Calculated Risk*. If need be, she could further adjust the angle, so that their apparent time passed even more slowly relative to the time passing beyond the mouth of the wormhole, but she very much hoped that Bel, Iekanjika and Saint Matthew were only in the past for a few days subjective. Time was exposure and danger, for both Bel and Iekanjika and the *Homo quantus* in the freighters. She wouldn't have traded places with any of them. She wasn't a fighter.

To pass the time, Cassandra stayed in savant, gathering as much as she could from the racer's sensors. All of it could be analyzed fruitfully by the *Homo quantus* later. She didn't want to talk to Stills or anyone when there was data to be mined, but her internal clock ticked more and more ponderously as she realized that there might be some social obligation for her to even just check in on him. Finally, she exhaled heavily and switched on the inner comms system.

"Does the environment bother you?" she asked.

"Nothing bothers me, princess."

Cassandra slipped out of savant reluctantly. She didn't want to offend him inadvertently, so she'd need all her social skills. And she didn't understand his tone. Most people might think he'd just taken a low-tech text-to-voice program. But the *Homo quantus* were very good at frequencies and there were more frequencies and even speech speed differences in what she heard than would be found in simple software. There were layers of meaning in his speech, something he'd encrypted into it, but it would take a sophisticated computer, or a very bored *Homo quantus,* to decipher them. This was another instance of the *Homo eridanus* being anti-social.

"Not even hyperspace?" she asked.

"Whatever the fuck is outside *The Calculated Risk* doesn't translate well through the flier's sensors," he said "but it doesn't bother me. I flown higher than this."

All notions of analyzing and decrypting the tones hidden in his mechanical speech halted.

"What?" she said.

"What?"

"What do you mean higher than this?"

"Doped up, princess. High. Stoned. Baked. Drunk out of my gills."

"What? You're drunk?"

"Naw," he said. "Not drunk. Not stoned. Not high. Tripping out... yeah maybe. Even if I turn off all the feeds to my chamber, electrical echoes bounce around here, coming from nowhere, doppling back and forth, side to side."

"You've been flying like this in hyperspace?" she asked in disbelief, a cold sense of doom settling in her stomach.

"Shit, sweet-cheeks! This is nothing. Once I strafed a Second Bushido base so hammered out of my skull that I heaved up everything back to my first meal, right in my chamber. Gastric acid burns like hell in the eyes and I might have been upside down, but I still dropped a pile of ordnance right on target. The hangover was worse though."

"Vincent! Focus! Can you fly now?" she demanded.

"*Merde,* princess, don't tie your panties in a knot! Never said I couldn't fly. I'm hearing weird-ass interference patterns in cock-eyed dimensions when we're standing still, and EM signals coming straight through the walls and floor from angles they shouldn't when I move. Yeah, it's like I'm flying after dropping a tab of acid. But no one can fly better'n me on acid."

"Have you tried?" she demanded, hearing a note of panic in her voice.

Nevermind.

Nevermind.

She and Bel would have to handle hyperspace. Their brains could think hyperspacially. They'd hoped Stills could handle it.

"Why didn't you say anything sooner?" she demanded.

"Do you have another pilot?"

She rubbed the heels of her palms into her eyes. All they had to do was sit here. In a pinch, she could program in navigational corrections if she needed to. It was slower, but she could do it. And once Bel was back, they could slowly pilot back to the futureward mouth. This was their fault. They should have tested this more first, but there'd been no time.

"You don't get your freak on much, do you?" Stills said.

"What?"

"Party," he said. "Cut loose. Dance on tables. Smoke weed in a wriggly group grope."

"No!"

"*Coño!* What do you do for fun?"

"I think," she said in a tone she hoped conveyed the obviousness of her answer.

"Really? Sounds like a waste. But I mean you must be hot, right, with your two legs?"

"What?"

"Mongrels got no legs, sweetie. Makes a world of difference for getting it on. There ain't a lot of make-out songs with 'hey baby, sit your cloaca down right here'."

She wasn't sure if he was genuinely making conversation or just trying to revolt her.

"Lemme get this straight," Stills said. "Prancy-pants is the funnest you quantum people got?"

"No," she said indecisively.

"I seen him gambling and breaking laws. I'm sure he was up to no good while he was shacked up with the Puppets, if you know what I mean."

Her stomach turned over.

"If you don't know what I mean, I'm talking Prancy-Pants Puppet-poki—"

"Vincent, why do your people stay on Indi's Tear?" she interrupted.

"There's only so many shit holes the mongrels can survive, sweet cakes."

"It sounds confined."

"Sort of. If you don't mind being squashed into paste, you should come visit," he said. "It's dark. And smelly. Like sulfur and ammonia and old dead things. Imagine hell burst a big urinal pipe. That's the ocean on Indi's Tear."

"Why don't you colonize a gas giant?" she asked.

"Did you drop some acid too?"

"If you need eight hundred atmospheres of pressure to live, any gas giant will have that at some altitude. That pressure band would be much larger than where you live now, and if you find a giant close to its primary, you'd get plenty of light."

"We don't breathe air, stupid," he said.

"So wear wing suits with water respiration systems. In a gas giant, you could easily pressurize water habitats to eight hundred atmospheres and those could move around in the clouds. You don't need to live in the stink and the dark."

The silence lengthened and she mentally rechecked her pressure and luminosity calculations in case she'd made a mistake. In principle, what she'd just described was no different than what the Congregate did with their habitats in the clouds of Venus.

"Shit," he said flatly.

She wasn't sure how to take that.

"Shit!" Stills said, now angrily. "We got a hail!"

"We've got a what?"

"Incoming comms."

"Is it Bel?" Cassandra asked.

"Fuck," Stills said. "*Câlisse! Puta! Zarba!*"

"What is it?" Cassandra demanded.

The cockpit speakers activated. A sepulchral voice spoke in last century's French. "Union ship carrying Belisarius Arjona, this is the Epsilon Indi Scarecrow. Power down and slave your controls to my ship. Any other course of action will result in you being fired upon."

"How did a Scarecrow get in here?" Cassandra demanded.

"Get into your acceleration couch!" Stills said.

Cassandra fumbled with the straps and then leapt from the pilot seat to the line of coffin-sized chambers. In the first, she sealed her suit and struggled the tight hood onto her head.

"Where did it come from?" she demanded with shaking hands.

"Skip the plumbing!" Stills said. "Just flood your chamber."

Cassandra slammed the door of her chamber, attached the neural jack and punched the button to fill the chamber with gel.

"Our sensors are all fucked up in this space," Stills said. "I can make out a low-profile shape about a kilometer away. Can't tell the design with this resolution. Can you use your quantum magic to see what the fuck we're dealing with?"

"That's not the way my senses work," she said through the jack as she fought instinct and inhaled thick, choking gel as fast as she could cough around it.

"Of course it isn't," Stills said. "You quantum people are all deadweight when the chips are down. Fuck. Fuck. Fuck. A Scarecrow."

"How bad is it, Vincent?"

"When I flew for the Congregate, my job was to fuck up their enemies. The Congregate sends in Scarecrows when they want to fuck up their friends."

The low, dead voice spoke again. "You have ten seconds to power down and turn over your ship's control. I am fully armed."

Cassandra tuned the telemetry resolution to maximum input and slipped into savant. The world became pattern-rich and logical, built of linear, geometric and exponential relations, accented with fractal patterns and edged with chaos.

"It looks like a missile, Stills."

"Fuck."

"One missile doesn't make sense."

A searing line leapt the kilometer of hyperspace from the Scarecrow's vessel. An explosion on the surface of the racer shook them.

"Holy shit!" Stills said. "He's shooting anti-matter! That was a warning shot. He could have destroyed us right there."

Cassandra's brain churned out calculations, the energy required to produce the observed acceleration and vibrations, factoring in dispersion on the hull of the racer. "That was a few micrograms!" she said.

"This is your cue, big brain."

"My what?"

"I'm just the fuckin' hired help, princess, an' I got no fuckin' weapons. I can evade, but tell me how you want to deal with this and do it quick."

The racer moved dizzily, so hard that even in the acceleration gel, her chest crushed tight, taking the air from her. At least thirty gravities, in-mixed with angular accelerations. Even with telemetry fed into her jack, position and velocity in multiple dimensions jumbled. The racer couldn't keep track of all the dimensions in here. Only she could.

"Stop moving!" Cassandra said. "Stop moving! You'll get us lost!"

"Lost ain't our problem, big brain!" Stills said, turning again, making the other ship vanish, but forcing her to desperately track their movements with her brain. "One real hit from the AM this *malparido's* throwing and we're dog food."

"This is a twenty-two dimensional region of space-time with no landmarks!" Cassandra said. "We're navigating by dead reckoning!"

"Then you better reckon, *ostie*, 'cause I'm supposed to die in an ocean!"

"Come to a full stop!" she said. "Full stop right away! Then rotate forty-five degrees across the p-axis, then forty-five degrees across the v-axis!"

The crushing pressure on her ribs and joints mounted, vanished, then shot up again.

"He's following," Stills said.

Cassandra's brain raced, calculating their position and velocity at the same time as she constructed a better pattern of the Scarecrow vessel based on the slim sensor readings. She diagrammed it and projected it in Stills' display.

"Does this make sense to you?" she asked.

She'd drawn a missile, nineteen meters long, plus or minus sixty-three centimeters, by one hundred and sixty centimeters in diameter plus or minus nine, studded with protruding straight edges.

"That's a *casse à face* missile," Stills said with distaste. "Fast bugger."

"Someone is riding it?"

"A Scarecrow is an AI mounted in a robot, baby, not a somebody. He doesn't need life support. And if you take the warhead out of a *casse à face*, you get a shitload of space for weapons."

"He's following, making the same rotations," she said.

"That's probably how he got here," Stills said. "It wouldn't have taken much for a low-profile missile to be sensor-absorbent. He must have matched all our maneuvers all the way through. Come up with either run or fight, big-brain. I can't do this all day."

She'd never been in combat. She'd navigated the movement of the Sixth Expeditionary Force across the Puppet Axis. She'd escaped from the *Limpopo*. But most of that had been Bel's plans. She'd never *fought* anyone or anything.

But this Scarecrow thing wanted to hurt *her*.

"Let's see if he can follow this," she said.

CHAPTER THIRTY-SEVEN

BELISARIUS FOLLOWED IEKANJIKA as she drove the remote control surface truck about a kilometer from the ground HQ, on the other side of the *Hortus quantus* herd. While she programmed the different robotic drill components, Belisarius' brain snuffled at something to keep it occupied. Predictably, he gravitated to the *Hortus quantus* again, testing patterns, relationships and analogies. The more he thought about their perception of time, the more alien they seemed.

To the *Hortus quantus*, eleven years in the past and eleven years in the future might feel adjacent, maybe even simultaneous. They signaled one and received signals from the other. But the years in between, say 5 years pastward and futureward, must not be invisible to them. That would make little evolutionary sense.

They knew what happened in the intervening spaces, but that knowledge wasn't observational. They probably worked like a radio telescope. The most cost-effective way to build a radio telescope was not to build a single large one, but to integrate one image out of many small images from an array of smaller telescopes. That was also the way the hundreds of millions of magnetosomes in his muscle cells worked. Each one was a microscopic magnet. Each measured only the tiny magnetic environment around them, but all their inputs came together in Belisarius' brain as electromagnetic maps of exquisite resolution. It was also the way Cassandra had used entangled particles to see the space-time environment across the distance of hyperspace when she had guided the Expeditionary Force across the Puppet Axis. Except that the *Hortus quantus* were not summing observations across space. They were integrating information across a twenty-two year wide simultaneity.

But what did the *Hortus quantus* see? They weren't sending electrical patterns or pictures across their array. Gene combinations that were mal-adapted for the future were selected out and not sent back in time. They saw their environment in the abstraction of gene frequencies. They saw their environment in terms of how they themselves evolved to it. They might not discern the unevenness of the ground before them, but the immensity of the picture they saw through their genetic telescope shivered a chill up his spine.

They were tremendously alien, peering at abstractions rather than the world itself. He and Cassandra might have more in common with the *Hortus quantus* than he did with Iekanjika or any other human. It was a dizzying, frightening thought. The *Hortus quantus* were far more valuable to him and the cosmos. He had to talk to them again.

He set his comms to link only to himself and AI.

"Do you think I'm crazy?" Belisarius asked Saint Matthew.

"How do you want me to answer that?" the AI replied.

"I mean about the *Hortus quantus*."

The AI was silent for a time.

"You've asserted some incredible things about them, without evidence, which is rare for you," Saint Matthew finally said.

"I'm relying on how I think they work," Belisarius said. "I haven't tested it. I'm not even sure how I could."

"I'm not sure you'd like any of my ideas on this."

"What do you mean?"

"You're the quantum expert," the AI said. "You don't believe in fate, but you made a pretty speech about my place in the cosmos when you were trying to convince me to leave Saguenay Station and help you with your con."

"Yes?" Belisarius said warily.

"You don't believe in fate, but other *Homo quantus* believe in Einsteinian block time, that the future and past are written and that free will is an illusion. But that belief can be rephrased in terms of fate. What some call fate, I call the hand of God, and some *Homo quantus* call block time. And I think it's real. The Union has been here for months, but only Belisarius Arjona could have noticed the nature of the *Hortus quantus*."

"What are you getting at?"

"The hand of divinity can move in ways that even saints can't understand."

"You have a role in this?" Belisarius asked.

When Saint Matthew finally spoke, his voice carried a note of discomfort. "Mister Arjona, we find ourselves with the *Hortus quantus* at their crossroads. I don't understand why we might have been sent just to witness an extinction. Although you don't believe in God, I feel His hand around us."

"Then his hand has put us somewhere between an extinction and genocide."

Iekanjika's voice broke into their conversation from the common channel.

"Saint Matthew. How certain are you of this plot to assassinate Brigadier Iekanjika you found in Rudo's encrypted files?"

Belisarius and the AI switched to their common channel.

"I don't believe it was planted there, if that's what you're asking," Saint Matthew said. "I have no doubt she's involved."

"In my history, there's no indication she was involved," Iekanjika said.

"History is just a narrative that may or may not be faithful to a set of observations," Belisarius said. "What you've been told may have been modified in the records, perhaps by Rudo herself. None of us has observed her pulling the trigger on the gun that killed Brigadier Iekanjika. Or it might be that your presence here persuades Captain Rudo not to join this plot or even delays it long enough for you to be born."

The light from the brown dwarf, faint red like a heat lamp, changed subtly. His ocular implants detected a brief doubling in luminosity, too low for the human eye to notice and a spatter of x-rays. The flare event was building deep in the magnetic tangle beneath the clouds.

"Are you speaking to Captain Rudo about this?" Saint Matthew asked.

"There could be a hundred explanations for what you found," Iekanjika said. "Conditions and opportunities change. The assassination might be delayed on its own and never involve Rudo. Maybe she's a bit player."

"You're gambling more than your own life on that, colonel," Belisarius said. "Like it or not, you're now a central figure in Union history. If you aren't born, our timeline is shot. You must know Rudo well enough to reach the woman she is now."

"Drilling your core samples will take three days," Iekanjika said. "You stay here. I'll speak to Captain Rudo."

Belisarius looked uncertainly at the big truck and mobile drill tower and the dozens of programmable robots.

"No problem," Belisarius said.

Iekanjika turned and walked off towards the buildings. Belisarius switched off the transmitter so that he and Saint Matthew were alone. This might be his best time. Days of mind-numbing work would be performed by machines. This was his chance to try to know himself again, and to know the *Hortus quantus*.

"Can you run the robots?" Belisarius asked.

"Why?"

"I'm going to try to see the *Hortus quantus* from the fugue," Belisarius said.

CHAPTER THIRTY-EIGHT

IEKANJIKA HAD MEMORIZED the layout of the base, the standard operating procedures, the top hundred officers and NCOs on the surface, and had passing familiarity with another hundred secondary people and projects. She knew that Captain Rudo was active during Iekanjika's two waking shifts and that she usually worked from the tiny space she'd been assigned. But she found Rudo's office empty. So she sat to wait.

After half an hour, the short prodigy appeared, a bit breathless from wherever she'd been rushing from. Rudo didn't bother to hide her disappointment in finding Iekanjika there waiting. A moment of dissonance washed over Iekanjika. Sometime in the next twenty years, Rudo would become the unflappable, confident officer. This young incarnation of her, with her mix of arrogance and insecurity, was a doppelganger she couldn't match with the older woman she knew. Rudo closed the office door and sat.

"What are you doing here?" she said in a low voice. "I gave you the authorizations and equipment."

"We're drilling now," Iekanjika said.

"You shouldn't be in here."

Iekanjika sat back and crossed her arms. "I need to talk to you about the future."

Young Rudo shared the mannerism of narrowed eyes with her future self, but the rest of her face belied the flinty scrutiny. Rudo's instinct was to command the situation, or at least approach it on equal footing. But she was the junior here, in experience and knowledge.

"I have tools to break files encrypted forty years in my past," Iekanjika said.

Rudo sat straighter.

"For reasons that contribute to the mission you yourself gave me thirty-nine years in the future, I looked into some of your files here," Iekanjika said. "I saw what you and a few others have planned for February 28th."

"I don't know what you're talking about," Rudo said.

"My concern is not for my mother," Iekanjika said.

The younger officer didn't squirm, but it was a close thing.

"I never knew her," Iekanjika said. "I'm concerned with two parts of the timeline. Firstly, I was born on February 34th. Secondly, you had nothing to do with the brigadier's assassination. If I die, some rather large successes thirty-nine years from now will be in jeopardy. And if you're associated with the assassination of Brigadier Iekanjika, your career will stop. And you're far more important to the history of the Expeditionary Force than I am."

This seemed to deflate the young captain, as if this kindness were proof that Colonel Iekanjika really was from the future, the full weight of which was far more than the thought of murder. The captain's lips pressed tight.

"I don't know what you have to do," Iekanjika said, "but I need you to understand the stakes. Don't do it. Or change the date so I at least have time to be born."

"I have to deal with this now," Rudo said leaning forward with a fervency in her voice, "or we don't get to have your future. The Expeditionary Force is on the verge of breaking apart."

"You have to keep yourself clean. You got us the drilling equipment. We need a few days of cover and then the permits to go back near the time gates," Iekanjika said. "I don't know if you're the key to preserving the Force now, but your help directly affects the war effort in the future."

Rudo stared straight into her. "War effort?"

"You have to excel both now and tomorrow, captain."

Rudo's eyebrows rose in a familiar manner; not quirky or curious, but deadly dangerous.

"*Captain*, is it?" she demanded. "Pulling rank, *colonel*? Fuck you! I don't know you from shit. You might be from the future, but you might not be on my side then. For all I know, you captured me in the future and tortured my real name out of me so that you could coerce me now."

Iekanjika's hands had gradually tightened on the arms of the chair. "I don't know what you're dealing with in the present, captain, but in the future, we're about three months away from being overwhelmed by the Congregate. Even if I get back with the core samples instantaneously relative to my time, I don't know if it will be in time."

"You have a time machine, *colonel*. Use it."

"It doesn't work that way. We can only travel to certain places and times."

"There's not enough time here either," Rudo said. She worked at a peeling seam on a datapad and lowered her voice. "I've cast my lot with Major-General Takatafare's faction. My senior wife and middle husband haven't committed to either one. They're trying to maintain their independence, but there are no independents."

"This is politics. It will wind itself out."

"This doesn't look like politics at all," Rudo said. "This looks like where I come from."

"Where Vimbiso Tangwerai comes from," Iekanjika said in a low voice.

"I spent time in the slums of Harare. This struggle in the Force has all the characteristics of a gang war, yet the factions approach it like a political fight. That will drag it out. We'll lose ships and years, maybe forever."

A chill snaked up Iekanjika's spine. Losing ships was unthinkable, not only because all twelve had survived to cross the Puppet Axis in the future, but after that they needed everything they had for the war effort.

"You can fix this?"

"Gang wars are never about ideology. They're about money and control. Fighting costs money and dead men don't get rich. They make deals or they solve things fast through other means."

"I've given you more information about the future than I should have," Iekanjika said, standing. "You and I are critical to the timeline. Don't do anything to take us off the board. Losing in the future is just like losing now."

She opened the door and left.

In the icy stairwell leading up from the offices and cubicles, a sudden trembling overcame her. For fifteen or twenty seconds her hands felt frozen, and she fought an unnerving dizziness. She knew the signs. Officers were trained to spot it in their crews, and sometimes in themselves.

Shock.

She knelt on one knee and lowered her head. Somebody descended the stairs and Iekanjika made as if she were adjusting an ankle seal on her suit. They passed her without paying attention. Iekanjika rose, heading for the airlock where she'd left her helmet.

Shock had hit her before: from injuries, from acceleration damage from failing gel chambers, but she'd never gone into shock just from mental trauma. Time travel. Meeting her youthful future wife. Discovering the plot to assassinate her own mother. What had she expected?

Time travel wasn't part of her profession. She soldiered. She could face danger, fight any enemy, and stick to the parameters of a mission profile. But time travel wasn't just another battle. Meeting young Rudo and finding out over the last week that her wife carried a terrible secret had deeply shaken her faith in her future wife.

And her mother? Her mother was alive, right now. Her brain could think the thought, process it. What had her heart expected? That she could walk on the same world as her and not feel it rip at her? Ayen Iekanjika had grown up rootless, another orphan in the Force, raised on the *Mutapa*, apprenticed to anyone who needed an extra pair of hands. She'd known her way around the *Mutapa* by the time she turned six, and could fix anything on it by her fifteenth birthday, like all the children who knew they would have to take up jobs in the fleet.

No one visited the platoons of orphans or brought them presents or told them they loved them. None of that had bothered her, growing up. She'd known who she was and what she was. Her father had been a criminal, executed months before her birth. And everyone knew her mother had been assassinated and vilified after the fact. It wasn't politic for Ayen to try to find out who her mother had been. So she'd grown from child to adult without context or reference to anyone.

The idea that she had a chance to know her mother kicked her hard now. Know her for real. Not through the dry administrative recordings the fleet carried on file. She knew where her mother was. The unexpected ache to meet this long-dead person strengthened. But realistically, she couldn't get within a dozen meters of the brigadier. A corporal in the Union navy trying to approach a general officer with no reasonable business would be shot or jailed. Her fake identity would survive casual inspection, but even forty years ago, the cross-referencing in the secure areas would spot her in a second. And what could she even say?

I'm Ayen, your daughter from the future?

Would her mother think her mad? Maybe not. Doubt her, yes, but the Union had the time gates, even if they didn't yet understand how to use them. The idea that in the future their descendants would have figured it out couldn't be outside the realm of possibility.

I'm Ayen. Your daughter.

I don't know you.

Iekanjika didn't like these thoughts. She didn't feel like herself while she thought them. She hadn't been trained for this. She screwed on her helmet, hopefully sealing out the dark thoughts that kept trying to infect her. She cycled through the airlock.

On the surface, under the spongy red light. The black surface crunched under her boots and flakes of the all-covering plants came away, revealing the bright surface beneath. The layers fell away to show the true world. Bright truth was important, but there was something artful and vibrant about the layers that obscured the truth here. She missed her innocence and the honest trust she'd offered.

The drill towered above the horizon, hammering downward in a faint booming that was louder in her boots than in her ears. Arjona stood nearby, watching the robots load the next section of tubing. He saw her and approached. He wasn't responding to radio or laser. She got ready to draw her sidearm or fight him down. Instead, he pulled a fine wire from his suit and offered it to her. Direct cable. Used to transfer software or data between suits. Also useful for private communication. What did he have to say he couldn't tell her by laser?

"I wasn't sure you'd gotten out," Arjona said. "I didn't dare signal you or leave the work site."

"What is it?"

"Saint Matthew left some one-time electronic alarms in the network to let us know if Rudo's group continued its plotting."

Her heart thumped faster. "They were detected?"

Focus on the mission.

Assess risk.

"No," the AI said. "The Expeditionary Force doesn't have anything in this era to detect my programs."

"What happened?" Iekanjika said.

"Captain Rudo was arrested," the AI said, "for treason."

"I was just there!"

"It just happened," Saint Matthew said. "If you'd stayed a few minutes more, you might have been arrested yourself."

Worry made her stomach clench. Not just for the mission, but for Rudo the woman, no matter how infuriating she was at this age, no matter who she really was.

"She was arrested by Takatafare's MPs for treason?" Iekanjika said. "But she's working with Takatafare's faction against Brigadier Iekanjika."

"The use of the code Lieutenant-General Rudo gave us was detected," Arjona said. "From when Captain Rudo went into the network to create our identities."

"We did this?" Iekanjika demanded.

The implications for the future swam in her mind, dizzying.

"We don't know," Arjona said.

"Are we compromised?"

"Not yet," the AI said. "Security detected an authentic code coming from a remote location. It will take them a while to figure out which actions were Rudo's and which ones were ours."

"They caught her based on just that?"

"No," Arjona said. "They found the same code had been used again."

"When we looked to see if she was moving on the drilling requisition," Iekanjika said as a finger of horror slid along her spine.

She'd done this. It had been Arjona's idea, but this was her mission. She'd authorized it. She'd stopped trusting Rudo and now the future commander of the Expeditionary Force was in the brig, with enough evidence to bust her to private or to get her executed.

"Is this a change in history or was this episode in the books?" Arjona asked.

"Of course it wasn't in the books!" Iekanjika said. "An officer doesn't get arrested and then fast-tracked for promotion."

"We've changed the timeline," the AI said.

"Smaller bits of the timeline may be flexible," Arjona said, "and not recorded. This may be what really happened in the past and no one knows."

"We changed the past, Arjona!" Iekanjika said.

"We don't know that! Our arrival may have delayed the assassination attempt on your mother, long enough for you to be born."

"Causality doesn't work that way. Trust me. The Expeditionary Force has spent a lot of time thinking about avoiding paradoxes."

"And the *Homo quantus* couldn't have done better. But the *Homo quantus* examine the nature of reality. Causality isn't just linear. It can branch in lines, forward and backwards in time. It can take other geometric forms: two-dimensional sheets, solids, and in cases involving time travel, it could exist in closed loops like eddies and open loops like spirals."

"I'm not looking for a lecture in graphs, Arjona!" she said. "Do you think this arrest caused the delay in the assassination to allow my own birth?"

"If Rudo gets out of jail with no charge, or a minor one, then it's self-consistent, constructive interference," Arjona said. "Imagine it like the interference patterns you'd see in electromagnetic waves. Going a step further, the fact that you're still here to ask the question means that Captain Rudo's initial plan didn't work."

"What can your AI really do?" Iekanjika asked. "How deep can he get into our networks without passwords, without getting detected?"

"I can break through some layers of security," the AI said, "but lots of important things aren't visible on your network. It's like your network security was designed by paranoids."

"With reason," she said.

"What do you want Saint Matthew to do?" Arjona asked.

"Can he fabricate evidence to show that Rudo was framed?"

"Maybe," the AI said. "Who would I point your investigators at? Whoever I do, they'd likely be executed, no?"

"The Expeditionary Force has few innocents," she said.

"It's not my job to see that anyone is punished," the AI said.

"The alternative is messing up the timeline and the future," Arjona said.

"But hacking will only get us so far," Saint Matthew said. "A determined investigator will look for physical evidence too. We can't fake that, so even if, in the short term, we get Captain Rudo free, she might just end up back where she is now when our fabricated evidence meets real evidence."

Iekanjika inhaled slowly and deeply, but her head swam, like she was underwater and no matter how much she clawed for the black surface, it remained just out of reach. She walked back towards the base.

CHAPTER THIRTY-NINE

BELISARIUS' MOOD WAS not much better than Iekanjika's. While listening to Saint Matthew's news about Rudo, he'd started to rethink his views of predestination and free will. With their knowledge of the future, Rudo and Iekanjika were as constrained as Belisarius by his genetics, but he didn't want to be as trapped as them. He was moving away from the idea that he couldn't control his curiosity. He had to believe that he was more than an automaton, wound at birth through genetics and development, going through the motions of a clockwork life until his spring wound down.

But the price of believing he was free was responsibility. He really was responsible for every choice he'd made, from fleeing the Garret all the way until the present moment. That stuck him with all the consequences of his mistakes, in a place his talents meant nothing. A con man in a culture he didn't know was close to useless. A contemplative among hard-bitten soldiers was no better.

He switched off his transmitter as the drill rumbled on.

"Are you shutting down?" the AI asked.

"What?"

"A response to prolonged stress in humans is apathy and depression. You can't care anymore."

"Are you counseling me, or worried about my soul?"

"I've always been worried about your soul," the AI said, "but you need to be functional for a while longer, at least until we get out of the past. Even then, the *Homo quantus* need you for months, maybe forever. That kind of pressure is hard to bear."

"I survived the con and travelling through time."

"It's different when you're alone," Saint Matthew said. "Your mind has a pressure release valve. When the pressure goes on too long, your brain can start to accept that death or some other outcome is possible and make peace with it. But you can't make peace with the uncertain fate of all the *Homo quantus,* which is now tied to the future of the Union rebellion."

"We're getting the core sample," Belisarius said. "We'll save the *Homo quantus*. Right now, I need to go into the fugue."

"That's a different Belisarius Arjona than I've known for years."

"I want to see if there's some way to help the *Hortus quantus*."

"The *Homo quantus* don't run into savant and the fugue to hide from the world," Saint Matthew said. Belisarius had never known the AI to be openly sarcastic, but there's a first time for everything. After four point four seconds, an eternity for both of them, Saint Matthew said, "What can you do?"

"I don't know yet."

The ember shine of the brown dwarf cast only faint shadows, creating a dreamy aura around him. Only the harsh spotlights in the distance gave any feeling of solidity, and it wasn't solidity he was looking for.

"I do need to understand what I've become, what it means for the subjective me to coexist in one brain with an objective intellect," Belisarius said. "Although I don't like it, Cassie is right. I might be a new stage of *Homo quantus* evolution, if I can make it work. If I go back and I bring the *Homo quantus* data on how my brain works, they'll be happier."

"How much of this is real and how much of it is just your curiosity? Could you hurt yourself by entering the fugue? You did before."

"I should be okay, and the risk ought to be worth it, if I can do something to preserve the *Hortus quantus*. I'm just one man, but I need data."

"One man who has to carry back coordinates that will help his people escape."

"You're fussing like a mother hen again," Belisarius said.

The brown dwarf's magnetic field trembled. This gas giant equivalent of a minor earthquake was small in astronomical terms, but heralded a much larger readjustment only months away, and perhaps extinction for the *Hortus quantus*.

Not extinction exactly. The oily black plants slicking the frozen surface could be considered a variant form of the *Hortus quantus,* or a segment of their life cycle. But that sessile form wasn't intelligent or conscious. The consciousness of the *Hortus quantus* seemed centered on the time gates, which the Expeditionary Force were taking away.

In a way, it was an act of genocide, perhaps not intentional, but not entirely innocent either. It was too facile of the Union to claim that they were saving the time gates from an ecological disaster; the time gates must have experienced dozens or hundreds of flares while the *Hortus quantus* were evolving.

What could he do? He had the time gates now. When he was done, might he figure out a path back to save them? If not all of them, the part of them that was intelligent? Many creatures and species lived and died in the cosmos, but these beings were the only others he'd ever known who lived with some part of themselves in the quantum world. They might hint at the future of the *Homo quantus,* something that, despite all his differences with his people, carried the echoes of a kind of inner peace for him.

He didn't enter the fugue, not exactly. The existence of the quantum objectivity in his brain no longer required the extinguishing of his subjective self. The quantum intellect ran all the time and it was partitioned from the parts of his brain running his subjective consciousness. Otherwise he would collapse the superimposed probability waves the quantum intellect perceived.

Belisarius diminished and the quantum intellect expanded, consuming his processing resources, even his senses. The two of them, subjectivity and objectivity, could not coexist, so the wall between them was high. A soft numbness seeped into him as the quantum intellect rerouted more than ninety-nine percent of the electromagnetic sensations to itself. The richness of sensation from the hundreds of millions of magnetosomes in his muscle cells faded. And although he couldn't see it, the interacting, overlapping waves became quantum data, superimposed, with multiple states existing at once.

Perceptual sensitivity has dropped, the quantum intellect said in Belisarius' thoughts. The voice was his, though toneless and eerie. *Recommend de-partitioning the brain of the Belisarius physicality to increase sensitivity.*

The drop in perceptual sensitivity the quantum intellect referred to was the leakiness of the partition, allowing him to feel the faintest breeze of the magnetic sensation against his arms and legs. The quantum intellect couldn't be distressed; it wasn't conscious. Nor could it be described as self-interested. The term had no meaning to an intellect with no sense of self. But it had the same priorities and objectives as him: to learn as much as possible of the world and the cosmos, at almost any cost. The intellect was looking to increase the efficiency of its senses.

But the leak through the partition gave Belisarius a pinhole view of the quantum world, like it had in the hyperspace of the interior of the time gates. Every brief glimpse, only a tiny fraction of all the overlapping probability waves, caused a minor collapse in the superposition of states as his attention forced the cosmos to decide on one set of choices instead of others. But his engineered brain was fast enough to make sense of those strobing glimpses of the quantum world.

A vast cosmos, a thousand cosmoses written over one another, frothed as quantum states indecisively looked through all possibilities inscrutably, selecting between reality and discarded might-have-beens. In the past, the quantum intellect had viewed the quantum world, and Belisarius saw only its memories. Even those feeble memories had been awe-inspiring, frenetic, second-hand peeks into what really made up the cosmos.

But those memories paled in comparison to this glimpse through whatever separated subjective selfhood from the objective, unconscious world. That tiny fraction of superposition he saw collapsed, but the vastness out there felt incalculable, the superposition seeming constantly to be replenishing itself. He was looking at divinity through a pin hole. All pain and worry receded, collapsing behind him; discarded possibilities. Belisarius stepped forward in wonder, one slow step after another.

"Mister Arjona, you're moving away from the drilling equipment," Saint Matthew said. "I'm no con man, but I don't think this will help our cover."

"Inverse-square law," Belisarius whispered. "I need to observe from closer."

The vast herd of the *Hortus quantus* was only two hundred meters ahead, slowly-moving black shapes trampling fine bushes and grasses of oil-covered ice. But it wasn't what he saw with his eyes that gripped him. Webs of tangled probability, fractally layered, described orbits around the herd. The vanishing glimpses started adding to a nearly hypnotic eleven-dimensional picture. His brain, engineered for curiosity and discovery, looked for patterns and relationships feverishly. Something was building around the *Hortus quantus,* a sense of their connectedness.

And more moving yet, he was glimpsing the quantum world directly, not filtered and abstracted. He saw frames of a jerky, interrupted film of the wonder of the cosmos undecided and debating, waiting for some consciousness to announce that the debate was finished so that reality could come into being. And as soon as he saw it, the debate collapsed.

Belisarius stepped closer. His fever and breathing were rising, starting to fog his faceplate. But that didn't get in the way of him *seeing*. He wasn't looking with his eyes. The fragments of the quantum world he saw before he collapsed the crashing probabilities were electromagnetic. His brain constructed images from the millions of magnetosomes in his muscle cells, but he could see snapshots just as his attention dissolved them.

Trillions of lines of quantum entanglement surrounded the entire *Hortus quantus* herd. Infinitesimally fine lines of entangled probability threaded through the time gates trillions of times and back through individual *Hortus quantus,* making loops with no beginning and no end. The *Hortus quantus* were entangled, through the time gates.

The entanglement of the *Homo quantus* wasn't just through space. The two faces of the time gates reached forward and back in time. Their lowest energy orbit through the hyperspace was eleven years, but there were other pathways through the time gates.

So, the entanglement might link to *Hortus quantus* far into the future and far into the past. The waves of entangled probability interacted with each other, and even with less than a hundredth of the perception, he saw new lines of entanglement diving into the time gates every moment, dragged along like kite strings by frozen grains of pollen. Entanglement was knitting all the eras of the *Hortus quantus* together, perhaps even across periods where flares had melted the entire species, preserving their information through time.

It was so beautiful that tears blurred his vision.

No wonder the Union scientists had had such trouble sending information back in time. The odds of any unpowered object navigating the hostile interior of the time gates were vanishing. But entanglement guided the pollen from the *Hortus quantus* in a process almost like quantum tunneling, past destructive regions and back out. The *Hortus quantus* existed like a giant superposition of uncollapsed quantum states. And the nature of their consciousness was quantum. They existed in a kind of natural quantum fugue, without collapsing quantum fields.

But humans did. The scientists of the Sixth Expeditionary Force had observed the pollen. They had collapsed the superimposed quantum probabilities, interrupting the flow of pollen. Each observation the Union made on the *Hortus quantus* reduced the quantum superposition. Humanity and its subjectivity was caustic and destructive to these sublime aliens. The Union wasn't really to blame. How could they have known?

The *Hortus quantus* were slowly recovering. Pollen was finding its way through the interior of the time gates, on feeble lines of unobserved entanglement. If the Union were not taking the time gates, eventually, the pollen stream would be reestablished. Genetic information from the future would arrive again.

But with the gates gone what would happen to the *Hortus quantus*? Was this really genocide like Belisarius thought?

Quantum entanglement was independent of distance and time. Maybe as long as the time gates existed, the weave of entanglement through them would serve to hold the *Hortus quantus* together through all eras. It was comforting to think that there might be a kind of eternal consciousness in the universe, eschewing limits of time and distance; a consciousness woven into the fabric of space-time. He stepped forward another uncertain step. The strobing feel of the lines of quantum entanglement began to falter.

Destroying, destroying, the quantum intellect insisted in a toneless, terse voice.

Belisarius closed his eyes.

"What is it?" Saint Matthew asked.

The *Hortus quantus* had stopped moving. He knew it even without waiting to measure their slow procession in glacial time. The cataracts and surging ocean of entanglement were gone. All the superimposed quantum probabilities in the icy vacuum under the baleful stare of the red dwarf had evaporated. The weave of countless infinitely thin waves had dispersed.

"What is it, Mister Arjona?"

"I..." Belisarius began.

The ache in his chest overwhelmed him. He tasted his own tears on his lips.

"I just killed them all."

"I detect movement," Saint Matthew said.

"No," Belisarius whispered, dropping to his knees. "No, no, no, no."

Destroyed, his own voice said tonelessly in his head. The quantum intellect, without sense of self or guilt, could make assertions of fact. Destroyed.

"They're alive, Mister Arjona."

Belisarius' stomach lurched. He breathed unevenly.

Hyperventilated. He was too hot. Far far too hot. Or he was just feeling the cold of the world against his ever-fevered skin? Belisarius forced the words out. "Walking is the least important part of them. I collapsed their quantum environment. I destroyed them more thoroughly than flares or the Union ever could have."

"You didn't stop the pollen," Saint Matthew said softly. "It stopped almost a year ago."

"I observed their quantum state," Belisarius said through a painfully tight throat, "and that broke the quantum scaffolding the *Hortus quantus* live on through time."

He heard his own sobbing in his helmet. Distant.

Any human could have observed the *Hortus quantus* and done minor damage, as the Union had done. Any *Homo quantus* could have observed them safely from within the quantum fugue, doing no damage at all. Belisarius was the only being in all the cosmos who could have collapsed the entanglement that knit them into a vast group mind through time.

And he had.

CHAPTER FORTY

"FORTY-FIVE DEGREE clockwise rotations through s-axis and u-axis!" Cassandra said through the neural jack. "Ten seconds forward on twenty gravities, then a complete stop over two-point-four seconds! Then forty-five degree counter-clockwise rotations through the x-axis and the z-axes!"

"Got it," Stills said, with what sounded like effort. Despite what he'd said earlier about the hyperspace giving him some sort of psychedelic trip, he'd completed every maneuver with breath-taking, if foul-mouthed, precision. Any AI, even Saint Matthew, would have faltered before now over piloting compensations that she couldn't have ordered in time. No *Homo quantus* had the reflexes or the cool-headedness under the pressure to carry out her navigational orders.

"I'd rather this be a straight on fight," he said. "If this *pedazo de mierda* had any weapons, I could fillet even a Scarecrow like a fish."

"I know," she said for the third time. She grunted in the shock gel at the violence of his flying, nothing he could hear.

"Why are we doing forty-five degree rotations?" Stills continued. "You had me doin' ninety-degree turns through this maze."

"We took the straightest orbit on the way in," she said. "Forty-five degree rotations through hyper-dimensional space-time will involve fractal dimensionality. I want to confuse the Scarecrow."

"I don't understand one thing you're saying, so you may be onto something."

Stills finished the maneuvers. A kilometer behind them, the *casse à face* missile casing rotated into the dimensionality the racer occupied.

"*Zarba!*" Stills said. "Where to, big brain? I wanna lose this afterbirth."

"One hundred and eighty degrees clockwise across the q-axis. Accelerate at twenty gravities for five seconds. Full stop. Rotate ninety degrees clockwise across the p-axis, then ninety degrees counter-clockwise across q again."

"You know what I want?" Stills said. The force of his rotations compressed her spine in directions evolution had not prepared her for. "I'd like to know if all this driving is doing anything useful, or if you and the Scarecrow are just doing a geometric circle jerk."

"I'm hoping the Scarecrow can't follow the math," she said.

The *casse à face* missile casing rotated behind them, still a kilometer away.

"That artificial foreskin keeps lickin' my ass, big brain!" Stills said. "An' while I appreciate a good rim job, I'd like a little romance first, you get me?"

Cassandra ignored Stills' words. Although Bel's paranoia about his quantum objectivity had led him to say a lot of things she didn't believe, she trusted one of them to be true. Bel said that ultimately, a subjective consciousness could discern the algorithms making up even the most advanced objective system.

As they played cat and mouse, she modeled the movements

and tactics of the Scarecrow. However intelligent, no matter how much human patterning had gone into its programming, the Scarecrow was still just a big computer, hard- and soft-wired, without the creativity of subjectivity. It could follow any maneuver they made, blindly, without understanding the nature of the hyper-volume of space-time around them. She needed to beat it on the field of machine versus subjective person. Bel had talked about it in terms of cards, but she didn't know cards. She knew space-time, though.

"Princess!" Stills said as he completed their maneuvers. "I'm lookin' for a little advanced warning on what you need me to do. Hit me or I take over and drive the bus wherever I want."

"Do the reverse of what you just did," she said. "Do it exactly."

"Will that help?"

"I just need five seconds to think through something."

In normal space-time, she could lead the Scarecrow through a series of obstacles and hope to lose him there. In this hyper-region of space-time, she couldn't do that. But if she was crazy enough, she could make her tracks disappear.

"Vincent!" she said after two point eight three seconds of hard thought, "how brave are you?"

"*Câlice*, sweet-cheeks! Ain't no call to besmirch a dog's honor. I never back down."

CHAPTER FORTY-ONE

IEKANJIKA ENTERED ONE of the tool sheds, opened a rack of drawers and found a few multipurpose data-pads. These were ubiquitous on the base and in the fleet. They interfaced with most equipment, and best of all, all keystrokes were recorded, so MilSec could always recover any misuse and even do a fair bit of intel gathering and forensics if a sleeper agent used one. For this reason, they weren't tightly secured. Iekanjika keyed the access code Lieutenant-General Rudo had given her.

This would be its third use, the second from outside the main headquarters. Iekanjika knew enough about the systems to reroute it through a few nodes within the base. The code got her in, but MilSec would be monitoring any use of the code, laying in wait with a trap.

After her commissioning as a second lieutenant, Iekanjika had been assigned to Auditing Section. She'd been tragically disappointed at the time. She'd worked hard, outperformed every other recruit to try to escape the stigma of her heritage, and she'd been rewarded with an assignment in Internal Affairs, far from combat, command, weaponry or engineering.

Iekanjika hadn't learned until years later that the assignment had been Rudo's idea. She hadn't known then that Rudo herself had also risen from Auditing, hand-picked right out of the academy by a senior auditor. Nobody liked auditors and it wasn't a job from which most officers could hope to jump to combat or command.

But as an auditor, Iekanjika had learned to read human flaws. Everyone had done something wrong; everyone had something to hide. Few indiscretions concerned Internal Affairs, and she didn't personally care if a corporal and a lieutenant fraternized in a storage closet. But she found out she ought not to care *much* if the quartermasters skimmed a percentage off supplies. The black market gave officers and crew a sense of freedom at little cost to the Expeditionary Force, and it generated small sins that could be used in coercion when real investigations were at stake: dereliction of duty, falsified records, cover-ups.

Auditing had also taught her how criminals and traitors circumvented surveillance. Iekanjika had personally rooted out a number of innovative dead drops, extra-network communication patches and exploitable system vulnerabilities, none of which would be invented in this time period for another decade or more. MilSec couldn't be ready for them yet.

This was the first time she'd ever used the tactics she'd caught others using. She patched into Captain Rudo's virtual office to follow the electronic traces of her co-conspirators. It took a bit of doing, but she soon figured out the identities of the other three. MilSec hadn't picked them up yet. She could try to penetrate MilSec systems to see if she could find out where Rudo was being held, but her entry would have to be much more intrusive in those hardened systems. Lieutenant-General Rudo hadn't given her any passwords at that clearance level. But this second look into Rudo's files with the same password could help build a case that someone was trying to frame Rudo.

The next step was to get herself some allies. She rose, put on her helmet and headed to the airlock. On a battle cruiser in a theater of war, the gulf between officer and crew was relatively deep, but bridged with hundreds of discreet relationships. In an espionage and counter-espionage environment, those relationships were a strength and a vulnerability. Deeply embedded spies, whether occupying roles of officer or crew, could use those discreet bridges to conspire, but counter-espionage could create better and larger informant networks.

A stray corporal ought not to frequent the officers' quarters, but one never knew if this might not be an informant, reporting to their handlers. Iekanjika entered the plastic-walled hallway of the officer quarter during the evening watch. The heaters worked hard here, making the air feel thick and humid, smelling faintly of machine lubricant, ammonia and burning. Colonel Okonkwo and Major Zivai ought to be in the suites they shared with their youngest wife, Captain Rudo. Iekanjika knocked on the hard plastic of the door.

"Come in," a woman's voice called and the door lock clicked.

Iekanjika slid it open, came to attention and saluted. A woman in her late thirties sat at a work table set with holographic arrays—long lists of line items too small to read from the door. Colonel Okonkwo squinted at her through the smoke from the cigarette in her lips. She stood slowly and saluted back. It wasn't a textbook salute and the hard muscles of a combat-ready officer didn't seem to be driving the woman's movements. But the pistol holstered at her waist was unclasped. Okonkwo sat back down, slouching slightly, extinguishing her cigarette and motioning her in. Iekanjika stepped through and closed the door uncertainly.

"It's late, isn't it, corporal?" Okonkwo asked.

"Yes, ma'am," Iekanjika said. Now that she was here, all the words that had sounded plausible in her head felt flimsy, insufficient to hold the weight of what she was trying to do.

She'd read Colonel Okonkwo's personnel files as part of her mission prep. Okonkwo was a special kind of officer. Despite only modest accomplishments, she'd been chosen at mid-career to be the middle wife of the previous colonel of auditing. When the old colonel had died early in the Union's time on this ice world, Okonkwo was promoted two grades, from major to colonel and given a commendation. Her personnel record was utterly silent on the reasons behind those honors.

Militaries reserved such explanation-free commendations and promotions for people possessing extraordinary and secret accomplishments. Although she'd never been in command or weapons or tactics, a few weeks after the death of Brigadier Iekanjika, Colonel Okonkwo would be promoted to brigadier and given command of Bioweapons Research, a post she would quietly and efficiently occupy to the end of her days. Okonkwo was a layered officer whom it would be unwise to underestimate. Yet Okonkwo's stare was soft and patient.

"Could I speak privately with you, ma'am?" Iekanjika said.

Okonkwo gestured to a chair and Iekanjika took it and dragged it closer to the colonel.

"What's your name, corporal?" Okonkwo asked.

Iekanjika took a deep breath.

"I'm Colonel Iekanjika," she said.

Okonkwo's hand drifted to the butt of her pistol and her eyes narrowed through the cigarette smoke.

"You look like her," Okonkwo said, "but we both know there's only one Iekanjika in the Force, don't we, corporal?"

The essential madness of this conversation hit her all at once and she wanted to run, retreat back in time five minutes and erase it all.

"I've come back in time thirty-nine years, colonel, through the time gates. I've been sent here on a mission by the Commander of the Sixth Expeditionary Force."

Okonkwo's hand rested lightly on the butt of her pistol. She took the cigarette from her lips. Anyone close enough to the Expeditionary Force Command had seen or read about the early experiments in sending information back through the time gates.

After lasers and other EM signals hadn't survived, they'd tried floating metal blocks back through the gates, with information encoded in the spacing of microscopic perforations. Lieutenant-General Rudo still had such a block in her office. On its exiting from the gate, they found the disfiguring abrasions weren't just on the outside of the block; the *inside* itself was abraded, as if the scouring forces had bypassed the external surface.

The interior of the time gates was destructively abrasive in dimensions of space-time the Union could not access. At times, talk around the tables in the officer's mess might drift to what they would do if they ever encountered evidence of more substantive time travel, but that was always just talk. In a way, she could understand Colonel Okonkwo's feelings.

"Now would be the right time to show some evidence to back up your astounding claim," the colonel said.

"I had proof, but it would be meaningless to you, and maybe even unhelpful," Iekanjika said.

"That's not much to go on. Surely you planned better than that?"

A cautionary note hid beneath Okonkwo's light tone, along with a slight widening of her eyes; the deep fight-or-flight response struggling to overcome the skepticism of the modern mind.

"I gave the proof to Captain Rudo. She issued us with a couple of temporary identities and some work orders. Unfortunately, she's been arrested and can't help us anymore."

Okonkwo stiffened. Anger washed over her face.

"Why?" Okonkwo asked.

Iekanjika could only hang her head as if this were her shame. However, both of them were married to Rudo.

"The unauthorized use of a MilSec pass-code," Iekanjika said.

"Where did she get it?"

"I gave it to her. The Commander of the Sixth Expeditionary Force in the future gave it to me, dug from MilSec auditing records."

"You really are from the future? And you're incompetent enough to get a stupid innocent caught?"

"Rudo isn't so innocent."

"What?"

"MilSec doesn't know, and history doesn't know, but it looks like Rudo is involved in a plot on Brigadier Iekanjika's life."

Okonkwo's expression crumbled. She stood unsteadily, still facing Iekanjika, fingers twitching over the grip of her pistol. She sucked on her cigarette, staring at Iekanjika through coils of smoke.

"Are you serious?" she whispered. "Your mother?"

In Iekanjika's own past, key officers took standard Safe Use of Future Information courses, no different from the yearly review modules on the safe handling of radioactives or biohazards. For thirty-eight of the forty years they'd been on the run, information from the future had simply been another controlled asset, requiring handling protocols as strictly administered as weapon launch permissions or engineering specs. It was reassuring to see that discipline all the way back here.

"So you have no proof of your story?" Okonkwo said.

"My commander didn't prepare me for this. My history doesn't record Rudo being arrested. My presence here may have changed things."

"Being the daughter of Brigadier Iekanjika, you were raised as fleet royalty, no doubt? First choice of all assignments and groomed for command from an early age? What are you, a warship commander or a staff officer?"

Okonkwo's reaction stung her. Iekanjika had not indulged in many fantasies of what it would have been like to have grown up with a mother, much less what it might have been like to be raised by the second-ranking officer in the whole Expeditionary Force. It might have been a childhood of privilege and influence. And she had been groomed, by Rudo herself. But was it for command, or to come back in time, to prevent a grandfather paradox?

"I'm the Chief of Staff," Iekanjika said quietly.

"Put your sidearm on the table, corporal, and I'll take a blood sample."

Iekanjika pulled her pistol out and set it on Okonkwo's desk. The auditor slid it away from her, leaving her hand on the butt of her own sidearm.

"Rudo in the future warned me that a genetic query on the brigadier might be noticed," Iekanjika said.

Okonkwo's eyebrow rose. "Rudo is just starting as an auditor. She doesn't know about every audit I do or what records I have access to as a matter of course." Okonkwo pulled out a small case from a cupboard and slid it across the desk. "Swab," she said.

Iekanjika opened the case, revealing a field DNA sequencer about the size of her fist, surrounded by sample collection tubes. She broke the crinkled wrapper around one rough plastic stick. She scraped it along the inside of her cheek and held it out to the auditor. Okonkwo let the device run while she reconfigured her desktop. Different yellow holograms appeared, diffusing into foggy halos in the lingering cigarette smoke and the clouds of their breaths.

After a moment of waiting, Okonkwo pulled a small metal case from an inner jacket pocket, tapped it, and held out a hand-made cigarette. Iekanjika hadn't had a cigarette in days. Okonkwo lit hers, then resuscitated her half-smoked cigarette from the ashtray. Iekanjika took a cautious drag and coughed.

"What is it?" Iekanjika asked.

"What do you smoke in the future?" Okonkwo asked.

"The Expeditionary Force grows its own tobacco," she said, grimacing. "Better than this, sorry to say."

"We weren't meant to be out this long. Six month mission, sooner if we took too many losses. It's been a year. Hobbyists made these by synthesizing tobacco DNA from records."

Iekanjika took a longer drag, and held it up. "You can look forward to this getting better."

The holograms over Okonkwo's desk started moving, listing, drawing linkage trees. Iekanjika resisted the urge to lean in. Okonkwo's half-smoked cigarette drooped in her lips.

"*Câlice,*" the auditor said.

Iekanjika exhaled a cloud of stinging smoke and waited.

"You *are* her daughter," Okonkwo said wonderingly. "With Colonel Bantya."

"What? Who?" Iekanjika said, sitting forward. "I'm sorry. I never knew my father. I've never even heard that name."

"Colonel Bantya isn't your father. You have two mothers."

Okonkwo faced her. Sympathetically? Kindly? Pityingly?

She had two mothers. Such a thing was certainly possible with artificial help. She hadn't known that the Force had carried that tech, and that, more than anything else, made her realize that she'd never seen a fully kitted Expeditionary Force. Two mothers. And she finally had a name for her second parent. She felt hollow and full at the same time.

"I was told my father was an executed criminal."

"Colonel Bantya was the former Chief of Staff to the late Major-General Nandoro," Okonkwo said, referring to the original commander of the Sixth Expeditionary Force. "She was convicted of treason six months ago, busted to officer cadet and executed."

The world tilted and swam before her eyes. Iekanjika slumped back in her chair. Okonkwo scanned the analysis listlessly for errors, double-checking telomere lengths and time-dependent methylation patterns in the DNA for proof of aging.

"*Câlice*," Okonkwo whispered.

"*Câlice*," Iekanjika repeated.

A silence settled over the women. They smoked their cigarettes, staring into space. Iekanjika's stomach did slow painful turns. Two mothers? She'd known her... other parent had been an executed criminal, but that she'd also been the Chief of Staff... That meant that Iekanjika was the direct professional successor of one of her mothers in some strange echo across the decades.

They shared the ashtray until they finally crushed out the butts.

"Why go to Rudo?" Okonkwo said. "Why not someone more powerful?"

"Rudo is still alive forty years from now," Iekanjika said.

"The little traitor is alive? Isn't there justice?"

For all the auditor knew, Rudo spent the next forty years in the brig. Okonkwo looked like she wanted to ask real questions about her future, but she didn't. Iekanjika would have. She hoped no one from the future ever visited her.

"Why did you come back?" Okonkwo said.

"In the future, we need fresh core samples of the surface of Nyanga."

"The fleet didn't keep the core samples."

"Data yes. Samples no. We have new tools in the future to extract additional information."

"And you couldn't take a new sample forty years in the future," Okonkwo guessed. "Not so soon after the flare."

"Something like that."

"You came through the time gates. So in the future, we learn to travel through the time gates themselves."

"We're drilling right now," Iekanjika said, "using work orders from Captain Rudo. We haven't been bothered yet, but we'll need authorizations to get the core samples through the security perimeter and back to the gates so we can carry them through."

Okonkwo's eyes widened slightly. "Not a small request."

"I have a bigger one. Rudo can't be convicted of anything. That's not part of the future I come from. The only thing I can hope for now is that the charges are dropped or turn out to have been falsified."

"Are they false?" Okonkwo asked.

"Maybe not."

"If I'd known she were this kind of person, I never would have married her."

"I... sympathize," Iekanjika said.

Knowing what she knew now, would she still have joined Rudo's political marriage? It startled her to have to ask herself the question.

"We need to worry about the timeline first," Iekanjika said.

"I don't have any power to get her out of the brig."

"You're a highly-placed auditor. Evidence can be planted. Erased."

Okonkwo straightened. "You can't be serious!"

"Rudo has nothing on her record in the future."

"Maybe she should, but that's for a court martial to decide! There are some things that officers don't do. That *people* don't do."

Iekanjika didn't disagree. Lieutenant Nabwire lived and he

would be tried under the Code of Service Discipline. Just like Okonkwo could be if she falsified evidence. What was Iekanjika becoming? Morals mattered. But did they matter as much as causality?

"I'm sorry to have to say this about your mother, but Brigadier Iekanjika is an awful person, a brutal officer obsessed with advantage and politics. But her murder would be worse."

"We're all political," Iekanjika said without conviction.

"Maybe you are, and maybe most of the officers are," Okonkwo said, "but it doesn't have to be this way, if people believed in some higher goal."

"Do you really believe that?"

"Yes."

"You're a rare officer, then," Iekanjika said.

Okonkwo's hands shook. She flustered another cigarette out of the beaten little metal box and lit it; her cheekbones reflecting the glowing ember. She looked away, tapping desultorily at icons. Thirty and forty years from now, the Expeditionary Force would be different. Officers would be different. The majority of those alive and serving when the Expeditionary Force broke out of the Puppet Axis had mostly grown up in a strengthening belief in the mission and the dream. Where had that dream started? From what she'd seen, it hadn't been born in Rudo's heart. Colonel Okonkwo was part of the Union's political elite, and she carried parts of it. At the very least she believed in morals bigger than herself.

Okonkwo cleared the holographic display.

"Aside from your worry about Rudo and the timeline, you must be relieved your mother will survive," the auditor said.

Iekanjika had not worked Internal Affairs and Auditing as long as Okonkwo, but the best of them were keen investigators. Okonkwo's statement was a probe.

"What Rudo did transcends military law," Iekanjika said. "This mess was caused by my presence. The Expeditionary Force has many trials ahead of it, but after a lot of sacrifice, we end up in a good place. That's in jeopardy. Rudo is important to those events."

"Rudo and some co-conspirators had been planning murder on a fellow officer before you arrived in the past," Okonkwo said. "That's unconscionable."

"She made a mistake," Iekanjika said. "Don't let a focus on that one mistake undo the sacrifices of decades of loyal officers and crew."

Okonkwo considered her for a long time.

"I'll help you, but I won't cover up anything for a criminal. Rudo can hang."

CHAPTER FORTY-TWO

BELISARIUS HATED THAT he existed. His self-loathing radiated fever-hot. If he'd been born human, or mongrel, or even a Puppet, he couldn't have been more miserable, but neither would he have wreaked so much destruction. He gasped, as if the weight of his guilt were a physical, crushing force.

He stepped towards the *Hortus quantus* herd.

They were still. No amount of waiting would make them move before his engineered eyes. He turned away and walked as quickly as he could to the tool sheds without drawing attention. The chest plate translator he'd used to speak with the *Hortus quantus* was still there. He signed it out, and strapped it on as he rushed back.

"What are you doing?" Saint Matthew asked. "You're looking conspicuous!"

"Maybe I'm wrong," he said. The con man in him heard the desperation in his own voice.

He stopped at the edge of the herd, as if it were no longer a living field but a cemetery with a sanctity to be violated. Guiltily, he picked his way through the frozen, alien bushes and grasses, towards the small rise where he'd spoken to the *Hortus quantus* elders. The herd stood eerily still.

He recognized the one who had spoken the most: one point three six meters tall, not including fronds that clawed another seventy-one centimeters into the faint wind, and small horizontal lesions in the black skin of the forward right leg, where scraping had exposed the unliving ice beneath.

Elder, Belisarius wrote. The chest plate hissed as piezoelectric stomata released the scents. For long minutes, the word was alone on the screen.

What had he done to their world? The *Hortus quantus'* present had been twenty-two years wide, perhaps far more; mediated, he now understood, not just by the pollen from the future and sent into the past, but by a tapestry of quantum entanglement. Their present now might just be a moment wide, like his; strobing flashes of a world moving too fast, bereft of context and relationships. It might feel to them like it felt for Belisarius to step down from the quantum fugue or savant to being just baseline human.

Belisarius' chest plate registered incoming scents, but instead of turning into words on the inside of his faceplate, whatever was said made his word *Elder* fade. The elder had sent the negative or opposite of elder, had rewritten the conversation to not have occurred.

Help, Belisarius wrote. The word was semi-faded, half there, half not there, a question.

Another word appeared beside his. Then another.

Dark. Alone.

Tears stung his eyes. His stomach churned. The *Hortus quantus* had been a communal being, knit by quantum entanglement into a greater consciousness, and now he'd broken them into a series of solitudes. Unprotected by each other, cut off from each other, the world now inflicted itself upon them. He wanted desperately to be punished, with any sentence, if this could just be reversed.

Belisarius erased the word *Alone*.

He would help them, somehow.

Tribe, he wrote where *Alone* had been. *Regrow* he wrote next, although it sat ambiguously in the lexicon with other end-of-life meanings that the Union researchers had never puzzled out.

His chest-plate chirped softly as different receptors received new smells. He waited for the message, but *Regrow* began to fade. And new words appeared, orbiting the word *Tribe*.

Wrong-parentage/wrong pollen, which was the *Hortus quantus* conception of falsehood, pictured as inappropriate genes being sent to the past, not truly preparing this generation of *Hortus quantus* for the future.

But the elder continued modifying it before his eyes, using combinations of smells as qualifiers, something the Union had never before observed.

Wrong-parentage/wrong pollen faded, and became *No parentage.*

Belisarius didn't know what to make of this. It was beyond the borrowed lexicon. Pollen and genes and truth and perception were conceptually synonymous to the *Hortus quantus,* encompassing a general meaning of rightness and visionary hope. This was the opposite: a feeling of wrongness and despairing blindness.

Help, Belisarius offered. *Regrow,* he insisted.

But the *Hortus quantus* did not even bother to erase these. What was Belisarius to them but a bright angel of destruction? He'd lobotomized them, extinguished their communal soul. They didn't owe him an answer.

The other elders weren't moving. No melting of joints with anti-freeze proteins. No slow lumbering in the faint gravity. The black photosynthetic skins clung to statues of ice, performing mindless metabolic functions. Their thoughtful essence had bled away, leaving this vast archipelago of lonely islands.

He couldn't do anything. He could make entangled particles, but he couldn't entangle the *Hortus quantus* to each other, much less to the tribes of the future and the past.

He couldn't look at them. Seeing the results of his crime was too much to accept. But turning away couldn't help him. His perfect memory preserved them in his mind's eye, like a slideshow of the moments of horror as he realized what he'd done. His memory was a curse in this moment, as it had been when he'd seen the Garret destroyed. He staggered away from the living graveyard he'd made.

"They were thinking and talking," Saint Matthew said softly in his helmet.

"I destroyed their soul," Belisarius said, his voice cracking.

The saint was silent.

"They were unique," Belisarius said. "Transcendent. They really existed beyond the material. I destroyed the part of them that was eternal."

"Mister Arjona," the AI said, "Belisarius. You couldn't have known. You didn't mean to."

"It's not about knowing. I did it. But so did the *Homo quantus* project. The *Hortus quantus* would still be alive if I'd been less curious, more cautious. The *Homo quantus* would still have a home if I could control my instincts. Our instincts, requisitioned by Banks, were made too strong to be safe. I wasn't strong enough to stop mine. The *Homo quantus* as a species have to share in this guilt, but most of it is mine."

Saint Matthew spoke in his ear, but Belisarius wasn't listening. Oddly, his brain had stopped recording. Parts of him were shutting down. He walked without counting the steps, measuring the distances in millimeters. Then, Saint Matthew appeared in the heads-up display in his helmet.

Belisarius closed his eyes and kept walking, following the mental image of the surface he'd recorded in his mind. He wouldn't listen to the AI. He walked, acidic grief blocking everything out until he was wrenched by someone grabbing the chest straps of his harness.

Iekanjika's fist was bunching his harness and a drawn sidearm was in the other hand.

"What are you doing over here?" she demanded by tight suit-to-suit laser. "I left you with the drill."

His crime was too big to repeat, a lump too wide to fit past his throat.

"What happened?" she demanded.

"There was an accident," Belisarius heard Saint Matthew answer. "He was examining the *Hortus quantus* from within the fugue. Something went wrong with them."

Iekanjika didn't lower the sidearm. She squinted at the field of *Hortus quantus*.

"Did they react to him?" she asked. "Something the Union will notice?"

"I killed them all," Belisarius said.

"They don't look dead to me," Iekanjika said.

"They really were quantum lifeforms," Belisarius said. "They possessed a true Cartesian dualism of mind and body. Their essence wasn't here. It was in the interacting entanglement across space and time. I observed it. I collapsed all of it, all the miracle that couldn't be seen."

Iekanjika holstered the pistol and gripped the sides of his helmet and forced him to look up, her helmet light shining through his faceplate.

"Are you sure?" she asked.

He nodded awkwardly in his helmet, closing his eyes against the light and her look.

"That's... terrible, Arjona," she said, "but this herd of vegetable intelligences wouldn't have survived more than a few months anyway."

"They would have survived. Their entangled consciousness would have survived the flare. It would even have survived the theft of the time gates."

"Let us hope the same can be said of the Union."

"Everything I've touched has come out wrong. They engineered me to be the exemplar of my generation, and instead I became a con man. As a con man I betrayed my clients and used my friends, which endangered my people. My meeting of the *Hortus quantus,* one of the only untarnished moments of my life, was poisoned by my engineered curiosity and obsession."

"You need to bring the core samples back," Saint Matthew said firmly. "You can save the *Homo quantus.* And one day, you might do something for the *Hortus quantus.*"

"Do something?" he demanded. "I collapsed the quantum entanglement! That can't be uncollapsed."

"Arjona," Iekanjika said, "I'm the last person who ought to be comforting you, but put this in perspective. This is not normal causality. We're moving around events in space and time. The vegetable intelligences died long before you knew they existed. If what you say is true, you've come back to a time before they went extinct, and maybe you discovered that you caused their extinction. That doesn't change anything. Whether it was an asteroid, a solar flare or a single *Homo quantus* visitor, in our present, they were dead before we came, and they're dead when we leave."

Belisarius hesitated. She didn't understand. No one but a *Homo quantus* could.

"You can't do anything for the *Hortus quantus* now," Saint Matthew said. "You'll know more in the future. And you'll

have people to help you. You and Miss Mejía have to lead your
people now. This trip into the past has shown you other ways
of being. Hundreds of hyper-intelligent *Homo quantus* working
on reversing this event will be very different from you thinking
about it alone right now. And you'll be bringing home pollen
samples from across thousands of years."

"Dreams don't all come true, Arjona," Iekanjika said. "What
you eventually make might not be what you dreamed, but if you
care, it might be better than nothing."

CHAPTER FORTY-THREE

IEKANJIKA DIDN'T KNOW what to do with Arjona. He shouldn't have been her problem, and yet somehow he was. She knew little about his stability, how quickly he might bounce back from this, whether it might break him, or whether that had already happened. She set him to focusing on the core samples. It was boring work. She didn't know if that would help, but right now she just needed to keep him out of trouble.

"Arjona," she said. "I need your AI."

"What?" Arjona said, touching his wrist self-consciously.

"I need to find some way to get Rudo cleared of these charges. History has to be put back on track."

The augments in Iekanjika's eyes dialed up the light sensitivity. In grain-washed detail, Arjona looked uncertain.

"I can't do it without him," she said.

Arjona unwrapped the service band from his wrist. She gave him hers.

"Stay here," she said. "Keep the drill working. Don't do anything else, no matter how you feel."

Iekanjika left Arjona and marched back to HQ maintenance.

"Where are we going?" the AI asked in her helmet.

"Will he crack?"

"Imagine you just accidentally annihilated a habitat with thousands of innocent people inside."

"If he cracks, can you take over for him?"

"The drilling and getting the right sample? I don't know. If he shuts down, we have to do our best and then get back to Cassandra and the flier. She'll know what to do."

"If we get back," Iekanjika said.

"What do you mean?" the AI said.

"I don't know how to fix the timeline. I don't know where or how to create evidence without getting caught doing it. I contacted someone who could help, but they won't help either."

"What are you hoping I can do?"

"The high-level codes that Lieutenant-General Rudo gave us are limited. I need more. Arjona said that you're one of the most advanced AIs in all of civilization. The security around the Expeditionary Force shouldn't stop you."

"Maybe so for electronic security, but I can't reach stand-alone systems in the high security areas."

They arrived at the maintenance HQ. Iekanjika cycled the airlock.

"You should be able to reach Captain Rudo's virtual office from here," she said.

A collection of worn-looking privates and corporals were cooling their heels inside. Some diced. Some smoked. Three napped. She knew this kind of crowd. As a young teen, she'd been a private-in-training, working hard on getting at least a technical rating, making her way into the officer corps. She'd spent time in crew bays just like this, with moderately or completely unmotivated crews, not working for anything, not themselves, not even the dream. Just people who'd signed up for a three-year hitch in a bad job, suddenly finding themselves trapped in it forever. And they knew people like her too, people on the way up, driving themselves.

Iekanjika found a hard stool by an empty terminal, close enough for the AI to establish a tight data beam. She lit one of the cigarettes Okonkwo had given her. The user access screen brightened, querying for authorization.

"Turn her office upside down, without anyone noticing you," she whispered.

"One of these day," the AI said in her implant, "I'm going to do something good for someone's soul."

Iekanjika puffed quietly, assuming the cautious ease of NCOs and crew anywhere officers might walk in unannounced. While her cigarette burned down, she plotted escape routes in case MilSec somehow traced back the AI's access. After some minutes, the AI started speaking painfully loud in her audio implant. She gritted her teeth and dialed down the volume as she tensed to run.

"What is it?" she whispered. "Were you found out?"

"I don't think so. Captain Rudo has some strange things in her virtual office, things no one has seen yet, not even the MPs."

"What things?"

"I snuck around the hidden directories she used to meet electronically with co-plotters. Hidden under those were whole processors that aren't accounted for anywhere in the network. Not only that, but the power draw and connectivity of the system is very efficient, efficient enough that a routine scan wouldn't notice that other systems were running."

"What does that mean?" Iekanjika asked with a sinking feeling. "Is this an auditor thing?"

"The system architecture isn't typical of Union design. It matches Congregate system architecture. Worse yet, it doesn't look forty years old. I saw designs like this ten years ago in Congregate military systems. There must be another set of time travelers here, from the Congregate."

She took a long draw on her cigarette as the full implications sank in.

"No, there aren't," Iekanjika whispered. Her heart started breaking. "Forty years ago, the Congregate were using their cutting-edge tech to spy on their client nations. That equipment and those designs wouldn't be phased into regular units for twenty or thirty years. Are you sure it's hers?"

"It's bio-coded to her DNA and thought-locked."

"The Union doesn't have thought-lock tech," she said slowly. "Even now."

"What does this mean?"

Iekanjika tapped out her cigarette and crushed it under her thumb until the paper fragmented and the dried leaf powdered. It wasn't hitting her yet. She was reacting in a kind of combat consciousness that filed facts and prioritized information. Emotional reactions were crowded back until the adrenaline dropped. Right now, her adrenaline was surging.

"It means that Rudo is a Congregate sleeper agent," Iekanjika said woodenly.

"The Commander of your Navy? The one who destroyed the *Parizeau* and stole the Freyja Axis from the Congregate?"

Iekanjika slumped. This revelation was enormous, bigger than the impossibility of traveling back in time, bigger than breaking through the Puppet Axis. Forty years ago, the woman who called herself Rudo had been a Congregate sleeper agent.

"Who is Garai Munyaradzi?" the AI asked.

"I don't know," Iekanjika whispered. "Why?"

"His bio-ID is over many of the secret files. I can access the Force' original manifests from here. He appears in the manifests, but his personnel record isn't stored with the other personnel files."

She didn't answer. Pieces were falling into place too quickly. Rudo's original story, that she'd hacked the military academy's systems at Harare was hard to swallow. A civilian shouldn't be able to do that. But Congregate agents within the Union bureaucracy could. Easily. Maybe they'd even helped kill the original Rudo.

It was overwhelming. Forty years from now, Kudzanai Rudo was arguably the most powerful person in the Sub-Saharan Union. She commanded the navy, and *de facto* the armed forces. The officers and crews gave their loyalty to the hero general who'd brought home a fleet lost in history and who had led it in its first battle against the most powerful navy in civilization. And she'd won. She wasn't just the inspiration and the cult worship figure of the fleet; she was a national icon.

And she'd been a Congregate informer and spy.

More dangerously, maybe she still was.

It seemed absurd to think that a sleeper agent could choose to be activated after forty years, but the Union was losing the battle. Without any change in the strategic terrain, they had eighty to a hundred days. It would be very tempting for Rudo to switch sides, or even lead the navy into a disaster. She could defect with the inflaton drive tech straight to the Congregate. As a reward, she would live in a palace in the clouds of Venus. Or if she wanted, the Congregate could give her governorship of the Union, backed by Congregate marines and navies. Even after all this time, Rudo had everything to gain by betraying her people to the Congregate.

Only Iekanjika knew all this, and she was conveniently trapped in the past, with no latitude to do anything. She couldn't shoot Rudo here. In fact, to protect the timeline, she had to do everything in her power to get Rudo cleared of charges and properly launched in her career. To do any less could trigger

a grandfather paradox of catastrophic scale, stretching across
four decades of time and three hundred and eighty light-years
of space.

CHAPTER FORTY-FOUR

THE BROWN DWARF glowered accusing red down as Belisarius watched meter after meter of drill grind its way into concrete-hard ice. The grinding vibrated through his boots. Thousands of years of pollen impregnated the ice, every grain of it disconnected and disentangled from every other, like sand, instead of being part of a great quantum consciousness.

His mind drifted numbly, floating on slow-moving misery of a kind that had never seized him before. He stayed in his baseline mental state. His feelings were too raw to go into savant, where emotions, while distanced, could abrade more harshly. Nor did he want to go into the fugue. After what had happened with the *Hortus quantus*, he couldn't really be sure what that might do to the world around him. His thinking stalled, repeating, unable to break the knot of algorithms, like a computer program.

The unmodified human brain had instincts and protocols for withstanding situations too large or too painful to process. It shut itself down when it needed to, like an injured leg or spine. It dulled the emotions, disassociated and disconnected from horrific experiences. His mind could easily fracture. It came in pieces already. He would welcome the disintegration of self if it took away the anguish in a soul he hadn't known existed before now. But he couldn't. If he gave in, if he let himself crumble, his people would be carried away into captivity or death, just like the *Hortus quantus*.

The slow tide of misery washed around him, resonating with the cadence of the thrumming ground. He didn't notice Iekanjika return until she touched his shoulder. They looked at each other for long seconds. Even in its numb state, his brain assembled patterns, analyzed, honed with a decade of experience as a con man. Something disturbed her, and not the normal anxiety of a military op going south.

"What's wrong?" he asked.

"Nothing," she said, in a fair attempt at a lie. Her face, pixilated by his ocular augments dialing up their sensitivity, hardened and softened by turns. "We're quits, Arjona."

"What?"

"You owe me nothing anymore. Maybe you wanted the time gates for yourself. Maybe you wanted to keep them out of the hands of the Congregate when we inevitably lose our war with them. Whatever our differences before, keep them. Take them as far away from humanity as you can and keep on running."

A tiny sense of relief blossomed in his chest, bobbing on the guilt; the edge of loneliness a little less hard.

"Is the war going to get worse?" he asked.

"War becomes a wild animal as soon as it's born. You can guide it, fence it, tame it, but it has no master until it's done."

"It sounds like mathematical chaos."

"Or quantum reality."

"Thank you."

"We're awake past our shift," she said. "You need rack time, but I don't know if I can trust you inside by yourself."

"I won't get in trouble."

"When I left you before, you wandered out to see the vegetable intelligences."

"No danger of a repeat," he said bitterly.

She gave him back the service band containing Saint Matthew.

"You can get a half shift of sleep. Shower. Eat up. Get back here. Don't talk to anyone."

Her orders were brisk and persuasive. He started obeying before he realized it. The world was foggy, but she spoke with stony certainty. Belisarius trudged back along the black-slicked ice towards Barracks D. But no matter his condition or exhaustion, he couldn't turn off his brain.

It switched to quantum logical pathways, superimposing possibilities in his thinking, blurring and broadening his sense of the present, to better consider the question of whether the *Hortus quantus* might ever live again. The *Hortus quantus* had been created by miraculous accident, much like the time gates. Might the nature of the universe allow an observation to be unmade? Or could miracles be reproduced?

"Do you want to talk, Mister Arjona?" Saint Matthew said, breaking into his thoughts.

"I don't know," Belisarius said, slowing his progress. "I wonder if you could be right, that there might be some way to bring the *Hortus quantus* back."

"Do you have any ideas?"

"I may need a miracle."

"Are you and I talking about God?"

"Collapsing a superposition of quantum states is irreversible, at least to the observer who collapsed them. You can't open the box on Schrödinger's Cat, see the cat dead, and then go back to the superposition of quantum states that existed earlier. Observations can't be unmade."

"And the *Hortus quantus* can't exist without the unobserved superposition of quantum states."

"Yes."

"You can't break physical laws, Mister Arjona."

"Everything outside of what we're capable of understanding is where a god could exist," Belisarius said.

"The Final Observer philosophy offered by some *Homo quantus*?" the AI asked.

"I observed the quantum entangled nature of the *Hortus quantus*, and forced the system to choose one state. But from Cassandra's point of view, nothing has been chosen. I'm part of the quantum system that is the *Hortus quantus* and I've collapsed the probabilities. I'm the cat in the unopened box."

"Miss Mejía can't undo this observation," Saint Matthew said.

"The principle of expanding concentric circles of consciousness collapsing ever more complex quantum phenomena and determining reality may still stand. The universe may be a patchwork of determined and undetermined reality. The only truly real things might be those tiny patches illuminated by the observation of a subjective consciousness. But that's the problem with the quantum anti-realist philosophy; there's nothing to connect those patches causally, or even to make the far past and far future of the universe real. A Final Observer, some consciousness so vast that it could collapse all the superimposed possibilities of the cosmos, might really be needed to make the universe itself real."

"Do you believe in the *Homo quantus* god?" Saint Matthew said quietly.

Saint Matthew's question was profoundly simple, yet as insightfully rigorous as any posed by the most studied Puppet theologian. The answer could transform a life, a philosophy, all belief, and yet was also binary and mutually exclusive in the most classic quantum sense. The question was all the more profound when directed at a *Homo quantus*. Belisarius' brain partitioned conflicting logical positions and probabilities to sustain quantum logic. One part of his brain could be the hard-nosed realist who thought that a vast universe-creating consciousness was too much to accept. Another could embrace the hope of a Final Observer who might bring back the innocent beauty and peace of the *Hortus quantus*. Both beliefs existing at once had the same implications as a cat both dead and alive.

"Only a god could fix what I've done."

CHAPTER FORTY-FIVE

Iekanjika verified the programming in the drilling equipment. It ran smoothly. The loader of the truck contained ten thousand years of clean, stacked sample. Within six hours, their core would extend back fifty thousand years. In the distance, the time gates loomed dimly under rings of lights.

She'd done the right thing, if bitterly. The time gates were too powerful. She didn't trust much, but compared to the Union and the Congregate, the *Homo quantus* might be the least destructive owners for the gates.

Her service band chirped. A message from Colonel Okonkwo waited: a summons. A chill tickled up her spine, and wondering dread about who she could and couldn't trust. But twenty minutes later, she was knocking at the door to Colonel Okonkwo's suite. A tall major opened the door and Iekanjika saluted. He eyed her carefully, looked back at Colonel Okonkwo who was occupied at her desk, and then stepped out of the suite. Iekanjika stepped in. He closed the door and she was alone with the colonel.

"Major Tinashe Zivai, I presume?" Iekanjika asked. The middle husband to Okonkwo and Rudo.

"I told him he couldn't stay," Okonkwo said without looking up. "He didn't like it, but I'm the colonel."

Iekanjika sat in an empty chair without moving it closer. Okonkwo shut off her display and turned.

"I have news for you. My sources informed me that MilSec cracked Rudo's office. They found the information on the plot. Her three co-conspirators have also been arrested," Okonkwo said. "I have no indication that your temporary identities have been compromised yet, but you never know what Rudo might reveal under interrogation."

Iekanjika wasn't sure how to feel. In a sense, justice was working. But the timeline was ruined. And Okonkwo hadn't said anything about Rudo being a Congregate sleeper agent. She didn't know. They didn't know.

"The plot on Brigadier Iekanjika has been foiled," Okonkwo continued, "and I should be the first to say happy birthday, colonel."

"What?" she asked in a bit of a daze.

"Brigadier Iekanjika just had her baby. She named her Ayen."

"I'm Ayen," she said numbly.

"I would like to say that everything has been fixed, but things are much worse. The plot on Brigadier Iekanjika and the apparent plot by Lieutenant Nabwire to frame her has inflamed tensions in the Force. MilSec has been here twice in the last four hours. I'm being summoned to a hearing at three this afternoon. And I've had some discreet inquiries from warship commanders. People are picking sides. The Force is eating itself from the inside."

"Why do you tell me this?"

"I can't ask you what the future is supposed to look like," Okonkwo said. "But as things stand now, Rudo will likely rot in prison or be executed. I don't know how to get her out and, frankly, timeline or not, I know I don't want to."

"I know what you mean."

"No one is essential to history. The universe can't be so inconsistent that it would allow a time travel device to exist and yet be vulnerable when causality twists and eddies."

"It could be."

"Have you tested that in the future?"

She shook her head. "We didn't dare."

"I believe that history must be fluid, otherwise creatures like the vegetable intelligences couldn't exist."

"But you have no proof either."

"The people filling history might be as replaceable as officers in a navy. Some of the details might change, but the timeline will survive."

She didn't know what to think. Okonkwo might be right. What needed to be done would be done by someone. And to save Rudo would put the Expeditionary Force in her hands for decades, making her grip on the future unbreakable.

Yet the Rudo timeline had produced Ayen Iekanjika from its web of causality. Her own existence was in play, along with all the Union successes of the future. If she didn't fix the timeline, she saw no way to fix causality. All of it would change to avoid a multi-layered grandfather paradox with no guarantee that it could actually be fixed.

If Rudo was tried and executed in the coming weeks, no one would have sent Iekanjika back in time to tell the Force that when the time came, they should seek out Arjona. But if she didn't come back in time, Rudo would not have used the command code from her office, thereby drawing the attention of MilSec. The last forty years of history might turn into a Möbius strip of unstable causality constantly rewriting itself.

No one knew what a grandfather paradox would really do physically. If information theory was the best model, history was nothing more than all the information contained in all the particles involved in that history. Rewriting history meant erasing the information in those particles and overwriting them with new information. But a grandfather paradox was not a single rewriting event. The rewriting cycled, a toggling between the two histories forever.

But erasing and rewriting was computation, and computation took energy. They'd never been irresponsible enough to try it, but they theorized that the repeated rewrites might suck energy out of a system until it created a four-dimensional region of space-time colder than a black hole. And this was no simple desktop experiment of a grandfather paradox. The four-dimensional region influenced by Rudo and Iekanjika would be forty years in duration and almost four hundred light-years across; a swath of destruction too vast for the human mind even to picture.

"Who is Munyaradzi?" she asked.

Okonkwo couldn't mask her surprise.

"I stumbled across suspicious files with his name in them," she added, "but his personnel files have been pulled."

"It's hard to keep in mind that you're from the future," Okonkwo said wonderingly. "You don't know Bantya. You don't know Munyaradzi."

"But you do."

"Colonel Garai Munyaradzi was my senior husband, the man in charge of Internal Affairs before me. But he was a Congregate sleeper agent, the highest ranking one in the Force and a very successful one. He was found out. He was executed."

A slow breath leaked from Iekanjika, one of anger and sympathy. "I'm sorry," she said finally.

"I'm not. They saved me the trouble of confronting him myself. You can't imagine what it's like to live with the knowledge that your spouse is a traitor to you and your people, that the affection or love you thought you felt was all wasted."

Surprisingly, Okonkwo wiped the back of her hand across an eye.

"You didn't deserve that," Iekanjika said.

"I don't believe in *deserve* anymore."

Iekanjika stared at her hands, thinking of all those who didn't deserve. Her. The vegetable intelligences. All the crew and officers who had worked so hard their whole lives to bring the Expeditionary Force home for their war of independence. Okonkwo.

"Have you found a way for me to get the core samples near the time gates without being observed?" she asked. "Maybe in eight hours?"

"Some people aren't going to be happy, but I can authorize a relatively large spot inspection of the security systems in the MP tower. I can time it for you."

"Thank you," she said, synchronizing the time on her service band to Okonkwo's.

Iekanjika stood, but didn't move to the door. Okonkwo looked up at her.

"You don't know me in the future, do you?" Okonkwo said.

Iekanjika shook her head. Okonkwo looked wistful for a moment.

"I'm glad to have met you now then, Ayen."

CHAPTER FORTY-SIX

To HIS SURPRISE and bafflement, he'd passed all the tests; but whatever this new thing was, built on the scaffold of 1D446, he was not yet a Scarecrow. He'd been equipped with processors, armament, armor, sensing equipment and vast arrays of intelligence reports. But he was just a machine, a tool without function. He'd not been invested with the authorities that would make him useful to the Congregate, and would make him real. He was in between. Interstitial. Not alive, nor useful, but not dead, or lacking value.

The old, second-generation Scarecrow summoned him back to the interrogation chamber, a diamond bulb distending off the upper curve of a big defense facility floating in the hot murk forty-two kilometers above the surface of Venus. Beyond the window, misty in the distance, were sentry drones, spheres of sensors and weapons beneath glassy surfaces slick with condensing sulfuric acid. He was home.

Two armed human operatives stood behind the second-generation Scarecrow, over a bound human. Pictures shuttered past in his processing, seeking matches. The two armed human operatives were members of a Scarecrow support team, seen many times, identified almost instantly. The last human, face

327

bloodied, hair hanging across forehead and eyes, was slower to match: almost a second.

"Adéodat," he said, stopping, looking in confusion at the second-generation Scarecrow.

"Kill this one."

"What did he do?"

"Nothing. No ties to your past should survive the vitrification process."

"He doesn't need to die. He's a citizen of the Congregate."

The second-generation Scarecrow stamped closer on piezoelectric muscles. Camera eyes swiveled, reading him, accompanying an invasive digital search of his processors and memories, an examination of his thoughts and motivations. He had nothing to hide.

"One life is a small price to pay for a new Scarecrow," the second-generation Scarecrow said. "You have decades of service before you, protecting the Congregate from enemies. If you pass this test."

"What are you testing?"

"Loyalty," came the cold digital reply, not even by sound, but inserted directly into his thoughts. "Many are relentless, but not all are loyal."

Why me? Why did you pick me? Relentless? He didn't know. Loyal? Surely others were more loyal. But he didn't say these things. He wouldn't. But it didn't matter. The older Scarecrow was reading every one of his thoughts, every output and algorithm within his processors. Why wasn't the older Scarecrow failing him? His hesitation was obvious; he couldn't kill his own brother. Yet he was trapped in this digital body and mind, incapable of expressing emotion.

"The vitrification process specifically deletes markers and identities," the second-generation Scarecrow said. "We are too powerful to possess any side loyalties. The Congregate is too important for one life to endanger it."

"I don't want to," he said. "Adéodat deserves to live. He's who I've been protecting. We've all been protecting him. I didn't want to be a Scarecrow."

"The Congregate is ringed on all sides by enemies," the second-generation Scarecrow said. "You have been summoned to serve."

Why? Why did he need to become a Scarecrow?

Adéodat looked up in fear, alone, all of the electronic conversation silent to him.

There could only be one reason he'd been summoned to serve as a Scarecrow. Not because he'd been gravely injured. Not because his analysis was irreplaceable. Not because he'd outcompeted all his nameless colleagues who'd wanted to be Scarecrows. It could only be because his mind was attuned to loyalty, above all other factors, above humanity and pity. How many Scarecrows were grown and yet never passed this point? Was he one of them or was he like the older Scarecrow? The Congregate was greater than any single person and any single life, and worth preserving at all costs.

Adéodat looked in wordless terror from one Scarecrow to the other, believing himself to be trapped in some mistake, without a friend in the world. The thing grown on the template of his brother stepped closer and lifted a mechanical hand of wire and servo-motors and piezo-electrics.

A bullet fired from the hand into Adéodat's heart.

The younger brother bled to death, gasping in disbelief.

CHAPTER FORTY-SEVEN

BELISARIUS SLEPT POORLY amid the snoring, snuffling, sleep-grumbling of a barracks full of strangers and their cold, humid smells. He felt no less a monster, but he was strangely more open to taking some comfort in this uncomfortable press of humanity. They all sheltered temporarily on this icy world, vulnerable to the elements. The very existence of humanity in this place was a hopeful statement in itself. That thought alone let him sleep in some kind of internal cease-fire with himself.

His mathematical dreams calculated death rates among the *Hortus quantus,* extinction curves, wobbling gene frequencies as the population dropped precipitously and was finally wiped out. His dreaming mind calculated the constellation of interacting probabilities required to make the quantum minds of the *Hortus quantus,* and the time required before those factors would be logically expected to appear. Then, Iekanjika was shaking him awake. It was still the middle of the sleep shift. He'd slept a broken total of seventy-one minutes.

"Suit up," she whispered.

He groaned, dressed and met her in the commissary where she was pulling out more rations on their ration cards. They didn't speak until they could laser in the airlock with their helmets on.

"Give me your AI," she said. "Go to the drill site. In five hours, take the samples and walk them out to the time gates and go through."

"What about you?" Arjona said as he handed over Saint Matthew in his service band.

"I'll be with you," she said as the airlock opened to the near-vacuum. "In case I'm not, go. If you have to leave me here, make sure you pay my people for what you've taken. Your people are not the only ones on the verge of destruction."

"I will," he said. "What about Saint Matthew?"

"The preservation of the timeline has become far more dangerous. I need help."

"What are you going to do?"

"Get your samples through," she said. "Find our Axes. And don't double-cross us on this one."

Then she walked away from him, and he stood alone on the slick black of the surface he'd rendered lonely.

CHAPTER FORTY-EIGHT

"WHAT ARE WE doing?" the AI said into the implant in her ear. "I was safer with Mister Arjona, wasn't I?"

"History as I know it," she said as she stalked towards the maintenance HQ, "has been changed by our arrival. Rudo was never meant to be arrested. And the plot on Brigadier Iekanjika's life has been foiled. Those major events will undo my history and the history of the Union."

"We don't know what will happen to the future now that it's changed," the AI said. "Rudo is a Congregate sleeper agent. And your mother will live. You'll be raised by her."

"You're not going to argue to save the timeline? What of your future?"

"What is my future? I'm an Apostle. Who knows if this isn't God's way to lead me to some revelation. I don't fear the future. His ends will have out."

"You're mad, AI."

"We might all be mad, waiting on a moment of spiritual epiphany."

"We all have to struggle with the ambiguities life gives us," she said. They'd reached the airlock to the Maintenance HQ. "Now I need to plant evidence that will show Rudo is innocent."

"She's not innocent," the AI said as the airlock cycled.

"No. No one is."

"Aren't you?"

"This is my deal with the devil."

They emerged into the large storage area, the server banks and smoking crew.

"What evidence are you planning to plant?" the AI said into her implant.

She took a seat far in the back by shaking a private awake. "Sleep somewhere else," she said. The private walked away sullenly. She sat and glared down the curious looks sent her way.

"Can you make Munyaradzi's secret files look like Rudo has never accessed them?" she asked the AI quietly. "Better yet, could you make the files look like they've been used by someone else to frame Rudo?"

"Probably, but that won't undo what the military police have already found."

"We need to make it look like a good attempt to frame Rudo by someone who is continuing Munyaradzi's work, someone who's attempting to assassinate Brigadier Iekanjika."

"That would also free her three co-conspirators," the AI said. "Is that what happened in the real history? You would be releasing at least one Congregate sleeper agent and some of her helpers into the Expeditionary Force. With complete cover."

"One thing at a time. Do you need me to decide how to make it look like a frame-up on Rudo?"

"Sadly, I've spent so much time with Mister Arjona that I probably know the way," the AI said. Iekanjika sat back and scanned the maintenance HQ. Only the private she'd manhandled was still staring at her. She held his gaze until he looked away. The rest minded their own business.

She pulled a last cigarette from a hard pocket and lit it.

Happy birthday. February 34th. The day everything changes. New context. New reality. New her.

She'd come on this mission as Colonel Iekanjika with orders; a mission and scope to adapt. These were the walls and roof of the soldier's life. But she'd walked so far beyond that structure that she no longer had the authority for any action. She'd gone from bringing a specialist on a sample reconnaissance to trying to protect the history of the Expeditionary Force four decades in the depths of space.

In what way could she legitimately consider herself to be Colonel Iekanjika on a military mission? She had no superiors, no backup, no legal or military authority. Hiding her discoveries from the responsible authorities, even here, was a crime. The Government of the Sub-Saharan Union hadn't even authorized this mission because Rudo didn't trust them. But who was it who withheld her trust in the government? Rudo the patriot or Rudo the sleeper agent?

She exhaled a cloud of smoke, the acrid bite of the synthetic tobacco stinging her throat. Everything was smoke. Ayen Iekanjika didn't trust Kudzanai Rudo—captain or lieutenant-general. Maybe the theorists were wrong and a grandfather paradox would sort itself out in some other way. Maybe all she needed to do was to leave things and get the hell out with the samples. Rudo the Congregate sleeper agent would face a court martial. That was the purest thing to do, an isolated moral choice divorced of cost.

And she might return to a different world, a different set of memories filling the last thirty-nine years. The Ayen Iekanjika she was now would be smoke, drifting away on the faintest of drafts, lost in time like pollen. Some other Ayen would exist; perhaps a colonel still, perhaps a warship commander, or perhaps a general officer already, propelled by her mother's influence.

But the Expeditionary Force wouldn't be on the other side of the Puppet Axis. Maybe the Expeditionary Force wouldn't have even survived that long. Even in a rewritten future Major-General Takatafare and Brigadier Iekanjika still didn't trust each other and in another history might have destroyed each other, or fractured the Force.

Where did trust come from? Rudo trusted Ayen to preserve the timeline. Ayen trusted Rudo for the next thirty-nine years because she didn't know all the secrets buried in the past. People were frozen into decades-long actions and pathways. Knowledge of the future ensnared them in something very much like fate. She wiped at the dampness in her eyes.

"I've modified Munyaradzi's files and work," the AI said. "It will now look like the secret communications in Rudo's virtual office were an effort to frame her and three others."

"I'll need this to be discovered in about ten to twelve hours."

"I can modify the power usage profiles of the system, as if it's glitching. The sub-AIs in military security will detect the anomaly quickly."

"Thank you."

"So we've saved Rudo and we can go?" the AI asked.

"That was just the start."

She struggled to prevent her voice cracking. That she was an officer no longer mattered. No officer was trained for this. No one was really responsible for history.

"I need you to get me into the surface headquarters."

"I can't do that!" the AI said in her implant. "That's the most secure part of the base. Military Security, the MPs and the brig are all there. We don't have the codes. The security forces aren't relying on just pass-codes and electronic authorizations. They'll carry out visual inspections and check biodata."

"This isn't your first time in this situation, is it?" she said. "You accompanied Arjona onto the *Mutapa* when he stole the time gates. He didn't overcome the security on the flagship. You did, didn't you?"

The AI offered a pause all the more significant because he thought so much faster than she did.

"I came to help you with Rudo, but getting into the headquarters is a different story, a different level of danger," he said.

"Rudo isn't safe, not yet, nor is the timeline. And I have no intention of leaving until the future of the Expeditionary Force is assured. If that means missing my departure time with Arjona, so be it. I'm a soldier."

"I'm not!"

"Your god is guiding you," she said quietly. "If you're not certain he intends you to be captured by the Expeditionary Force decades before you were invented, then you'd best help me. I need you to use whatever methods you used on the *Mutapa* to get me into the surface headquarters."

The AI made no answer. She waited.

Who was she? Was she Colonel Iekanjika, protégé of Lieutenant-General Rudo? Was she Ayen, the daughter of a politicking Brigadier? Or was she neither? Ayen alone had no identity, no purpose. If she stood in neither shadow, she was utterly, terrifyingly free, with only the consequences of her choices to deal with. Millions of lives depended on what she chose next.

"Alright," the AI said. "No wonder He never reveals his plan to me. I'm unworthy of grace."

"We're all unworthy of grace," she said, rising.

CHAPTER FORTY-NINE

THE STREAM OF anti-matter cut too damn close to the racer; some of the particles, probably anti-protons, sizzled against the hull. Goddamn Princess Cassandra had a plan. She had a plan, and Stills wished she'd stop shit-grinning and come out with it. He was pulling hard enough on the stomach-twisting turns and bone-bending accelerations that they even tickled his cock. He hoped he hadn't knocked the princess out.

"Vincent," she finally said. "I haven't had you rotate around the r-axis or the u-axis."

"You collecting the alphabet, darlin'?" Stills said. "Never mind. I don't give a shit. Just tell me your plan."

"After the next maneuver, come to a stop, rotate one hundred and eighty degrees around the r-axis and then one hundred and eighty degrees around the u-axis."

"The Scarecrow has followed us through every rotation and acceleration so far," Stills said, gunning the racer through her contortions. "I bet he's close to as smart as your batshit crazy AI."

"He won't want to follow us on this one, or even understand where we went."

Stills grunted, pushing harder on the next set of maneuvers—twenty gravities of acceleration.

"You still conscious?" he said. Some people couldn't take the acceleration, even in shock gel.

"I'm... okay," she finally answered. "I can do it."

"You know Arjona talks this cocky." He decelerated off their last maneuver so fast that the racer creaked. Full stop.

"I'm not cocky," she said. "I'm scared out of my mind."

"Not what I'm lookin' to hear! *Puta!*"

They rotated into a full view of the Scarecrow missile, bow to bow with only half a click of space between them. Point blank and nothing to shoot but his cock. A stream of particles glanced off *The Calculated Risk*'s cockpit from high behind them.

"What the fuck?" Stills demanded, looking through his sensors and even the rearward cameras. Nothing behind them.

The particles bouncing off their cockpit ricocheted straight at the *casse à face* missile, shooting into a cannon barrel poking out the front, clean as a whistle, not a single particle scattering over the half kilometer. Then, the Scarecrow's missile rotated away and vanished.

"What the fuck?" Stills yelled. "Where did he go? Why did he go? What the fuck was that shit shooting into his guns? What did you do?"

He hadn't asked so many questions at once since he'd woken up deep in the ocean under Claudius, hammered out of his skull, floating in a tangle of sleeping mongrels, two pressure-crushed Congregate officers, a half-eaten Claudian tuna and a weird ache in his ass. He hoped this was gonna be easier to explain.

"We rotated through two dimensions I'd been avoiding," Cassandra said a little dreamily. "We reversed our parity and time."

"What did I reverse?"

"Vincent," she said, like he ought to have known this, "the conservation laws of the universe apply everywhere, whether in eleven dimensions or just the four we were born in. Time, charge and parity are three qualities conserved together. We rotated across a temporal axis to reverse our arrow of time, and we rotated across a spacial axis to change left to right. Because of conservation laws, doing those two things automatically also reversed the charge on every particle in us and the racer, in the Scarecrow's point of view."

Stills' brain worked overtime trying to keep up with her craziness. She was talking one hundred percent cock-eyed nonsense. But he couldn't explain what had happened with the Scarecrow, with or without her explanation.

"Okay, big brain, I give up. I don't understand a single piece of shit comin' out of your mouth."

"We're anti-matter now, Vincent," she said, "mirror images of ourselves, moving backwards in time."

For long seconds, Stills tried to process that.

Mirror image. Charge reversed. Moving backwards in time.

"*Osti de tabarnak de câlice!*" he said.

"Are you okay, Vincent?"

Was she on drugs? Her voice was completely normal, like she was asking about altitude or flight speed. In what fucking reality was any of this okay? He felt a shiver of fear, the first he'd felt in a long time. But he tamped it down. He wasn't going to be weirded out by anything a *Homo quantus* girl could do. If she could go there, so could he.

"I'm... anti-Stills?" he asked slowly.

"Yes," she said. She paused. On the camera image, she was smiling. "Maybe this means you'll be more polite?"

"Fuuuuuuuck," he said slowly. "We really must be anti-us if you just cracked a joke."

He took it slow; trying to see if slow would let the whole of it sink into his skull. He was made of anti-matter. He was literally Anti-Stills. She was Anti-Cassandra. They were in their Antiship. And they were living backwards in time.

Nope.

Nope. Nope. Nope.

Puta.

Puta. Puta. Puta.

These shit-eating, pretentious, wordy, contemplatives were... What the fuck were the *Homo quantus?*

He increased the oxygen mix in his tank and dropped the temperature. Deep, cool breaths washed over his gills. Icy, rinsing, refreshing. And it all felt normal. And it couldn't be that she was shitting him. He'd seen the Scarecrow living in reverse. Deep breaths.

"So if we touch shit," he finally said, "we annihilate ourselves?"

"We won't notice anything different in ourselves, but the rest of the universe will look pretty different."

"I'm left-handed Stills," he said, swishing his thick, blubber-covered fingers through the water. They didn't feel different.

"Left everything," she said, "down to the chirality of every amino acid and nucleotide in your body."

"And when the Scarecrow shot anti-matter at us..." Stills said hesitantly.

"It didn't do anything," she said, like a know-it-all. "We're made of anti-matter, so his anti-matter just bounced off the hull like dust. And we're time-reversed. To us, it looked like a video running backwards."

"What?"

Princess two-legs started explaining again, repeating the exact words, but slower, like he was an idiot. Maybe he was, but *calvaire!*

"*Coño!* You fucking *Homo quantus* are dangerous! You can turn people into anti-matter!"

"We've never done it before," she said. "I just thought of it now."

Just fuckin' thought of it now?

"Why the fuck haven't you conquered civilization yet?" he demanded.

"Why would we do that?"

"Of course," Stills said disbelievingly. "*Zarba*. Of course why would you do that? I just... I don't..."

"Are you okay, Vincent?"

Stills didn't often feel out of his depth, so to speak. He was smart. Smarter than most. And he'd occasionally served smart officers. But sometimes it was best just to keep his head down and do the grunt work and try not to absorb the big picture. This might be one of those times. He didn't want to go nuts. But... *fuck!*

"Alright," he said finally. "Never mind. I respectfully propose to your air-sucking highness that we go after that ass-licking Scarecrow."

"We can't," she said. "We're in our own past right now. What we just did is experimental enough. I don't want to risk a real causal violation. Besides, we have no weapons."

"You can stay on your mountain top thinkin' your big thoughts, princess," he said, "but get me into the Scarecrow's future, then leave the flying, fighting and fucking to me."

"Matter and anti-matter larger than the size of particles shouldn't be interacting, Vincent. You'll see the future. Effect before cause. You'll make mistakes."

"Look brains, as long as fuck-face is in here with us, we're in danger, right? You, me, Prancy-Pants, Iekanjika and by fuckin' consequence all your contemplative circle-jerk friends. Military rules are pretty simple. Fuck up the enemy before they fuck you up."

"We're not even moving in the same direction of time, Vincent."

"So he'll never even see us comin'."

"He will. He'll see our future and we'll see his."

"Yeah, but we're the only ones that'll know what the fuck is going on."

She finally agreed and gave him a set of navigational instructions. Stills hoped he was right. He was within a half-fuck of not understanding anything. But they couldn't leave the Scarecrow armed in here. That goddamned electronic afterbirth could happen onto them by accident, or onto their past or future selves, as welcome as a finger up their asses. Even worse, what if the Scarecrow exited the time gates in the past or future, maybe fucking them up in time? Too many possible surprises. The best way to avoid surprises was to shoot them in the head.

Cassandra's navigational instructions were easy compared to what he'd been pulling before. Following a dimension was easier than rotating across it, even a time dimension. He didn't know where and when to find the Scarecrow, but she did.

"The event of the Scarecrow watching us disappear was defined in time and space even if it was in a twenty-two dimensional space-time hypervolume," she said, as if that was useful information to him. He let it go. If he answered, she might want to expand on her point.

"How much time do you need to do your thing?" she asked.

"Give me a ten second window and I'll shove his head up his ass."

"What are you going to do?"

"Follow the Way of the Mongrel, baby. *Bite every hand. Piss on every leg.*"

She didn't ask again, but navigated them along one of the time dimensions of the hyper-volume, carrying them into the local future, before calling for a stop.

"We're up-future of the Scarecrow's last known position and time," she said. "We're off by one spacial dimension. When you rotate ninety degrees across the x-axis, you'll be about three hundred meters in front of the Scarecrow, moving backwards in time relative to him. At ten seconds, you have to rotate back across the x-axis, otherwise we'll see ourselves in our past, and we already know we don't see that."

"Don't worry your head a thing, sweet-cheeks," Stills said. "I can't understand shit of what you're saying except that I got to insert, shoot my load, and bail in ten seconds. Mongrels call that mission profile a teenage fuck, so let's pop the Scarecrow's cherry."

Stills listened to the electrical waves in his chamber. The telltales were all green except for some minor damage on the rear dorsal plating. Congregate ships carrying anti-matter always made him twitchy, not 'cause he was scared they'd hit him. Anything could hit him. Orbital debris in the wrong spot could do as much damage. He worried more about whether the *comemierdas* carrying the AM knew what they were doing. If they blew themselves up by mishandling the AM, they were as likely to take out the surrounding battle group.

And now he was anti-matter.

Time to feed someone a shit sandwich.

Cassandra was worried. Fine. He didn't need her to have nards for this. He just needed his window. She was scary though. She'd turned him into anti-matter. *Puta!* Would'a been nice to brag about this. But even if he survived this shit-show, who the hell would believe him?

"Hang on tight, princess," he said.

He twisted his controls, rotating the racer ninety degrees through the dimension Cassandra called the x-axis. He flinched, blinded by the spray of photons and hot plasma outside the racer. Then, the cloud and light retreated, shrinking, collapsing in on a chaos of fire around a spinning, exploding *casse à face* missile.

Fuck, it didn't get trippier than this.

Welcome to Wonderland.

Snort deep, grab your cock and do what you gotta do.

Two seconds done.

Stills' chamber was connected to the racer's life support. Prior to filtration and recuperation, biological waste was stored in a tank. Before making the last rotation, Stills had loaded his waste into a service port and pressurized it. Now, he opened the port. Pressurized anti-piss leapt into the near-vacuum of the hyperspace outside the racer.

The spray froze into an expanding torrent of anti-piss, with the momentum it had when it emerged from the vent. The snow raced towards the conflagration shrinking around the Scarecrow's spinning, approaching ship.

Five seconds done.

Just as the fiery blast shrank to nothing around the Scarecrow's ship, the spray of anti-piss collided with it. Then the Scarecrow's ship was pristine and whole and still in one spot.

Seven seconds done.

Alarms went off as a scatter of anti-particles bounced off the racer and shot back into the barrel of the Scarecrow's anti-matter cannon.

Nine seconds.

Rotate. The pristine missile ship shrank and vanished.

For a moment, the incredible weirdness of his battle flummoxed him.

"I... uh, got him, right?" he asked.

"Seeing effect before cause is confusing," Cassandra said,

"but you hit his ship with grams of anti-matter. If you want to see it in a way you'd understand, and the way the Scarecrow saw it, play the recording backwards. Then you'll see the Scarecrow spotting us, firing an anti-matter stream, which bounced off *The Calculated Risk*, right before you sprayed him with a cloud of anti-matter."

"I thought I'd invented weird watersports," he said, "but anti-Stills takes the cake."

"Let's get back to the pastward mouth to our waiting spot," Cassandra said. "We still have to very carefully turn ourselves back into real matter on the way."

"I ain't ever doubtin' your navigating again, princess."

CHAPTER FIFTY

"You'd better get the recognitions right, little saint," Ayen subvocalized, "or I'll be killed for a spy."

"Blame Union paranoia," the AI replied softly in her ear, "for extra layers of authentication."

Ayen and the AI had penetrated the main HQ housing MilSec and the generals. They'd passed check-points with fabricated electronic authorizations. The AI's ability to pass their strongest defenses terrified her. If the Plutocracy actually had more AIs like this, the Union had another terrible enemy in addition to the Congregate. In the top secret area, they came to the secure doors beyond which Brigadier Iekanjika, her staff and her bodyguards lived and worked.

MilSec had set up their systems so that authentication could only happen at the doorway, in full view of the cameras. The mad AI had modified a virus to mask them on the networked cameras, the same he'd used on the *Mutapa* thirty-nine years in the future. This gave the AI some time to try to break through to the command algorithms of the door. But their entry depended entirely on how many people might be monitoring the closed circuit feed which the AI couldn't hack. The longer they stood here, the more likely they would be noticed.

Seconds dragged.

Finally, the door chimed and slid open.

Ayen stepped into a hallway with three doors on the right wall. The floor was grippy plastic and the walls naked ice. One camera at the end of the hall would be tied to the closed circuit system.

"How many?" Ayen sub-vocalized.

"White noise generators are running all over the place," he said. "I don't know."

It didn't matter much. There would be no fooling anyone anymore. Her cold sidearm weighted heavy in her hand. The first door opened and a head peered out.

Her hands betrayed her. The quiet plasma beam hit the man's neck instead of his head. A loud pop of instantly-boiling blood and flesh sounded. She ran close and caught him, looking into the office, where a captain rose from eating.

He only had time to cry out and half-draw his sidearm before Ayen's plasma beam hit his forehead, painting an instantly-frozen mess on the wall and ceiling. The captain would have been the general's aide-de-camp. The soldier she lowered to the floor would be a bodyguard and all-purpose aide. The tangy saliva that came before vomit slicked her mouth.

She'd fought battles before, but never murdered. She was a naval officer, not an army grunt. Her weapons were warship guns, fired through gun commanders and their crews. And as her career had progressed, increasingly her weapon had been her brain. Naval tactics. Squadron strategy. Movement, positioning and logistics. Not boiled blood on door frame and ceiling. She wasn't this kind of skulking killer.

She swallowed down the rising bile.

A voice called from the next room. Ayen stepped quickly and silently to the general's door. It was locked. She held her service band containing the AI against the sensor pad. It chirped and the door slid open.

The bedroom was small, much smaller than Ayen would have thought for a brigadier: a single bunk, a tiny plastic crib and night table. The haggard woman sitting on the bed had a tiny bundle suckling at her breast. With one hand she reached for a holstered sidearm on the night table. Ayen met her eyes over the shaky aim of her pistol, and the brigadier froze. Ayen stepped in and the door slid closed behind her.

Bags under her mother's eyes and a sallowness to her skin pointed at a hard birth, sleepless nights and even malnutrition. Despite this, there was a staring-in-the-mirror strangeness to the encounter. Some of this woman was in her. Ayen stepped close, taking the weapon from the night table and dropping it in the corner. Then she and her mother stared at one another in horror for long moments over the sound of a baby sucking.

"Colonel," Saint Matthew sub-vocalized, "we've only got ten minutes, maybe less."

Ayen swallowed.

"I'm sorry, brigadier," Ayen said. Her voice choked and her eyes teared.

"You fucker!" her mother said. "Who are you?"

The force of Brigadier Iekanjika's personality, the righteous anger, propelled the words. But they both saw that the woman accustomed to command and obedience was on the wrong end of the pistol. Hints of fear shot through her expression. Ayen recognized those hints, the tiny flinches, too small for others to see. In her darkest moments, she saw them in the mirror. Ayen's aim trembled. They both saw it.

"It doesn't matter," Ayen said, her voice shaking.

"You don't have to do this," Brigadier Iekanjika said haltingly. "You're troubled. We're all troubled. You may succeed here, but you can't escape. This doesn't make sense. Whatever they're paying you, I can double it, and protect your life. I can hide you on one of my ships."

One of my ships.

It really was a fleet divided. Ayen wiped at the tears on her cheeks, without shifting her aim.

"I have to do this," she said.

"Why? For Takatafare? Will she do better than me?"

"For someone else. I have to do this for someone else."

The brigadier's shoulders slumped.

"Please don't hurt my baby," she said.

Ayen had to remind herself to breathe. Her throat ached. Her eyes were hot and wet.

"What's her name?"

"Ayen."

"Why?"

"She's not involved in any of this. She's innocent."

No, she's not.

"And I love her," the brigadier said.

Tears cooled Ayen's cheeks, meeting under her chin.

"Is there anything you want her to know when she's older?" Ayen asked. Her voice trembled.

"Please tell her how much love I wanted to give her."

Ayen couldn't speak. She tried to stop the tears. She took a shaky breath. "She'll know."

Brigadier Iekanjika hugged the baby tightly and then removed her from her breast. Baby Ayen whined softly. The brigadier set the baby beside her. "Goodbye, Ayen," she said, stroking the baby's head.

Ayen had always wondered whether her mother would have loved her, or what life might have been. This is what it would have been like. A warm hand stroking her hair, calming her.

"I love you too, mother," Ayen said.

She pulled the trigger. Brigadier Iekanjika's head snapped back. The baby Ayen began crying.

Ayen stood dumbly, listening to her own cries; to the frightened, orphaned baby. She stepped closer to the bed and looked down at herself. Baby Ayen cried louder.

Saint Matthew whispered in her implant. She swallowed.

"I can't hear you, Saint Matthew."

"I'm praying for your mother's soul."

"Thank you." Ayen released a shaky breath. "Pray for the baby too."

"I have been for months," Saint Matthew said softly.

In that moment, she felt fooled, or maybe she let herself be fooled, into thinking that the mad AI had feelings, and that his prayers would help. Ayen desperately wanted life to mean something, for this sacrifice to mean something. It didn't mean anything to anyone, except her, and what did she matter?

She took a shaking breath and then walked out of the room. Her anger had a clarity now. Her pain had a focus. She understood her own history now, and the history of the Sixth Expeditionary Force, and the last acts needed to ensure its survival.

"Clear the way to the detention area, Saint Matthew," Ayen subvocalized, although she mightn't have needed to over baby Ayen's rising cries. "We have to clear Captain Rudo of the suspicions against her."

"How?" Saint Matthew asked.

Ayen didn't answer. Saint Matthew opened the door out and projected a map, showing the safest route.

Captain Rudo was in detention, not the actual prison that held the political commissars and sleeper agents. The detention area was largely automated, being nothing but a row of insulated, plastic cells set into the ice. The cells were not wired, to prevent hacking or escaping. A single MP station controlled access to the area. Saint Matthew opened the final doorway. Ayen walked to the MP station as if she belonged, and then shot the corporal and private manning it. The corporal's ID card opened the door to the cells.

She opened the first unlit cell; it contained two of Rudo's co-conspirators, curled on the icy floor. She checked the terrified faces, and then fired one shot into each of their heads. Blood steamed and froze onto red ice. Saint Matthew continued his nearly sub-vocal prayers. He might have prayed silently. It wouldn't have mattered to his non-existent god. But his indecipherable words comforted her.

The fourth cell was Rudo's. Ayen unlocked the door and switched on the light. Rudo shivered on the floor with hands bound in front of her. The last of her co-conspirators lay beside her. Ayen looked at the co-conspirator's face and fired into her forehead too, splashing blood onto ice.

A look of confused fear wrote itself onto Rudo's face. This was the end. The lowest level for the woman who had been her superior all her life, and her spouse. Rudo had no power anymore. Her lies lay exposed and she was helpless.

Ayen reached the tiny officer in two steps. Ayen grabbed Rudo's short hair and tugged her head back so that Rudo had to stare straight up at her. Tears ran cold on Ayen's cheeks.

"Colonel, no!" Saint Matthew said. "Don't!"

Ayen ignored the saint, and pressed the muzzle of her pistol against Rudo's head.

"My mother is dead," Ayen said. "I killed her. For you."

Rudo was so small and Ayen so big that Ayen could have beaten her within an inch of her life, even if the captain hadn't been bound. Ayen was in the prime of her military career, seasoned, experienced. Rudo was an overconfident imposter, a traitor, a precocious youth, whose machinations had created the conditions in which the only way Ayen could give a chance to their rebellion was by murdering her mother. Rudo would continue, over the next forty years, to create those conditions that made the removal of Ayen's mother essential to history.

"I loved you," Ayen said. "I looked up to you for everything. And in return, you used me as your dirty assassin."

"I don't understand," Rudo gasped. "Ma'am."

"Your future self used me. You needed this done. You needed me to kill my mother so that you could rise, even though you're a Congregate sleeper agent. And you told me nothing about it so that I would be here, stuck with your mess to clean up. Now my mother is dead."

Ayen laid the barrel of the pistol at a glancing angle along the left side of Rudo's head, where in the future no one could ever look and forget that a Congregate sleeper agent had failed to assassinate her.

Rudo's eyes widened.

"No," she gasped, genuine fear in her eyes, crowding out the calculation, the confidence. "The timeline...."

"We'll finish this conversation in thirty-nine years, when you answer for your crimes."

Ayen pulled the trigger. Rudo's head jerked sideways in Ayen's hand, blood gushing from a long, glancing slice along the left side of her skull. Ayen released Rudo's hair and the captain slumped against the floor. The cold would keep her alive until someone found her.

CHAPTER FIFTY-ONE

SOME SILENCES WERE unlike others. The drill lay folded on the truck bed beside a ton of samples. The lonely hiss of oxygen feeding into his suit interrupted the silence fitfully. Belisarius had sat in the slow, green quiet staring over the grassy hills of the Garret after a descent into the fugue. He'd stared at the stars from the cockpit of small ships speeding through the vacuum. He'd sat in the black cold of his apartment in the Free City. And now he stood on the mindless plain where before the *Hortus quantus* had thought their strange thoughts, had looked at the world disconnected from his time, without all the anchoring insights of consciousness and self-awareness. Their intelligence had emerged from the interstices of complexity, entirely leaping over the definite, classical world of neurons and chemical memory, creating a consciousness through time out of entanglement itself. And Belisarius had created this new quantum silence on Nyanga.

In the distance, from around the tool sheds, a figure approached. The figure wore a sidearm that glowed hot orange in the infrared, the heat of recent firing. Iekanjika.

What had she done? And was she going to do it to him? He didn't know why the thought came to mind. He'd double-crossed her a month earlier. She might double-cross him now and leave him and Saint Matthew charred on the ice, taking the samples back to Cassandra to figure out. Not payback, but revenge. And he would die alone, cut off from everyone who knew him, the way the *Hortus quantus* had.

Iekanjika stopped in front of him. He dialed up the gain in his eyes to see her face within the helmet. She looked disturbed. In pain? Injured? She held out the service band containing Saint Matthew.

"The timeline is safe," she lasered to him. "A sector of cameras around the time gates will be down for inspection in eight minutes. We have to move."

Iekanjika took remote control of the truck and they walked beside it in silence. The *Hortus quantus* were statues, photosynthesizing in brute silence. Belisarius had tossed the translator chest-piece among the samples in the back of the truck. He didn't know if the Union would miss it. He was bringing it into the future. The only way he could go on is if he believed, even against all facts, that he might speak to the *Hortus quantus* again.

Belisarius protested too late to stop Iekanjika's hand from snaking around the fronds of a *Hortus quantus* and breaking them off. The soundless chandelier-glass snapping hurt to watch. She handed a dangling shard to him.

"You broke it!" he said.

"They're all dead, Arjona. Every last one will be melted in three short months. Taking this one piece won't affect them, but it may affect you. You'll need more than pollen to remake the vegetable intelligences. You need the female portion too."

The tangles of thin ice shone on oily strings of black. He held them up and the tiny cylinders caught the light—from the truck, from their suit indicators, from the spotlights in the distance, compressing each source into a hard focused point among which his brain began drawing patterns. Patterns of lights like those that played on the surface of the Garret. Beauty for the sake of beauty. Life within ice. Mysteries in the tarry black. He set the broken fronds gently in a cold drawer of the chest plate.

No MPs were in sight. They drove the truck right up to the edge of the pastward wormhole where no pollen emerged. Iekanjika programmed the truck to drive back on its own to the tool shed and then gripped the straps around the ton of ice cores, and hefted them high with a combination of weak gravity and military-grade muscular augments. She maneuvered the ice cores across the horizon. Belisarius grabbed the chest plate.

Holding onto each other, they hopped into the eerie vastness within the time gates. Most light vanished, but the haunted blue Cherenkov radiation made hyperspace itself luminesce in dimensions that were hard to see. *The Calculated Risk* hung in the gloomy emptiness, about fifty meters ahead of them. Its running lights winked red.

They each grabbed the straps around the ice cores and used their cold jets. The mass of the samples made this slow work. *The Calculated Risk* neared. Long bright scars marked the hull in some places. In others, what looked like burn splashes blackened the cowling.

"Antimatter weapons leave marks like that," Iekanjika lasered to him.

Belisarius' brain had already analyzed the spray patterns and come to the same conclusion. But there were no weapons in this hyperspace, nor had he seen any natural sources of antimatter.

The doors to the lower cargo area, where Stills' pressure chamber was kept, opened. Belisarius clamped down the ice cores while Iekanjika shut the bay doors. In a small way, he was home, a cramped box of a ship in which he could flee faster than anyone could catch him. They cycled through the bay airlock and into the cramped cockpit.

CHAPTER FIFTY-TWO

CASSANDRA HUGGED BEL as he emerged from the airlock, not even giving him a chance to take off his helmet. He hugged her back, uncertainly at first, then with a kind of desperation.

"You fuckers better have had a good vacation," Vincent called back, "'cause we been eating shit out here."

Iekanjika and Bel got their helmets free. They were both sweaty. Bel had started to lose some of the extra pigment they'd used for his disguise.

"What happened?" Bel asked.

"Fuckin' Scarecrow!" Vincent said.

Bel stared at Cassandra questioningly.

"Fuckin' Scarecrow," she said, and laughed.

"Don't shit your pants," Vincent said. "We nuked the electronic felcher."

"With what?" Iekanjika asked.

Vincent explained, fouling and rendering crude what had been a relatively straightforward geometric set of events. Bel looked at Cassandra wonderingly. Iekanjika shook her head and took a seat. Something in Bel's expression was dark, mourning. Iekanjika was also in a mood. She strapped herself in and turned immediately to look out the cockpit window, into a geometric immensity unhealthy for baseline humans to ponder too long.

"I'll navigate us to the other mouth," Cassandra said. "Come on. Strap in."

Bel nodded and she brushed his face once with her fingers, before she took the pilot's seat and started issuing instructions to Vincent to carry them to the other side of the hyperspace. No one else spoke.

Cassandra had Vincent park them about five hundred meters from the futureward horizon, about twenty minutes after they had entered so they would not encounter their past selves, or the Scarecrow. To keep them in place, she'd had Vincent bring the racer to a step in a set of dimensions that included a time axis perpendicular to the one they'd followed in. Here they could look for the other wormholes of the Axis Mundi. She unstrapped and floated back to Bel.

"Ready?" she asked.

He nodded.

"How long, Mejía?" Iekanjika asked.

Cassandra shrugged. "A few hours, I hope."

The colonel didn't look impressed and turned back to the window. Cassandra and Bel moved through the galley, then to the airlock to the cargo hold. They were out of earshot.

"What's wrong, Bel?"

He pursed his lips and looked away. She pulled his face gently around. He was crying.

"What is it?"

He slipped his arms around her and held her tight. She whispered in his ear, the way she had when they were children, frightened and dislocated by their first steps into savant and the fugue, soothing, stroking his face. Then, slowly, in hoarse fragments, he told her everything, of who he had found and what they were, and what he had done. Each word seemed to expand the cosmos and all its possibilities, until they all collapsed.

Humanity had found microbial life exploiting other environments. Some patron nations were rumored to have even found other intelligent life forms, but there was no proof and no hint that other life forms might be more like the *Homo quantus* than baseline humans. Other quantum beings were such an unexpected discovery that it was difficult for even her engineered brain to contextualize it.

And Bel had destroyed them.

"It's not your fault, Bel," she whispered.

"It's either my fault or the fault of the whole *Homo quantus* project," he said bitterly.

"You didn't choose for this to happen, Bel. You weren't reckless. If you had known, you would have done anything to prevent this."

"Those are just words, Cassie."

"They're more than words, Bel! The region of space-time occupied by the *Hortus quantus* is bounded in time, just like everything else, including us. They have a beginning and an end. The presence of any human, and especially a *Homo quantus*, was destructive to them. But your specific presence there also had a remarkable outcome. You saw what they were. You saw what kind of an intellect could be formed with quantum processes. And before they ended, you took away gamete samples. They were going to be set back to zero by the flare and the loss of the time gates. Now you have the gametes and the time gates. The *Hortus quantus* may be important to the cosmos and you might be the mechanism by which their seeds are carried to new environments."

"The cosmos has no purpose, Cassie."

"It has whatever purpose we give it, Bel. You might be less a destroyer than the bird who carries seed to new lands."

"I would love that to be true."

"We'll make it true."

He nodded and she held him again.

"Let's cut up the ice cores," she said, "so we can find ourselves some axes to help the Union and our own people."

CHAPTER FIFTY-THREE

AYEN STEWED IN the straps of her seat, waiting one hour, three, six in the unwholesome space within the time gates. The pair of *Homo quantus* had been busy for hours. Stills was silent and inscrutable in his steel chamber in the lower hold.

She'd written and rewritten her mission report, boiled it down to just notes, but finally erased everything and shock-wiped the pad's drive. Nothing she'd seen or done could genuinely be adequately expressed in words, and who would read it? Rudo, the once—and perhaps future—sleeper agent? The questionably competent Minister for the Navy? The Union Cabinet, wracked by infighting and lack of resolve?

Two weeks ago, everything had seemed clear, at least for her. She'd lived safely within a rational, loyal chain of command with a very specific mission. But since then, she'd been dislocated in space and time and authority, and neither space nor time was that difficult to come to terms with. She'd struggled with having nothing but gray moral positions to stand upon, no higher authority to whom to cede decisions beyond her rank.

She'd been solely and entirely responsible for handling risks that faced not only the Expeditionary Force, but the entire Sub-Saharan Union. She'd been thrust into a surreal adulthood where she parented the parents, punished them, and made choices that would create or end her nation, and the kind of people they were. She didn't want this responsibility. It was hard to understand what set of looping causal factors had led her to this existence, and she didn't know the way back to normalcy. Or if she even had a life to go back to.

Lieutenant-General Rudo was cunning. She'd had thirty-nine years to think about the last time she'd seen Ayen, thirty-nine years to plan for their reunion, and had all the power of the Union to execute her plans. Rudo knew that Colonel Iekanjika had gone from being the most loyal of her supporters to being someone who now had to consider assassinating her. All her life, Ayen had been prepared and groomed for this formative moment in Rudo's past, and now her purpose had been fulfilled. The plant that had thrown seed to the wind could now be plowed under.

Her life and loyalty might mean nothing. Through no fault of her own, the best thing for the fleet and the Union after she gave over the coordinates of the ten Axes Mundi might be her own death. She'd always been ready to die at the hands of an enemy. She'd been ready to die for strategic advantage in a battle. She'd even resigned herself to the fact that her life might end in friendly fire. It was harder to swallow the idea that a death might be needed for political and organizational, rather than strategic or tactical, reasons.

But she wasn't ready to lie down yet. She had no idea if the Union was in safe hands. Maybe Lieutenant-General Rudo was no longer to be trusted, and maybe the Union Cabinet was uncertain ground upon which to lay a foundation. Of her own loyalty she had no question. If she belonged to no authority structure, and those at the top of her nation were unreliable, what would she do to save her people?

That wasn't a question she would have asked even a week ago.

She would seek allies, powerful allies.

The Union Government had been tentative in their diplomatic overtures. Ayen could imagine what they'd do with the coordinates to ten mouths to the Axis Mundi. They would imitate the patron nations and keep them secret.

But the Expeditionary Force had, of necessity, created new ways of thinking about risk and advantage. They'd had to think of new ways of fighting, sometimes even changing tactics and remodeling strategies on no other merit than that they differed from what had come before. The Union was too small, floating on a sea of giant patron nations; it could never afford to be predictable. Secrecy would not turn the new Axes Mundi into strategic advantage.

"Stills," she said finally.

"What?"

"What is the goal of the mongrels? What do your people want?"

"I'd like people to stop trying to slip their cocks into my ass."

"I'm serious, Stills," she snapped. "What are your people doing? Do you want to work for the Congregate forever?"

"I ain't workin' for the Congregate now. Although I ain't rightly workin' now. This is another one of those shut-up-and-wait missions that's borin' the shit out of me, hyperspace or no."

Stills' obtuse attitude would make him a fine negotiator.

"How many mongrels could we peel out of Congregate service if we had enough inflaton fighters?" she said. "You brought thirty. We're still outgunned."

"I don't know. Lotta the dogs like a good fight, but yours doesn't look so winnable right now."

"Numbers," she pressed.

She imagined thousands. That would be terrifying, if they could build enough inflaton fighters. They'd built all their kit with multiple self-destruct systems, but with that many fighters in play, their systems would eventually fail, and the Congregate would capture and eventually reverse engineer the inflaton drives, and the inflaton cannons. Still, that was almost a problem for another year. They needed to survive this year.

"You pay right, you might get two, three hundred."

"How many does that leave in Congregate service?"

"All over? Shit. Maybe fifteen hundred?"

Not thousands. She'd hoped for squadrons of mongrel fighters swarming Congregate positions like wasps.

"How do we get them?"

"You have to fuckin' win."

She took a steadying breath. Speaking with the mongrels was always difficult.

"We invented a lot of new tactics for our cruisers," she said. "You've improvised new ones for the inflaton fighters. I'm wondering what I could learn from you if we were to apply mongrel tactics to the war cruisers."

"I seen some of what you guys did when you took Freyja," Stills said, for the first time with a note of cold admiration in his false voice. "It might be interesting to see what the mongrels could do with one of your big ships if everyone onboard could pull thirty gees."

"Or more. How many mongrels have you got on Indi's Tear? Can we have some of them?"

"If you want to scrape the bottom of the barrel, you might pull another couple hundred, but inexperience may be just as likely to get some of your experienced mongrels killed."

"What's the training time for a mongrel?"

"If they're luggin' big ass *cojones,* a few months. Mongrels already come with some serious three-dimensional spacial awareness from living in the oceans, but piloting is about the hardware and the fine control of the electroplaques. Not every mongrel has it. Your recruiting plans would have some serious hard upper limits, added to the fact that you'd be laughed out of every pitch."

"What about if they were crewing the cruisers?"

"*Mierda,*" he said. "That might be deadly. Two or three mongrels in command positions, calling the shots, navigating. Leave the numpty mongrels as gunnery crews or engineering. Interesting. But I still don't know that you'd get that many."

"What if I sweetened the deal?"

"Talk, sweet-cheeks."

"How would the Mongrel Government react to the idea of their own Axis and a permanent alliance with the Union?"

"Slow down, sweetheart. What government?"

"The Mongrel Government."

"Ain't no such thing. In case you ain't guessed it, orders give us dogs a rash."

"How do you get anything done?" she asked, wondering if he was lying.

"What would we want to get done?"

"Defense, finance, laws, health, education, everything."

"Shit, we don't do that. And who would invade? We live at the bottom of an ocean in a system filled with asteroidal debris. The closest thing to a government we got is gettin' together for fucking and birthing. We aren't clients of the Congregate, 'cause who the fuck would sign an accord? Every pilot has an individual contract."

She was baffled. How could anyone survive that anarchy?

"So there's no point in offering the tribe an Axis," she said.

She felt herself slump inside. She felt boxed in. Even if she survived the week, the Union wouldn't survive the year.

"I don't know," he said. "We own some things. Fucking equipment and birthing equipment. The tribe has never had to come together to defend anything we own. Seems like a shitload of work."

"I'm surprised."

"I didn't say fuck off. I just said it don't feel intuitive-like, right? Where would we live?"

"I suppose I assumed that you'd worry about that on your own if given an Axis. Bachwezi system doesn't have any heavy water worlds like Indi's Tear."

"Lemme give it a think."

"It may come to nothing anyway."

"I didn't think you were authorized to make these kinds of big deals anyway."

"Big things are moving," she said, "and I don't know where they'll stop."

"I don't give the Union more than six months," Stills said.

"Three months for the Union. And I might not survive the week."

"Did you fuck up bad?"

Interesting question. The dimly luminescent dark beyond the cockpit, and its sudden, dizzying shifts in perspective, stared back at her. Yawning nothingness.

"I found two very important people in the past and shot them both in the head," she said.

A sound came through the speakers. After a moment, she realised it was laughter.

"Huh," he said. "Maybe you are somebody the mongrels could work with."

CHAPTER FIFTY-FOUR

HE AND CASSIE had done all the preparatory work, had measured the lowest-energy time through the time gates with the pollen in the ice core, but it had taken far longer than they'd wanted and in the end, they needed sleep. But they were within the time gates, and he quickly found that it was no fit place to sleep. Even Belisarius' baseline human senses tilted unnervingly in a way that had nothing to do with gravity. In this region of uncurled space-time, electrical signals in the neurons had a richness that was difficult to describe, adding a kind of echo to sensation.

And motion mattered a great deal. They were four-dimensional constructs in a region where they could accidentally begin to rotate through any of the seven other dimensions. It didn't happen often, but when it did, the sense of dislocated falling overwhelmed everything else. And all these effects multiplied in sleep.

Being *Homo quantus* made it worse. Millions of magnetosomes made their homes in his muscle cells. Within each, a tiny coil of iron could rotate in cytoplasmic fluid in response to the ambient magnetic field or to the electrical current he could send from his electroplaques.

Most of the time the interior of the time gates had no real

magnetic field, but sometimes the effects of EM fields in other subsets of hyperspace turned some of his magnetosomes in nonsensical directions, giving the EM world a sense of false texture that woke him with magnetic hallucinations.

And worse, he replayed with photographic clarity, waking and in nightmare, the moments he observed the Garret being destroyed, and the terrifying moment when all the superimposed probabilities knitting the *Hortus quantus* together collapsed. The interior of the time gates lent a tactile texture to his recurring nightmares.

In the sleep bag beside him, Cassie moved restlessly and finally, they decided to give up on sleep. Belisarius didn't ask how Iekanjika had slept, or worse, Stills, who also had magnetosomes, but far cruder than those Belisarius and Cassie carried. He didn't want to know what a blurrier sight would do to the nightmares of someone trapped within the body of a *Homo eridanus*.

"Are you scared about going into the fugue, Bel?" Cassie said from very close.

He shook his head and sealed his fugue suit. "I can't hurt myself anymore, although I don't know if that even matters to me."

"Don't say that, Bel!"

"Now that the intellect is running in me all the time, I won't be as good as you, and I might interfere with what you can see in the fugue."

"If you do, I'll tell you to get out," she said finally, tugging at a strap on his suit and sealing it. He checked her suit.

Cassie was warmer, more alive, caught up in an endearing, infectious excitement.

"We're going to look at the universe for the first time through a new kind of telescope, Bel!" She grinned.

He kissed her and they sealed their helmets. They cycled through the outer airlock and emerged on the outside of *The Calculated Risk*. Intermittent magnetic fields pressed at them, deeply textured, a language of hyperspace they could not speak. They clipped themselves to the rings around the airlock and moved away from *The Calculated Risk,* which interfered with their quantum senses.

Belisarius expanded his weird quantum fugue. To prevent his subjective consciousness from collapsing probability everywhere he looked, most of his magnetic sensation narrowed, rerouted to the quantum intellect. Less than a percent of all sensation reached him, but even this fraction was still a vast canvas.

And as he felt even this tiny fragment of the world, it collapsed in layers. But he wasn't looking at a fragile form of life on a single dark planetoid; he stared at the cosmos. He was the fragile thing here, on a sea so vast that even the largest, widest perceptions of his quantum intellect were but glimpses of dust motes in the cathedral.

Beside him, the laughing and curious Cassie vanished. The subjective self, the consciousness that had been Cassandra had extinguished, giving her quantum intellect space to take control of her sensation and perception. He was alone out here, although he took a strangely powerful confidence that she would exist again. The fugue was a temporary pause to her subjectivity.

Maybe Cassie's way of looking at the *Hortus quantus* did contain some hope. Perhaps they were only gone until he could bring them back. The *Hortus quantus* had existed naturally in a quantum consciousness. The extinguishing of that state might be analogous to what Cassie was now: gone, but soon to return. He didn't want to write meaning into the world, but his brain obsessed in its searches for patterns and parallels.

He closed his eyes and let himself feel with just his

magnetosomes. He stretched his arms wide, making his muscles and their embedded magnetosomes into a larger telescopic array into the quantum world. His world expanded. Only flashes of collapsing probability waves struck the subjective, conscious part of him, but even at that, the world became larger and larger as more distant quantum effects raced into his senses at the speed of light. He perceived in strobing imprecision the outside of the time gates, out to eight light-seconds. Each second he saw a light-second farther. But that was not why he and Cassie had set up this observation from within the time gates. From here, they could see the entanglement of the Axis Mundi.

The quantum intellect inside Cassandra looked at the entanglement of the time gates to each other and to all the other wormholes of the Axis Mundi. The quantum objectivity running in Belisarius' brain found the vanishing threads of entanglement within the morass of quantum phenomena. The one-in-a-thousand snapshots, collapsing as quickly as he saw them, built a picture.

Cassie had not been able to communicate the scale of the network of entanglement earlier. There hadn't been enough time or study. When he'd first been on the *Jonglei* those months ago and first tried to navigate a ship across space by following lines of entanglement, his quantum intellect had almost instantly perceived the whole of the pathway in space-time, without waiting for distant signals to reach him; no waiting light-second by slow light-second. That was why he'd seen nothing like this.

Quintillions of bits of positional and quantum information flooded into his brain, only the thousandth fraction of what the two quantum intellects perceived. A subsurface gravitational and space-time web covering a wide swath of the cosmos was illuminated in his mind in strobing flashes speckling in a pattern very much like the distribution of galaxies. And it was bright, bound by not a few dozen entangled particles or waves, but by threads of entanglement beyond counting.

What could have bound the wormholes so tightly? They might have been created all in one spot, of one origin, but entanglement decayed over time, and the degree of entanglement he saw was more than he would ever have predicted for a set of objects created together. The Axis Mundi network of wormholes became *more* entangled with time, not less.

And it was vast, so large that he could perceive no edges or end to it. His brain recognized the distribution patterns: the walls, the filaments and the sheets of the galaxies, all the way up to the largest structure in the known universe, the Hercules-Corona Borealis Great Wall.

But parts of the vast web didn't follow super-galactic structures.

As he focused on these anomalies in the starless voids between the strings of galaxies, he found more and more. They were smaller and less resonant with the rest of the web, bound to the main web of the Axis Mundi by fewer lines of entanglement, making them harder to see. Why would these be darker? Was the Axis Mundi powered and recharged by stars and galactic activity? The more he looked with his limited, strobing vision, the more he noticed that this dark web was entirely contained in the voids between the filaments, walls and superclusters of galaxies. None were part of the visible structure of the universe. The patterns of entanglement showed these other wormholes in the inter-galactic voids knit together into their own web.

For a moment, his conscious self couldn't absorb his brain's own theorizing.

There was an entire second Axis Mundi network, separate from the one they knew.

The realization, the epiphany, the sudden access to the truth of the cosmos, was like touching infinity. His engineered brain, over-curious, thirsting for understanding with a passion that bordered on vice, was for once slaked. His brain was full. It had reached beyond what even the engineers of the *Homo quantus* project had asked for. A religious ecstasy filled him and he let himself feel it. It was a *Homo quantus* miracle.

And in a world where miracles could exist, he might really find a new home for his people. In a world of miracles, he could find a new garden for them to make beautiful with light and to hallow with quiet contemplation. And within that garden, they could plant new seeds and hope for new miracles, like the resurrection of the *Hortus quantus*.

CHAPTER FIFTY-FIVE

THE PAIR OF *Homo quantus* were breathless and overwhelmed. They weren't collapsing with fever the way Ayen had seen them on the *Jonglei* and the *Limpopo,* but Saint Matthew had brought both in when their temperatures had reached forty and a half degrees and their fugue suits had run out of antipyretics.

Ayen couldn't assess the military threat the *Homo quantus* posed to the Union and civilization at large. They seemed to be pacifists, if inclined to thieving. Their fragility and tendency to fever limited them. But she recognized their usefulness as tools. Fragile tools to be sure, but their accomplishments were stunning.

These fragile geniuses had stolen the time gates from the tightest of Union security, discovered how to use them to travel back in time, and then figured out how to find the wormholes of the Axis Mundi. They were not tactical resources. The *Homo quantus* were strategic assets to entirely change the field, if only she knew what they really wanted and needed.

Arjona's hands trembled. Mejía was more feverish, and wouldn't make eye contact with either Ayen or Arjona. Was this savant again? The *Homo quantus* were incomprehensible.

Mejía took a data pad and input a series of numbers. Her

movements were frenetic for the dozens of seconds she was typing, until finally she thrust it at Ayen almost aggressively. Ayen took it. The display showed a simple array, twenty rows of coordinates, in familiar solar relative units with galactic relative units in brackets. Twenty rows.

"What is this, Mejía?" Ayen asked.

"Axes Mundi," she said distantly.

"Twenty?"

"Twenty," Mejía said. "Bel still feels bad about taking your time gates. We agreed to give you twenty wormholes."

Ayen regarded the array again. What startled her more? That Arjona was sorry? Or that the Sub-Saharan Union, if it survived, would be vaulted into the first rank of the powers of civilization? Or, more disturbingly, that the locations of the wormholes were of so little value to the *Homo quantus* that they casually doubled her share because Arjona felt bad?

"Can I talk to you?" Ayen said. "Are you in savant?"

Both *Homo quantus* shied away from her words, as if uncomfortable with her even asking about their mind state. After a few seconds, Arjona gave a deep sigh that shook and transformed into a fevered breath. Mejía looked up at her next. Ayen strapped herself beside them.

"I told Arjona that we're quits, Mejía," she said. "I don't know what I'm doing to humanity and civilization, but the time gates are probably safer with the *Homo quantus* than with the Union. We can't use them and not all of us are to be trusted."

"Why the change of heart?" Arjona asked.

"I'll gladly take all twenty wormholes. They may serve to help us make some alliances. I don't know where you'll both go or what you'll do, but it may be that someday you need an ally with a navy. If the Union survives, I would like us to be that ally."

Arjona wiped at the drying sweat on his forehead.

"We're taking the *Homo quantus* far away," he said. "We may not ever see civilization again. We just want some place as quiet at the Garret."

Ayen shook her head. "You're no contemplative, Arjona."

"I have a lot to think about."

"My offer stands," Ayen said, "hopefully longer than three months. But in the meantime, take me home. Stills and I have a war to win."

"Fuck yeah!" Stills' electronic voice said.

CHAPTER FIFTY-SIX

CHAPTER FIFTY-SIX

STILLS DID NOT pilot Ayen back to the Freyja Axis. Ayen let him go with Belisarius for whatever piloting the *Homo quantus* needed to hide his people. And she needed to show Stills more trust. Another mongrel pilot came for her.

Ayen was drained, colorless, both certain and uncertain of what she'd said to Arjona and Mejía. In just forty short years of possession of the time gates, the Union had become the most technologically advanced power in human civilization. What might the *Homo quantus* become given four decades?

Perhaps gods.

And gods lived best on high and distant pedestals.

Ayen's problems were both closer to home and more immediate.

What was she going to do? Beneath her vacuum suit she had the data wafer. She'd encrypted it, and was certain that only she could open the encryption. On her waist outside her suit was the pistol she'd used to shoot Rudo in the head.

Ayen's pilot signaled the fortifications at the Freyja Axis and they were cleared for passage through to the Bachwezi side. The pilot darted them through the eerie quiet of a proper wormhole with a proper throat of just four dimensions. On the other side, the flier angled into the shadow of the long cylinder of the *Mutapa,* ducking out of Bachwezi's hot light. This battleship had been her home for most of her life, yet it didn't feel like a homecoming. A funereal pall hung over her mood.

Deck crew and officers saluted her. They had to, of course, but more than that, she'd earned their respect. The fleet did not turn just to Rudo. Among the youngest of the colonels in the navy, Ayen possessed the rank and training to command any of the Union's warships. And yet she was *prima inter pares* among the colonels. She was the younger spouse of the Commander of the Navy. If the Union survived, everyone would remember that she'd been instrumental in the legendary crossing of the Puppet Axis. She'd been embedded in Arjona's crew. And yet ironically and bitterly, no one would ever know that her greatest contribution to the rebellion was matricide. Her future held death or bitter honors.

Outside of Rudo's quarters, Ayen found not only a trio of MPs, but the fleet's MP commander, a resolute young lieutenant-colonel. He saluted her crisply. "The Lieutenant-General is expecting you, ma'am," she said, "but I'll need your sidearm please."

Ayen wasn't surprised. Thirty-nine years ago, three days ago, Ayen had promised to finish their gunpoint conversation. Times to pull out tools and times to put them away. Perhaps it was time for Ayen to be put away. One did not lean on an untrusted tool. Ayen unbuckled her holster and handed her weapon to the MP commander. With a trace of embarrassment, the lieutenant-colonel signaled for her to wait while he did a body scan. The MP commander saluted and the door to Rudo's quarters slid open.

Ayen drifted in and waited for the door to close behind her before she met Rudo's eyes. The Commander of the Navy sat strapped to a chair at a small meeting table. Her short gray hair curled tight. The plasma burn along the left side of her head was as Ayen had always known it. Familiar wrinkles surrounded Rudo's sad brown eyes, but Ayen saw another Captain Rudo laid over this one. Past and present co-existed.

"Nice touch with the MP, commander," Ayen said, omitting the respectful *ma'am* she'd previously used even in the privacy of their joint spousal quarters. Ayen pushed off the wall to a chair at the table opposite Rudo.

"I wanted to stop you from doing something that would hurt your career," Rudo said.

Ayen maneuvered into the chair and strapped herself in. Her mood was still dark, and she didn't try to hide it.

"If you want to kill me," Rudo said, "don't do it in a moment of unplanned anger. There's no point in the Union losing both of us. You're skilled enough to assassinate me in a way that won't implicate you."

This wasn't the answer Ayen had been expecting.

"That's the way they took care of Colonel Munyaradzi, isn't it?" Ayen asked.

Rudo's eyes widened, then looked ashamed.

"I haven't heard that name in a long time," she said in a small voice. "I didn't know you found about him."

"But he made you, didn't he? Did he help you kill the real Rudo, or did he only take advantage of the fact that you had something to hide?"

Bitter heat radiated from her words.

"I killed her," Rudo said simply. "My handlers promised me a fast track through the ranks. I owed nothing to the Union. The political class didn't want people like me for anything. And then, as now, Union politicians were incapable of unifying behind a single purpose or policy the way the Congregate could.

It was the right deal. I would have had a good career if the Expeditionary Force hadn't found the time gates."

"The Congregate must have known of you then," Ayen said. "They must know you now."

"No doubt."

"Are you theirs?"

"I haven't been theirs since you shot me."

The air thickened between them. It was all just words. What proof did Ayen have? She'd started her career as an auditor. She knew what evidence was. But there was no evidence for loyalty.

"And Okonkwo?" Ayen said.

Rudo shifted uncomfortably. Then shook her head.

"I disappointed her. And Zivai," Rudo said. "She told me that she'd met you. She despised not being able to seek justice for what I'd been planning. She dissolved my marriage to them. Okonkwo was promoted and took over Bioweapons Research."

Replacing your mother remained unsaid.

"You lost," Ayen said.

Rudo pursed her lips.

"Major-General Takatafare knew I'd been involved in the assassination. More than that. I told her that I'd been visited from the future, that I'd sent someone from the future to kill Brigadier Iekanjika. I had evidence. Nothing else could explain it. Takatafare's hands were tied too by that knowledge. She promoted me to a major on her staff."

There was a look of deep pain on Rudo's face, something Ayen had never seen. Was that it? The fate of the Union depended on whether Ayen believed that Rudo was being honest? It was astonishing. Their whole future could not depend on belief.

Ayen's anger at Rudo deflated. She hadn't the energy to sustain such an assault. Only so much of her world could crumble at once. Rudo had lied and conspired to murder and she'd been promoted. Ayen could not have justice any more than Colonel Okonkwo or Major-General Takatafare.

And what justice could be just? Rudo was a product of the political gangsterism of the Union and heavy-handed political interference of the Congregate hegemony. But on the other side of the scales, she was the architect of their emergence from those times. And architects could only use the tools they knew. Impersonation. Murder. Intimidation. Extortion. Lying. These had been Rudo's tools.

Until, somewhere between becoming a captain thirty-nine years ago and becoming a lieutenant-general a few weeks ago, a tool had fallen into Rudo's hands, a tool called Ayen Iekanjika. Rudo had created circumstances where the tool would be best positioned to hold up the sprawling edifice of her rise.

Had Ayen ever been a prodigy, a trusted officer, a valued younger spouse? Or was she just a critical cog in a device? Ayen was used to battle plans, with soldiers and officers and warships assuming specific roles at specific times, sometimes dying, often killing. But time and history gripped Ayen more powerfully than any battle plan.

Failure to play her part could cost lives or even the entire battle. Failure to play her part might have ripped time. She hadn't believed in destiny or fate before, but how could the first thirty-nine years of her life be anything but pre-destined? It had been Ayen's destiny to murder her mother to clear the way for Major Rudo. Colonel Rudo. Major-General Rudo. Lieutenant-General Rudo. She hadn't been strong enough to try fate and time itself. She'd done what she'd had to do.

And now, for the first time in her life, she was free to choose?

She didn't know for certain that Rudo was loyal to the Union. And if she toppled Rudo, if that was even possible, what then? They were in the middle of a war. Precipitating a leadership crisis in the general ranks was no way to win it.

And what was more galling, what ate at her insides, was that none of what Rudo had done was reproachable. She'd gotten them here. She'd destroyed the *Parizeau*, and taken the Freyja Axis. What were soldiers in that context, but acceptable losses? Or a mother? Would Ayen have chosen any differently? She would like to think so. She would have said before that no murder was ever acceptable, but she'd murdered six people to save the timeline. She'd gotten results. Like Rudo.

The only thing that mattered was whether Rudo belonged to the Union or to the Congregate. And Ayen had no information. This could only be settled by trust. There was no evidence. Just instinct. And yet Rudo had built Ayen's instincts too. She was in a decisive battle for the future of the Union, and the only tool she had at her disposal was talking.

"And so began the rise of Rudo," Ayen said bitterly.

Rudo shook her head helplessly.

"You saw it," Rudo said. "The Expeditionary Force was coming apart thirty-nine years ago. We had the greatest military asset ever discovered by humanity, and it was about to be lost because everyone wanted the crown."

"So you made the fighting go away?" Ayen said derisively.

Rudo had the grace to look ashamed, regretful.

"Takatafare was trained to the kind of military politicking which, even after the death of your mother, gave her no advantage on Nyanga," Rudo said defiantly. "I grew up watching gangland positioning."

"From gangster to traitor back to gangster."

"I consolidated the Expeditionary Force under Takatafare. I'm not proud of everything I did, but I kept the Expeditionary Force together."

"I'm sure the Old Lady was very pleased with your loyalty."

"She didn't trust me, but she needed me. And she eventually brought me into her political marriage as her junior wife."

The silence between them stretched. Ayen fidgeted. What did Rudo want from her? Was this a gangland tactic too? Putting Ayen off-balance before having her eliminated? Or was she hunting forgiveness, as much as Arjona, or Ayen herself?

"Takatafare wanted to refit the fleet with better weapons and propulsion systems, but she didn't know what to do with a new fleet," Rudo said softly. "I did. I made the plans. I invented all the strategies. I trained the Expeditionary Force. I moved new people into the right commands."

"Including me," Ayen said bitterly. "I thought you invited me into your marriage because you saw something in me. And then, not even weeks ago, I realized you'd only married me to avoid a causal violation. That was a step down from pedestal to floor. But the last few days have pulled that out from under me too. It wasn't just a causal violation you were avoiding. You couldn't trust me knowing what I know. I'm dangerous to you and yet I couldn't be eliminated. So you made me your junior wife. It's all a lie."

"Your last words as you shot me were *we'll speak again*. I would have been negligent not to have taken a hand in making you."

"You didn't pick me to find Arjona and work with him because I was good," Ayen pressed. "I was the only person you knew for certain would survive."

"You're an excellent officer. Look what you've done with Arjona for the Union. Time travel makes a mess of orders and choices, but it doesn't take away what you chose to do in each moment."

"None of that makes me less dangerous to you though, does it? Our time debts are quits aren't they? You can finally eliminate me without endangering the timeline."

"I don't want to," Rudo said. "We have a common dream, you and I, and I have no more secrets. You know everything about me, ugly and good. No one knows me better than you do and I've had four decades to think about who I was when I met you, and who you were. You were the first honorable person I'd ever met, the first who showed me a dream I should carry.

"I'd been like everyone else, looking out for myself, trying to pick sides and hedge my bets, and you made me ashamed of that. You showed me a larger dream and you showed me the kind of people who would reach it. I didn't want to be left behind. When I became a major, I knew I didn't want to be like Takatafare; I wanted to be like you. If I haven't ruined everything between us, I still want you leading my staff. I still want you as my junior wife."

"To help you with more assassinations?"

"You told me we're losing the war. Outgunned, outnumbered, and led by a Government trained for subservience to the Congregate. Even the officer corps Bachwezi has developed is composed of people with the right political connections to get into the academy and get promoted."

"What are you proposing?"

"I don't know yet. I don't know if some shock to the system will show them how to pursue the same dream. I don't know."

Ayen didn't know either, what to do with the larger Union culture they'd rejoined, nor what to trust in Rudo. The fire was there, the fire of the dream. Her faith wasn't knowledge. She really believed. Ayen had made her believe. And belief was all the Ayen had.

"Swear to me," Ayen said, "that you aren't a Congregate sleeper agent and that you'll never betray us to them."

"I swear it."

"And swear to me that there will be no more lies between us."

"I swear it."

Ayen slowly nodded. The ache and grief still throbbed, but like a lanced infection, the pressure started receding.

Ayen took a data wafer from her pocket.

"This is from Arjona," Ayen said, "the coordinates of twenty mouths of the Axis Mundi."

She plugged it into the table and unlocked it. The coordinates showed geometrically in a hologram between them. A magically expanded world, a whole new kingdom. They both regarded the projection with some wonder.

"Thank you, Ayen," Rudo breathed.

"This was a long op," Ayen said, floating away in the zero-g. "And I need to clean up and finish absorbing all this."

Rudo looked small sitting strapped in her chair, in some ways as beaten as Ayen herself. The scar of crinkled skin running across her scalp like an ugly, but effective weld, reflected the lights in the room that seemed sharp after the faint red glow bathing Nyanga.

Rudo was welded together. This Kudzanai Rudo was born of the murders of the previous Kudzanai Rudo and of Brigadier Iekanjika, as well as her betrayals of the Union and Ayen. But like the vegetable intelligences, Rudo was born of more than past. Information and perspective from the future was as much part of her, and that was as heavy a secret to carry as murder. Kudzanai Rudo the patriot and leader had not existed before the imperfect welding of future and past.

And if Rudo was created like the vegetable intelligences from past, present and future, Ayen was created from nothing at all. Ayen the honor-bound officer had been raised in Rudo's dream, yet Ayen herself had given the dream to Captain Rudo. Ayen came from nowhere.

"In a few hours," Ayen said slowly, "we should discuss new alliances."

Rudo smiled guardedly.

Rudo was only sixty-two years old, but her age was concentrated in the sadness in her eyes. She was still paying those costs she'd incurred early in her life. And as if Ayen really could peer straight into her heart, Ayen knew that Rudo wouldn't kill her. It was the opposite. She really would have let Ayen kill her. Rudo was aching for a redemption she couldn't reach. Her only hope for inner peace was the gift of absolution only Ayen could give.

CHAPTER FIFTY-SEVEN

BELISARIUS AND CASSIE were on the bridge of the *Red*, as they emerged from the third Axis Mundi wormhole transit of their voyage. Saint Matthew was with them, as were Simón and Letícia, two younger *Homo quantus* learning to be pilots. The cockpit windows polarized and their ocular augments stepped down their sensitivity under the sudden blaze of yellow-white light. The two other big freighters, *Blue* and *Green*, carrying the rest of the *Homo quantus*, emerged from the Axis behind them.

The automated navigation and piloting systems scanned the new system telescopically across a range of wavelengths. The holographic displays began filling with data. A big G-type star shone blindingly about half an AU from them. Radiological alarms sounded. Radio emissions and x-rays forced the sensors to repeatedly rescale their displays.

The Axis mouth they'd just emerged from was just above the plane of the spinning lighthouse beam of a pulsar. X-rays and radio waves flowed around the freighters, some of it penetrating. The three ships thrust hard, lumbering towards solar north as more information came in. Radio and x-ray emissions dropped.

The system was a binary. A white dwarf orbited the misshapen G-type star, slowly cannibalizing it. The stellar hydrogen falling onto the white dwarf fired the blistering x-rays and radio beams from the spinning poles.

Belisarius hadn't expected the Axis Mundi mouth to be so close to the plane of the pulsar. That was another mistake, but not one that had proven too costly—yet. He and Cassie had to take care of them all, for a while. The politics of civilization were far far behind them now. Their future was going to be engineering more than anything else for a while, the creation of a home. All of the *Homo quantus* could be very capable engineers, if they stopped looking at patterns for a bit.

The tiny convoy had passed through the secret, unguarded Axis in Epsilon Indi that Belisarius had first given to the Union. They'd emerged into Kaffaljidhma in Gamma Ceti, a triple star system with a quiescent neutron star. Around this neutron star orbited three other mouths of the Axis Mundi network, which would all belong to the Union when they took possession of that system.

The fifth mouth of the Axis Mundi around Gamma Ceti was in a distant, chaotic orbit of the F-type star. Cassie hadn't given its coordinates to the Union and they would likely never find it. Through that Axis that only they knew of, the *Homo quantus* had arrived at Alpha Ceti, a system with five mouths to the Axis Mundi whose coordinates Cassie had also not given to the Union.

A last transit through the third of those brought them here, to J2307+2229, where five wormholes of the Axis Mundi orbited a pulsar. This was a fresh start in a solar system that didn't even have a name. And they might not name it. The *Homo quantus* liked numbers better than letters and words.

He took Cassie's hand with a sigh of relief. J2307+2229 looked inhospitable at first. The active pulsar spraying x-rays and a close, hot G-type star created orbital chaos and prevented planetary formation. But initial telemetry also showed millions of asteroids, both chondritic and iron-nickel, which would be everything they needed to build a new home, hidden from all of civilization. Cassie squeezed his hand and pointed as telescopes in multiple frequencies showed fast-moving objects darting from one of the Axis mouths.

The objects were small, only two to three meters long, flat and triangular. The skates were a kind of unintelligent photosynthetic life-form of ceramic and metal seen around some Axis Mundi nodes circling pulsars. They were utterly alien, but alive.

The *Homo quantus* had never had access to the skates to study them; the patron nations guarded all knowledge of the Axis Mundi as state secrets, even the flora and fauna that sprouted around them. Now the *Homo quantus* could know them, with their own unique senses. The nature of the cosmos was not just quantized and probabilistic, but it was also fecund, ready to allow life in the eddies of moving energy.

Cassie switched on the public address system for the three ships.

"We've arrived," Cassie said to the *Homo quantus*. Her voice was even, if a bit shy. "We've reached J2307+2229, a pulsar-G1 binary, twelve hundred and thirty light-years from Epsilon Indi."

Saint Matthew was helpfully feeding all the bridge telemetry and astrometrics into the comms systems of the three freighters. How many *Homo quantus* listened to her and how many were calculating orbital periods in their heads might be debatable.

"It will take some time to build a new Garret, but no one will ever find us here. Not the Congregate. Not the Banks of the Plutocracy. There are five mouths to the Axis Mundi here for us to study, along with the time gates. And the pulsar itself will be a telescope to peer into our world."

So much of the *Homo quantus* project had been simply building themselves and their new senses. They hadn't gone anywhere, nor looked at anything new before developing their tendencies for quiet and shyness. Now, they had this whole system to themselves.

"And we also have neighbors," she said with a tiny lifting in her voice. "Skates."

They had not come to a dead system, but a living one, however strange the life they'd found. Cassie was looking at him now as she spoke. "And we'll have others someday if we can succeed in resurrecting the *Hortus quantus*."

She shut off the address system and took Belisarius' hand. They looked out at their new home.

CHAPTER FIFTY-EIGHT

THOUGHTS CRACKLED. THE error messages were supposed to blink once per second, with metronomic precision, but the flashes came too quickly, or carried the pause far too long. The Scarecrow could not immediately tell if it was damage to the missile casing or to himself.

The force of the matter-anti-matter explosion on the skin of the missile casing had been so powerful as to bend the steel frame. The Scarecrow had only survived because the initial explosion had thrown the hot wreckage of the *casse à face* missile casing clear of the rest of the wave of incoming anti-matter, and because most of the annihilation products had been in the gamma spectrum. The Scarecrow's hardened circuitry and carbon neural webs had shut down briefly. Twice. The damage to the AI was likely significant, perhaps irreparable, depending on how long before he'd rebooted. No clocks could be trusted here.

It was difficult to think. Many things made no sense. Internal pingbacks were full of errors. The sensors could not establish the speed at which the bent missile casing was traveling, but it was spinning fast enough across several axes for the Scarecrow to feel a high apparent and varying gravity.

Sensors finally failed. But the Scarecrow wouldn't give up. He could not. He was built to be relentless, untiring and unfailingly committed to wiping out sedition in Congregate territories. Not only had the *Homo quantus* helped the Union's rebellion, but they were bringing new and dangerous weapons.

The *Homo quantus* had carried enough anti-matter in their tiny ship to be used wastefully. The anti-matter hadn't even been loaded into a weapon and launched precisely. The Scarecrow could not fully grasp the mind of someone who had so much anti-matter that they were free to splash it. How had they not been destroyed?

The Scarecrow was trapped in this strange hell in the interior of a wormhole, but he would get out. He would alert the navy to all that had happened, and the full weight of the Congregate would fall on her enemies.

ACKNOWLEDGEMENTS

I DEEPLY APPRECIATE the business and editorial guidance of my agent, Kim-Mei Kirtland. I also owe a debt of gratitude to the considerable editorial expertise marshalled on my behalf by Solaris editors Jonathan Oliver, Michael Rowley, and Kate Coe. I wish also to thank Rebellion publicist Remy Njambi and cover artist Justin Adams.

DEREK KÜNSKEN

Derek Künsken has built genetically engineered viruses, worked with street children and refugees in Latin America, served as a Canadian diplomat, and, most importantly, taught his son about super-heroes and science. His short fiction has appeared in *Analog Science Fiction and Fact*, *Beneath Ceaseless Skies* and multiple times in *Asimov's Science Fiction*. His stories have been adapted into audio podcasts, reprinted in various Year's Best anthologies, and translated into multiple languages. They have also been short-listed for various awards, and won the *Asimov's* Readers' Award in 2013. He tweets from @derekkunsken, blogs at BlackGate.com, and makes his internet home at DerekKunsken.com.

FIND US ONLINE!

www.rebellionpublishing.com

/rebellionpub   /rebellionpublishing   /rebellionpub

SIGN UP TO OUR NEWSLETTER!

rebellionpublishing.com/sign-up

YOUR REVIEWS MATTER!

Enjoy this book? Got something to say?

Leave a review on Amazon, GoodReads or with your
favourite bookseller and let the world know!